Groverle of America

Yearning To Touch The Sky

www.groveronline.de

Order this book online at www.trafford.com/07-2994
or email orders@trafford.com

Most Trafford titles are also available at major online book retailers.

Note for Librarians: A cataloguing record for this book is available from Library and Archives Canada at www.collectionscanada.ca/amicus/index-e.html

ISBN: 978-1-4251-6493-5

We at Trafford believe that it is the responsibility of us all, as both individuals and corporations, to make choices that are environmentally and socially sound. You, in turn, are supporting this responsible conduct each time you purchase a Trafford book, or make use of our publishing services. To find out how you are helping, please visit www.trafford.com/responsiblepublishing.html

Our mission is to efficiently provide the world's finest, most comprehensive book publishing service, enabling every author to experience success. To find out how to publish your book, your way, and have it available worldwide, visit us online at www.trafford.com/10510

www.trafford.com

North America & international
toll-free: 1 888 232 4444 (USA & Canada)
phone: 250 383 6864 ♦ fax: 250 383 6804
email: info@trafford.com

The United Kingdom & Europe
phone: +44 (0)1865 722 113 ♦ local rate: 0845 230 9601
facsimile: +44 (0)1865 722 868 ♦ email: info.uk@trafford.com

10 9 8 7 6 5 4 3 2

To All Messengers of God

Book I

America

1. Brother of the wind

Clarence said he had a story to tell. He started by declaring he was aware few people would be interested in what he had to say, since he was a "black man" and fewer would be interested in what a "gay black man" had to say. "You see, we're not part of the mainstream. We shouldn't even exist!" He explained, asserting he had resigned himself to his marginalization. He said he wanted to tell his tale in the belief he had a right to be heard. "My earliest recollection was that people called me dream dancer for whatever trivial reason. I was seeking the impossible...flawlessness in the wrong world. A fortune teller once told me I was brother of the wind with the wind in my bones, which would blow me from one place to the next. He prophesied there would be no place in this world I would be able to call home," Clarence said. Then he took a seat in the corner of my living room, smiling his charming smile...looking deep into my eyes. I could see having a home was very important for him. "This fortune teller proved to be right in his assessment of my life," Clarence continued. "I later began to understand I had no native home, except the one which existed in the breath of my soul."

As story teller, one should start at the beginning...with Clarence's childhood. Clarence Hill was born at the end of WWII. He tumbled into a cold world on the night of a moon solstice, landing in the Deep South of North America...spitting, hissing and puffing like a mad engine, crying for the moon. It was an unwilling entry into an arena of champions and cowards, those who existed on a playing field for the vulgar. He found himself surrounded by wicked men and women, with cynical minds, who like gladiators in a deep pit, were striving for hero epics. Clarence, unfortunately, did not desire to win, or to be a hero. He was just a puny queer, who heard a rhythm that only queers can hear. It took him what seemed like an eternity to hear this rhythm. But once he began to hear it, this rhythm, he began to live. Sometimes one can find luck in an unlucky fate. Clarence was lucky to have been born on the shores of the Gulf of Mexico, and not in some ghetto of some urban sprawl on the East or West Coast of America, where he would have been forced to squabble in street battles for a small turf, to battle for gang rights. The coast of the Gulf of Mexico offered him enough elbow room. His playgrounds as a child were the white sandy beaches of Northwest Florida and the emerald green waters of the Gulf of Mexico. He bathed his lonely soul with the rhythmic tides, frolicking on the wet shore at low tide and wandering between the dunes at high tide. Oftentimes, his fantasies floated out to sea with the flood and he imagined that at the bottom of the Gulf laid a sunken realm of splendor, a treasure similar to the treasure that *should* exist in the hearts of men and women.

During such moments of reverie, colossal tankers sailed pass him, sailing to faraway places, cruising under a free sky. Clarence followed their course out to sea, pondering how the rest of the world looked. Was it similar to his world under palms? Were people in other parts of this world, as trifling and brutal as the people in his hometown? Of course, a couple of palms on a white sandy beach did not make a paradise. If this would have been the case, every corner on this planet would be a paradise. It is people who create realities, and not trees, nor beaches or mountains. Sometimes, one is placed in the wrong world, as the one in which one should have been born. One believes there is more than this cruel world; that there is a better world to discover. Because of this belief, Clarence spent most of his time on a green island of cool fantasies, pleasure wandering in a magical kingdom of his own. He was hunted most of his life by memories of his past, recollections of his hometown, which was a sleepy small southern town with fleeting charms, a place where time appeared to stand still. The town had a natural Elysian beauty like in a fairytale book. It laid off the beaten track, nested in a picturesque landscape. Clarence often thought about it with nostalgic longing, but not for very long. Because quickly other memories struck him like a blow in the neck, and he remembered how suffocating life was in this town. He remembered that behind the deceptive facade, the deceiving pictures, the charmed view, were wounded people with coarse manners, natives to spiritual darkness. These were people, who fought with hard bandages, who desperately made him want to leave, to find an oasis of peace, or a beautiful space.

On every corner of his hometown stood massive Magnolia trees, like charming old ladies, creating a deficiency of light. Migratory birds had a reserved seat on their branches. The Magnolia trees towered over small wooden rectangular houses and narrow streets, which were named after Native Americans or Spanish conquerors. The trees were mammoth, silent observers of the tragedies and comedies of the inhabitants in the shotgun houses. The family of Clarence lived in such a house...his father and mother, his grandmother and his brother. It was located not far from the waters of the Bay. If the Magnolia trees could have spoken, they would have been able to explain the logic of the world...this complacent order in a fluttered chaos. When the wind blew through the branches of the Magnolia trees during summer storms, it sounded like the birth of an ocean. The trees swayed with the wind. The wood houses under the trees appeared to become ships that floated on the white crest of waves, drifting in the Gulf of Mexico. Seagulls dived into the waves without a sound. In such times, Clarence imagined that he could grab the seagulls from the sky; that he could even move heaven and earth. In such moments, he trusted his own strength.

The Magnolia trees were the first to bloom, to awaken to life, when everyone waited for spring, for a chance at a new beginning. With the change in season came a change of mind. The flowers of the Magnolia trees scented everything with a honeyed smell. It was an intoxicating scent, which animated the superstitious dwellers of the wood houses to sleep at night with their windows opened. Some folks even slept on their porches, believing that the perfumed scent of the Magnolia flowers could induce sweet dreams. Black folks claimed the trees burned in the night. Everything planted into the ground grew copiously here. Nature triumphed over men. The tiny wood houses were surrounded by unplanned luscious gardens. The gardens grew wild, naturally in the game of chance. Pink and purple cluster blossoms of Rhododendrons competed with yellow and orange Azaleas and crimson red Hibiscus blooms. Wild orange, lemon, plum, cherry, peach, fig and pecan trees hung heavy with fruit. They beckoned to be picked. There were Oleander, Juniper trees and Marjoram hedges. A wedding of flowers grew on vacant lots; fields of red Poppies, wild Begonias and white Lilies. Evening Primrose bushes sprouted on the side of the road, surrounded by a kaleidoscope of wild Impatiens and Verbenas. The tropical weather and the unspoiled nature made this spot appear as an unblemished creation, a scene to dream upon, a treasure closet of colors and smells, a Garden of Eden.

Clarence drowned in the colors of the primrose bushes, robbing their delicate petals on his daily route to school, plucking them, placing them in his ears in a valley of fantasies, stretching his eyes with pleasure. Their evanescent beauty mesmerized him. They appeared to be tiny ballerinas, who danced elegantly, dangling in his ears. It was enough to make one dizzy. Who knows how a personality arises? There are many things, incidents, and experiences that go into making a person into an individual. If you believe at the beginning is a point, then the Primrose bush marked the cognitive beginning of Clarence's personality, of his long path to self-realization. But the catastrophe began with the primrose bush. None of the other boys placed primrose petals into their ears. They fancied harder poses, John Wayne postures. They preferred wild, dangerous and impulsive games. The other boys were thrashing and cutting, constantly seeking big points, playing master of the fields. They scratched at Clarence soft image, unmasking him as a lah-de-dah, a softie, a sissy, and a pervert. They expelled him from their circle of insiders, because he was naturally different.

With the primrose bush a quiet rebellion against the society began within Clarence, a solitary march on a long path to an identity that was worth defending. The strange pictures in his head would not fade of an unblemished world of human beings, who live and let live. Existential questions, such as, who am I and why am I here, preoccupied him. He did not know at the time that philosophical questions always remain unanswered. The only thing he knew was he wanted to become like the primrose petals which he put into his ears. They dangled and danced so elegantly, like ballet dancers. But odious boys tried to rob him of his belief in his worth. Not long after Clarence started playing with the primrose bush, his teachers began to complain about his lack of attention in the classroom, his inability to follow simple instructions. They declared him beyond the reach of understanding. There were certain things you could not hide in the South. Everybody seemed to be familiar with everybody else's business, even when they did not know each other personally. This was a consequence of living in a small town. The rumor spread quickly throughout the neighborhood Clarence was a strange fruit, a ding-a-ling, impeded in his mental development, who heard drum music and saw the world in a blue light. The fantastic was normal for him. In other words, they labeled Clarence as not normal. These rumors made Clarence the center of children's ridicule. They sprinkled flowers in his path, playing naughty pranks and antics with him...with no consideration for his fragile feelings. The adults regarded him to be slow and simple, on a pink cloud, someone from another shore. It was easier for them to declare persons like him a problem person. Clarence had no worth for most of them, not even as a human being. He was considered to be ballast for the community, a persona non grata. They wanted to throw him overboard, to get rid of him. It did not occur to them it would be better to accept and to tolerate a person that fell out of the framework. They themselves had limited freedoms. But isn't this the tragedy of all strange birds? They are forced to walk on a tight rope? The entertainment value is the hope they will eventually fall on their nose. Nobody expects such types to soar, to climb into the sky.

Some folks see gloom, while others see gleam. The black school authorities, the principal and guidance counselor of Clarence's junior high school, were the former types. They summoned Clarence's mother to the school one day to inform her that he was mentally handicapped. They spoke like God and advised her to place him in special education classes. This was a hard stone for his mother to swallow. Special education classes were special classes for children, who were deemed to be slow learners, children with a fart in the mind, children with behavioral problems. Such children supposedly had no luck with abstract forms. They were like budding flowers that were literally placed in a stone desert, to wilt and shrivel for lack of attention. Clarence's mother understood putting Clarence in a special education class would be like placing a train on the wrong track. After his education, he would be qualified enough to dry coconuts in the sun. She felt southern white folks were always trying to keep black folks down, and even some black folks were stupid enough to pull other blacks down, especially those who were trying to get out of the pot.

Clarence's mother was at war with southern traditions. She was a small, strong, valiant woman, who was nicknamed, Venus, because of her uncommon beauty. Most folks erroneously mistook her for a white woman. She was what they called in the South, a banana, a light-skinned Negro woman. Everyone joked that this was the reason why she had such a scurrilous tongue, since if she had been born pitch black like the night, she would had learned how to be humble and submissive like the black maids and chauffeurs were expected to be. There were few critical minds in this small southern town, neither among the blacks, nor among the whites. If one asked why the world turned on its axis, or why black folks lived on one side of the town and white folks on the other side, then you were looking for trouble. Such questions were considered to be irrational. The answer was always "because that is the way it is!"

Some folks believed in fighting for their rights. Clarence's mother was one of these types. She was ready to pay with her own blood, if need be. She knew the price one had to pay, but she was not afraid of bucking Jim Crow, of going against the system. She rejected the system which limited her horizons or the horizons of her children. She would not allow anyone to delegate to her a status of second class citizenship. She argued she was nobody's servant. She intended not to allow anyone to expel her from society. By the same token, she refused to allow Clarence and his brother to be discouraged, or denied opportunities she felt they were entitled to. Her two sons were the source of her joy. She claimed she would have climbed Mount Everest for her children. But she did not know where Mount Everest was located. This was something she had heard somewhere. The only mountain she knew was Stone Mountain outside of Atlanta. She was a prophet of light for some of the black folks in town, who craved for little improvements, for integration. Most of the folks in the black population, however, lived in naked fear of the consequences of demanding too much. To tread disrespectfully upon southern ways was dangerous. Clarence's mother was the only one, who dared to jump into the raw wind, to go against a collective insanity that held everyone enslaved in a southern drama. They had to be frightened awake. She appeared to be the only one who dared to call into question the monopolized privileges of the well-breed white sons and daughters of the South. She argued at the peak of insanity, for she had to be insane to make such a claim, that if her children had the same opportunities which were provided for the white children, they would be able to excel just like the white children did. This was not an incidental remark. She believed with her heart and soul not only white people existed in a valley of talent. She would not accept any allegations that Clarence was in any manner, retarded. She was an optimistic woman with a liberal vision, who was not crazy, just addicted to justice and she relied on the justice of her cause. "De truf iz uh invenzion," she said, speaking with a lazy mouth. It was not the Queen's English. But this did not matter. She lectured to anyone who would listen to her. "It sho' didn't fall outer heben. De truf iz dat de black man works ta no purpose, bein' barely able ta bring home de groceries and de white man farts in hiss face, whin he grins. He iz de joke of hiss hiss-story, lak uh ship witout uh compass," she preached, curling her lips in scorn. This was a sharp criticism of an uprooted species.

Clarence's mother was a simple woman. She spoke in such undressed language, especially when she talked about rights, about justice, and freedom from prejudice. She fought the system, as if she was a mouthpiece for the weak, as she gave vent to her frustrations and battled for the future of her children. "Clarence iz mah son," she said. "Ah brought him into dis world. Althou' it wus uh mistake, dat cin't be undone now. He walks upon dis world and Ah intend ta see dat he walks uprit' and 'riteous...wit enou' air ta breathe. Ah kno he iz differen' from de others. He iz slow, but he ain't wacky," she insisted, angry with hope. The family was poor with dreams on a long line, reduced to want. They lived much of their lives on an installment plan, in the trailer of life, from great dreams and small emotions. But his mother was determined to spite fate. She grasped one had to take life into one's own hand and shape it according to will. Even though they could not afford a doctor, she took Clarence to a psychiatrist, a half-god in a golden stool, who performed many tests, searching for the origins of his problem. He concluded there was nothing mentally wrong with Clarence, except that he was hard of hearing. The psychiatrist told his mother to take him to an ear doctor. The ear doctor peered into Clarence's ears with a long instrument which he had tied around his head with a tiny light at the end, as if he was looking for Dinosaurs in a dark hole. "Oh, my God...!" He exclaimed. "Son, it is a wonder you are able to hear anything at all." He discovered a bed of flowers in Clarence's ears. His ears were packed full of wilted primrose blooms and old wax. Clarence never told anyone he could not hear and he never complained. It was not a serious problem for him, not to hear what others said. The world he lived in was separate from the real world. It was a world between reality and dream. He was on an expedition in a world of plants and existed in a valley of magic flowers. Clarence's problem was that he was born too sensitive for the real world and the grave mistake he made was to believe everyone was just as sensitive as he was.

The ear problem was a small accident, but the catalysis for a large change. Clarence's mother decided not to send her children back to "black schools". She said black schools were snake holes. She decided to place her children in "white schools", arguing the quality of education in black schools was low and the teachers were too eager to declare her children as retarded. She placed on an invisible armor, declaring war on the system. She suddenly became a reformer, trying to improve the circumstances of the black race. Her decision to place her children in white schools caused a small drama in the town. Suddenly she was confronted with a crusade of white Christians. The quietness in the small southern town dissipated into thin air and it was Clarence's mother, who fired the first shot. She began a march on a lonely battle against iron white men of authority, who lived on inciting fear. She enrolled her children in a white school, although she was advised not to do so. She suddenly found herself as a single fighter against an unjust system and she realized she had to have a great amount of bravery, to be ready to fight to the end. She was ready to attack southern taboos, which meant she was also ready to die for a cause, not that she did not want to live, but she was not ready to live a lie any longer.

Legally, white public schools in the South were obligated to admit black children. The separate, but equal gibberish of the South had been declared by the US Supreme Court to be illegal and although black folks spied a New World before their front door, they were still afraid to claim their constitutional rights. They knew oftentimes a blood sacrifice was necessary to gain one's rights. The crafty, cunning and deceitful white men, who called themselves school officials, were bloodhounds on a great hunt, using every trick in deception they could think of, to defend southern values. They quickly established a test bar for new students, the purpose of which was to eliminate black children, because they knew the level of education in black schools was low and they assumed black children would not be able to pass the test. This is the absurdity of the thing. They had kept blacks down for so long; they thought all blacks were dumb and stupid. The school authorities also planned for the eventuality of a black child having an above average intelligence and passing the test. They agreed with each other to inform the parents the child had failed the test. They hoped everything would then remain as it had been in the small southern town. They wanted to keep the blacks in their place, to throw dust in their eyes in order to guard an absurd belief.

The white authorities soon informed Clarence's mother both of her children had failed the test to enter white schools. They attempted to spin a blue fog, consciously breaking the 9th commandment of their own religion, "thou shall not lie," to protect their white dream, their golden mountain. Clarence's mother was not persuaded. She gave little credence to the half-truths of "stupid white men". She called them scoundrels, rogues and rascal, who would do everything they possibly could to doom blacks to a pit hole, where they could burrow the rest of their lives. Since she was a stubborn woman, she decided to do a war dance for tolerance. She unintentionally became a freedom fighter, trying to make the world safe for her progeny. She sat down one night under current, with Clarence and his brother, asking them how they felt about the test...if they thought they had failed the test. Clarence and his younger brother, Burl, said they thought they had passed the test. She believed her children. When Clarence's father returned from work that night, sitting at the kitchen table, reading the newspaper, the mother appeared to be a picture of calmness, a goddess with an apron. This appearance was deceiving. This was a fragile peace. She walked around in the kitchen, building up the steam pressure. Suddenly the words burst out of her. "Ah receivt uh letter from de school board, which claimts de children failt de test ta enter white schools." The father did not say anything for awhile. Then he spoke. "If dey failt, dey failt," he said with a confident voice. He made a wry face, shaking his shoulders as if he didn't care, since he knew his fiery wife and was afraid of what she would do next. "Yo cin't break uh brick wall wit yur head, wuman!"

The father was absolutely against her idea to register the children in white schools. His language was simple and to the point. He lectured about black folks staying with black folks and claimed that there was an army of differences between black and white folks. The father preferred in reality to live a lie than to fight for a right. He did not like the vision of an integrated world, because his eyes couldn't bear the light at the end of the tunnel. He had decided to remain in the hole. The mother and father measured their strengths against each other, two squabble roosters damned to dialogue. The father did an egg dance out of fear. The mother called him a dummy, who had been enticed to his own death. She tried to break through the murdering wall in his head...unsuccessfully. They went to bed that night without discussing the matter any further. The father tried to dismiss the thing from his mind. The morning after, the demons returned.

"Ah don't wanna cramp yo style, bud muss yo always tak' de easiest way out, shunin' trouble? Iz all yo kno ta do iz ta stoop, ta duck, ta creep and ta crawl?" Clarence's mother asked his father. She was tired of sneaking, cowardly black clowns with their traditional submissive spirit. This was a heavy rebuff of the father, whose failures were ignored for a long time by her. "Ah intend ta git uh lawyer. Ah will fight it," she stated. This was a declaration of war. She knew the law did not just fall from the sky. Normal men and normal women made the law. Wasn't Jim Crow a law? Her belief in her children helped her in her fight against the system. Clarence's father, whose only symbol of success was his automobile, shivered with fear at the thought of what would happen, if they went against the system, if they started to rock the boat and became identified as a people who did not know its place. He was afraid of respected white folks, who were terrorists in the name of racism. "Jus' don't yo jump off de deep end. Yo iz uh silly wuman," he said, laughing, crying and stuttering, with death in his eyes. He clothed his fear in words, afraid of becoming a prey to terror. "Dey will make sure dat we lose our jobs. Dey will burn our house down...jus' fur revenge. If we survive, we'll hav' ta leave town." The father stood in the kitchen, rooted to the spot, foaming with rage. He heard the whizzing of the bullets. He was fearful of the naked force of power, afraid of a conspiratorial bunch of white men, who could inflict a penalty. He tried to knit a stone net, fighting for a lost position. The thought of leaving their little town was a horrendous thought, similar to contemplating the end of the world. They had lived in this small town for generations. The spirits maintained a delicate balance between Clarence's father and his mother. His father attempted to patch his nerves, for he was less courageous than his mother. It was the season for war in the family.

Clarence suspected his father was not a noble animal. He suspected his father was afraid of dust storms and war howls and preferred to live in the dark past. On this night, he saw how chickenhearted his father actually was; perfectly camouflaging his fear in a clock of concern for the family...being a master of concealment and self righteous in his ignorance. In the little histories is the larger story. Because of his mother, Clarence gained great respect for women, mothers and daughters, for the world of women. "They are nobler, and more courageous than men," he said. His mother planted a golden Lotus in his soul...which never withered during his short life on this planet. Her strength and belief in herself and her support for those she loved was an enlightening lesson. This lesson...to never give up, to believe in something, to never surrender principles, to always fight for justice...was of real significance for Clarence's life.

The white school authorities became entangled in contradictions before the lawyers. They retreated quickly. Clarence and his brother entered white schools the following fall. Nothing adversely happened. It did not rain fire and ashes. The storm of integration passed over the South. This was a victory for the sparrows. As if a miracle had occurred, Clarence began to bring good grades home. A tree began to grow out of his window. His mother was proud of his accomplishments, but his father, whose eye could capture only still moments, was surprised. He hid his face in shame. Being placed in white schools was the best thing that could have happened to Clarence. It was a somersault to a new height, a window to a New World. He was suddenly taken out of a brutal black world, which was the main reason for his withdrawal and placed into a cruel white world, which ostracized him. This was a bad awakening. The eyes of his new white classmates and white teachers branded him unwelcome and a great silence befell them. They punished him with isolation, as if he was beneath contempt. They could not accept the end of segregation. They did everything possible to make him feel dumb, stupid, and insipid, lonelier than lonely, like a fish in an aquarium, in a human zoo. Clarence became more isolated and he tried to deal with intolerance as best as possible. But he was flabbergasted in the face of its expanse, and it was impossible to blend out violence no matter how hard one tried. Clarence turned to his grandmother for advice. She was a plump Mulatto woman with a quiet dignity and wisdom of age. She sat in a wooden rocking chair in the living room, ritually rocking as a fixed point in life. A soft, warm light seemed to shine constantly over her head. She was born of a freed slave with an unshakable belief in God. She said she believed in the coming end of the world, preaching to all who was willing to listen to her that God would shine a light into all the dark corners and the brighter the light, the deeper the shadows. She was proud of the fact her father was a white man, even though his father was a slave owner. "De master's hand iz seen in de finisht work," she stated, giving Clarence a bag of wonders for his spiritual life, telling him about the dynamics of intolerance. "Don't yo be put out, mah sweet child. Yo don't becom' strong throu de weakness of others. Dose white folks wanna continu' ta sang old songs. Yep! Dey wanna' hide in de last hole dat dey cin find," she said, in a flight of words. "Dey iz proud of uh villainous past.... Dey want yo ta feel low and despised, ass if yo haz uh rat's tail, 'cause dat iz de way dey feels. Uh huh! Dey hate yo, caus' of deir own low-self esteem. De ones dat call yo charcoal Nigger, uh ape, uh darky, uh coon, uh dinge, uh goon, lampblack and pumpernickel, dey all iz red necks, dat yo should avoid at all cost, mah child! Dey iz fillt wid grudge and ill will.... Dey wanna put yo down, caus' yo haz more dan dey do. Yo iz intelligent and yo haz talent. Dey feel dat youse not entitle ta it. It iz de end of uh myth fur dem. Dey thought dat yo wuz stupid. Bud remember, mah child, de whale and de hippopotamus iz related."

This was the advice of a wise one about the truth. Clarence quickly noticed with time his grandmother was right about the lies of things and the things of lies. He observed on a daily basis what she had told him about the light and dark sides of life and seeing was different than being told. The rich white children at school ignored him if they could, being at the boundaries of politeness and courtesy. He just did not exist for them. He was not a threat. When they were forced to confront him face to face, they smiled embarrassed, showing traces of teeth, putting on their second face... in a land of a thousand mendacious smiles. It was all the same for them, whether it was genuine or false. The poor white children, on the other hand, saw him as a threat. They showed him open hatred. They schemed to make his life painful, trying to humiliate him, to bring him down low. It was painful for Clarence to notice he was not only different from the other black children, but that he was different from the other white children. This realization brought him down to the ground, provoking him to question himself....why it was like this? "Don't yo cha try ta fathom dey mind of dey Lawd," his grandmother said to him one day in a cozy chat. "Everyding haz uh reason and uh purpose, mah child. Dey stars in dey heben iz witout boundaries. Command yo yur ways. If yo walk in dey breathe of dey Lawd, yo gointer be all right, sho'nuff! Yu strut yo stuff and trim yo sails ta de wind." Clarence's grandmother had knowledge of stars and men. Clarence decided to listen to her, turning his eyes towards the heavens for answers, as he prayed for a new morning to begin.

2. What happened to the heart was a marginal theme

It was difficult for Clarence to talk about his mother. Her early death had a great effect upon him. He said he would like to think his mother's death was sweet, despite the fact she died of a broken heart. But death came suddenly to her, ending the suffering of life. She died of high blood pressure at the age of 54. Clarence was bitter of this fact. "How is it possible in a country as rich as America is, that someone should die of high blood pressure?" He asked rhetorically, knowing the answer to this question. In a land, where millions of people were without health insurance, she was unable to afford the necessary medicament for her ailment. "My mother probably died of a broken heart more than from high blood pressure," Clarence declared. "Let's say it was the broken heart that caused the high blood pressure, although my mother insisted there was no such thing as a broken heart. The real pain for her was learning the truth of life, after the end of all truths. She could not forgive the man, who she once fell in love with, the man whom she married; in the belief it would be a union for life. She could not forgive this man, my Dad, for abandoning her to poverty, to the travails of life."

Clarence said his father possessed vices like most males in the circle of men, allowing his vices to control him. "They called him the bull in our town. Drinking alcohol was a religious ceremony for him. He was not only an alcoholic, but a habitual gambler looking for Eldorado. He was a jealous man enchained to a pile, who was a life artist like most black men of the times, expecting enlightenment to fall from the sky. I often wondered why my parents married, since they had nothing in common." Clarence said his mother, on the other hand, was not a complicated woman. "She did not seek the source of life nor did she seek to caress the moon. Her dreams and goals in life were realistic, down to earth. She sought a place of peace, a refuge. She wanted to get out of the trench. She wanted a good education for her children and she hoped for a house and a home... a little brick house in the suburbs, family luck under a palm tree, a calm and simple life. She spent all of her time and effort working, saving every penny in order to buy a house with a small garden on a quite street under a Magnolia tree, pursuing the American Dream." One could see the pain on Clarence's face, as he spoke about his mother. "Life is unfair. It gives to some fantastic palaces and fertile gardens and to those, who need bread and salt just to survive, who dream, hope, and scheme in chicken stalls for a better life, luck is denied. My family had to struggle hard to survive," Clarence said.

Clarence's mother forgave his father for being an alcoholic, a gambler and for being a jealous man. It was normal and expected that women forgive, bear and forbear. She even forgave him when he treaded the boundary of decency, abused his position on his job and stole money from his white boss, which he used for gambling. But when he had to flee up North in the dark of night, in order to escape prison, abandoning his family, she could not forgive him. He had fallen from her grace. "Yo see dat's jus' how stupid yur daddy iz. He wuz afraid ta demand from de white folks uh good education fur hiss children, but courageous enou' ta steal from dem," Clarence's mother said one day to him, summing his father up in a sentence.

Her love turned like a slow freeze to hate. She gave up preserving lost causes, capitulating. She questioned with time whether it was true love. This thought came from her stomach. Maybe she had convinced herself it was love, to conceal the reality of her situation. As she became pregnant in her last year of high school and did not know a solution to her problem, she grabbed the first solution offered to her. Clarence's father was a good-looking brown-skinned man, a self-crowned prince, who came from a middle class family. His father was a Baptist minister in the local church. Clarence's mother never knew her father, who was a Mexican migrant worker. Her mother was a cook in a Greek restaurant. Clarence's mother was well aware of his father's vices, his shadows, before she married him. She willingly lost her virtue to him, hoping her love would be stronger than his vices. But many arms fed his mouth and their life moved back and forth between love and hate. They married with fury and delight for pleasure. He rolled the red carpet out for her, for she was a high yellow-skinned girl. This was the time before the slogan "black is beautiful" appeared. Black men at the time used black-skinned girls for play, but hunted yellow-skinned girls for marriage and building a family. Clarence's father considered himself lucky to have caught a yellow-skinned girl to play with, a virgin in wait. He saw only the female form. He would have preferred a dead woman to one who wasn't a virgin or a woman who had at least lost her virginity to him. He pursued and courted her like a Crane dancing before mating, because she was a pretty little thing, spicy and piquant, and they made a handsome couple. When she became pregnant in the first coition, on a picnic, he married her, making empty promises and more promises for a future in misery.

In moments of madness and for lack of a deeper meaning, he later in life regretted having married a pretty yellow-skinned girl. She was the object of men's attention. He guarded her on the alert, as if she would be his property. The thought she could be sleeping with another man was unbearable. It caused him mental agony. If he caught another man smiling in her direction, he would explode in jealous anger. This anger rode him like an ogre. He lost the ability to think, as if he was doped. They fought often, rendering a perfect private performance, scrambling like two chickens about nothing. He wantonly threw her naked out of their house one day and brazenly locked the door, preferring to hang their embarrassing underwear out on a telephone pole for the entire world to see. Looking for a reason to brawl and underway in insanity, he accused her of sleeping with his brother, claiming she was an adulteress, that his younger son, Burl, was not his son. This was a labyrinth from which he never escaped. If it had not been for the constant intervention of his own mother, Clarence's grandmother, they would have killed each other. The grandmother was the mediator in disputes. She was the only one he listened to; the only one he respected. She defended his brutality, for he was a mama's boy. She told everyone stubbornness was in his blood. His father, despite the fact of being a Baptist preacher was also an alcoholic and a fool.

"Yur' fatha' sometimes act lak he done wash hiss head under' de pee of uh cow," Clarence's grandmother said. "Try ta forgiv' im. Despite all of hiss imperfections, he still iz yur fatha! He's de one, who fathert yo," she said, as if this was an achievement. The grandmother made excuses to others for her son's irrational behavior. She tried talking to him, telling him he should stop listening to gossip, stop seeking his buddies among the vulgar, who led him down the wrong road. She called them Satan boys. They were evil and ugly black men.

Twenty years later, the father returned from up north like dust from the moon, as if only a season had passed, as if the only thing needed was a fresh shine for a windjammer and an old screw. The way back to his family was barricaded. His children were all grown, had gone on paths of their own. He returned home, trying to court his former wife in the fall of their life, his last instance, believing marriage was irrevocable. He beat the drum in the night, arguing they were both old, and needed somebody, needed companionship. It was not important anymore, whether they loved each other, he stated, apologizing for his past mistakes, yet not realizing they were more than blunders. Clarence's mother refused to speak to him, refused to acknowledge his existence. She never forgave him for his negligence. Clarence witnessed these lost years and asked his mother before she died, why she would not give their father a second chance. "Only uh fool thinks yo git uh second chance in life," she replied. She had zero tolerance for a fool. This was a revelation for Clarence, as if the sky had opened and the heavenly father spoke, as the wind fluttered in eternity. There was no such thing as redemption. Happiness was something hard to capture in life. It existed at the most only in fiction. Clarence's mother died on Ascension Day in a melancholic end. Black birds sang a requiem for a lone freedom fighter, a black woman, who believed she had a right to justice.

Clarence said he secretly wished for another father, one with commonsense, one without a cold heart. He could not understand his father's wantonness, why he preferred to exist between threats, conspiracies and self hate. Clarence understood that many black men sought refuge in alcohol, the devil's crutch, and black wracks in America were part of the scenery. But why his father preferred a life of guzzling and gorging remained a puzzle, an enigma. He was an embarrassment, worse than his reputation, the perfect villain, and a consummated buffoon. Clarence did not love nor like him. He did not like his chain smoking, his stinky feet, and his macho black man type of behavior. "Ah'm de only real man aroun' here. White men ain't real men and dere's only two types of black men...real black men and sissies," his father often asserted. Clarence detested his 'I know better than thou' attitude' and his cowardliness in the face of adversity. "Only sissies run from fights! Real men don't cry!" The father claimed.

When he was asked what is a real man, he said that a real man was one who was 'tough as leather, quick as a greyhound and hard as steel'. This was something he had heard somewhere, from one of his buddies, who himself had heard it somewhere. Clarence learned later in life this was what Adolf Hitler claimed a German man should be. Clarence's father and his buddies were all birds of misfortune with no sense of shame. They talked a lot about manhood, pride and dignity. But they were not gentle men. They could not trust each other. They were all lonely and bitter black men; men who decided at an early age to waste their lives away in alcohol. They were fellows, who drank themselves into a delirium. They had a heritage of alcoholism and a tradition of recklessness. It was the simplest escape. Alcohol loosened their tongues, allowed them to loose their timidity and inhibitions. Words then came easily. They would say rude things. They were never the right words. They were hurting words. Their attempts at tenderness were awkward. Those, whom they supposedly loved, became their victims. These types of men believed life without dignity wasn't worth living. And yet they lived undignified lives and were too cowardly to put an end to it all. Clarence was surprised the day he caught his father weeping, as if it was time out for machos, after he had declared real men did not cry. It was the day they assassinated Martin Luther King, Jr.

Such bitter experiences forced Clarence at an early age to have thoughts of travel. His favorite game was packing and unpacking his mother's suitcase, simulating travel, not playing the game of the victors and the vanquished, which the other boys in the neighborhood preferred to play. Clarence could not understand why men preferred such win/lose situations. "Ah'm catchin' de next train out of here," he said, when asked where he was going. These childhood trips were imaginary; a departure from the present, a pause from life... trips to the roof of the earth, to the center of his heart, trips to fantasy lands, where he discovered he was emotionally different. He just did not know what it was called. But he resolved not to be like his father, not to have his father's fears, not to travel bleak and beaten paths and not to create victims along his path. It was fear, which slumbered upon his father's shoulders like an old scarecrow. It was an affliction without a remedy. Fear was an intimate friend of his father. Fear was the mute tyrant, suffusing his spirit, fomenting his ruin. Fear encircled and bound him. It saturated his mind with demons. It haunted him at night. It stalked his every movement. It saddled him like a cowboy mounts a wild stallion and rides it to the ground. The darkest spot on the planet was his soul. He never experienced the bliss of true love, only the appearance of love. He never learned how to fly in pursuit of his dreams. When the rooster crowed and he awoke to find himself an old man, a fallen patriarch without friends and family, alone with no one to console him, to wipe away his lonely tears, he sought to swim in a sea of sympathy, to roll life backwards. It came to him suddenly that the game was over. Emptiness came nearer. His heart had been broken, as well. He failed on his own system, blockading himself. The fool had dismantled himself. In a fleeting moment of solitude, the futility of his life was revealed. This was not a unique drama, but an insignificant family tragedy in the American South...a drama in an endless loop, where pain and joy were private things and where what happened to the heart was a marginal theme.

3. Seeking freedom in a cock

Clarence's biggest tragedy was being born with a penis, not that he hated it. He disliked the responsibilities and expectations which went with being born a man. He felt women had a much easier life. The expectations for them were not as high as they were for men. Women were expected to get married, to have children, and to attend to their households. Men, on the other hand, were expected to live up to a myth...the myth of a real man. He wondered, what was a real man? Something else disturbed Clarence, besides the thing that hung between his legs. It was the luggage he carted behind. Clarence had an ignominious and notoriously round ass, which set perched in the air and poised like a monument on presentation. It swung from side to side, depending on the tide and the phases of the moon, whipping thin air in space, causing traffic accidents. Normal people, if such a species exists, called him a "faggot". They said his ass was too perfect for a normal man. Being called a "faggot" was the worst thing one could be called in the American South. It was worse than being called a "nigger", because a "nigger" had, at least, a right to life, even if it was a subservient life as a second class citizen on the margins of society. But a "faggot" was considered to be a pervert, a distortion of nature...a freak. A "nigger" had to deal with deprecation, discrimination and disrespect from the so- called "white folks". But a "faggot" was free game to be hunted and killed by all sorts of fellows. A faggot had no rights. They appeared to exist somewhere between the earth and the sky...yearning to touch the sky, to fill their dreams with meaning. They were compelled to live their life in a glass box in which others placed them and forced to fight the rest of their lives to be free, to express themselves as they willed. Faggots were not men-at-arms, who chased demons, but rather, they were colorful butterflies, hunting nectar in melancholic fields. Semen was sweeter than blood for them. The title "queen" sounded better in Clarence ears than the word "faggot". Flaming queen was more appropriate. A flaming queen was a fairy. He was one, who could not hide who or what he was. He was one, who swaggered with a natural elegance and pranced with the grace of a Giselle, resembling a long-necked, long-legged crane strutting across the Savanna. This strut was a God given talent and not affected. It was considered unnatural and awkward for a man to walk in this manner. Men were supposed to saunter with aggression, to walk with their legs wide apart, allowing their club, their weapon...their penis, which was their most valuable asset, to swing from side to side. But queens appeared to demystify the essence of the courageous knight with sword and shield, riding his horse for the triumph of the holy cross. Flaming queens sucked their pistols. This was more than subversive. It was an insidious trampling upon the status quo. As a result, they were banned from respectable society and damned to dwell in a house of exotic wishes; to wander an endless path of ridicule and danger the rest of their lives.

Clarence was a novelty. When he looked into the eyes of others, their eyes showed disgust, revulsion and hatred. Their cold disapproving eyes compelled him to dishearten in his budding identity. The first person, however, to call him "faggot" was his father. His wrath was caused by Clarence refusal to drag the wretched and retarded Mary Sue, his childhood playmate, under their wood house and do with her between the debris what the other boys in the neighborhood had done, to abuse her. "If yo wanna be uh real man, uh top dog, yo hav' ta learn ta take from gals whut yo want and demand whut yo need," his father declared. It was a pretext for a wicked mind. Clarence's father told him Mary Sue was just one of the many huddles he would have to overcome in becoming a man. He told him if he didn't abuse her and use her, he would be considered by all to be a faggot. This insult from his father was quickly forgotten by Clarence, since he did not know what exactly a "faggot" was. The best strategy was to conceal his hurt. He went to his grandmother for consolation. She was a religious woman, who lived a life of service and devotion, declaring she placed her fate in God and love...not in foolish men. She was the organist in the local Baptist church, in which her husband, before his sudden death, had been the pastor. She never missed a Sunday morning and was constantly preaching God is love; and love lights the night. She believed there was victory in faith. Clarence stated that his grandmother never used a vulgar word nor raised her voice in anger. He said she tried to treat all men and women the same, irrelevant of their failures, treating all with patience, with sympathy, and with affection. She tried to soothe his pain. "God don't (*doesn't*) lak de ugly," she frequently said in southern Black English.

Everyone in the family and in the neighborhood appeared to love her for her gentleness, kindheartedness, and generous soul. Clarence confided to her what his father had told him to do to Mary Sue. He told her his father had called him a "faggot". "Sticks and stones cin break yur bones, Clarence, bud words shall never hurt yo," the grandmother responded in a laggard languor that was typical for the South. Months passed without an occasion for healing wounds. The entire family gathered to celebrate Thanksgiving. The grandmother waited until everyone was seated at the dinner table. She then turned to her son, the younger of her two spoiled sons...Clarence's father. She asked in a loud, resonant voice which came from deep within her and that was loud enough to be heard by everybody. "Does uh man hav′ ta be pussy crazy ta prove he iz uh man?" She asked. Clarence's father almost choked on his drumstick upon hearing his own pious mother use such words. The women at the table flamed red in embarrassment and all the grandchildren snickered and giggled with amusement. They intently watched the spectacle as the two quibbled about whether the expression "pussy" was an appropriate word to use at the dinner table, in front of children. "It iz ok ta be uh sissy," the grandmother later murmured quietly and confidentially to Clarence. She used the word sissy instead of faggot because during her time sissy was what they called gay persons. "Live yur life ass best yo cin. Shine ass brightly ass uh star! Bud hide in de shed wen it rains," the grandmother advised Clarence.

From that moment, this is exactly what Clarence decided to do...to shine! He heard a ragamuffin rhythm that fell from the sky; a rhythm, which only queers could hear and upon which they appeared to pirouette with esprit, dreaming of being serenaded by hung stallions. Clarence grew up and soon found that life in the small southern hick town didn't allow him to shine at all. The setting was wrong. You couldn't be grand around tattooed red necks and docile colored folks, whose vision of a better world were to do battle under Old Glory and to fight for anachronistic slogans created for herd mentalities; to die for a cause and hope to go to heaven...where there was one heaven for "niggers" and one for "white folks". It was dangerous to walk through these red neck gardens, perilous to step on their toes. Being tarred and feathered, lynched or beaten ripe like a Georgia peach, were the vile games they played with each other. Since neither of these choices was preferable for Clarence, he took the first train out of the South going North to New York City...the heaven for "faggots". New York City allowed types like Clarence to blossom as a flower in spring, to sleep under satin sheets of black palm trees between perfumed pink roses, to become a grand queen and with all the other dainty queens, seeking freedom in a cock, delighting in every moment, from place to place, from bed to bed. But Clarence soon recognized life was not just about diversion and entertainment, or even about sucking a cock. Nihilists, injured souls and cracked psyches could be found everywhere, and one could not escape brutality.

4. I love New York

Clarence found himself an adult man, as time fluttered away, living and thriving in the big city. He was told one could love and hate New York City at the same time. Clarence wondered how this could be possible. He observed quickly that life in New York City was similar to a toboggan without end and those who wanted to survive could not rest long in the city. One had to have a thick skin...a tough hide in order to survive. Clarence awoke this morning like every morning to the noise of the traffic outside his window, which appeared to know no boundaries. Its' constant droning drove him insane, penetrating his mind, making the houses on the street vibrate and the windowpanes rattle. Every passing truck rang brooooommm in his ears. He dozed half awake and half asleep, cozily submerged under the covers of his bed, trying to ignore the restlessness of the ticking clock on the floor. The clock shrilled suddenly a metallic noise, sending a reverberating sound throughout the room, which bounced off the walls, slapping him in the face. Clarence got out of the bed and walked into the bathroom. He could hear the banal and irritating rituals of his neighbor on the other side of the wall. She was a single female and a nurse at Harlem Hospital. She gurgled, making exaggerated, preposterous sounds, purling like a strangulated chicken. Clarence surmised this was her favorite diversion in the mornings. He speculated her gurgling was a joyous substitute for a disturbed sexual life. She needed a man like so many single women in New York City. But who didn't need a man, he contemplated? Even men needed a man, sometimes, to confess their sins to, to brag about their conquests...as a pal and as a companion. From the pipes of the radiator in the living room, a lustful groaning floated up into the room. The groans were infecting like a bacillus of pleasure, hanging in the air, waiting to infect Clarence with desire. "Oh, Mon Dieu...! (*My God...!*) Mon Dieu! Mon Dieu...!" It was Monsieur Albert screaming in rapture, climaxing in a delirious vertigo, calling God's name in vain. Monsieur Albert was an old Haitian man, who lived in a tiny room on the first floor, directly under Clarence's apartment. He was 82 years old with a lot of erotic energy, spending most of his time and retirement money for passion and lasciviousness. He engaged in sexual intercourse with different, drug addicted young girls. Despite his age, he was more agile in bed than most young men. Clarence wondered how this was biologically possible. Monsieur Albert bought sex from the drug addicted girls, as if it was a commodity, like any other commodity, and consumed it without becoming involved in the human factor, the tragedies behind these poor girls. After he climaxed, which he did almost every morning, he paid the young drug addicted girls and threw them out unto the streets.

In the other tiny room on the first floor, lived an alabaster matronly white lady. Her name was Mrs. Holstrom. Mrs. Holstrom played her radio very loud every morning. Although Clarence could not see her in her room, he knew what she was doing. He knew she was sitting in her kitchen with a tired look on her face, nursing a cup of coffee, listening to her classical music, which competed with his butt shaking funk and soul. Their music filled the space. Clarence's one bedroom apartment, which was located on the second floor, was also quite small. It included a minuscule bathroom, a small kitchen, just off of the living room and a modest bedroom. The apartment was sparsely furnished. It was plain and without charm. There was a table in the kitchen. A worn couch filled the living room. In the bedroom was a futon bed on the floor. The radiator was under the bedroom window, where most of its heat escaped. In front of the radiator was a row of vases with Asian plastic flowers. Exotic posters of swarthy men in colorful robes hung on the four walls of the bedroom. A poster of African herdsmen hung on the wall directly across from the futon, which presently captured Clarence's fantasies, stimulating him to daydream. "Africa! Africa! Africa!" He repeated the words softly to himself like a magical sound, as if he was riding on a breath. Clarence was not yet entirely convinced he would soon be going to this place, called Africa. He was already in Africa in spirit, expecting miracles to happen, with a vision in his head of how it would be ... this rendezvous with a continent and a legend. How would it be to sail for a faraway land, to a land of giants? Would the welcome be joyous, harmonic? Would he find there a place for his lost soul, something for his heart? Visions of god seekers, under colorful umbrellas, with flags and banners, embraced Clarence. His head was filled with images. He saw dark men and women celebrating with a lot of fanfare, playing under the shadows of a Baobab tree and sleeping under the moon on warm nights. A virile Shaka Zulu with antelope horns materialized before his eyes. Clarence allowed the Shaka Zulu to seduce him and he imagined a new life bloomed out of ruins. He envisioned them building a hut on a hill and eating together on banana leaves. Then he saw a group of dusky herdsmen marching pass his futon. Over their heads rained corn and hops. Beer fell from the sky. The herdsmen rode camels under a royal blue sky. In their haste to reach their next encampment, they appeared to be too busy to see the beer falling from the sky. They were merchants of spices and herbs, selling, dealing, negotiating treaties between Timbuktu and Mauritania. They conversed and drunk tea in the barren desert. They sought the marguerite sun and allowed themselves to burn crispy black. The sun was a calabash. The herdsmen followed it, stamping dust in each other's faces. Their children wore tin pans for hats. Their wives wore soup bowls, with necklaces of amber and earrings which hung down to their navels. They shook their asses on command, rattling brass anklets to songs, dancing in circles, concealing charming smiles behind dark scarves. They appeared to Clarence to be masters of the universe, as they rode their camels, swinging their whips in their hand...in their yellow turbans and green robes. Their faces were decorated with dots and circles. Their lips were painted purple. They, like Clarence, appeared to yearn to kiss the sky, heeding the call of the wild.

Clarence snapped out of his reverie, returning to the reality of New York City. It was time to prepare for the daily struggles of urban life, to place on an invisible shield and armor...to go into battle. It was not the time to cruise through the galaxy of fantasies. This could be done another time. He did his morning hygiene. Then he proceeded into the kitchen to make coffee, checking the mice hotel on the floor under the table. He lighted two candles on a petite altar in the living room...to the spirit of his mother and grandmother. Outside the living room's window, he could see it would be another gray day. He decided not to let the weather disturb him, tangoing back into the bedroom, singing to himself. He thought about how a lot of people in New York City suffered from depression and how many were on valium and other types of psychic drugs. He was thankful to God that he did not have a depressive type of personality.

Clarence seldom complained or grumbled about personal problems, or worried about his fate, which was wrapped in obscurity. Clarence had never been anxious about his existence, like a lot of people he knew, nor was he afraid of what the future would bring. He believed in destiny. He confronted the problems as they occurred. This positive attitude is perhaps the attitude of a field rabbit, but why do humans think that they are more significant than a field rabbit? He dressed into an outrageous costume, which was very loud with illuminating colors. As he looked at himself in the mirror, jumping from pink to purple, from lime to orange, he appeared even to himself like a paradise bird or a carnival figure from Rio de Janeiro. The funniest part of it all was, he knew it was all insane...this crazy life he lived in New York City. It was only a performance...a festival of vanities. After admiring his striking image in the mirror, he departed his little apartment, shutting the massive steel door behind and checking the numerous padlocks and bolts at the door. When he was sure they were securely fastened, he leaped down the steps of the apartment building, out into the busy streets of the city, sashaying down 141st street, existing between magic and geometry, and yearning for style. "Real men" whistled out of their car windows, as they drove up and down the street, making catcalls in his direction, using abusive language. Voluptuous women with too much make-up on their faces, strutting on their way to work, surveyed Clarence with envy. They looked at him with grudging eyes...the slender form of his body and his perfect round ass. They made him feel accused. Clarence would have given his last penny for an acceptance. But he knew it would never come. There was no pardon for those, who fell from the frame....certainly not for a sissy like him.

It was a cold January morning. A soft snow shower embraced the city. On the corner of 141st street and St. Nicholas Avenue, an unsophisticated black female positioned herself on top of a makeshift platform, taking up space, trying to make a buck, some pocket money for her next fix. She recited a libretto about New York City, something she had written herself. She had a plastic "I love New York" bag pulled down over her head, and she screamed against the clamor of the morning traffic, captivating a small crowd of people. They surrounded her, listening to her prose in suspended animation. In the "I love NY" plastic bag, she had cut two holes for her eyes and a larger hole for her mouth. Clarence concluded she was either crazy, addicted to crack or cocaine or some other drug, or she was another black deranged homeless person of the countless thousands in the city, screaming about mythological catastrophes. Who else would think to pull a white plastic bag over his head? "Ode to New York...! I said, Ode to New York, yo'all!" The deranged woman hollered. "I love New York, I love New York! I love the smell of piss in dark corners, the crack heads, the homeless and the ostentatious display of wealth. I love its banditry and its glimmer." She gesticulated with her thin fingers. "I love to ride on the Staten Island Ferry, to take the A train to Harlem. I love the pornography on Times Square and the pornographic managers of Wall Street," she shouted, shaking her emaciated body. "I love the bright lights of the city, the pimps with their prostitutes and the faggots on Christopher Street. I just lovvvvvvvvvve this city!" She looked at the folks around her, the ones who had jobs to go to, praising New York without restraint. Her enunciation indicated that although she obviously lived on the street, she was educated... an educated fool or a schizophrenic intellectual. Clarence dropped $1 dollar in a tin can in front of the wood case, ignoring her insult, her comments about faggots, and then he proceeded on his way, quickly forgetting the superfluous remarks of a redundant person, who seemed to be still fascinated with the bright lights and the fast crowds of the city. But in one thing she was absolutely right. You could be in New York

City, what you wanted to be…free and liberated. Clarence's small town blues disappeared in the city and his small southern hometown seemed like a bad dream…some ill-defined place.

St. Nicholas Avenue ran parallel to St. Nicholas Park. A virile young man sat in the park perched on a massive rock, holding an umbrella over his head to protect himself from the snow. He looked like a picture post card of the King of the Blacks. Clarence did not fail to notice him. The young man sat on the same rock every morning, as if he was waiting for an angel to fly from the clouds. Every morning, he smiled at Clarence rushing past him on his way to work. Sometimes, he would signal with his fingers if Clarence had a cigarette for him. Other times, he would play with his penis, as if he was baiting a fishing rod to lure a fish. Clarence knew he was the fish. Clarence would not have been a queen, a cream puff, a fag, a la-de-dah, if he would not have been attracted to the virile young man. That is what made him a pervert with perverted desires. It was better to pretend, to try to ignore him. But a star had fallen into Clarence's heart and he lost a soft battle against fear. How could a queen ignore a robust man on the hunt, soliciting himself to the highest bidder? He was what they called a real hunk, a large piece of meat as opposed to a morsel, a tidbit. He was for sell for a mere song, a penny dropped. There were no boundaries to Clarence's longings. This hunk placed him in a trance, making Clarence wish penises had wings and he could play their flute softly in apple fields. Clarence indulged in such fantasies, until he realized he had a job to go to. St. Nicholas Park was a disreputable park. It was crime infested, reputed to be the meeting place in the evenings for solitary young men and their purported trade. It was the stomping ground for Clarence. The young man on the rock unquestionably captivated him, making him want to taste him, to savor his virility. He sat on the rock like a hesitating falcon, cruising exclusively in the mornings. Subtle intuition told Clarence the young man was a thug. But he was a good-looking one, a potential bedroom servant. Clarence imagined him as a reclining nude, rubbing his private part, indicating he was available, for sale. He continued to daydream on the hunk, envisaging a hot chocolate man on a white sandy beach with a racy wide nose and sensual thick lips, with a slender black body of enticing loins and a sexy round ass. He imagined their bodies pressed black against black. He was enraptured with a manhood, which possibly lay hidden behind a strip of cowhide. He fantasized of dark glowing shadows. He pictured himself as the queen of vaudeville, pampered by some God of beady hair and shiny dark skin, murmuring into his ear, displaying his infinitely long black penis, which knew no beginning and no end. He longed for a Mapplethorpe Black man to appear, a meditative brother with fire in his head; one, who perch on his throne of ostrich feathers, splendidly broad of chest, and adorned with red and green beads, brass jewelry and geometric chalk figures, would squeeze, embrace and seduce him. He longed to spend the night with such a man, counting his natural muscles, running his hand down his smooth curves, pinching his nipples till they turned purple, visualizing such a man in beads of sweat, working in the sugarcane fields or picking cotton, as he waited in anticipation. Clarence felt weak and delirious as their bodies intertwined. They made love, smeared with ochre and animal fat, frolicking among oxen, bulls, goats and sheep. After their mad act of love, they strolled hand in hand under the oblique rays of a setting orange sun. Then Clarence snapped back to reality again, feeling fantasy was better than reality and he returned to the slanted house in the desert of dollars and cents, to rationality and common sense. He ignored the young man sitting on the rock in the park, rubbing his penis…his toy, because it was too cold to get an erection and too wet to copulate under trees.

5. The myth was uncovered

The winter became fluid, melting into dirty water, which flowed into the gutters. The polar cold departed and another winter of catastrophes passed away to be forgotten. Nature awoke in an explosion of colors...in a labyrinth of flowers. Spring appeared from its' winter sleep, awakening a craving, the hunger for color and a little tenderness. A sweet, warm breeze blew from the south, stirring lustful desires. The tulips and narcissus in the parks competed with each other for attention. The trees were no longer disrobed and barren, but clothed with delicate lime leaves. They soared up into the sky. A succulent growth stretched across the parks of the city, making them appear as a green oasis. Clarence sauntered through St. Nicholas Park in Harlem, after a long day of toil. He sought to escape the drudgery of routine, strolling between the tulips, smelling and picking them....gathering them into a bundle. St. Nicholas Park was a private jungle for him. He usually went there cruising on warm nights, when his body burned with desires and beckoned with silent entreaties. In such moments, he was on the hunt for horns, centaurs and supermen. The rock, where the young hustler sat in the early morning hours, was now vacant. Clarence strolled through the park, meditating on male gallantry, inhaling the various fragrances in the air. It was a warm late afternoon...framed in rare harmony. The worn brownstones of Harlem below the park could be seen through the roofs of the trees. The skyline of Manhattan glimmered in the distance under the setting sun. The sky was a bluish blood orange, enticing Clarence to dream about yellow hills, wild jockeys, and untamed cowboys on polka dot horses, riding in lavender fields...scenes of a far away place. He removed his leather coat, reclined on a massive rock, and allowed himself to bask in the evening red, totally surrounded by nature. He was happy to have such a park in the neighborhood. He cherished the few minutes of peace in this natural environment and craved for a love, someone God created especially for him. Clarence felt lonely in such moments and wondered how native New Yorkers could live their entire lives between concrete buildings. Did they not miss the feeling of nature under their feet, the sensation of walking across damp grass as the fog rose, the luxury of being able to recline and to dream under a massive Oak tree, the thrill of watching cows grassing in the fields? Maybe this was why the parks in New York City were so loved. Some said they were the hearts of the city. But the city parks were not an alternative for rural tranquility. They were not playing fields of nature, but lurking places for bandits, cunning robbers and evil midgets. Those who had money like hay, the rich, could afford a glittering escape. They were not stranded in the city. They owned entrenchments in the Hamptons on Long Island, where they fled the sharp edges of the city for the quiet solitude of the privilege. Working-class people like Clarence, could only flee within themselves, within their inner space. Workers rarely have the time for such escapes. They are too busy trying to survive.

Clarence sprawled out on the huge rock with images in his mind of a lost paradise, images of blooming trees and tousled dark people floated though his mind, of zebras racing across the Serengeti, of elephants grassing and leopards relaxing lazily in the sun. He imagined little Negritos in crimson red and gold, carrying bananas on their heads and muscular fishermen, pushing their boats against a silver tide. He thought he heard drums beating in the distance, summoning ancient spirits. He saw with his inner eye ebony women, braiding their hair in gold, and humming a mysterious melody to themselves. Clarence imagined himself standing in the mist of a public gathering and drowning in an ocean of colors, forms and chalked bodies. He saw himself canoeing across a lake with brawny indigo warriors in imposing turbans with bows and arrows, as thousands of naked bodies bathed and fished around him. Their nets and calabashes reflected the evening red. "What's up, bro?" The voice came from nowhere. It was rough, as rough as the man was, who uttered it. He stood in front of Clarence, waiting for a response to his idle question. An accurate answer was not expected, just a response. Clarence roused from his reverie to observe the man, standing in front of him. "What's up, bro?" The man said again. In gay circles, this would have been the moment to turn on the automatic. A clever queen, who knew the secret of picking up a man and didn't hesitate or waited long, would have responded to the question in the following manner; "You, baby! It's all about you!" This was how the game of seduction was played in Harlem...similar to jazz. "Hi!" Clarence responded. "Where's the action at?" The man asked. "Action...?" Clarence queried. "Yea, I'm looking for some action." The young man shifted his body, taking a stance that indicated to Clarence what type of action he meant. "Well, I guess you found it with me." Clarence indicated with his eyes that he was interested. A soft wind blew from below the park, as a circular conversation began between Clarence and the man, which resembled a religious ritual. One had to be cognizant of the right questions and the correct responses in this seductive game. Clarence, although he had lived in New York for a long time, had not become accustomed to the nuances of the rite. He often retorted with, "hi" or "hello". This sounded like the white boys, who lived downtown. It was the worst thing a black male could have said. Often Clarence introduced himself and inquired: "What is your name?" This turned the black boys off. They were against animal seriousness. They were not seeking a chaste Mary, who did not know how to catch a male or how to give an anonymous blow job. They lost interest quickly and would ease out of the situation by saying: "I'll check you later," drifting away with the wind. Most love yearning queers in the city and the males they picked up from the streets, their trade, were not looking for the blue band of romanticism. Sentimental drivel was not in demand. Those, who were fixed on being rough, would continue on their way, shopping for another partner, or trick, one who would manhandle them or one whom they could manhandle. After "shooting their guns" (orgasm), they would swiftly walk away without uttering a word, leaving their partners in shame, with their pants around their ankles.

But Clarence was ready for a little flirt this late afternoon...on the edge of night and he had resolved not to let this young hunk slip through his fingers. Screening was half of life in the gay scene. Clarence focused his attention on the man, eying him from top to toe, and he suddenly noticed this was the young man in the thicket of youth, who perched himself every morning on the massive rock in the park...the one Clarence often observed on his way to work. It appeared as if St. Nicholas Park was this young man's runway, his stomping ground. Clarence observed him. He was more gorgeous in evening red than in the early morning light. He was like a wild animal with green eyes. He stood in tight jeans like a half god before Clarence, posing for prosperity, exposing everything he had to offer. It was an erotic view. Clarence imagined such men fell from the sky and prayed to God to bless him for he was about to sin. Wondering how to maneuver this stallion into the bushes, or to more private quarters, where he could check the product before taking it home, Clarence dismounted the rock, approaching the young man, who stood erect like granite with muscles of steel, like a master of the fixed moment. Clarence gazed into his eyes and although they were beautifully green, he was shocked to see that the eyes of the young man were like an empty space, devoid of warmth and tenderness, lacking humanity. The young man had nothing which was valuable. He was not a hero, but only a bandit. Yet Clarence horniness rendered him blind, like a luckless beggar and beggars couldn't be choosy.

"You want some of this?" The young man spited the words out of his mouth, while grabbing his penis in his hand. The expression on his face was indifferent and unconcerned, but he was very aware of the fact his impressive penis was a weapon, and his penis was, what made him a "man". He presented himself to Clarence like a priceless Stradivarius. Clarence desired him, doing a minuet around the young man, letting his hormones control his mind. Moving closer to the young man, he placed his hand on the young man's private part. It was soft like a rotten banana. Clarence throttled his tempo, disappointed. He suddenly realized the young man did not desire him and he was plagued by second thoughts, thoughts about whether it was a good idea to continue this game. He started to gather his belongings and attempted to make a quick exit from the young man and out of the park, as a blow struck him suddenly to the head, rendering him unconscious on the ground. Corn dust floated from the ground into the air. Clarence laid prostrated for less than a minute, then he opened his eyes, staring at the orange sky above, wondering what had happened. He had been robbed. His leather coat and his wallet were missing. He grabbed his briefcase in a state of confusion, fixed his clothes, brushed the dirt off his pants and shirt, polished his shoes with a handkerchief and patted his hair into place, rubbing his face clean; making sure he was presentable. Then he started to yell at the top of his voice. "Help me! Help me! Oh, Lawd! Somebody please help me!" He said whatever came into his head, expecting spectators and onlookers to rush to his aide in order to push his derailed cart out of the dirt. But nobody came to his rescue. "I've been robbed! Can somebody help me?" Clarence screamed again, swaying from side to side, offering a dazzling show, dizzy from the depth of his fall, disappointed, because he was so near to triumph only to fall into a bottomless pit. "Oh help me, please!" His yells were perceptibly weaker. "Somebody please help me!" His desire to get lost was greater. No one was in sight. No one happened to be on the same cross road as he was. It was his luck to be in need, and to have no one around to help. He stopped screaming, realizing it was futile. "He called me brother! What type of brother is that?" He said to himself, disappointed with black males in general. There was no trace of brotherly love.

Clarence marched out of the park into St. Nicholas Avenue and walked up 141st street, searching up and down the street for a police car. There was not a police car in sight, only the dilapidated gypsy cabs could be seen, which were often driven by immigrants on their flight from hunger and war, dreaming of a better life in a rich land. He looked down Convent Avenue and saw young students rushing to City College. Most of them were also foreigners, seeking a window to the future in America, a career perspective. He decided to stand on the corner of 141st street and Convent Avenue, filled with anger. He improvised, waited and hoped a police car would eventually pass. Clarence did not know how to play the vanquished, the victim, or the humiliated, since he had never been physically assaulted before, never had anything violently taken away. He wondered if this was how bruised and battered women felt…vulnerable, debased, without any rights, like a dog that had just received a swift kick in the butt? He debated with himself the pros and contras of telling someone what had happened. It was an embarrassing situation. An elderly lady approached him, noticing his misfortune, his wounded appearance. "You poor child," she said in a sympathetic manner. "Have you been robbed?" The elderly lady sought to soothe his suffering. Her brown eyes were warm, reflecting the evening sun. She carried her groceries in her arms and appeared as a black dairymaid. She reminded Clarence of the old black women that he knew from the south....the ones with bent backs from a life of working for white people. He wondered if she was a phantom; if she had just walked out of a fairytale. How could she tell the nice mess he had gotten himself into? Did his face look benighted? Did it reflect his misfortune? "Yes! I've been robbed," he replied. "I was mugged in the park!" The old lady shook her head in amazement at the emotion of the moment. "You'll get over it," she said. "I've been robbed five times!" She seemed proud of this accomplishment, proud of being a victim. Clarence looked at her in bewilderment. How could one be proud of being robbed? "Don't fret. God is the chief, the creator of heaven and messengers, the calm listener in every conversation, the observer of every ordeal. Time will heal your wounds," the old lady said. "Time doesn't heal all wounds," Clarence responded. Happy were the people who believed in this bull shit, lucky in their ignorance and simplicity, he thought.

A police car cruised down 141st street at this moment. Clarence waved it down. The car parked at the corner of 141st street and Convent Avenue. Two officers got out of the car. They were white, cute and masculine, very feudal in their uniforms...just what white sissies dreamed about. "I've just been robbed in the park!" Clarence proclaimed. The policemen queried if he was injured and if the assailant had a weapon? This was an embarrassing question. Clarence was forced to admit he had not seen anything, to admit he was knocked out on the ground. This meant explaining how he allowed his assailant to get close enough to assault him. He prevaricated. Did he know the assailant, the police officers asked? How long did he and the assailant carried on a conversation, they interrogated? The police officers asked, if he wanted to fill out a report? "Yes," Clarence replied. They escorted him to the car. Clarence was reluctant to get into the police car, thinking what his circle of friends and colleagues would say, all the scandalmonger queens, if they saw him, sitting in the back seat of a police car like a criminal and a convict. It would be food for their fantasies. He was a respectable, middle-class person...a teacher. He had a reputation to protect. The police officer suggested it might be better if they rode around the corner several times. "Maybe you will be able to recognize your assailant on the streets, Sir." The officer said Sir sarcastically. Clarence agreed reluctantly. They turned on Convent Avenue and drove down Convent Avenue through the campus of City College, then they drove pass St. Nicholas Park. They turned on 130th street and drove down the hill, turned on St. Nicholas Avenue and drove slowly up the avenue, alongside the park. On the corner of 139th and St. Nicholas Avenue, there was the young man sitting on the same massive rock. "There he is!" Clarence shouted. "The nerve of him...! I can't believe he would be so stupid to rob someone and return to the scene of the crime!"

"These boys are bold, Sir. You are probably not the only one he has robbed today. They prey on people like you. Because no one ever reports it, they feel relatively safe. It is easier than picking mangos." Clarence wondered what the police officer meant by the phrase "people like you". The police car abruptly halted on 140th street. The officers leaped out of the car, scurrying into the park with their gun drawn, geared for killing. It was worse than a Hollywood western or a thriller. Clarence heard the roar of the guns in his imagination...the police officers and the young man battling at the intersection... the young man bathing in his blood. He visualized a pink funeral with all his fairy friends dressed in pink, with pink flowers, a pink casket and pink limousines. He contemplated getting out of the car and running for safety. After a while, the officers returned with the young man. The young man strained his head to see who was sitting in the car. Clarence tried to hide his face, wishing he could turn himself upside down and pack himself into a box. The policemen requested for Clarence to get out of the car, to identify the young man as his assailant. He got out of the car, looking defiantly into the young man's face. The young man was visually shocked to see him again, having believed they would not cross fronts again. His green eyes became watery. His brazen face softened and he began to cry like a baby, melting into tears. "Is this the man who robbed you?" The police officers asked. Clarence hesitated. It was pitiful to see a grown man cry. He felt empathy for the fellow, realizing they were both black and the policemen were both white. He felt guilty, like a traitor of the race, somehow. The young man prostrated himself in front of Clarence. "Please, mister, don't do this to me." He felled on his knees as if in prayer, begging. Fear was in his eyes. "I'm sorry, mister!" He lamented. "I'm sorry!" He sobbed, being desperate, afraid. He placed Clarence in a distressing dilemma, being torn between being responsible and following his emotions. Clarence's heart bled for this young man. He was a young black boy, he thought, rebelling against morals and order. He was just a young boy, a robber of eggs, who was trying his best to survive and homosexuals were easy targets, fair game. His dilemma was between self-interest and species preservation. His belief in crime as a way out of the chaos was the wrong way. There was for such young men, in reality, no choice...not even a choice between good and evil. Wantonness was a necessity, when one was forced to live a life from hand to mouth. Clarence knew all these things. "Yes, that's him," he said. "Where are my things, my personal belongings... my leather coat...my wallet?" The green eyes of the young man quickly turned to hate, scorn, and loathing. He became the monster he hid under his skin, a vulture with sharp eyes and wide wings. The police officers placed him quickly in handcuffs and threw him into the car. They inquired if Clarence wanted to press charges. "Yes, of course!" The police officers filled out a printed form. They handed the form to Clarence to sign, telling him he would receive a letter from the attorney general's office and would be invited to testify against the young man. They then thanked him and got into their car, driving slowly up St. Nicholas Avenue. As Clarence braved a last look at the young man, sitting in the back seat of the police car, he gazed at Clarence with anger in his face. It was a face that had changed so quickly from pity to brutality. The young man drew his finger across his neck in a gesture of evil, indicating to Clarence, his victim; he was just as good as dead.

Clarence lingered on the avenue, watching the passing cars, while pondering why he did not feel relieved, why he felt burdened, tired, disappointed and disgusted with life. He was given the opportunity to help a lost soul and he failed. Feeling dejected and alone, he walked slowly up 141st street. Was his outlook, his way of looking at life wrong, he asked himself? He could not deal with all of this brutality. He stopped exhausted under a marquise with "Sullivan's Apartments" written on it, resting on the stoop, observing the heavy traffic, the pedestrians, absorbed in their daily routines. After he regained his composure, he entered the brownstone under the marquise. A church bell sounded in the distance. There were loud voices in the vestibule. "Please, please, leave me alone," a female voice pleaded. "Sweetie, let me in," a male voice intoned with galloping seriousness. "I have a nice gift for you, if you give me a kiss." Clarence looked through the glass door to see Mr. Sullivan, his landlord, surrounded by the stinky smoke of his cigar, and standing at Mrs. Holstrom's apartment. Mr. Sullivan's foot was in the door, preventing Mrs. Holstrom from closing the door. His broad body cast a long shadow on the wall of the vestibule. Mrs. Holstrom peeped from the side of her apartment door. "I wish you would leave me alone," she cried. Mr. Sullivan leaned with his weight against the door. He was a huge man, who was tame only in the lap of a willing woman. Clarence walked into the front entrance of the apartment building, where the mailboxes were located. He looked into his mailbox and quickly closed the mailbox, walking then into the vestibule. He looked sternly at Mr. Sullivan, who appeared not to be embarrassed by his presence. He acted as if Clarence was invisible, hoping he would fade away or silently climb the stairs and go to his apartment. But he underestimated Clarence's sense of righteousness. "Mr. Sullivan, why don't you get in your car and go home," Clarence suggested, noticing Mr. Sullivan was intoxicated.

"You fucking faggot, get out of my face," Mr. Sullivan replied, exposing Clarence to ridicule, striking a defiant pose. He took his foot out of the door, turned towards Clarence, intensifying his assault. Clarence observed him standing in front of his face. Clarence concluded this was a shallow man, biting, vain, immovable, and he quickly resolved he would use the Chinese vase on the large oak table in the corner of the vestibule, to defend himself. "You're not the first one to call me a faggot and you probably won't be the last one, Mr. Sullivan. If you are trying to insult me, you are playing the wrong card," Clarence said. "I know what I am and who I am. That is not what I can say for you." He held this man to be presumptuous and ignorant. "I will smash your face in this wall, you fucking faggot!" Mr. Sullivan hollered, pointing at the wall. Clarence decided to show this muddle-headed fellow that being a sissy with a twirling stick did not mean he was a punk. Brutal men have to be taught there is a stronger one. "I'll bite your peter off, Mr. Sullivan...the very one you're trying so hard to utilize," Clarence said, considering Mr. Sullivan to be the type of stupid black male, who lost his common sense in the face of a white female. "That white woman don't (*doesn't*) want to hear anything that you have to say."

"You fucking faggot! I'll throw you out on the street! This building belongs to me!" Mr. Sullivan was raving. Clarence reminded him this was New York City and he was in a New York state of mind. "If you continue to threaten me, Mr. Sullivan, I will report you to the New York City housing authorities," he informed him. "It is your responsibility to fix the toilettes, to provide heat when it is needed and to put a new lock on the front door of this building, to keep drug addicts and uninvited guests from walking in from the streets." Clarence hoped Mr. Sullivan would not believe he was telling fibs and stories or that he had an emblem of fear on his face, because he was gay. He was dead serious. Drawn out of his room by the loud shouting, Monsieur Albert shuffled into the vestibule on his cane. "Mon Dieu...! Quel clamour!" (My God...! What noise...!) He exclaimed, playing the house angel, the Good Samaritan. Monsieur Albert was the old Haitian man, who lived in a tiny room on the first floor. "Monsieur Sullivan, I think you go now. Tis' better for all," Monsieur Albert pleaded. He opened the front door of the vestibule and held it open for Mr. Sullivan to leave. Mr. Sullivan walked out of the door...moon mad. He got into his Lincoln Continental, cursing Clarence's soul. "Monsieur Hill, go to your apartment, s'il vous plait (*please*). Tis' no good to fight," Monsieur Albert said to Clarence. Clarence followed his entreaty, climbing meekly up the stairs to his apartment, as if they were ladders to heaven, wondering about the logic of conflict and why men went to war. He rested this evening on his futon. His need for friction and antagonism was covered. His nerves were wracked. His feathers were plucked. During the night, Nubian men came to him in sleep. They were different from the ones that said 'brother' and meant 'fiend'....not like the ones who prey on queens, the ones which could be bought on the cattle market like a commodity, where the price and quality were the only things of importance. Clarence wondered about his queer friends, who thought they were lucky to have a male, even if it was the semblance of a man, more like a thug or a bandit. They often times acted as if they had won a lottery when they had found one, a man. But in reality, they spent their entire lives seeking quick sex as an anesthesia against timeless eternity and took all the steps to insignificance to achieve it. The myth of freedom was uncovered. Clarence thought that they were not free.

6. All roads lead home

In his moments of loneliness, Clarence dreamed of undressing Antoine. He pictured him standing in the silver shimmer of the moonlight. Antoine was a muscle bound black Olympian, a wavering colossus. He was a Jamaican man with the face of a king, who had left the shadows of his Caribbean nightmare in search of the American Dream. He spent most of his time, striving to become one of those successful black men at the top, with a bright future. He whipped himself forward with ambition to the peak. But his success left ruins and there was a cost for success. Antoine was a psychologist at Columbia University. Although he was able to decipher other persons, he remained a puzzle for himself. He could not explain his shattered marriage; why his beloved wife threw him out of their marriage bed for a less successful gigolo, or why she preferred the low life of carnal pleasure and delight. Her unfaithfulness left bruises in his psyche. Antoine played the abused king with a disappointment behind him. He fanatically lifted weights at the Harlem YMCA after work, groaning and believing he could become a special class of men, Herculean, alone and free as a tree. He praised the things, which made men hard. He wanted petite Barbie dolls in costumes to droll over his body. But he was only interested in feeding, mating and copulating with them. Antoine had actually sealed the entry to his soul, seeking revenge on all females.

In Clarence's eyes, he exuded a virile manhood, which was his attraction. He was the portrait of a muscular male in repose. His muscles were hard as a rock. When quibbling with his buddies, he often slapped his muscle bound thighs to stress a point. His biceps and calves were spacious. They quivered when he walked. The winding lines and semi curves of his body made him appear as a sculptured statue… an Adonis in bronze. He gave to all the impression of being hard. But Clarence knew that there was a soft spot somewhere in his soul. Antoine and Clarence met at the Harlem YMCA, which Clarence joined after his fairy friends, the ones, who lived for moments of ecstasy, the ones, who were always open for a new amusement, a new kick, told him that the Harlem YMCA was like a fruit bowl filled with apples and oranges, all ripe for the picking by hungry faggots like himself. It was a garden of twisted bodies lifting weights, where frustrated queens tangoed around muscle flexing men, looking for attention, yearning for warmth. Clarence joined the Harlem YMCA with the intention to train his slender androgynous body, giving it some type of manly definition, training every evening and putting himself to the rack. After the incident in St. Nicholas Park, he decided to become a dragon that other men feared, struggling in vain to give his slender body some type of definition, mimicking strength and power.

It was his greatest delight to watch Antoine training, to observe intently the esthetic of his movements. Clarence considered Antoine to be a hot thing with an alluring curvature of the spinal cord, which ended temptingly in a faultless firm round ass. It was a pleasure for his eyes and soul. Antoine and Clarence began chatting in the sauna of the YMCA, becoming muddled and entangled in the mechanics of language, while dripping in sweat. It was a ritual for the men in the hot sauna to carry on intense political discussions about people, power and markets, about the unimprovable state of the nation, about the race problem, and about the boundaries of morals. It was an honorary round of middle-class black men, who perspired, parleyed and disputed with each other in cheap polemic. Antoine talked a lot about Africa. He was an African buff…a black nationalist… a Pan-Africanist. He was the one, who implanted into Clarence's mind the bizarre idea of going to the 'Dark Continent'. Antoine described to Clarence breathtaking landscapes created in heat and drought, magnificent mountains and spacious rivers, while Clarence laid naked on one side of the sauna and Antoine reclined naked on the other side. "Listen to the signals from your heritage," Antoine said one day. Clarence did not immediately respond, because he did not understand in which direction Antoine was heading. "What heritage?" Clarence later asked in a rhetorical manner. "You didn't just fall into this world, Clarence. Somebody is responsible for you being here…just like somebody was responsible for your parents and your grandparents. People die. The spirit continues to live," Antoine told him. "What spirit? I don't believe in any spirits," Clarence said. In reality, he did believe in spirits. He remembered the day his mother died, as he was sitting along in the Cathedral of Saint John the Devine on the upper Westside of New York City…the very moment his mother died thousands of miles away, the moment her soul left her body and travelled thousands of miles to him. He remembered the silence and the feeling that he had at that moment, while sitting in the Cathedral. "You only know what you see and you only believe what you see, Clarence. You have ancestors!" Antoine insisted, trying to convince Clarence. "That might be the case. But they are all dead and can't do anything for me. I don't believe in dead heroes," Clarence responded. Antoine had a disappointed look on his face upon hearing Clarence's comment. "I'll pray to our ancestors that you change this view, my brother," Antoine uttered.

When Antoine spoke, his eyes glimmered like gems. He had a gift of the gab, speaking with intellect. Despite his small foibles, such as, his macho behavior and his belief women were made to serve men, he seemed to possess sense and understanding in other things. He appeared to be a sensible black man. This was the internal contradiction within him. He was a black man, seeking a culture. It was important for him to have roots and a history. "The roots of a tree can destroy a wall of steel," he said. He saw himself somehow as a torchbearer for a forgotten wisdom, for dead ancestors…the keepers of the sun. "Trees die as well," Clarence responded.

"We are a part of the past and a part of the future, but because of our short memory, we have become prisoners of the present, afraid of listening to our ancestors. The search for our lost souls begins in the dark," Antoine said. When he described Africa to Clarence, it appeared to be a land like a poem, a wild land with a wild heart. Clarence could hear the trembles, the drums, the belafons and tambourines playing. He saw images of naked men and women kissing the ground in ecstasy. His soul floated with harmonic sounds and loose rhythms. Antoine called it Akebu-land. Clarence wondered how Antoine knew so much about Africa. "It is Greek and means land of the blacks," he declared. Clarence heard his message. Within him the cool birth of a need stirred. "The greatest freedom black folks have in America, is in their cage," Antoine said. He grabbed Clarence around the ankle to emphasize his lack of freedom, his shackles. Antoine later invited Clarence to come to the 'African People' seminars on Saturdays at the Lutheran Church, the Chapel in the Field, which was located in Harlem on the corner of 145th street and Convent Avenue. It was an institution in Harlem, more than a church… a sanctuary for those who collected dreams. There the dreamers were among themselves, engaging in a healing hour with the spirits, searching on thin ice for the secrets of the past. This was the place where Antoine had learned about Africa. A dark man, who looked like an alligator, guarded the front door of the church.

Clarence struggled with phantoms. Half ghosts floated through the air of his apartment. They danced sometimes in the twilight, striving to persuade him to visit the seminars. He often observed on his way to the subway, the patrician men and dazzling black women standing on the Avenue in front of the church, as if they understood better than others did, the power of light and air. They were rooted in the earth of their forefathers. The descendants sought their dreams in the ruins of Africa. They were lordly and grand in their resplendent African dress, in their multicolored cloths and glittering head turbans. They appeared like kaleidoscopic butterflies that flew from the page. A torch light procession in honor of mother Africa occurred. They intimidated Clarence. He knew they were intolerant, seeking revenge on their oppressors from earlier times. He knew they rejected his lifestyle. He was in their eyes, a harlequin, one who breaks taboos, and for whom nothing is sacrosanct. He could not be saved. One Sunday morning, Clarence hurried along Convent Avenue on his way to church, in search of answers. He encountered underway, the demons which hunted him, the rascals who preached wry mouthed about truth. A babbling and adulterating rat catcher, yearning for death, stood on the trottoir, on the corner of 145th street and St. Nicholas, preaching about virtue. He fervently proselytized, giving out pamphlets. He was dressed in an African costume and tried to recruit black men and women for what he called, "the birth of a new existence, a rebirth as African men and women." The man preached as if he had the entire world on a wire, praising heathen ancestors and pagan ways, raging about Jesus, Buddha and Mohammed. Clarence tried to ignore the tirades of the preacher. He believed the truth was located in the middle, somewhere between heaven, hell and nirvana. "Every problem has a solution," the man screamed. "There are only two versions of truth, the right version and the wrong version. Black folks have to rediscover themselves." He preached against sexual deviation in the white man's society and claimed, "Homosexuality is a white man's sickness. It is a phenomenon of decay." The preacher threw stones in Clarence direction, who suddenly remembered his student days, when the young communists on campus claimed homosexuality was an affliction of capitalistic decadence. "What if your brother would be gay?" Clarence inquired with a nimble tongue, standing between a hard rock and a hard place. "I would do what a man has to do. I would kill him with my own hands," the sermonizer replied, becoming offensive and public, as if murder was a commodity. It was a declaration of love for insanity. "Isn't killing a cardinal sin?" Clarence asked. The young black man gazed at him in disbelief. Gray clouds covered his head, blocking the sun. "Brother, homosexuality is a cancer. It eventually will destroy the body and society," he said, fire flaming in his eyes. Clarence confronted the devil. "I'm gay and I don't believe that I'm sick or decadent," he proclaimed with a trace of self-irony. Upon hearing what Clarence had said; that he was different than the others and he was not seeking quick salvation, the street preacher raised his voice, calling the ravenous beasts, a pack of hounds, and his followers to the kill. "Brothers and sisters, here is a brother who is a faggot and proud of it," he screamed loudly, shooting sparrows with canons. Roaring was half of winning. The ghosts and the phantoms assembled from all sides. A bell clanged in the tower of the Lutheran church on the hill, shaking the windows and arches, the houses and the street. Since it was senseless to blow wind in someone's ear or to swim against a current, Clarence decided to flee this circle of villains. They congregated in their net of violence and passion. They knew only the fist rights of freedom. Clarence hurried to catch his subway. It was the wrong time to fight a long battle for nothing. Clarence did not intend to confess his sins to those who were of sin in a sea of sins. He also would not allow himself to be reprimanded for having flexible identities, nor would he allow himself to be abused by a bunch of black lambs with white vests, who thought they were blacker than thou, experts for history and feelings. You couldn't break a brick wall over people heads to make them tolerant. You could not remove the walls in people heads. They saw ugliness, where there was beauty. For some people, stations of beauty were unknown. It had to be sketched onto a blank canvas.

Antoine regularly asked Clarence why he had not seen him at the seminars. Prevaricating, Clarence said he was busy and promised to come the next time. He darned a patchwork of white lies, instead of telling Antoine the truth. He was afraid of being branded and choked under the public eye, of being whipped naked for entertainment. He believed fanatics were the greatest danger for the environment and there could be no reconciliation, nor friendship between the hunted and the hunters.

It was the Easter holidays. The Pope prayed for lost souls at the Vatican and true believers showed devotion. Clarence stole away to his dreary apartment, where the weight of the world appeared to rest upon his shoulders. It rained for one week. Clarence counted the raindrops on excursions of the mind, wondering when it would stop raining. The streets were vacuous with little trace of life. The houses appeared forlorn. His secret friends, the uncrowned queens, the accidental queers, the dukes, the countesses, the witches, the fairytale gentlemen, and all the other flaming creatures had returned to their little towns in Pleasantville, from whence they came, leaving Clarence to deal with the anatomy of melancholy in the city. He walked in the mornings along the cliffs on the Hudson River and hid in the afternoons in a dark corner of the Cathedral on 110th and Amsterdam Avenue, listening to heavenly organ music and the melting serene sounds of young choirboys. Then it occurred to him, a secret dawned upon him that even when one is forced to travel endless curves, to walk crooked lines, all roads lead home. And this home was only a corner of the total. He took a trip into his own past and realized all of his life; the only thing he wanted was a place to breathe, to exhale freely. He had had enough of boredom. He decided to visit the African seminars on the following Saturday. There he sat in the middle of their splendor, equipped for all chicanery, overcome by the emotion of the view. It was a festival of butterflies, free in color. Here were a people on a long march to liberation. They mourned for an ancient past. They remembered a lost world and created new myths to live by. They sought answers to their predicament.

Clarence felt as if he was without a face for the occasion. These children of the African Diaspora were deep and emotional. They had a memory of pain and suffering. They were a small minority, looking for a new beautiful beginning in the distant future, in a land of great peace. They fought against the corroding majority. The surf would wash them away. A sad thought occurred to Clarence, while sitting under the arches of the small church, observing this splendor of color. He thought, they all lived as a people together in one land, in one nation under God, as they say, and yet they, white America and black America, remained strangers to each other. A woman of mahogany wood greeted everyone at the seminar. She requested for the oldest woman, the oldest man and the youngest member in the church to stand. The entire congregation applauded. They prayed for reconciliation, for a healing process to occur. The moderator asked if there were any 'new' beautiful sons and daughters visiting. Clarence remained sitting, afraid of being flagellated, afraid of being hung on the gallows, of becoming the scytheman. He knew there were serpents under every leaf, behind every tree ready to attack. Everyone held hands and gave thanks to their ancestors, commemorating their sufferings and accomplishments. Clarence was convinced they could tell he was homosexual. He attempted to act unnaturally butch, manly and rough. This meant overpowering his éclatant behavior, concealing his natural grace and elegance, trying to walk without shaking his ass. This was a stressful situation for him. It was normal for him to look at and appraise hot men, to pick out the raisins, the ones worthy of a prize. He did this automatically, similar to the way men appraise women. He wore dark sunglasses to conceal his eyes. Since this was New York, no one thought it odd that he would be sitting in a church with sunglasses on. They thought he was just being grand.

In the seminars, Clarence learned a lot about African philosophy, African nature and African esthetics. He became absorbed in African mysticism, and religion. It was a cerebral and spiritual exercise. A flame for knowledge was ignited within him, a burning desire to learn more. Here were a people, who yearned to create the birth of a new existence in common. They sought a rebirth...to give their life meaning. They yearned for a renaissance of an ancient civilization, of traditions in another time. They sought refuge in the heritage of their forefathers. They were all searching for a utopia. "Those who have nothing to lose have to depend upon their belief, and hope that tomorrow a new wind will blow," Antoine told him.

Clarence surmised in the end, the final decision would be one of living a life of rationality or living a life of devotion and spirituality. The Pan-African seminars organized guided summer trips to Africa. Clarence yearned to go, to wash his soul in a deep river in Africa. But he feared that traveling with a group of judgmental homophobic black folks would be bloodletting. It would be an existence in hell. He would be a nuisance for them. There was no salvation for types like him. They lived in a separate world as the normal one and would always be considered outsiders. Since this was the case, he decided to search for another group with which he could travel to Africa...one in which he could allow his secret 'perverted' desires to play free, without shame. Actually he should have traveled to Africa alone, but he was afraid to travel there on his own. He discovered by chance the New School for Social Research on 5th Avenue offered summer trips to Africa for artists. He booked immediately without second thoughts. He then informed Antoine he would be going to Africa in the summer. Antoine congratulated him, inquiring who would be leading the group, thinking the Pan-African group at the Lutheran Church organized it. "I am not going to Africa with them. I'm going with a group from Parsons," Clarence said "Are they white? Antoine asked. "Yes!" Clarence sheepishly answered. "Clarence, let me give you some advice." Antoine waited a few seconds before he spoke. "If you were Jewish, would you go to Israel with a bunch of Germans?" He asked, trying to show Clarence his discrepancy, to give him insight into an unavoidable conflict. "No, I guess I wouldn't. It wouldn't be appropriate." Clarence blushed. "Well, going to Africa with a group of whites is the same thing. These people will not see Africa the way you will," Antoine said. "They will not understand the deep emotions you will be having, the purity of your feelings," he continued. "You will be returning home after centuries of the Diaspora. They will be going on an exotic trip for the sole purpose of diversion, seeing Africa on a Safari. It will be a collision of perceptions." Antoine reclined on the wood bench in the sauna, closed his eyes and spread his legs wide, sovereign-like. Clarence thought of another diversion, while lying on a bench across from Antoine. His thoughts were free. Antoine was oblivious to his desires. Clarence wanted Antoine, but he was too shy to tell Antoine how he felt. He waited for Aphrodite's lightning attack, observing Antoine's masculinity with his tongue hanging out, pondering if at the end of the rainbow, such a man would be waiting for him. He turned over on his stomach, stuck his ass in the air like a pyramid and hoped Antoine would at least out of the corner of his eye notice his presentation. He was hanging his hopes on a windmill. He was fishing for a King on a throne. How could he tell Antoine he was from the other shore, a freak, and an outsider? A storm raged within him. Antoine became his friend, but gave him no indication he wanted more than friendship. Antoine dreamed of nude girls; nude girls behind the curtains; nude girls in the sky; nude girls on the beach; nude girls shooting bow and arrows; nude girls swimming in a lake, relaxing between dunes, surrendering to the sun. It was an obsession with Antoine, as it is with most men. Clarence thought that if he could transform himself with witchcraft into a nude woman, Antoine would most certainly have raped him without hesitation in the sauna. But then he remembered that to be a woman, one had to learn how to suffer. He brooded over the creation of Adam.

As time progressed, Antoine started his own Wednesday's discussion group on African history, philosophy and culture at Columbia University. Since Clarence respected Antoine's intellect, he went to Antoine's discussion group. The discussion group was light, not as intimidating and stressful as the Saturday's seminars at the Lutheran church in Harlem. The church was a fortress for him. Antoine's charisma sparked in Clarence holy inspiration. He was a light tower on a cliff, which shined its light into the darkness. On their walks after the Wednesday seminars, Clarence wished Antoine would embrace him, but he was submerged in deep thoughts about the problems of the world, Antoine suggested one night to Clarence to teach African history, philosophy and culture at his job. Clarence informed Antoine that black history was generally taught in the school system in the month of February. Antoine responded that most people in America thought black people didn't have a philosophy or a culture. They thought one month was enough for black history. "It should be taught everyday!" Antoine said. "You have a view from a unique window and the rare opportunity as a teacher, Clarence, to give to our children a gift," he argued. "You can give our ancestors faces and contours. You can bring them to life for the children," he said. "You can teach them not to shoot into an empty space, not to exist in rooms with boundaries." Antoine continued. "You can teach them to stop believing on white fools and swearing on the devil. You can give them heroes like themselves, who will help them to their true soul and spirit." Antoine convinced Clarence of two things: (1) to go to Africa to find his true roots; and (2) to change the way he was teaching. Clarence always believed his roots were in the small town in the South, where he was born and raised. He felt he had little if any connections with Africa, because although a part of his ancestors once came from this continent, he also had ancestors from Europe and America. He considered his home to be America, land of the free and brave, where he presently vegetated. "Americans only believe in the power of the market," Antoine said. "They neglect the importance of culture." They shared glances. Fireworks exploded within Clarence. He felt faint hearted, wanting to cherish, to nourish and to embrace Antoine. He felt Antoine held the key to the gate of a road which led directly to his heart. He desired Antoine greatly. But Antoine was oblivious to his longings. Oh! Agony! Oh! Alleviation! Agony and alleviation laid close together.

7. Wood can not lie in water a long time...

Two black men bantered and joked with each other under the sun. They tarried on the corner of 145th Street and St. Nicholas Avenue, as if they were waiting for a magic hour to come...playing cards in the meantime. Clarence scrutinized them, pretending to be making a telephone call. He blew invisible kisses from the telephone booth in their direction. In his eyes, they were like black knights, who rode white horses at night. Clarence sensed that they could be armed and dangerous...warriors, who dreamed of war, and washed their feet in another man's blood. It was difficult to grasp the labyrinth of such men's minds. These were the types of fellows that demanded things with their sword or pistol drawn. They were also searching for a beautiful field, but were willing to step over bodies to get there. These were the types of males, who bickered and quarreled with each other, dividing the world into victors and the vanquished. What the world needed was more love...not hate and brutality. And love was like a pair of pink glasses. When you put them on, you discovered a new peaceful game with different rules. Clarence walked out of the telephone booth, leaving the two black knights digging for luck in their ghetto. He descended into the subway station on 145th Street and St. Nicholas Avenue, where he caught the A train...downtown. The subway accelerated through the dark tunnel like a magic bullet. Clarence rested on a bench in a corner next to the coachman's cabin, fantasizing about his intended trip to Africa. Images drifted through his mind. He imagined a boat carrying him down a rapid river, gliding pass clay huts and minarets, which dotted the river shore. He visualized a camel caravan, which trotted over sandy dunes in the distance. River barges materialized in his mind's eye, filled with corn, rice, millet, salt, coffee beans, tea leaves and exotic fruits. Pink flamingoes flew over his head. He envisioned a small village with dusty streets and clay houses without windows with dirt roads that led into other dirt roads. An empty alley twisted to the center, where a slender, thin charcoal man dressed in purple rested his head under a shed, guarding his load and drinking peppermint tee. Clarence saw the charcoal man, as if he was real. Another swarthy man emerged from a stone garden, covered with metal bells, nails, hide fur, and feathers. He grasped Clarence by the hand, tenderly leading him to an oasis of palm trees, orchids, and mango trees, where he offered Clarence a cup of palm wine and a gold pillow with a dancing deer to rest his head upon.

"The gods are asleep. Overpowering the buffalo will bring grief," the swarthy man whispered into Clarence's ear. "Let us sleep and walk together in the wind." Clarence closed his eyes, meditating on dark men drinking tee, and naked African males, collecting cacao fruits. The subway came to a halt at Fourteenth Street, ending abruptly his reverie. Clarence disembarked from the subway station, submerging himself into the city crowd. The street was engulfed in the clamor and yells of Dominicans, Puerto Ricans, Africans, Asians and Mexicans...refugees and immigrants. All of whom had escaped their tropical sun. They considered themselves lucky to be in America. They stood on 14th street, shouting. "Check it out! Check it out!" They sold everything under the sun....cheap wares produced in China...just a lot of junk. Clarence meandered between them. He finally entered a gray building on the corner of 14th street and 5th Avenue. A small group of people sat in the auditorium of the building, talking excitedly. He concluded that this was the group, with which he would be traveling to Africa. There were 12 persons in the group. Most of them were young white dames of fortune... silly young white girls from protected families, most likely spoiled and unsympathetic, Clarence thought

"There are over 70 some tribes in the Ivory Coast and 4 major linguistic groups," a white overweight man claimed, standing on the stage, giving a lecture. He said that he was professor for African history and art at NYU and that he would be accompanying the group on its trip to Africa. "The Ivory Coast, unlike other African nations, had a short colonial period from 1880 to 1960, when it gained its independence from France. It is an agricultural land and its cash crops are cocoa and coffee."

"African art is not an esthetic phenomenon," another white intellectual-looking man reported. He looked Jewish in Clarence's eyes and smoked perpetually cigarettes, while blowing circles of smoke that twisted above his head. "African art has a functional utility. African masks are primarily used for masquerade performances. The Golli mask of the Baule people represents an evil bush spirit. The Baule believe that evil is mutable and can be eventually changed. This is similar to the slave's belief in the eventual goodness of the slave owner. The Baule and Senufo people, another ethnic group in the Ivory Coast, make a distinction between village human beings and bush persons. Village human beings are men and women who are social, orderly, controlled, law-abiding, human and productive. Bush persons are savages who cannot deal with the necessities of group living. They are antisocial, arbitrary, dangerous, lawless and non-human," the white intellectual-looking man said. Clarence thought about the young black man that robbed him in St. Nicholas Park. He wondered if this young man could be identified as a "Bush Nigger". "We recommend that everyone in the group bring a first-aid kit, extra batteries for your camera, a cassette recorder, and a mosquito net for your beds. Malaria, Diarrhea, and sleeping sickness are widespread in Africa. We advise you not to eat contaminated food or to drink impure water, not to swim or wade in fresh water. We recommend that everyone buy malaria prophylactics," the overweight white man said, implanting fear into the hearts of the members of the group. "A Baule proverb says, wood can not lie in water a long time without becoming a fish," he said, trying to ease the apprehension in the group. "I can tell from some of your faces that you are all afraid and that you are probably asking yourselves, if you should have booked for this trip. Don't be afraid! You will all survive in Africa and quickly adjust to it."

Clarence was scared. The next day, a guided tour was given of the African exhibit at the Metropolitan Museum of Art. Clarence went to the Met, but avoided the guided tour of the African exhibit, preferring to form his own interpretation of African Art, instead of the misinterpretation of a white tour guide. He strolled meditatively between the wood figures with elaborate coiffures, elongated necks, round, well paced buttocks and scarified faces. Suddenly he stood in trance in front of an impressive statue of a hornbill. It was an exquisite bird with multicolored wings, whose beak touched its thigh. Clarence imagined it flying in the African sky. The Hornbill was dead wood that suddenly came alive before his eyes. He lingered then before a Golli mask, which depicted an animal spirit with braided grass for hair. He imagined it strutting and beating a whip across its back. "Yoop! Yoop! Yoop!" The beak of the Golli was colored red, white and black. Its pointed red tongue was luscious and still, as if it was waiting for the kill. Its big white eyes frightened Clarence. He sought to run, but there was no place to run or to hide. Thus, he decided to get down on his knees, as the Golli approached him slowly, placing its paw upon his head, appearing to bless him. Clarence saw in his mind his fathers and mothers, his ancestors, dancing in celebration, singing in joy: "Golli! Golli! Golli!" As he opened his eyes, a young blond woman with blue eyes stood behind him, observing him in his reverie. She seemed to be following him. Every time he jumped, she would jump. When Clarence turned to see if his shadow was still there, the young lady would also turn to see if hers was there. They encountered each other in front of a statue of a kneeling mother with child. Clarence studied the scarified face and large breasts of the statue. The blond woman came closer. She stood beside him, whispering gently. "Mother and child," she said. Clarence turned to observe her. She was a young woman, dressed in an alternative style with silk Indian scarves around her neck, in a long printed dress. In the flash of a moment, Clarence remembered what Antoine once told him in his incessant litany about women. "You can tell how a woman lives by how she dresses," Antoine claimed. "But her underwear reveals her character."

Clarence wondered what kind of underwear this woman wore...if she wore any at all. They exchanged embarrassed smiles. "African art is beautiful," she replied, waiting for Clarence to respond. But he did not say anything. "You're not taking the guided tour?" She asked. "No, I want to feel the statues, to let them enter me and make me understand," Clarence said. The young blond woman appeared to be sympathetic. Clarence hoped that she was not like the last white woman that he met in a bar downtown. "I like black men!" The woman declared to him, while rubbing his arm. "I like them too," Clarence retorted. "That makes two of us," she said. "Yes, that means you're in the right church, but in the wrong pew," Clarence quickly responded. He felt that sometimes, one had to be direct, telling white female pursuers that he, unlike some black men, didn't feel as if he had seen the light or become enlightened just because he had a fair lady on his side. He felt, in general, ambivalent toward both black and white women. He did not dislike them. How could he? He loved his mother, and his grandmother. He was not sexually attracted to a woman...that was all. He was convinced that it would be a waste of his time to seek female companionship. Women, he believed were interested only catching a man, in having a home and children. They wanted to be hunted, caught, pampered and spoiled. Clarence wanted the same things.

"You can only understand African art experientially," the young blond woman said. "It is a mistake to try to abstract it." Clarence nodded his head in agreement. He often contemplated why the "white man" abstracted the world; why he always attempted to explain why the cat was in the window; why he thought that everything had to have an abstract meaning. Couldn't it just be for enjoyment? "Is this your first time traveling to Africa?" The young blond women asked, staring into Clarence eyes. "Yes!" He responded. "You will love it!" She assured him. "You will not want to leave it." Clarence looked at the young woman in surprise. "I have already heard this before," he replied. "It is true. I've been to Asia, South America and to Africa many times. Africa is somehow different. It is not just the abundance of wild life and the breath taking scenery, nor the beauty and joy of the African people," she raved. "There is mysticism in the air and a sensuality that one feels especially on warm evenings." Clarence could see that this young white woman was in love with Africa. "That sounded interesting what you said about the experiential versus the abstract," Clarence said. "What do you mean exactly?" They sat on a bench in a corner of the museum. The young blond woman crossed her legs. "By the way, I'm called Ellen," she said. "My name is Clarence." They shook hands. "Well, there are two ways of understanding the world, the abstract and the experiential way. The abstract form of understanding the world is based upon analysis, that one can understand something by analyzing it, by attempting to break it down into its parts and by studying in detail the individual parts…by identifying and defining. It is believed that with this method, one will eventually understand the whole." Ellen paused. After the silence, she continued. "This world view was concisely described by René Descartes, who claimed 'Cognito, ergo sum.' This means I think, therefore I am." A discourse occurred in body language between Clarence and the young lady. Ellen crossed her legs. Clarence observed that she wore Birkenstock sandals, toe rings and silver anklets. "The experiential methodology is based upon a spiritual approach. Experiential means to experience something," Ellen said. "One can understand something by experiencing it." She kicked her legs rhythmically up and down, up and down, as if she was kicking the sky and stomping the ground. Clarence folded his arms across his chest like an impenetrable fortress. He was not interested in girls.

"The philosophy behind the experiential method could be put in short as, I feel, therefore I am," Ellen explained. "The abstract method is European and the experiential method is African." That sounded logical to Clarence. This young lady was not tedious like most women, he thought. She knew how to elucidate theories, to hold ones attention. She was not dull. "Because the Europeans don't believe in the spirit or in the soul, but only in that which can be rationally explained, this has led them to unfortunately neglect their spiritual development, which is the reason for the widespread dehumanization and spate of psychological disorders in Western society," she stated. Although Clarence and the young lady were carrying on an intellectual conversation, there was still an undercurrent male/female game which simultaneously occurred. They played Tom and Jerry (*cat and mouse*) with each other. Clarence pondered if she had finally noticed that he was not interested in females. He knew through experience that women only see what they want to see and only hear what they want to hear. "The most rational behavior is increasing one's material well-being. This is why the market is so important in our society. It is the conduit for wealth, but it has led to the rat race that we see around us," Ellen said. "And in which we are captured as prisoners," Clarence added. "Do you think the experiential method would have led to another way of living?" Clarence allowed his hand to go limp at the wrist, which was typical of sissies. He wondered if she had caught the message by now. He thought that she was swimming blind. Then he thought of the French saying, 'honi soi qui mal y pense' (*shame on those who think badly*). Ellen continued to lecture on the abstract and the experiential. "Yes, it would have led to a more holistic approach to the world, to a more social society, as opposed to civilized society. The environmental problems that we have today would not have happened, nor the destructive wars, the holocaust, pogroms or incidents of mass genocide, which are all a result of profit addiction, power striving and envy. We would be materially poorer than we are today, but we would be happier."

Clarence and the young lady walked through the Metropolitan Museum of Art, comparing their notes about the state of the world. "You know, in the school where I work, I have tried to introduce this experiential approach to learning. I have noticed black children in particular respond to this method better than the abstract method."

"Are you a teacher?" Ellen asked.

"Yes!" Clarence replied. "I teach in Harlem."

"I have always wanted to go to Harlem. Teaching there must be very challenging," Ellen said.

Clarence was shocked by Ellen's statement. She was a New Yorker, who had never been to Harlem. How is it possible, he asked himself, that one could live in the same city and not be the less bit curious to see how the other side lived. "I think that teaching is my fate! Sometimes it is a little too challenging. It can be bizarre," Clarence explained. "You know, the public school system is organized to systematically miss-educate people, not just black people, as Carter G. Woodson claimed. My problem is trying to break through these barriers. There are some people within the system, who want to prevent this from happening, because for them, teaching a poor black child or young black adult, the underdogs of the underclass, to think critically, to understand and to critically analyze his or her situation within society…is subversive!" Clarence raised his voice with the word subversive and said it as if he was spitting it out of his mouth. They stopped in the middle of a huge room of the museum, starring at each other.

"Gosh!" Ellen exclaimed. "It isn't easy to break through the class system."

"No, it isn't." Neither is it easy to break through the race system or this system of sexual identification and exploitation!" Clarence declared.

Just thinking about these things made Clarence agitated. As if caught in a circle, Clarence and Ellen surrendered to helpless laughter. Then they continued their tour of the exhibit, realizing it was fruitless to talk about such social torments. "What is it that you do professionally?" Clarence asked Ellen. He thought about another question…*what is it you do, besides chasing black men and monkeys that climb trees.* "I'm an art historian at the Louvre in Paris," Ellen answered. "Are you American?" Clarence asked her. "I have American and French citizenship," Ellen said. "I thought you couldn't be all American, since what you just said is totally un-American. To be against the market or modern society is similar to being sacrilegious. If you voice such opinions loud enough here, you will be branded a neo-communist, an anarchist or terrorist and burned at the stake," Clarence told her. Ellen laughed. She had a strange laugh that indicated she was just a little bit crazy on a high niveau.

"Parlez-vous français?" (*Do you speak French?*), she asked. "Bien sûr!"(*Of course!*) "I've been to Paris a number of times." Clarence was proud of the fact that he could answer this question in the affirmative. It proved somehow that he was not from the bush. Ellen told Clarence that she lived in Versailles and had an apartment in New York on 5th Avenue, which belonged to her parents. They later drank cocktails in the restaurant of the Met, standing apart from the rest of the group. Ellen spoke of her adventures, of her wonderful encounters in Africa, of extraordinary friends, who made music in the face of the night and sung like exotic birds under Baobab trees. They parted in the late afternoon on the steps of the Met. "A bientôt en Afrique, Clarence." (*See you soon in Africa*) "A tout à l'heure en Afrique" (*See you soon in Africa*), Clarence responded. He watched Ellen, as she walked down 5th Avenue and disappeared like a phantom into the crowd. Light felled from the clouds, illuminating the concrete and steel of New York City.

8. Dance of the victims

Clarence grumbled with himself about how to transform Antoine's unique idea into a reality. It was a great idea to teach African philosophy, African culture and African history in the public school where he worked. But that was all it was…just an idea. Clarence in reality was fighting with his fists and his feet just to survive as a teacher. His school was not a place of peace and goodwill. Yet he somehow believed it was his obligation to do something constructive in life, to try to help those who had less than he did...to try to make the world just a little bit better. Clarence did not want to be complacent in the madness of this world. It was naïve to believe in a just world. But he thought it better to believe in it, and to try to achieve it, than to be self-satisfied. This was why he became a teacher and why he worked in a public junior high school located in central Harlem. It was a shock to him to later realize the school was an Amazon house...a place of sneaking mistrust. The school was called P.S. 129. The initials P. S. did not mean postscript. It meant public school. It could also have meant postscript, because it was an afterthought institution, the hoarding place for the sucklings of the downtrodden, for those on the margin of ruin, for the rest trash of our society, who had no power, no money, nor a lobby in Washington...often referred to as the underclass. The school was located on 139th Street, behind the Harlem YMCA. A boastful statement was written in large bold letters on its side wall. "We play the best basketball in the country!" The sign boasted. This stinking self- praise perplexed Clarence. It was hollow bragging. There was no basketball, football or baseball team. The school couldn't afford a sport program. It couldn't afford computers, or even a library, and this in the richest country in the world, where wealth was not equally distributed and where there was no real concept of fairness, despite the constant gibberish of political officials about the equality of opportunities and the equality of chances.

The slogan on the wall of the school was an attempt by the downtrodden to broadcast to the wealthy white tourist that drove pass the school at accelerated speeds in crowded buses, that there were treasures even under the rubble. The underclass was tired of being recognized by its adversities and its defects. This was a kind of "think positive" or "I am somebody" strategy. The school was in actuality an island of lost desires, the last hole...a place which was frequented by poor Blacks, Puerto Ricans, Dominicans, Caribbean and other sluiced immigrants, who dreamed of turquoise seas, pastel wood houses, and fat bacalao mamas with coconut teeth. They were tropical souls, fantasizing in the hell of New York City about green bananas, salsa and calypso under Palm trees. The faculty consisted of Blacks, Latinos and lower middle-class Jews, who also somehow had all missed the boat into the mainstream. It was multicultural and therefore a colorful circus. It was the arena for a dance of the victims. Cultural conflicts occurred on a daily basis. The victims fought among themselves.

The children appeared to Clarence like encaged birds under a blue sky, with moving clouds. Poverty was boundless below the clouds...a material poverty and a spiritual poverty. These children were like hostages, who did a lot of roaring. They were sucklings in need of a wet nurse. They giggled and frolicked with each other, passing dirty notes to each other, ignoring with naked and open resistance the humorless and staid teachers in front of them, who shouted commands and orders. It was playing time for little pieces and great talents. The children were rich in tricks on how to kill and believed in self-interest before species preservation. They were like Viking youths at war. It was a torture chamber, a quagmire, a morass for the teachers and there was no escape, neither for the teachers nor for the children.

"Thomas, stop hitting Monique."

"Desiree, stop picking in your nose."

"Jessie, put your shirt into your pants."

"Stop talking!"

"Stop playing!"

"Stop breathing!"

Growth became a strangulated thing. Groups of children stood in formation on the playground...a formation of lips and proud, impudent sad eyes. One group stood with military composure, like black soldiers facing a wall. They were perfectly still. There was no jesting or silly laughter from their mist, but a concentrated self-restraint. A boy and a girl walked soldierly up and down the two formations, observing, surveying and instructing the other children. Clarence approached the children in the school yard. "Good Morning, Leo."

"Good Morning, Mr. Hill." Leo was the larger of the boys, in a position to demand respect from the rest. He was a handsome boy. The other children claimed he was Clarence's favorite. "Who is absent today?" Clarence asked, while observing the clouds. It was a wonderful spring day. "Rafael and Chantee are absent today, Mr. Hill," Leo replied. Clarence told Leo to lead the others into the building, into their classroom. Leo passed the order to a smaller boy that stood beside him. "Jeffery, lead the group into the building!" The children paraded silently into the building like tin soldiers marching to a drum. Clarence followed his group of children. He walked through the pandemonium, bedlam and hullabaloo of the other children. They carried on like monkeys and chimpanzees, jumping from trees, scrambling over bananas. The teachers were in the mist of the children, like battled victims in a war of nerves. They looked frustrated, screaming futile commands. This was indeed a cage of fools, where it was difficult to maintain one's balance. Clarence steered skillfully through the noise and chaos, embarrassed by the children's lack of restraint. He strutted down the hallway behind his formation of disciplined children, pretending to be oblivious to the whistles and catcalls, the sneers and ridicule. He knew that the others were not disciplined. They believed their individual rights were paramount and preceded the rights of others. Clarence ascertained that the children followed a mob-law of blood and iron, which they learned in the streets and at home. The one with the biggest fist was the one, who was right. They spent most of their time fighting among themselves like animals at the dump, exchanging insults. They held themselves to be the birth of the cool, competing with the latest fashions. Television was their navel and the trivial celebrities of the time. They exemplified America at its worse. The children had disastrous needs, but education was secondary for them. Their destiny, their future or their well-being were not a theme for mainstream America, nor was it a theme for them.

"Who needs an education? You can make more money selling drugs than you can on a 9 to 5 job," they claimed, looking for a comfortable alibi. The young boys idolized thugs, who drove Mercedes and BMWs in front of the school during the day. "Faggot! Faggot! Mr. Hill is a faggot!" There was this word again. It was a perpetual insult. Clarence understood its purpose. He knew men possessed words, which existed solely for the purpose of domination and subordination, words to control, to subordinate and to hurt. He knew how some folks were made to suffer. In the past, he was called a nigger. He responded as always that he was not a nigger. But he did not know an appropriate response for the word faggot. Clarence guessed he just had to accept it and not to allow himself to be put in a temper. It was best not to play the insulted one, to show that one was hurt, but it did hurt him to realize how intolerant people could be. These were the very same ones, who complained about racism and discrimination, about the white man's intolerance and yet they were just as intolerant in their way.

Clarence turned to see a husky built boy with a coarse tongue, guffawing in his direction, daring to insult him. It was Malcolm. Malcolm's parents named him after Malcolm X, with the hope and wish he would be worthy of the name. Clarence suspected Malcolm was borne to be a clown; that he would in all likelihood grow up to be a scoundrel, one who sat on other's coat tails and built useless cobwebs. He considered Malcolm to be a little smirk, a bandit, trying to get a nut. After an appropriate amount of time passed, in which everyone waited and wondered how Clarence would respond, he fixed the young boy in his gaze, spinning his mind in search of the right remark. Survival depended on being quick-witted. "Yea, you're right. I'm a faggot! And you were the best fuck I had!" Clarence replied in forward gear. This was a sharp attack. The boy turned purple, stuck his tail between his legs like a hyena, hoping he would suddenly evaporate. He was made a laughing stock in the eyes of his classmates. And the one, who laughed first, laughed the longest. The teachers pretended as if they hadn't heard Clarence's remark. It was ok to be called a faggot. It was one of the seven sins. But it was inappropriate to have said the four-lettered f-word in public.

Clarence remembered a conversation he had with Malcolm one day in the school yard. It was in the fall, just before Thanksgiving. "Son, what is it you would like to be?" He asked Malcolm, seeking to get to the bottom of the confusion in his mind. "I just want to be a millionaire," Malcolm said, revealing his pious dreams. "How do you suppose to get from here to there?" Clarence asked, wondering if Malcolm thought that honey flowed from the mountains. "I don't rightly know, Mr. Hill," Malcolm responded. "If I have to lie, cheat and steal to get here, I will." Malcolm intended to battle with the lion to get what he thought he deserved in life. "That's not surprising, Malcolm. That is how many people get rich." It surprised Clarence to see that Malcolm had already learned a valuable lesson. He knew that intrigue, plotting and scheming were the rules of the game. "But you seemed to have overlooked one difference between you and them, Malcolm." Clarence tried to deflate Malcolm's visions. Malcolm thought he could swim blind and win. "If you lie, cheat or steal to become a millionaire, you'll end up in jail."

"I don't think this gonna happen to me. I'm too intelligent," Malcolm said self-assured and sure of his success. "I will do what a man has to do," he said. "Intelligent black men are the one thing not needed in a racist country like America," Clarence replied, going to the core of the problem. "In any case, Malcolm, many intelligent black men, who had an arm full of tricks, are sitting in jail with garbled up dreams." Clarence knew Malcolm only wanted to be a winner, because winners were heroes. "That won't happen to me," Malcolm declared, without considering the risks. "Maybe you are right, Malcolm," Clarence responded, realizing it was useless trying to convince him to follow another road. The smell of money was stronger. "Before you begin your life of lying, cheating and stealing, why don't you consider another career? Become a folk hero... like Robin Hood. You can be assured of little competition in stealing from the rich to give to the poor." Clarence said, trying to show Malcolm the mistake of his simple logic. "The first person you can bestow riches upon could be yourself!"

"Naw, that is much too difficult," Malcolm quickly responded. "Besides, I don't have to learn how to steal from the poor. I see it everyday in the streets all around me. I won't need any training. But who's going to teach me how to steal from the rich?" Malcolm asked. He understood certain truths. He knew early practice was necessary for those who wanted to be master of the wild, alpha types, and warriors of tomorrow. The children watched as the storm between Clarence and Malcolm dissipated. It was for them a disappointment that Clarence did not fly into a passion in the heat of the moment. They stood gaping about. Then they retreated with their pigtails, dreamy eyes and easy smiles into the auditorium of the school. Their chaotic clamor suddenly became a melodic and harmonic clang, as they song in the words of a poet, one who dreamed of a black nation and spiritual enlightenment: "Lift every voice and sing; till earth and heaven ring; ring with the harmonies of liberty; let our rejoicing rise; high as the rolling sea. Sing a song full of the faith that the dark past has taught us; Sing a song full of the hope that the present has brought us; facing the rising sun of our new day begun; let us march on till victory is won!"

Clarence remembered these children were the descendants of Ham, the descendants of the builders of the pyramids and ancient civilizations, who were even lied to, to make them believe the ancient Egyptians were white and not black. Now they sung of an anticipated freedom and liberty in a bogus promised land. Their luscious physical features were a fascination for Clarence, as he meditated on a beautiful dark people caught in a new slavery, a folk not aware of the magnificence of their souls or the strength of their spirits. Instead, they blew their horn individually under the wide sky, trying to accomplish their MTV dreams alone. Solidarity for them was a foreign word in battling for the peak. There appeared to be few who were obsessed with the idea of community, few among them who dreamed of grabbing for the stars as a member of a group and not as an individual. For Clarence the word "individual" was a dirty word, regardless of what the liberals and neo-liberals claimed.

The melodic song of the children fell silent, as a plump lady, who was the principal and who was the size of a hippopotamus, walked onto the stage. She appeared like a Hottentot's female with a cold heart and huge junk food buttocks. She saluted the American flag, placed her hand on her heart and paid homage to the concepts of liberty and justice. "I pledge allegiance to the flag and the nation for which it stands; one nation under God; with liberty and justice for all," the woman growled in a shrill voice that felt like cold cream. The connections between liberty and justice were invisible. To have liberty did not mean to be free. How could a racist, class conscious society be a just society? The woman then dismissed the children and the teachers. They filed out of the auditorium, through the hallway into their classrooms. Clarence led his children quietly into their classroom, which was refuge and sanctuary, an oasis which sprung from his untamed imagination. He personally had decorated the room. A pink damask cloth hung on one wall. Yellow roses in a blue vase were on his desk. On the walls hung exotic posters of men in feather helmets and feathered coats. There were posters of Moorish dancers, and Amazon women, black nuns in white dresses with white candles, Imhotep, Hatshepsut, Makeda, the queen of Sheba, Piankhy, king of Ethiopia and conqueror of Egypt, Clitus, king of Bactria and the cavalry leader of Alexander the Great, Hannibal of Carthage, Mount Kilimanjaro and caravans of elephants grazing on the Serengeti. Over the blackboard, hung pictures of mysterious African masks, colorful thatch-roofed huts with geometric designs, of a nude woman in a field of lavender, and naked men and women dancing under a flaming yellow and orange sky. On the bulletin board, hung a poster of a naked black woman combing her hair, sitting on palm leaves. Every corner and space in the room enticed one to reverie, to think about a forgotten and glorious past, a lost paradise.

Clarence discovered with time that teaching in the public school system was similar to acting. He performed everyday like an actor. He pretended he was angry, when he was not. He acted as if he was happy, when he was sad. He played the general, the mother, the father, the friend and the Good Samaritan. He smiled when he wanted to frown and became angry and aggressive when he wanted to cry. The children, although they appeared to be small and sweet, were in reality cannibals, who enjoyed eating inexperienced and lenient teachers. They were wild, with no concept of discipline. They played sadistic games. They called it game farming.

"How do the fish survive in water?" Babatundi, the dance teacher, asked Clarence the first day of the school year. "By swimming," Clarence replied. "No, the big fish eats the little fish," Babatundi told him. "In this school it is just the opposite. The little fish eats the big fish." Clarence observed with horror how the children broke weak teachers, reducing them to a barrel of tears. They forced them to the end station for the broken, ruined...into nervous breakdowns. He resolved not to allow himself to be defeated. He felt that he could pluck any chicken in high heels. When it dawned upon him that it was either hunt or be hunted, then he decided to become a queen with a spear and javelin, who set out to tame the wildest of the beasts. He would not have been worth his weight in gold if he could not justify his title. With wit and a campy attitude, he navigated through stormy seas and cruised past islands of fear and brutality. He had always an appropriate response for every situation he encountered and he made sure he kept his foot on the ball. Clarence remembered their Christmas trip to the Hayden Planetarium, where "Gateway to Infinity" was being performed for the children. They were to learn about the wonderful chaos of the universe. Silence felled in anticipation of the program after the children filed into the auditorium of the Hayden Museum. A child in the class stood and shouted with urgency, as the lights were turned out. "Mr. Hill! Mr. Hill! I'm having my period!" This remark came from a tall, lanky dark-skinned girl, who was called Kimberly. Clarence liked Kimberly. She was intelligent, witty and beautiful. She enjoyed making jokes and wise creaks in the classroom. Clarence turned towards Kimberly. "That's ok, honey. I'm having mine, too!" He said. The children broke into wild laughter and pandemonium. Kimberly sat down, hiding her shadow. She had met her match in Clarence. He could be just as witty as they could. He often found the behavior of the children entertaining. They were little dramas in Harlem. Clarence had difficulties trying to understand the rituals and symbolism of the parents or difficulties trying to understand his fellow colleagues. The parents were pimps, drug addicts, prostitutes or plain hard working-class folks. It was difficult to work with such parents for the benefit of the children, since they were all victims of the street, all vulgar and ignorant. This was reaffirmed each day by bizarre incidents.

Clarence thought about Jesse, for example, a little boy that sat in the front row of the classroom. His big eyes were full of hope. Jesse was smaller than the other boys, but intelligent like Kimberly. All of the children, in fact, had surprisingly an above average intelligence, which was not reflected by the low scores they received on the standardized tests of the state of New York. For the officials from Albany, they were black cubes, who had a can of tools that was considered worthless for mainstream society. Jesse's mother came to visit in the fall. She was a fat mama, who worked as a cook for Harlem Hospital. She looked as if she ate half of what she cooked. She appeared in the classroom one morning looking like Amazon Gumma with a digger in her hand, as Clarence sat at his desk, drinking coffee. She complained about the amount of homework that her son, Jesse, received each evening. She was agitated. When Clarence offered her a chair, she refused to sit down. "Mr. Hill, I think you give my son too much homework," she stated, rolling her eyes. "Why do you think this?" Clarence asked, concentrating on her nostrils, which reminded him of a wild horse. He was insulted that an uneducated woman would have the audacity to come to his classroom and make such an assertion. He wanted to ask her what college she attended. But he held his tongue. He did not consider it to be fortuitous to wrestle with a Samurai wrestler so early in the morning. If she willed, she could have crushed him with her weight.

"Well, he ain't got time anymore to clean the house and wash the dishes," she replied.

"Jesse shouldn't be doing these things," Clarence told her, smiling at her temerity.

"If Jesse don't do it, who iz?" She asked, appearing shocked.

There were also moments of danger. Clarence refused to allow a child into the classroom, because he was chronically late. He asked the child if he collected twigs in the fields each morning. His father appeared early one snowy morning in the school, demanding to see the teacher. Clarence showed the man to the teacher's lounge, where he intended to discuss the child's problems. Clarence asked the man why the child was late every morning, informing him that school started at 8:15 and not at 9:15. "Can you tell me what Marcus does every morning that makes him late?" He asked the man, who was tall and unkempt. His eyes were red, blood shot. The man was nervous and kept moving around in his seat. "Well, he has to run my errands," the man said. It was apparent to Clarence from the man's aberrant behavior that he was high on drugs. "What type of errands?" Clarence asked. The man nodded his head. "Yea, Yea, Yea," the man responded, sitting in his chair half-asleep and half awake, nodding his head consistently, and having fallen into a drug trance. When the man did not respond in the expected manner, Clarence summoned the school guards, requesting for them to escort the man out of the school. The man suddenly awoke from his slumber, showing his third face. "Nigger, I'll shoot you with my gun!" He shouted, as he was being led out of the room.

Clarence had visions of blood, seeing apparitions of himself lying in a pool of blood on a pavement in Harlem. He could not concentrate nor teach the entire day. He had goose pimples. For one week, he was escorted by the police to his home every afternoon, but Clarence felt vulnerable for a long time. When he walked the streets, he looked behind to see if anyone was following him and from this incident, he decided to keep his classroom door locked, much to the chagrin of the school principle. The most absurd incident occurred with a sweet little girl, named Chantee, who reminded Clarence of a flower. She sat in the back of the class, because she was very shy. Her smile was like a gem seldom seen. She came to school each morning on time. She always attempted to put her best effort into everything she did. Clarence knew how difficult it was for her just to appear each morning. She tried her best to look presentable, but her cloths were dirty and she stunk. The other children made fun of her. They all talked about her circumstances. Everyone knew her mother was a prostitute.

The children were preparing for their assembly program in the winter. Clarence asked each child to bring to class the materials, such as construction paper and crayons, which were necessary to build the props for the stage. One of the boys in the class came to school the next day without the materials. "Woolworth don't accept food stamps for construction paper, Mr. Hill," he explained. Clarence was disturbed upon hearing this. After the boy made this comment in the classroom, the other children laughed. They made jokes about his family receiving food stamps. Chantee found courage to speak, since she also did not bring the requested materials. "My mama said dat she don't hav' no money for crayons," Chantee said in a mutinous voice. "Your mama should get a job," Clarence responded. He was in a moment of frustration, searching for solutions to immense problems. Somehow it became understood he had called or implied that Chantee's mother was a prostitute.

It was not long after his remark that Chantee's mother appeared in the school, blowing fire. Clarence was summoned to the principal's office. In the room were the principal, the assistant principal, and Chantee's mother, a tower of righteousness. She was dressed to kill. She balanced on high-heel shoes and wore a tight yellow body dress. Tons of 'dark and lovely' covered the ravages on her depleted face. The tight dress squeezed her breasts together like cherry blossoms. They appeared to want to jump out of the dress, to do a mating dance on the floor. Clarence walked into the principal's office at the peak of the storm. "So dis iz de son of a bitch, who called me a prostitute," she yelled, gasping and panting. She was both wild and tamed, a black dragon blowing fire out of her nostrils. The principal, Mrs. Hunter, advised her four-lettered words would not be used in the conference. "Why not?" She demanded, glaring at Mrs. Hunter, the principle, in disbelief, showing crocodile teeth. "Dey iz used everywhere else!"

Mrs. Hunter shook her head perplexed, trying to navigate between two worlds. How could you explain proper etiquette to someone who never heard of the word?

"I dare you call me a prostitute," she roared at Clarence, huffing and puffing.

"Who said I called you a prostitute? Clarence asked, wishing for a tamer, someone to domesticate her, being a coward against such breasts. He suspected the children instigated Chantee to believe he implied that her mother was a prostitute. They enjoyed playing vicious games with each other's feelings. They were like young soldiers with wood guns, who washed each other's clothes in a muddy river and hung them out to dry. "Mah daughter came home and told me, yu said dat Ah should git uh job," she stated, placing her hands on her wide hips and moving her head from side to side like a snake. "I did say that," Clarence embarrassingly admitted. He gazed at Mrs. Hunter, the principal and Mr. Drucker, the assistant principal. They were examiner and judge, looking for an excuse to outlaw him. They presently had him in their hands, over a burning rose bush. They would have loved to sacrifice him to this black dragon. Mr. Drucker, the assistant principal, hated his guts and Mrs. Hunter, the principal, abhorred his independence and pertinacity. They didn't like the fact that he was openly gay.

"Mister, I hav' a job!" The woman said. "I work every day just lak' you." She castrated Clarence with steel eyes.

"What do you do?" Clarence asked rhetorically. This was the moment of truth, a time when continents drift apart and oceans emerge. She either had to admit she was a prostitute or she had to lie.

"Why, Ah'm a whore! " She said with pride, which meant that she built her nest only for love and money was secondary.

The public school system of New York State developed a regional curriculum plan for the schools. In this plan, one month for teaching African American history was provided, one month for teaching Hispanic culture and history, one month for teaching Asian culture and history, and one month for teaching the Holocausts. They called the month of February "Black History Month." Clarence believed the low self-esteem of black children required the teaching of their history on a daily basis. He found he was fighting against a low self-esteem, which had its origin in poverty, but also against the negative images in the mass media which were being bombarded at children of color on a daily basis. The latent message of the mass media being transmitted was that to be white was the measure of all things. Clarence believed it was unrealistic to teach black children about the Holocaust, about Auschwitz, Buchenwald, and Sorbibor, about death marches, gas chambers, and mass graves or about the French Revolution or about Goethe or

Schiller. Clarence preferred to teach them about apartheid, glass ceilings, about miseducation, racism, sexism and homophobic attitudes, about black civilization and culture. He selected those cruelties out of the cabinet of human cruelties, which were closer to home, the heavy and oppressive burdens at home. The message he tried to get across to the children was that not only anti-Semitism and racism were wrong, immoral and evil, but sexism and homophobism could not be considered cavalier deeds. His arguments were held by some to be a new perspective on Jazz. Clarence had to take away his own clover leaf and identify himself as being homosexual, in order to be truthful about his motivations for defending such groups. The children accepted him readily. His colleagues were reserved and reticent. Being homosexual was one of the seven deadly sins. The administration resolved to get rid of him. They looked for reasons to dismiss him. His adversaries were the principal, Mrs. Hunter, and the assistant principal, Mr. Drucker.

Mrs. Hunter, the principal, was a fat black woman, who Clarence would have described as "a person without poesy". She knew neither the smell of mountain air nor the feeling of a salty sea breeze. She could not hear grass grow or birds sing. She did not believe a rose was a rose. She spoke with false tongue and possessed the smile of a snake. She anaesthetized herself with formalities, daily routines and treated her teachers as exchangeable parts. She was easily offended and she offended others easily. She thought running a school was like running a company. It was all just a question of management. She was authoritarian and acted more like the Pope than the Pope himself did. The teachers gossiped about how she got her job, since it was generally known by everybody in the neigborhood that she was not qualified to be a principal. It was rumored she slept with the superintendent and even had an illegitimate child from this man. Clarence tried to avoid her. He kept his classroom door locked to keep her from snooping around into his business. She would come to the classroom and knock on the door loudly like a police woman. Each time she did this, Clarence would count to twenty. Then he would open the door slowly. This augmented her anger. She saw black. Clarence had a general disrespect for the principal. She was a red headed lady who saw the devil in every corner, a housewife with chewing gum for a mind, who through hook and crook had managed to become a principal. Babatundi, the dance teacher, told Clarence that Mrs. Hunter had her bosom on backwards and carried her ass on her face. He claimed she didn't believe in angels, but believed in crucifying her enemies.

The assistant principal, Mr. Drucker was an overweight German Jew, who originally came from Berlin. Clarence observed him closely, surmising that he suffered from the burdens of Jewish history in the shadow of numerous Pogroms. He was exiled at home and carried a Holocaust memorial in his head, being tainted with what appeared to Clarence to be a hereditary disease...the belief the Holocaust was unique. It was really perverse. He had a special relationship with this man named Hitler, who had burned a swastika in his soul. Physically he had left Europe and Germany, but mentally he was still on the European Continent. Personally, he was a contradiction. He dreamed of bare breasted black girls with glass pearls, since he was attracted to black women and a job *not* in the ghetto. Mr. Drucker did not place great value on his physical appearance. His hair was greasy and uncut. He was unshaven. He wore baggy pants with colorful wide sweaters to conceal his obesity. He walked through the corridors like a spook, spying on the teachers. Every time he walked pass Clarence's classroom, Clarence instructed the children to break into the Jewish folk song.

"Hava nagila, hava nagila, hava nagila, venesimacha..."

Mr. Drucker considered this to be a cold slap in his face.

There was a disproportionate amount of Jews in the school. The greatest tragedy for the Jewish teachers in the school was to teach black children in the ghetto. Most would have preferred a one-room school in the desert or a pleasure garden in Israel. Clarence did not have anything against Jews. Growing up as a boy in the South, he did not know what a Jew was. They were as invisible as a group as black people were visible. Many of the teachers at the school argued that since African American didn't teach Jewish children; that there were no or few blacks teaching in Jewish neighborhoods in Queens or Staten Island and that Jews had no right teaching African American children. They were out of place. They were not brothers and sisters in spirit. And black people were tired of Jews presenting themselves as historical victims. Clarence felt all people constituted a piece of the puzzle and no one group had a monopoly on truth. But he did observe over time that the Jewish teachers were not really concerned with black children getting a good education. No one had a guide to paradise, not even Clarence. The problems in the school reflected those in society. Jealousy, envy, distrust, dishonesty, corruption, drug abuse, alcoholism, ignorance, racism, sexual abuse of minors, animosities, and hostilities beat against its roof. Sand battles occurred. Embers of passion flamed. Clarence believed they were all together in the catastrophe; that it was right to affirm one's culture, without scorning another culture; that the sworn enemy was ignorance and power hungry types.

9. Liberation was in their eyes, voices and souls

New York City was crowded with people, who treaded with hallucination through the unreality of the metropolis, hurrying to some point. They appeared under their dark umbrellas like crawling maggots, unaware of their Godliness, of their celestial purpose. Since their eyes could not bear the light at the end of the tunnel, they decided, therefore, to remain in the tunnel. They appeared in Clarence's eyes to grow like weeds through the creaks and the crevices of the pavement. These were feeble men and women, who climbed mountains competitively, whose religion was Darwinism. They walked a long path to a short freedom, spending most of their time with trifling dreams and paltry schemes, existing beyond magic. They were pitiable souls, who hauled their sorrows and dread of the future...concealed. They were motivated by fear. Dark clouds hung low in the city. A wind squalled and an endless cold rain pounded against the pavement, collecting into puddles on the pavement, flowing into the gutter. It seemed as if the winter had returned to claim revenge. It was a damp day. Clarence patiently passed the time by waiting for Babatundi, his friend and colleague. Babatundi taught dance at the school where he worked. It was foolhardiness to refer to Babatundi as a friend, since friendship was a word without meaning. New Yorkers said friend, when they meant acquaintance and employed the word acquaintance, when they meant foe. A friend was somebody special, somebody you could rely upon, not someone whose whims, attitudes and feelings changed with a breeze. Clarence could not call Babatundi a real friend, because he had no friends in the city, only acquaintances. Babatundi was like most queers in the city, charming, but with a heart of stone, concerned only about self. Clarence held him to be a queer that was far from being enlightened, because he was far too egotistical and incapable of seeing the world from another person's point of view. He noticed that Babatundi had little empathy with others, and that friendship for him was just a nuisance to be escaped...something to be avoided.

Clarence balanced himself against a street pole on Lenox Avenue in Harlem, waiting patiently for Babatundi, watching a pageant of the living which occurred before his eyes, the soap operas of the street, and the decomposing modern society of desperate people. He could see the despair on their faces, a desolation praised as progress. He looked into the eyes of several pedestrians, as they passed by and it was a cold view into a cold space. An old woman sold matches on the corner of Lenox Avenue and 127th Street, battling against the approaching scent of decay. Pimps hustled customers, who were in search of an eternal lust. The pimps greeted them with a grin and with tricks stitched in hems and seams. They tried unsuccessfully to hide their deceit and thievery from sight, nurturing their corruption within dark hearts, where it throbbed and pronged, clogging their arteries with thoughts of wealth and thoughts of an easy life. The greatest luck was a fiction. Three prostitutes posed on the street, spiting the rain, hoping for a golden hole. They did not know how to blow up the Ghetto, but dreamed themselves of an uninjured existence. An evangelist preached on the corner of 125th Street and Lenox Avenue, preaching relentlessly about the house of sins, about modern society's approaching collapse and humanity's damnation. His passion was the spoken word and he presented himself as a pious man, one who was covetous of lost souls, of saving the devil's children. The preacher offered a vision of a better world for the blind, but he himself was without bliss and harbored a baneful spirit, shrouding his lunacy behind a hypocritical smile, luring the passing pedestrians with a treacherous benevolence. He preached enraptured on a small patch of pavement about universal things, about God's kingdom and the desolation of hell. A small crowd surrounded him in the rain, shouting hallelujahs. Clarence walked up Lenox Avenue to Silvia's Soul Food Restaurant, standing in the front entrance, studying the tourists, who entered and left the restaurant. Clarence contemplated them. The tourists were predominately unattractive Germans and decorous Japanese in their ceremonies of control, who were on a Safari to the wild in the middle of New York City. They disembarked from shinny silver buses, like plastic soldiers, running under umbrellas into the restaurant, as the rain danced around their umbrellas. They were called the world's master travelers, traveling far and wide, but learning nothing. If it wasn't an adventure, it wasn't worth the trip. Clarence watched the German and Japanese tourists and he thought in this moment how they were known by the fruits of the past which they had brought forth, the suffering which they had once caused for millions of people; that they were identified by their historical fallacies, their pact with the devil, more than by their contemporary economic successes. And yet he knew that the German and Japanese tourists saw themselves in a more positive light than their victims or the descendants of their victims saw them.

Clarence also thought momentarily about Babatundi, while waiting for him. Babatundi was a black neurotic sissy that traveled as far as the wave carried him. He was always late, claiming you couldn't demand punctuality of a sissy, because they were too afraid of putting their face on wrong, struggling with glamour and decay, trying to scratch the limited boundaries of physical beauty. Like the men of the Gerewole, Babatundi also spent much of his time in front of a mirror, changing costumes and renewing his makeup. Clarence waited patiently for him, since he knew one needed much stamina for those who lived in a salon of vanities. Babatundi was like an exotic parrot, who was never quite satisfied with the way he looked. His concept of beauty was a fiction. He chirped about being wobbly and ugly, claiming he would have given all to the Gods to have been born gorgeous. Denied this blessing, he like Odysseus, went on a long lasting search for an exquisite form. He became a creation, who sought to change its body. He wore a carnival mask to please and his face for the disco bars at night became his face for the day. He had his nose cosmetically made narrower, his lips thinner. He had blue contact lenses surgically implanted. He bleached his dark skin to a lighter shade of brown. He was unaware of the fact that black men were an endangered species and he did everything he could to make himself less black. When Babatundi put his drinking horn down and was intoxicated, it was a time of self-reckoning. The demons of the past took revenge upon him. He took inventory of the magic circle in which he ran, being overcome with grief and sobbing that he did not know who he was. "You've put yourself together like a puzzle. Now you suffer from an identity crisis," Clarence told him with the reflex of a critic, knowing that Babatundi was seduced by the fairytale images of Hollywood and the white mass media with its beautiful shimmer; that he tried to live like the stars, shining every second of the day, an expert in the art of deception. Babatundi existed in an artificial world of his own making and complained about the bumps from reality, about his broken "I". This was his dilemma.

Babatundi finally arrived in the back seat of a yellow cab, which stopped in front of Silvia's Restaurant. He did not take Gypsy cabs, claiming they were dirty, smelled of chickens, hens, goats and were chauffeured by unfriendly immigrants. He had an aversion for immigrants, asserting that they did not know the rites of American civility. Babatundi also never drove his own car into Manhattan, because he was afraid of it being stolen, and afraid of having an accident. Since he was charmed with courtly splendor and luxury, and fascinated with the appearance of belonging to the upper class, he trained the yellow taxi drivers to open the door for him, for which he tipped generously. Babatundi stepped grandly out the yellow cab like the queen of queens, as if it was a royal ceremony and he was expecting an Oscar for his performance. Light stole the show from light. The most important thing for him was to be majestic, on earth as in heaven. Everything was theater. He performed every second of his life, as if he was on a stage in a play of fantasies, in a fable about Gods and heroes. A raccoon fur coat covered his broad shoulders, although it was not cold enough for such a coat. The raccoon coat hung down to his ankles. A Stetson hat crowned his head. Babatundi stepped grandly across the pavement, as if he was throwing roses to the downtrodden of Harlem. He was one of the lucky ones, who had accumulated a little wealth, owning his own house in the suburb and possessing an expensive European car with a sticker on the back window that claimed, "Poverty makes me puke." Babatundi spent most of his time, worrying about how to protect that which he had accumulated from being stolen.

"Babatundi, honey, you don't know where you're at!" Clarence admonished him as he approached. "This is Harlem, child! You need to be careful walking these streets. Somebody is gonna' take that raccoon coat right off your back. Besides, Miss Thang, it ain't that cold enough for a raccoon coat!" Clarence was afraid that Babatundi's luxurious ornaments could very easily become a dangerous pitfall. Sometimes, those who had much forgot the deprivation of those who had nothing. Babatundi sneered, lifted his right shoulder, and turned his head to the side, resting his chin on his uplifted shoulder, as if he was the birth of Venus. This was a typical Babatundi stance. "Are you talking to me? I dare you! Miss Thang, please!" He replied with a disgruntled charm. "I know how to handle myself on these streets. Besides, child, who are you, Miss Country Bumpkin from the South, telling me to be careful in a city in which I was born and raised?" They decided not to pursue the matter any further, strutting together into Silvia's

Restaurant like a flutter and a cream puff, posing momentarily at the front entrance, posturing and searching for a table, looking like two lost faggots in a blooming fantasy. Black gay men were always on a fantastic quest for a black sun, a dark prince charming, or Nubian wonder, which they hoped would soon appear in an evening suit.

Jamaican waitresses with wide asses, dark as the night, rushed from table to table, balancing trays on their heads, everything under control. They appeared to be dancing in slow motion. They were animators for all situations, scurrying and screaming their orders in Jamaican English. Babatundi and Clarence pranced between the tables of overdressed black women with too much makeup on their faces and stately black men in designer suits with high tastes, who appeared to be a people that had fallen from the sky, chattering with each other, eating soul food, and drinking Courvoisier Cognac...allowing the world to continue to revolve on its axis. It was a picture of the good life. Interspersed between them were white spots, alabaster European tourists, captivated by these exotic dark animals. The air in the restaurant vibrated with a dissonance of voices. A concert without musicians occurred. Babatundi and Clarence selected a table next to an adventuresome Japanese couple. The couple stared at them with awe in their eyes. Clarence stared back. He expected the Japanese man to ask him to pose for his camera, so that he could capture his noble image, like the cow with background and background with hills in the country side of the French Provence. They swapped smiles. Clarence wondered momentarily what it must be like to sleep with a Japanese man. It was rumored that they had little penises.

"Oh, you little Nymph!" Babatundi whispered to Clarence, noticing the twinkle in his eyes.

"What do you mean?" Clarence responded.

"Honey, you're a whore, who likes anything that wears britches, whether it's a cactus, an egg or a snail," Babatundi declared. "Besides, Miss Thang, Asians have little dicks!"

"Oh, he's not my type," Clarence replied.

But he had recognized the fire in the Japanese man's eyes. His narrow eyes were like eagles with flags. Suddenly the Japanese man overcame his speechlessness, accosting Clarence.

"I love black people!" He declared, gawking at Clarence, as if he expected Clarence to jump up with joy and scream hallelujah, just because he said he liked black people.

"Oh, you do!" Clarence exclaimed.

The Japanese man nodded his head in the affirmative, all the while beaming. His meek and mild wife fluttered in agreement. She grinned like her husband. This was an encounter of the third kind. Clarence pondered how big his erection was, phallic worshipper that he was. He was convinced that sex transcended culture, race, class or nationalities. Clarence imagined him seducing him, slow and romantic-like. Weren't the Asians masters of seduction?

"Are there any blacks in Japan?" Clarence asked.

"Oh, no! There are no blacks in Japan." The Japanese man replied, truly disappointed. His wife appeared shocked such a question would be asked.

"Well, you should import some from here. There are too many nappy-headed bimbos in America!"

The Japanese man and the woman laughed. Clarence wondered if they knew what a bimdo was.

"Oh, it is a funny joke. I like Jazz, Miles Davis, George Benson, Michael Jackson and Soul food." He then asked Clarence if he played basketball or a musical instrument. Clarence purposely ignored his trivial question and was annoyed at the same time that this man would think that all black people were entertainers.

"Good! Enjoy your meal," Clarence said.

He decided not to engage in a trivial conversation with this man, since he had already insulted him without even being aware of it. Clarence turned his back to the Japanese man, attempting to ignore him, but the thought would not let him go, why did "Caucasians" and "Honorary Caucasians" as the Japanese were called in South Africa had to establish the fact they were not prejudiced, that they did not come to baptize the black man or to save his soul; that they were not the executioners, the auctioneers on the slave markets, and that their historical collective souls were without sin. This guilt trip and culpability syndrome always occurred, when Caucasians or honorary Caucasians found themselves confronted with a black person on black turf, on the other side of the bar. They mimicked affability, expecting hostility. They thought they had to explain, to apologize, and to atone. It was similar to the way Germans acted when they were in Jewish company. They were in reality fearful, afraid of saying the wrong thing, apprehensive of their reactions, and terrified of being placed on the scaffolds for the deeds of the past. They came in groups and preferred controlled environments. Clarence knew no folk on this planet, who were without sin and he understood that there were many paths to enlightenment. But he wondered how was it that the hope of one group becomes the fear of another group.

Babatundi sat perched on his seat, balancing his weight on the tiny chair, playing with his fork. He started chattering about the school, which was something teachers did automatically, when they got together. He complained about the veil dance they had to do in order to make a living, going through the daily treadmill just to make a buck. Clarence thought about how he met Babatundi, remembering it was on a hot June morning. Babatundi skated down 5th Avenue in a white wedding dress with a magical fairy baton in his left hand. He wore red, yellow and blue flowers in his pressed hair. It was the day of the Christopher Street Day Parade, when the queers and their friends paraded down 5th Avenue like Bedouins for the beautiful mainstream people of New York. They danced to steel bands, and carried rainbow balloons and colorful banners demanding their civil rights, seeking a free place under the sun and craving for small freedoms. Liberation was in their eyes, in their voices and in their souls. Babatundi marched behind a banner with "Gay Teachers" written across it, which was behind a procession of nuns and priests, exalting the cross. He was the first to see Clarence standing on the curve in front of Saks. Clarence watched the parade every year, but he had not yet brought himself to the point, where he could participate. They gazed at each other in embarrassment, for both lived relatively discreet lives and had successfully camouflaged themselves in their struggle for existence. Babatundi then spoke one day to Clarence in the teacher's lounge, breaking the ice between them. They were alone in the lounge. "Miss Thang, your ass is like an eagle that flies too high. You couldn't hide that ass in a trunk, if you wanted to!" Babatundi said. "What man do you know walks around Harlem in ballerina shoes?" Clarence jokingly replied. He actually thought, 'what Samurai walked around in ballet shoes,' but he did not say what he thought. Babatundi was conscious of being overweight. He wore baggy pants with wide flowing silk shirts in order to try to conceal his belly. Babatundi was on an eternal virtual diet, but he ordered barbecue ribs with black-eyed peas and potato salad in the restaurant. Clarence knew that he would later complain about being too fat and about nobody loving him.

"A lot of the teachers have told me they won't be coming back next year," Babatundi stated. "I think Mrs.Hunter has alienated many of them. If you placed her in a room with a hippopotamus and a bull, she would come out first."

"Yes, I know, but the other half shouldn't come back or shouldn't be teaching at all." Clarence said. "They are not very well educated. I have always wondered why the most unqualified teachers are placed in black schools. Apropos, shouldn't be teaching…Justine Carter was in my classroom the other day. That woman is a nuisance. She uses her female charms to bend and capture men. She keeps inviting me to dinner at her place like hanging cheese in front of a mouse. I don't know how to tell her I am not interested without screaming it in her face. You would think she would be intelligent enough to see I am looking for the same thing that she is. Her problem is that she really doesn't like men and she uses her vagina to catch the one thing she would spend the rest of her life hating. She regrets the fact she was not born with a penis and her vagina is her shame, although she uses it as bait." Clarence said, acting as if he was agitated, because this was the way high-sprung black queers in the city talked to each other…bitchy and on the edge. Babatundi's cellar phone rang. He shouted a loud, sharp and unfriendly "hello" into it. "I told you about calling me on my handy, George," he protested. "I don't give a shit if it is an emergency!" Babatundi shook his massive shoulders for emphasis. "You son of a bitch…! I told you don't waste your time apologizing to me. You should have thought about that before you let him cap your gun (*give a blow job*) in my house!" Clarence gagged on his food upon hearing Babatundi scream such obscenities into his cellular phone. Everyone in the restaurant turned to stare at Babatundi, engaging in a verbal bullfight. "You're lying, nigger! How did he know you have a fucked up gun? Did he see through your dirty underwear?" Babatundi was fuming mad. "I don't care what type of situation it is," he snapped. "You should have thought about that before you decided to get a nut in my house, leaving your scent marks like a dog, George!" Babatundi snapped the cellular phone shut with a clipped "good bye". He shoved it into the pocket of his raccoon coat.

"That was George, calling from the police precinct at the Staten Island Ferry station. They arrested him for slugging an Italian boy on the ferry," he explained.

"What happened? Why did he hit the boy?" Clarence asked.

"He said the boy called him a nigger and spat in his direction."

"Well, that would certainly be reasons for hitting him. It is a reflex that is deeply rooted in black folks," Clarence assured him.

"Now he wants me to come to the precinct to help him, after he did what he did to me." Babatundi shouted vehemently, blowing his jars out like a soft volcano about to flow lava.

"Are you going to help him?" Clarence asked.

"Hell no, let him rot in jail, for all I care," Babatundi exclaimed. He changed the subject, concentrating on his barbecue ribs. "What type of man are you looking for Clarence?" Babatundi asked Clarence after he regained his composure. It was an evasive question. "I know that he will have to be self-confident to deal with a faggot like you!" He joked.

Clarence did not respond to Babatundi's question. Yet he knew exactly what he wanted from life.

"Don't waste your time with distressed women and wobbly men, who don't have any content of character!" Babatundi spoke out of experience. "For me, there are three types of men," he said. "The ones, who know how to fuck, but have no content of character; the ones who have content of character, but don't know how to fuck; and the ones that have content of character and can fuck well. The latter type of men is rare and we have to compete with women for them."

Clarence knew most queers accepted the first type, because they were afraid of living their lives alone. Their vision was missing, because most of them considered their sexual orientation to be a handicap. They adjusted themselves to the dictates of the market, where American dreams were made and they had become convinced that low quality goods with high prices were all the market had to offer them. They danced the blues and accepted the first hotchpotch king of emptiness who happened to come along. These men, pirates, bandits and Gauchos, were toys for queers. Babatundi was an excellent example of this type of neurosis. He was a successful gay man, petit bourgeois, educated, who delighted in the blessings of consumption, who owned his own home upon a piece of land to enjoy life. Babatundi lived well, but lived a hollow life. He cohabited with a man, who was no more than a thug, a parasite…a terror in person. Since there is always a breeze of hope, he frantically hankered for love over the long-term. But love never came his way. Clarence believed Babatundi could not love, but that he could only mimic love. Babatundi thought he could buy friendship and buy love. Therefore, he advocated the widespread installment philosophy of "dream here and pay there," that money could buy everything in the Promised Land. Babatundi hunted heterosexual men with nothing in their minds as a wall, who themselves were hunting for lost riches. He happened to meet them at dinky holes in the city with the scent of loneliness, where dreams become commodities. Like a proud hunter with booty, he enthralled them with expensive gifts, with cashmere sweaters, silk bathrobes, and trips to Las Vegas, concerts, and gems. The more sexual gratification they gave him in return for the gifts, the more they received. Being hurt became a ritual for Babatundi. These men all inevitably hurt him. Clarence was convinced one of these bandits would ultimately kill him. But Babatundi refused to see the color of truth. He bet against death, preferring to play the game of turtledove in love, biking and cooing, although he perceived in his heart that it was not love.

"How is George?" Clarence asked, although he was not interested in George's health. He thought it sounded nice to ask. George was Babatundi's present live-in courtesan. Clarence knew by asking the question that he was fishing in muddy waters.

"That bastard…! That prick…!" Babatundi screamed, while hissing his disapproval.

Clarence was not shocked to hear Babatundi refer to George with such names. He had heard Babatundi use other, worse names for George. He and George, to say the least, had a unique relationship.

"I hate his soul!" Babatundi said with credibility.

Babatundi and George had lived together for two years, fighting like cats and dogs, constantly engaging in power skirmishes. Babatundi told everyone how much he hated and despised George. They all asked the logical question: "Why don't you throw him out of your house?" Exiting from rationality, Babatundi explained he was raised in the choking grip of the church and his religion would not allow him to throw distressed persons in search of a rescuer out on the streets. His faith shined in his soul and it was the crutch of all crutches. "Besides, no man is flawless and perfection is not an embellishment," Babatundi would often say, meaning that he expected the men whom he met to have failures. Babatundi would tell people how he met George in the streets, hustling in the Village in downtown Manhattan, looking like a wanderer, which the rain buried. He said he took George into his house because he felt sorry for the guy, not knowing at the time that George was addicted to the holy drug, marijuana, and that he had no family. George's mother, who was a drug addict, died when he was a young boy. His father was sitting in prison and his sister was a crack addicted prostitute. He only had an aunt, who refused to let him into her house. Babatundi told everyone who was patient enough to listen to his monologue that he was just trying to do a little good in this mean world by taking George into his house. He actually believed himself to be a lifesaver and believed he could wash evil from the world, declaring that George like everyone was seeking healing, God and self.

"You can't do any good by feeding a snake," Clarence told him. "Why don't you put that freeloader out of your house?" Clarence considered George to be a fungus in search of a partner.

"I have put George out of the house several times, Clarence!"

"Why is he then still in your house?" This was a rhetorical question. Clarence was asking to hear the story about the black and the weeping clown.

"Clarence, the last time I put him out, he sat in the front of the house on the curb, crying like a baby. I ignored him the first day. Jazz and white ponies could not have gotten me to accept his apology. He sat on the curb of the street three days. Before I went to bed at night, I would look out of the window to see if he was still there. He slept against the telephone pole. What would you have done in such a situation?"

"I would have let him stay right there where he set up his camp. You will never be able to get rid of George. He acts as if he washes his head under the urine of a cow." This was something Clarence's grandmother would often say about his father.

"I am hoping he will one day go on his own accord. I know the wind blows the corn. He is so afraid of landing in the street again, having to survive by hook or crook. He spends his entire day in the basement of my house, his brooding nest, sitting on his Episcopal throne, watching cartoons and smoking dope. He doesn't clean up the house when I am at work. And if I cook anything, he eats it all up as if I cooked it for him. He walks around the house, moping and groping like a tower of frustrations, besieged by all kinds of demons. I told him to get a job, but he isn't interested in working. When he has a job, it lasts only a couple of weeks. He is usually fired for offending his coworkers or supervisor. The problem with George is that he has no social skills. I realized this one day, as I was sitting in my car in a queue, waiting for the traffic light to change. Suddenly I saw George ride pass my car on his rickety bicycle. He pulled up to the first car in the queue and spitted into the window of the car…in the face of some white man with his wife and two children, who sat in the back seat. I thought that I hadn't seen correctly. George is a mean son of a bitch. He pulled away on his bicycle, laughing loud. I know he must have been stoned to do such a thing and then to think it was funny!"

"But where does George get the money for dope?"

"He receives a small welfare check. When he runs out of money and dope, he gets aggressive with me. Then all he wants to do is fight, curse, doing much screaming, playing the little wolf. In reality, he is a wimp."

"You have bitten off more than you can chew this time, Babatundi. I would call the police and have him thrown out."

"That is well said. But who will bell the cat?" Babatundi was ashamed to tell Clarence that he had also tried this strategy, which likewise failed.

"The police told me he has lived in my house now too long for me to throw him out. They said he was like a common-law husband or wife and the only thing I could do, would be to get a restraining order against him."

"Did they really say common-law husband? I think they were pulling your leg, Babatundi!"

"You know they don't take us serious anyway!" Babatundi declared.

Clarence wondered why gay people got themselves in such perverted situations. They were not perverted, but the circumstances in which they existed were perverted. It was the tragedy of a minority. Clarence thought about another friend he once knew, who liked ruff Russian men, Perestroika boys, who were happy to be in America. He made the mistake of inviting these three young Russians, dreaming of the Volga, bread and caviar, to his home one night. They cut his throat, wrapped him in his oriental carpet and left it in a dark forest in upstate New York. Babatundi began to rage again, accusing George of misusing his friendship. He ranted and raved about "sneaky no-good gay friends," who act like they prayed at an altar of virtue and then when you turn your back in the light of the shadow, who would scheme and plot to get your man. "Miss Thang…let me tell you what happened last weekend." Babatundi began to explain the reason for his wrath. "I invited Duchess Jones over to spend the weekend at my house." The Duchess was a mutual friend. She was not a real Duchess. Among certain circles of black gays, a hierarchy of status was established and maintained. Those who were active in bed were called Princes, Dukes, Counts, and Knights. And those queens, who were passive in bed, were called Princesses, Duchesses, Countesses, and Dames. Babatundi loved to entertain, to show off his house and garden to guests, to show he had the hospitality of a princess. "I also invited my mother over for the weekend. She slept in the guest room upstairs. I told Duchess Jones to sleep in the family room in the basement," Babatundi said. He sucked on his barbecue ribs and gulped down his black-eyed peas, talking and eating at the same time. He licked his fingers and smacked his lips. "I let that bastard, King George, sleep in my room on the floor. The next morning I gets' up early to fix breakfast for everyone. Duchess Jones comes into the kitchen in a flimsy silk nightgown like the birth of a virgin," Babatundi fumed. "She proceeded to tell me that George slipped down to the basement in the middle of the morning, demanding her to give him a blow job, you know, like the president. I asked her if she did. She claimed that she did not. I then asked her why not and she said, 'because he has a phimosis and I don't like men with a phimosis. When she said that, I was certain she was telling the truth." Babatundi had worked himself into a frenzy, telling Clarence his never-ending story. Clarence refrained from giving him advice.

"I waited until George came down to breakfast. Then I asked him about it. He denied everything, standing there in his blue pajamas and you know, blue is the color of cunning and deceit. He claimed Duchess Jones was lying. I asked him that if she was lying, how then she knew he had a fucked up gun (*penis*). He started to cry about being sorry. I called that motherfucker every name in the book of four lettered words. My mother came downstairs. She told me I should go to church with her and pray. When she left for church, I kicked that bitch, Duchess Jones, out of my house. I then packed George's bags and threw him out, also." Clarence asked if George was finally of the past or if he was back in the house. Babatundi alleged George forced his way back into the house. "George waited at the front door and would not leave to let me open the door the next morning, when I wanted to go to work. I had no choice, but to let him back into the house. Clarence, what can I do?" Babatundi begged Clarence to help him. Clarence had often given Babatundi advice in the past, which he did not take to heart. He told him to stop giving gifts to men. He told him to stop entertaining queers in his house. When he was introduced to George, he told Babatundi that George was a straight, street-wise thug and that he should get rid of him. He warned him that George was a lazy man, who would do nothing, but lie in his bed and smoke pot, and that he would demand to be paid for every orgasm he produced. It was best not to give Babatundi any advice. He did not listen. He preferred to make his own mistakes. Clarence had the suspicion Babatundi enjoyed suffering and relished complaining about his love life to others. He watched Babatundi stuffing himself with soul food which would lie in his stomach like lead, giving him gas and he decided not to give advice to Babatundi this time, but to concentrate on his roast beef, potato salad and black-eyed peas.

"What happened to that guy, who robbed you in St. Nicholas Park?" Babatundi asked Clarence, visibly amused that he could talk about Clarence's weaknesses. "I thought that I had told you the story." Clarence did not want to dwell on negative incidents. "He was arrested and I pressed charges against him."

"No, you didn't, Miss Thang!" Babatundi exclaimed.

"Yes, I most certainly did."

"Child, that guy will seek vengeance and come back to kill you," Babatundi lectured Clarence. "It is very easy for them to get the address of their accusers. If I was you, I would get myself a weapon."

Clarence could not understand how New Yorkers, who were in everything else aggressive, could be so passive when they had been robbed or mugged. "It is my responsibility as a citizen to press charges. Because people are afraid to press charges, such thugs rob with impunity," Clarence responded, reprimanding Babatundi. "Do you have a weapon?" He asked Babatundi. "I keep a weapon with me," Babatundi said. "I don't believe it! You are so clumsy, Babatundi, you would either cut yourself with your own knife or shoot yourself in the foot." Babatundi could not allow this open insult go unanswered. "Girl, I might be a sissy," he said, "but I ain't a punk!" Clarence ignored his slap and continued.

"It is so absurd, it is almost unbelievable. Two weeks later, I was invited to the Attorney General's office for a hearing. It was downtown in a building across the street from city hall. When I walked into the office, there were all these white people and the black guy, Mr. Pacified, who robbed me, sitting serenely behind a bizarre mask. It was the club of the unsuspecting citizens, who were ready to dissect my story, to turn every word I uttered up and down for its veracity. They asked me to recount my drama. Then I was asked to leave the room, to wait outside in a cold hallway. I was called back into the barren room again." Clarence paused to let what he had just said settle in. "The attorney general asked me if I solicited 'love without words' from the guy. He was a born again Christian, who couldn't bring the word 'sex' over his lips. He was one of these trendy holy riders with a golden cross, who thought the sole purpose of life was to reproduce and multiply; that a woman's job is to care for the home and protect the tradition. I was the one who sinned in his eyes." Clarence acted as if he was shocked. "Apparently, this thief claimed I was the one, who approached him and solicited sex. It was his word against my word. I found myself sitting there, confronting this legend, and defending myself in front of these white people. I felt like Don Quixote, combating a stone wall which grew alone, a queer, seeking perpetrator protection. It was absurd. I was disgusted and so frustrated I went home and got drunk that night."

"You're lying, honey," Babatundi said. "You probably went back into that park, looking for another trick."

Clarence was not deterred by Babatundi's mockery. "No, I went home. I felt so bad and depressed. I was the one, who was robbed. I had to defend myself, as if it was a crime in America for being homosexual!"

"Girl…that is the way it is!" Babatundi assured Clarence. "If you would have asked for my advice, I would have told you this. And bashing cherries is only a bagatelle. It needs neither rhyme nor reason." Clarence noted Babatundi's little bit of wisdom and continued. "The following week, I received another letter from the attorney general's office. It informed me the charges against this guy had been dropped, due to lack of evidence."

"Yea, honey, didn't I tell you this would happen?" Babatundi spoke vehemently. He personally did not believe in the caravan of justice.

"Yes, you told me this, but I did not believe you. I had to make the experience for myself." Clarence admitted he had made a stupid mistake.

"I hope this guy doesn't seek vengeance, for your sake," Babatundi forewarned Clarence. "Then, you will not only have lost your innocence!"

"I saw him recently standing on the corner of 125th Street and 7th Avenue. I pulled my cap down and walked pass him," Clarence announced.

"Clarence, you are a naïve faggot, if I might say so myself," Babatundi said, pointing his finger in Clarence's face. "You need to come down from your island in the clouds."

They teased each other, tallying the gamut of negative names which they both had heard themselves called in life.

" Sissy, faggot, pervert, child molester, punk, maricona…,etc."

Clarence informed Babatundi that he, however, did not feel he was naïve. He told Babatundi he should also be careful, because it could happen to him, as well. "There are cunning windbags and slit ear bandits everywhere," Clarence claimed. "I am a New Yorker, darling," Babatundi responded with his hands on his hips. "I know how to survive in these streets. I know how to deal with bandits."

"Well, if you know how to deal with bandits, then you shouldn't have one living right in your home," Clarence enlightened Babatundi, making his point. Babatundi replied that he did not think George was a bandit, but just a sad lonely person, who needed help. "You might not believe this, Clarence, but I have never even allowed George into my bed. That is the difference."

"Babatundi, that is worse than I imagined. I thought you were at least getting good hot sex from this guy."

"No, George has a fucked up gun, as I said before. And I don't like men with a phimosis."

Clarence told him if he would have taken a man home and discovered he had a phimosis, he would have thrown him out the very same night.

"I can't throw him out now, Clarence. That would be unchristian-like," Babatundi said, leaning on his religion for support.

"It amazes me every time to see how you find refuge in your religion, when you don't know the way to go, or your way out of a difficult situation. They chased you out of your own church, because you're gay and the minister of the very same church is the last slut in the Bronx, sucking dicks right and left."

"Yes, I know, Clarence. But he lives a life of don't ask and I won't tell and I live an open gay lifestyle. And as you know, we are sitting ducks for every Tom, Dick and Harry to shoot at will. So you let me have my religion and I won't say anything about your spirits and voodoo bull shit." Babatundi had resolved that the problem was not his religion. "Without my religion, I would have killed that Nigger in my house long ago."

Clarence tried again to make Babatundi see the problem was George. "I think if you don't solve the problem with George, it will eventually lead to this. Either he is going to kill you in that house, or you are going to kill him!"

"It's ironic you say this, Clarence. Last week, I got a knife and threatened him. He kept cursing me, calling me fucking faggot and motherfucker, etc. He was just upset, because he hadn't had any dope for two days and didn't have the money to buy any. I told him if he didn't stop calling me those names, I would cut his peter off."

"What did George do?"

"He called the cops. He told them I was threatening him with a knife. They came later. They filed a report and left. It was a good thing I had threatened him, because he later went into the basement and stayed there the rest of the day, watching Buzz Bunny."

"I don't understand how George can call you faggot. What is he?"

"He thinks because he is a hustler, he is not gay. He sits around talking about chicks, fine chicks. George never had a woman in his life! Hell, he doesn't even know what a pussy looks like." Babatundi was visibly disgusted he had picked up a man who had never had a woman. He liked straight men or liked the illusion that there was such a thing as a straight man.

"Neither do I, for that matter." Clarence retorted.

"Hell, you are a pussy, honey! That's why you're going to Africa, looking for a screw king."

"I'm going to Africa to escape this soap opera life I live here." Clarence resisted any such claims, since they were not entirely true. "Here in New York City, everyone is an island. I just want to escape this existence."

"You are going to Africa with the hope you find a black sun to serenade you on dusty afternoons," Babatundi said, snappish as usual. "If you find one, Miss Thang, you will not only be a queen, but a grand empress on a Dark Continent." Babatundi snapped his fingers three times in the air to emphasize his point. "But I don't blame you. If you find more than one, bring him back for me. Then I will get rid of that dirty swine, George."

"Babatundi, I'm going to Africa in search of my roots!" Clarence was hunting for the last thing. He would need more than luck with the wind to find it. He convinced himself he was not going to Africa to look for a man. But he secretly hoped he would meet a nice fellow to pass his time away, to make his heart swim freely. Everyone dreams of a romance of fire and feeling during their vacation.

"I have often observed the African vendors in the open air Market on 110th Street. I think they are cute, dark and handsome. They are not like African American men, who oppress their hearts," Babatundi argued. "Shit, if you look longer than a second at a black man here, the first thing he will say is 'what you looking at faggot' as if the devil dances upon his head. When you look at an African man, he smiles unaffected. Isn't Mr. Junot at school African?" Babatundi asked.

"Yes, he is from Mali." Clarence informed him, knowing Babatundi had no idea where Mali was located, nor could he distinguish between Senegal and Benin. It was all Africa for him.

"Have you observed him in his tight pants, sitting in the teacher's lounge with his legs wide open, offering a rich bounty in a thick forest? I can imagine him in naked splendor. Do you think he is gay?" Babatundi asked.

"I don't know. I think he prefers women. But you never know, do you? It's nothing but a reflex." Clarence reassured Babatundi that the pursuit of Mr. Junot, the French teacher at the school, maybe would not be in vain. He knew to appear was more important than to be.

"Well, I have noticed him with his hands in his pockets, playing with his toy. You know, Africans are a nature folk. They don't believe in wearing cologne, or in wearing underwear," Babatundi claimed, hitting without pain.

This was an affront and provocation for Clarence. "That is not true! Where did you hear that?" Clarence was tired of defending Africa and Africans. He had never been there himself. Yet in his mind, it was a land of magic, charm and wonder. He felt obligated to defend the swiftly faded world of his forefathers, his archaic roots, which were defiled in the bloody fights of history. Africa's sons and daughters were the only thing left to him.

"They do!" Babatundi said. "And they live in huts in trees and are not very civilized." Babatundi was repeating clichés he had heard in his life on the train of time. "That is what I was told when I was in school," Babatundi declared, praising an institution which had failed as a system. Babatundi's remarks started a train of emotions in Clarence. He knew if one could claim that the Africans were uncivilized, a people of the cellar, then they were saying indirectly that he, the descendant of Africans, was also uncivilized. He wondered what civilization was. Clarence looked back at his desolate life as a child in the South and all those cruel ruffians who had walked through his life. He mused upon the barbarians dressed in monkey suits and ties, chasing wealth. He contemplated Babatundi and along the way the scenes from his bizarre life. He thought about the depraved children in the school, their spiritless teachers and the misanthropic way they treated each other, with their routine brutality, and their entrenched lack of social behavior. Was this civilization? Was civilization like a train which ran without a goal? Some claimed it was a train which had run amok, a train running through the chaos of the market system, in which we were all incarcerated like in a prison. Clarence preferred to fly.

"Yes, this is also what I was taught in school. I know it is a lie," Clarence said. "But what is the color of belief? I am going to Africa, to feed my curiosity, to learn the African esthetic, so I can free my spirit of fear and anxiety; so I can finally enjoy the blessing of a fresh wind and not allow white folks, or the West, as they call themselves, to tell me who I am, what I am, what I should expect from life and what I am capable of achieving." Clarence felt sorry for Babatundi, who was satisfied with momentary freedoms. "Even if Africa is in ruins, it will be ruins in which to dream upon," Clarence stated.

"Calm down, honey!" Babatundi attempted to soothe Clarence, to bring him back to the real world. "Don't give me a lecture on Africa. When you come back, then we can get together and you can tell me all about it. That is, if you do come back. You might get over there and decide to stay. Especially if you meet an African hunk, I am sure you will set up house in a little hut with him. You are lucky, child. You're going to Africa, while I will stay in New York City and occupy myself with summer puzzles, wriggling against boredom." A deceptive harmony reigned between them. They finished their soul food and departed. Babatundi threw his raccoon coat around his shoulders and pranced out the restaurant into the rain. Clarence held the umbrella over their heads. Babatundi searched for a yellow cab. Since he did not have an umbrella,

Clarence told Babatundi to wait under the marquise of the restaurant. He walked to the curb to hail a cab, holding the umbrella in one hand and his briefcase under his arm. He held his other arm in the air, hailing a cab, knowing it would be difficult getting a yellow cab on such a rainy day in Harlem. Numerous gypsy cabs cruised slowly by and stopped in the middle of Lenox Avenue, causing a traffic jam. They gesticulated wildly in their cabs that they were free. Clarence understood Babatundi's reluctance to take a gypsy cab. They were all weather-beaten and rundown automobiles. Their drivers were parasitic vultures. Clarence ignored the gypsy cabs, searching for a yellow cab. A yellow cab finally pulled to the curb. As Clarence opened the door for Babatundi to get in, he heard a loud scream. It was not a scream, but a squeal filled with panic.

"Clarence, help me, please! Help me, Clarence! Help me! Somebody please help me!"

Clarence turned around to see Babatundi and some black predator and poacher, a beautiful face with an ugly scar, pulling at Babatundi's raccoon coat. Babatundi stood at one end with his briefcase in one hand and a piece of the raccoon coat in the other hand. The black man pulled at the other end of the coat, trying to enrich himself through the back door. They dueled as if for a kingdom. "Are you going to get in, Mister," the yellow cab driver asked, oblivious of the drama presently occurring. Clarence slammed the cab door shut, rushing to Babatundi's side. He did not know how he could possibly help Babatundi, who was fighting, as if it was his last stand on Lenox Avenue. Clarence was afraid the black man could be armed and he decided not to engage in a tug of war with this man, not to grab the raccoon coat. Clarence stood next to Babatundi and held his rainbow umbrella over Babatundi's head, while Babatundi did an ecstatic dance, a bolero with this thug for the raccoon coat.

"Mister, let the coat go! It ain't worth it!" The thief said, in a tone of voice that sounded like it was somewhere between a bark and a howl. It was not a plea, but was said as a matter of fact. "Motherfucker, I will kill you!" Babatundi threatened, letting his briefcase fall to the ground, bluffing, as if he had a gun in his pocket. But strong words were not enough. The robber was a master hunter, who pulled out a silver dagger, which gleamed in his hand. Clarence shriveled in the face of danger with bombs in his stomach. He did not want to be like Sardanapalus with a dagger piercing his throat. Thus, he searched for cover and shelter from the wind, rain and the danger. "Babatundi, he has a knife in his hand! Let the damn coat go!" Clarence screamed in Babatundi's direction. In the flash of a second, Babatundi lost his concentration and his grip on the raccoon coat. The black man grabbed the raccoon coat, running into 127th Street. Babatundi ran behind the thief, leaving Clarence standing behind on the corner, bewildered and forsaken. He stood under his umbrella on the corner of Lenox Avenue and 127th Street, holding both Babatundi's and his own briefcase under one arm and the umbrella in the other hand.

The black man disappeared with the raccoon coat into a boarded up abandoned brownstone. Babatundi, like a daredevil, followed the thief in close pursuit, entering also the abandoned brownstone, and setting foot in another reality. It was pitch-black in the house, a dark maze. Babatundi could see nothing. Suddenly he felt dingy hands on his body, scratching, grabbing, and pulling at him. These were skeleton men and women, who looked like zombies. They tore at Babatundi's noble clothes, ripped his pockets out, ripped his gold chains from his neck, pulled at his diamond ring on his finger, tore his shirt from his body, and ripped his earrings out of his ears. Babatundi fought for his life, slugging in every direction, fighting for his head and collar. Only a blue shimmer separated him from the deadly vacuum of the universe. Babatundi noticed a staircase directly in front, leading to the second floor of the brownstone. He ran up the steps. His eyes were now adjusted to the darkness. He saw emaciated bodies in every corner of the room, the dead of Harlem, children of the hole, on America's dead-end street. The floor was littered with trash, condoms, injection needles, and crack pipes. The black man with his raccoon coat escaped through an opened window. He ran across the roof of another abandoned brownstone and disappeared. Babatundi regained his senses in the empty dark room of the brownstone. "I'll just have to buy another raccoon coat," he uttered to himself, realizing he couldn't conquer the underworld. He looked at himself. His shirt was ripped to sheds. The pockets of his pants were torn out. His jewelry was gone. He limped out of the brownstone to 125th Street, where he hailed a yellow cab, ordering the cab driver to take him to his house on Staten Island. There, he licked his wounds and dreamed of living a life without debts. Tranquility had a price.

It seemed as if it was raining steel and fire in Harlem. The rain splashed against the pavement, creating a rhythmic concert of monotony. Its sound could not be decoded. The city sunk under fog. Its wet expanse was unpleasant. The rain and the fog could not be ignored. Clarence suffered its discomfort, waiting patiently for Babatundi to return. A delicate yearning was frozen in the melee. The night approached. Death marched through the cold streets. There was no sight of Babatundi. Clarence hoped and prayed nothing terrible had occurred. It was not worth loosing one's life over a raccoon coat. Clarence realized that what had just happened was an earthly event, a drama which would not change the world. He hailed a gypsy cab. The mulatto driver was from the Dominican Republic. The dingy cab was an old Oldsmobile that appeared, as if it would fall apart in any moment. By each pothole, it rattled and shook. There was an altar on the dashboard, which was hung with Rosary beads around a miniature white Madonna. Incense stabs burned. Clarence instructed the driver to stop on Broadway and 140th Street. He wanted to walk a bit. He asked the driver what was the fare, being angry with himself for having forgotten to ask the price before getting in the taxi. The incident with Babatundi affected him psychologically. "$8.00 dollars!" The taxi driver said in a clipped tone with a foreign accent. Clarence told him he would give him $4.00 dollars and that he should be happy with this, since it wasn't worth more than this. The taxi driver, with his greasy black hair and greasy hands, took the money from Clarence. "Where is my tip?" He asked Clarence, after taking the $4.00. Clarence thought he hadn't heard correctly. Did this foreign taxi driver actually believe he was entitled to a tip? "What tip? Do you think you deserve a tip?" Clarence asked. The taxi driver was visibly agitated. He called Clarence, 'maricona' and several other things in Spanish, which Clarence did not understand. He threatened Clarence and warned him he had better get out of the taxi as quick as he could or else. His tone disturbed Clarence, who began to lecture the foreign cab driver about the correct way of acting in America...the land of unrestrained freedoms.

"This is America, my friend! It might be true that everything here turns around money, but you don't have a right to demand a tip, at least, not in America, "Clarence said. "Maybe in the Dominican Republic you can demand a tip, but not here!" Clarence was argumentative. Being a teacher, he felt it was his responsibility to educate others, especially those, who misunderstood the meaning of market economies, freedom and democracy. "Mister, I told you once to get out of my cab!" The cab driver said. "What cab?" Clarence demanded to know. "You mean this wrack. I wonder how you got a license to drive this wrack in New York City." The cab driver did not respond. He grabbed a baseball bat from under the seat, got out of the cab, walked around the cab to the right side. He snatched opened the back door of the passenger seat. "I said, get out!" The taxi driver spoke firmly. Clarence got out of the cab. He was flabbergasted that this immigrant, who just got off the ship, would have the audacity to threaten an American citizen. These were reasons for deportation.

"You have to be absolutely crazy! You can't threaten people with a baseball bat here. That is assault and battery!" Clarence said.

The cab driver stood with the baseball bat in his hand. He had no intentions of hitting Clarence with the bat. He only wanted to instill fear in his soul. He was frustrated with these spoiled, demanding New Yorkers. Just because he did not speak English like an American, did not mean he could be treated like a dog, he thought. Most of his clientele were Black Americans, who depended upon gypsy cabs for transportation, since most yellow cab drivers would not stop for them. The Black Americans, building monuments of thoughtlessness, treated such impoverished immigrants like dirt, as if they were no more than the shadow of a donkey. The taxi driver could not understand the reasons for their animosity, what ghosts rode their backs.

"Don't you get huffy with me, you pale-face dildo. Let me tell one thing, mister. My family has lived in this country for centuries, fighting just to be treated with human dignity. And you, dago (*a working class Latino*), just got off the boat and think you can talk to me like a twerp. I would recommend you put that baseball bat back where you found it," Clarence said, while getting out of the taxi. "Hunting turtles is different than hunting people. I have your name and number. I intend to report you to the New York licensing authorities and to the immigration authorities. Before you can say 'Jack the rabbit', you will be back in your dismal Caribbean paradise, on your island of joyful poverty." Clarence opened his umbrella. He bid farewell to the dampened Caribbean cab driver. Then he strutted up Broadway, as if he was blessed from heaven and honored on earth; as if he traveled a path on which the Gods wandered.

10. In the dangerous fantasies of a jungle

Clarence sat at his desk, hoping the unending retinue of routine would pass quickly and the day would be short and painless. It was a sonny June day...the last week of school. During the morning break, Clarence strolled pass Babatundi's classroom, trying to escape from the routine. Babatundi could be seen through the narrow window of the classroom door. He appeared like a sissy gladiator, pirouetting in ballerina shoes...a 250-pound orangutan with complete control of his dragon body, prancing in flowing silk pants and a wide silk blouse. "It's a light slide or brush on the floor. Start with the foot in the 6th position," he instructed the children in a Teddy boy voice. The children were composed mostly of girls. There were in the dance class one or two boys interspersed between the girls. It was difficult, however, to motivate the boys to learn how to dance...to learn the language of light, as oppose to spitting thorns. This was something, they claimed, only sissies did. When a brave boy dared the norm and registered for Babatundi's dancing class, it became a difficult task to get him to put on skin tights. Babatundi insisted all students in his dancing class wear tights. Clarence accused him of forcing the boys to wear tights only to bask upon their beautiful developing bodies. They were not quite colossal men and yet not little boys any longer. The boys gave promise of the men they would become. They were beauty in full bloom. "The foot goes behind, brushes the floor with a demi-point, toes flexed." Babatundi performed the position with elegance. "Bring the leg from behind, brush the floor and rise; step flat on the floor from the demi-point. The hip is pushed high to the side." Babatundi poked his big fat ass in the air. This apparition was too much to see without grinning. "Then change into the 3rd position, arms in the open basket handles, twisting the torso rapidly, head looking up; in 2 counts lower yourself, head on the knee, the hands slide along the thighs to the ankles; rise in one count, tremble in 4 counts," he instructed... looking like a well-fed chicken, trembling on a stick. "The trembling goes from the front to the back," he said. "The feeling comes from the small of the back to the shoulder and the neck. It is the shoulder movement from the dances of the forest."

Clarence left Babatundi to his positions, to his laborious search for a perfect movement, returning to his classroom, relishing a few quiet moments in which he found himself split in a wall of time. Babatundi had obviously gotten over the lost of his raccoon coat. Clarence was interrupted in his reverie by Justine Carter, a primary school teacher. She entered his classroom without being invited and besieged him, sitting herself in a child's chair across from Clarence's desk. Clarence noted she was a voluptuous woman with huge breasts. He wondered to himself, why women seemed to be attracted to him and sighed upon the thought. "Mr. Hill, I know you're on your break now, but I just want to ask you something," Justine Carter said, pulling her dress up to her thighs. Clarence saw that she wore no panties. Justine Carter sat self-confident and lewdly with her legs opened wide, wishing she was a sex symbol. All of her erogenous zones were on alert. Her heart drummed eroticism. A silent dialogue occurred. Clarence wanted to puke, thinking this was the best strategy. He did not want a pussy.

"Mr. Hill, you are too puny for me!" Justine Carter said.

"I know someone who likes it!" Clarence replied, suggesting a contented inner life. He lied. He didn't have a special one. He was looking for Mr. Special like she was...a keeper of the fire.

"What woman likes a puny man?" Justine Carter was like a dog in heat at the end of abstinence. Her scent pervaded the air. "Mr. Hill, I want to invite you to a home cooked meal," she said. She twisted her arms and legs around herself to hide her shame. She was almost a respectable woman. "I know you don't get the opportunity to eat good southern home-cooked food often. I want to help you gain some weight before you leave us for Africa." She licked her lips, batted her eyes. They gleamed with desire. "You like soul food?" She asked, wishing for an epoch when women wore petticoats. "Of course, you do, what southern boy doesn't like soul food? I want to cook you a meal before you go to Africa. When do you have time?"

Clarence thought to himself that Justine was not right of mind. She had to be blind not to have recognized he was not interested in women or she was stupid enough to believe all she had to do was to show a man what was between her legs and he would want to smell it. He despised normality.... normal men and normal women, since they were the ones who had caused him so much pain in his life. He usually did what was considered abnormal. Because he carried a stick between his legs, he wondered, why was it expected that he should use it to control, threaten and gain respect? Clarence was one, who did not take more than needed and he did not need a woman. He stood and walked to the window overlooking 138th street, imagining the Blue Nile flowing below, wanting to take himself out of Justine Carter's surveying eyes and placing himself in a position where he felt more comfortable. "Thanks for the invitation, Ms. Carter. I am very busy now. You know with plans for my trip and with the usual end of the year paper work... grades, report cards, etc. Why don't you give me a call next week and we can plan a date. I will be leaving on Saturday; maybe that Friday would be a good date to get together. Give me your telephone number," Clarence said, seeking time for evasion.

Justice Carter spent most of her time trying to catch a man. Clarence was sure she had gone through every male in the building and now she had decided to take on the homos. She was convinced with a certain amount of effort, she could make them normal and then she would have a good man for herself. She considered homosexuals to constitute an untapped reservoir of men. "I gave you my telephone number. Don't you remember?" She retorted.

"I probably misplaced it," Clarence said embarrassed, maintaining course. "Give it to me again. I promise not to misplace it this time." He walked back towards the desk to search for a notepad.

"I know it isn't important for you, Mr. Hill," Justine said. "You must have many ladies calling you!" Justine was a lonely woman for whom misfortune came in little bites. She hadn't had a man since the last blue moon. Clarence learned her sentimental story from the grapevine. It was said that her first man raped her in the bud of her life, in a public bathroom of a shoddy restaurant in Virginia. Justine told everybody in the small town he was her boyfriend, making much wind for a new love. It was a liaison with consequences. She was charmed behind the hills. When the rains came and she told him she was pregnant, he cowardly disappeared with the wind. She heard eventually he had gone to New York. After she gave birth to a girl, she packed her bags and followed him to the big city, hoping she would one day meet him on the streets of the city. She was a nice girl, who built her house too close to the water, as they say. She believed in a fictitious world from a picture book and wanted to be a woman of the world. Justine was not very intelligent, but intelligent enough to know how to survive. She managed to educate herself, while working in a factory at night. She dedicated the rest of her time and thoughts to catching a man. Because of this obsession, she could not live her dog's life in composure and calmness. She could not teach with vision. She could not think clearly or rationally nor behave sane. She became schizophrenic.

"Ms. Carter, I have no ladies calling me," Clarence said with severe earnestness.

"I don't believe it...a cute man like you! I bet you the women must be knocking your door down," she said.

"Ms. Carter, stop pulling my leg." Clarence sat back behind his desk, observing Justine with a stern face.

"I'm not joking," she insisted. "You're a good-looking man. Any woman would be more than happy to have a man like you in her pocket." Justine Carter did a rain dance and whackled her ass. She called on all the gods she knew to make Clarence attracted to her female charms. She cooed and giggled. Clarence actually thought he could smell her pussy and it was disgusting him.

"Now I'm too old. The children are calling me old maid. They are driving me crazy, really! Maybe during our dinner, you can give me some tips on how I can improve my teaching next year. Are you coming back next year, Mr. Hill? She changed the subject in order not to embarrass him. Her personal problems were general knowledge. She knew this.

"I don't think so, Ms. Carter. I've been offered a position at another school." Clarence was reluctant to tell her in which ape house he would be teaching next year. He knew telling Justine would be tantamount to broadcasting it over the radio and he did not want Ms. Hunter, the principal, the democrat with rooster claws, to know that he would not be returning next year or to know his plans for the future. His retreat was not yet official. He was being precautious, because he knew Ms. Hunter was a vicious woman with a soiled view of the world.

"You're a good teacher," Justine said. "You can go wherever you want to. You could even teach at a private white school or a school downtown. But I am stuck here. I only have an associate degree from City College. I'm now too old to go back to college to get a bachelor degree." Justine laid her grievance open for the world to hear. She wanted Clarence to say she was not too old and she opened the door for him to give her a compliment.

"You are not too old, Ms. Carter," Clarence told her with a smile of tenderness.

"Do you really think so, Mr. Hill?" Justine's face lighted up.

Clarence was aware he had made her day.

"Do you think I look all right…a little bit pretty, Mr. Hill?" Justine was hunting for orchids.

"You don't look that bad! Clarence said. "Of course, you could wear a little make-up and maybe change the way you wear your hair."

"How should I do it? Like this? That makes my face stand out too much. Don't you think so?" Justine pulled her long hair back into a bun. She revealed a breathtaking vista of wrinkles, dents and folds.

"Oh, you have an interesting face," Clarence told her, juggling wild with words.

"But my nose is too wide. It is so…Negroid," she replied, being wanton with her heritage.

"What is wrong with that? That is the nose you were born with, "Clarence said, returning to the constructive. Her comment shocked him and he wondered when would black people stop hating themselves?

"But black men prefer…." She uttered.

"I know what black men like," Clarence told her and wondered what she would have said if he told her the truth…that he had had more tasteless and beautiful black men in his life then she could even imagine. "You shouldn't worry about what black men like," Clarence said in a soft mellowness. "But you should try to be yourself, if anything."

"That's easy for you to say, Mr. Hill. You haven't been through the treadmill that I have been through with black men," Justine said on automatic.

Clarence really did not want to hear about female dilemmas. He had had his share of problems with black men, especially the macho types who loved to fuck sissies in the dark. "I can imagine it, Ms. Carter. I have heard the stories."

"You aren't like the others, Mr. Hill." Justine complimented Clarence under the line. "You're so sensitive and understanding." She touched his hand gently, allowing her hand to linger longer than it should. "I can't wait until you come to my house for dinner. We will have a lot to talk about and lots of fun. Now don't forget to call me and let me know when you can come." Justine stood after half of an eternity and whackled out of the door. Clarence escorted her. He opened the door and watched her walk down the hallway, swinging her ass and doing everything a lady could possibly do to attract a man, without appearing to be a slut. He was envious that Justine Carter swung her ass better than he did. He wondered if she would be willing to give him a crash course on swinging asses with wit and swing. Clarence later filled the final grades of his students into their report cards, hesitating once and awhile with those students, who were on the borderline, staring out of the window at the abandoned brownstones on 138th street. In such a moment, he drifted into dream. He flew away like the free birds in the sky, fantasizing he was sitting under a Baobab tree, painting his fingernails pink and contemplating the myth of creation. He pictured himself, listening to his Walkman and patting his feet to Prince; "all the critics love me in NY", humming with the melody and admiring his beautiful pink nails against the blazing sun. In the distance, he spied the specter of a caravan approaching across the steep. Waiting its arrival, he popped his fingers and shook his butt, imagining himself performing on a stage like Tina Turner, all legs and ass. Tina was his favorite star and if he had a choice of being born again, he would have wanted to be Tina Turner. He had even contemplated once dressing in drag as Tina Turner. He threw his hands in the humid African air and waved them like he just didn't care. "Hey mama, hey papa," he sang, twisting to the right and twining to the left, jumping to the front and jumping to the back. "Like a sex machine," he crooned. "I wanna get up and do my thang!" Clarence hopped around in his daydreams like the vermiculated blacks on MTV and Soul Train. He was hopping around like a rabbit when a caravan arrived of dark, handsome nomads, dressed in purple. They sat stately on their camels and spoke a language he did not understand. The handsome nomads wondered if he was human or spirit, and if he was a spirit, if he was a good or bad spirit. Clarence smiled, flirting with them. Suddenly a Herculean built swarthy man with the scent of the woods, dismounted from his camel, approached him. He grabbed Clarence up into his strong arms, carrying him back to his camel, and throwing him across the camel like a slaughtered antelope. Clarence squealed a weak protest, submitting to this noble exploitation, dreaming of living a life of love and sex in a hut in the Savanna, of being happy without illusions in a harem. He thought it was better to groove to devotion in the Savanna than living like Chaste Mary in New York City. The caravan continued its journey in a triumphant procession into the distance.

Clarence drank in a sea of fantasies and anticipation. His bags were packed. He was ready to go to a remote and faraway place, to a place at the end of the world. Energy pulsated and circulated through his blood, flowing through his veins to the tips of his fingers. The energy carried him from one moment to the next. He felt strange, as if he was floating in a high altitude. Clarence had traveled before, but he couldn't explain this excitement. It touched every fiber of his body, which prickled with expectation. His entire body beckoned with silent entreaties. Maybe it was the way people looked, when he told them he was going to Africa. They had a faraway look in their eyes. They looked at him, as if he had said he was going to Mars, or to Jupiter. Clarence knew that he was going to a place that none of his acquaintances in their wildest dreams would have considered traveling to, but their comments surprised him. One woman asked suspiciously: "What is there?" She advised Clarence to go to Disney World instead. "The best thing is to get a good insurance," a neighbor told him, adding with sarcasm "it is wonderful in hell!" Their comments frightened Clarence. They robbed him of the rest of hope. Had he not already paid for the trip, he would have withdrawn from the contract. Clarence had especially apprehensions about his sexual orientation. He complained often about New York City. But he knew that at least in New York City, he could live the life he chose. Gay people were treated like perverts and criminals in many places in the world. They were forced to wander their hidden lives in uncertainty. Honorable men and women decided their fate in a vile world.

Clarence sprawled out on his lime green sofa landscape between plush cushions, drinking a glass of Chianti, and reading the International Gay Guide. He was curious to see how homos were treated between the Sahara Desert and Cap Town, and he was shocked to read homosexuality was called forbidden love and was punishable in Saudi Arabia with the death penalty. He did not want to die for his sexual orientation. Clarence wondered what gave rude fellows, without measure or restraint, with bodies in their cellars, the right to deny the existence of others, to relegate others as irreverent, to place others on the pillory. These fellows claimed to have a heap of religion out of one side of their crooked mouths and out of the other side, they preached with a clear conscience that homosexuals should be hounded, imprisoned or killed. They were humans, who crawled while standing. They engaged in an undeclared war against phantoms and nightmares, blaming others for their own bed miseries. It was a cold shower for Clarence to learn that in Zaire, homosexuality could lead to imprisonment of up to five years. In Zambia, the maximum penalty was fourteen years imprisonment. In Cameroon, homosexuality was also punishable with imprisonment. Homosexuality was considered illegal in Kenya and harshly punished with a minimum of 5 years up to a maximum of 14 years. It was referred to as "carnal knowledge against the order of nature." The more he read, the more depressed he became. A great resignation set in. It portended a future of misery for chimeras like him, feeling like a bug against the rest of the world. You could not fight against the morals of men. He read that in Namibia, homosexuality was punishable according to the Sexual Offenses Act and in Nigeria it could lead to imprisonment of fourteen years. He was disheartened. All his fantasies about Africa dissipated in thin air. He searched for the Ivory Coast. It was encouraging to read that there were no laws restricting homosexuality in the Ivory Coast. But his heart fell to learn there was no gay scene in the 'Western' sense of the word. The Gay guide suggested that if open homosexuality existed, it would only be found in Abidjan or in some of the larger cities. He read that, in general, homosexuality in the Ivory Coast was still a taboo subject. There was a gnawing feeling of fear in his stomach...potent warning sign. Was he diving voluntarily into the catastrophe? Clarence reasoned he was not going to Africa to look for an African violet, to cruise in tropical forests under the African sun, to search for wild honey. He was fair of soul and had the honest skin of the chameleon. Of course, if it should happen by accident, he would not be indisposed towards such an encounter. Clarence rationalized he was going to Africa to look for the bones of his ancestors, for a dialogue, to find the source of a cool ground, in search of gods and graves, to return to the roots. He couldn't expect the rest of the world to be like New York. There was a boundary to light. He would depart cheerfully without illusion, realizing it was a long, long road to human rights and it would take an eternity for the world to learn what freedom means. The Arch of Noah was on a false course, he thought, still traveling the street of myths and false morals.

It was his last night in the city, and it was a warm full moon night. A soft breeze blew through the opened window, rustling the embroidered curtains, as it wandered throughout Clarence's apartment. The breeze stroked him softly across his cheeks. The scent of the honeysuckle awakened memories within him, whispered to him of his childhood in the South, the place of his earlier imprisonment. He remembered how on such nights, he and his brother would sleep on the veranda, counting the stars, idly talking nonsense about what they would own when they grew up. He was always considered the dream dancer. Clarence remembered how he would wish for a virtuous woman to love and a cozy home. His brother, on the other hand, who was considered the rebel and rabble rooster, would often claim he wanted in the river of life "a gun and a bitch to fuck". It was not about love nor about harmony he would say to Clarence, telling him that nobody would wait for harmony addicted suckers. The Gods in their heaven blessed poets like him, Clarence imagined. He was by nature a person who sought stability and security, trust and reliability. His brother, on the other hand, desired adventure and fun, wanting it all, while balancing on one leg in the steam bath of catch as catch can. Clarence's brother accomplished his dreams at an early age, landing in prison for perpetrators and masochists, the stomping ground for young, slick and clever black men, the ones who thought they could beat the system. In prison, they had more than enough time to exercise their minds. Clarence's dreams remained unfulfilled with the slight transformation of a new form in an old spirit. He no longer wanted a woman to love and a home. He now craved for a virile man to call his own, with which to be one heart and one soul, and he wanted a cozy nest for mating. These were moods of the heart. Chance determined their direction.

The warm summer breeze made Clarence nervous with thoughts of virile men. It pulled him like an invisible ray to St. Nicholas Park, promising him satisfaction...that a prince charming might be waiting for him under a tree, a private hero in the dark park. Clarence endless search for the seventh heaven was a kind of blues. The tepid night overwhelmed him with thoughts of sin and forgiveness, filling him with spirit and sensuality. It was the mating season for the light bugs. Clarence's bio-rhythm demanded a response. He eagerly put on his night splendor, his cruising costume and zealously followed the light bugs into the park, parading pass Monsieur Albert, resting on the stoop, relishing the warm night and lusting after the young girls, hurrying up and down the hill. He marched pass Mrs. Holstrom, promenading with her Pekinese dogs on Convent Avenue. Clarence greeted both of them in a neighborly manner, hoping they would be tolerant of his outfit...scanty hot pants with a skimpy tank top and combat booths. But he understood that they accepted his vampness, since they knew that he was familiar with their failings and deficiencies and because there were few secrets to hide, they all resolved to be discrete, not to linger on each other weaknesses.

Dark princes and princesses promenaded between the bushes in the park, whose desires were hidden by the darkness of the night. These were queers, who had left at home their demeanors of shame or opprobrium. Naked young men, who were human structures of the night, strutted down dark narrow paths, parading their nudity and using it as a marketing ploy. They targeted normal straight males and frustrated husbands, who were looking for a blow job or a quick fuck before they returned home to their frigid wives. Clarence ignored the nude fellows, as they strutted in phantom-like geometry between the bushes. He knew nothing was, as it was advertised on the package and he was also a little bit offended by their undeviating and minimalist approach to catching a man. They had reduced seduction down to an erection and a Vaseline greased ass. They were heartless and scheming queers. They were convinced men followed their erections first and foremost in their pursuit of a quick orgasm, in their desire to shoot their guns and spread their seeds. Sexual activity in a void could be found in the park. Everything revolved around the chase; the aggressive seeking of an expeditious climax, which left one disappointed and frustrated. Clarence engaged in tiny intermezzos, but he was unsuccessful in his chase for the right type. He, therefore, took a strong exit out of the park, deciding to return to his cozy apartment. As he rambled across the vacant City College campus, he stumbled upon Mrs. Holstrom with her Pekinese dogs. She rested on a stone bench in the small rose garden on the campus of City College. Clarence attempted to slither pass the rose garden unheeded, not wanting to show Mrs. Holstrom the frustration on his face nor wanting to give her the chance to comment on his outrageous and disheveled outfit. He also did not want to disturb her. She appeared to be meditating. She nodded her blond head of hair and spoke gently with her Pekinese dogs, lying at her feet. Clarence sneaked pass the rose garden, thinking that he had successfully escaped her attention, as Mrs. Holstrom called his name. She sung it like a short melody in a singsong. "Hello…oooo, Mr. Hill…ll," she sang. Clarence was startled by her mellowness. He fended surprise. It was astonishing to find a white lady sitting in a park at night in Harlem. He acknowledged her cordially, intending to continue on his way, but she invited him to join her in the rose garden. She did not ask Clarence directly to join her, but posed a question, which required an answer. "Isn't it a lovely evening," she asked. "It's a wonderful evening, indeed," Clarence responded. They gazed at the stars, the full moon over their heads. It was a pensive and melancholic night. Mrs. Holstrom patted the bench for Clarence to sit beside her.

The Pekinese dogs barked as he approached. Mrs. Holstrom tried to calm them in their excitement. They sniffled at his combat boots, his shaved legs. They smelled the semen and piss in the caked dirt around the soles of his shoes, the scent of numerous fingers that had touched, rubbed, patted and caressed his smooth legs. If the dogs could have spoken, they would have been able to give a chronology of lust, passion and sex. Clarence acted as if nothing happened. And yet he had not done anything in the park worth mentioning, worth bragging about. Of course, he would not have told Mrs. Holstrom about his vices anyway. It was the usual masturbation games, the usual voyeurism, and the usual market appraisal of men. He jerked off and allowed himself to be jerked off. He gave head and received head. These were the routine sexual practices in gay market places. They fell short of nirvana. They could not quench one's thirst and hunger for love, for tenderness, or for friendship. "Leave Mr. Hill alone," Mrs. Holstrom said, commanding the dogs to sit. She smiled at Clarence with whimsical eyes. Her breath reeked of alcohol, the local anesthesia. She was feeling well without consequences, euphoric. She looked unabashedly at Clarence hot pants and his ostentatious presentation of flesh. "You should be careful, my dear," she counseled him, emphasizing the word careful. She meant to be careful in general, careful of catching AIDS, of being robbed, of being victimized. Clarence expressed his gratitude for her motherly advice, remarking that he tried to be careful as a matter-of-course. He then changed the subject abruptly; declaring how happy he was summer had finally arrived and announcing he could hardly wait to enjoy it. Mrs. Holstrom told him that young people were usually impatient. "I know, I know you don't believe me, but I know what it means to be young and impatient," she said. "I was once also young and impatient."

Clarence complimented Mrs. Holstrom, telling her he did not think she looked old. She giggled like a young girl, grabbing his arm and leaning against him, not like a woman leans against her man, but as a mother leans against her son. "I envy you, Mr. Hill," she declared. "The way you live your life in the manner you chose." Clarence understood normal people thought that abnormality was a choice. He had often heard this comment before. His patent response was he did not have a choice. He would say he was born this way and he was not an expert for abnormality. Mrs. Holstrom was not deterred by his acerbity. She told him she found it wonderful how he had taken his fate into his own hands and turned what was a bad situation into an asset. "If I had taken my fate into my own hands, I would not now be vegetating here in Harlem," she said. "I am from Sweden. Do you know Sweden?" She asked. Clarence knew it was where the cold wind sprang. Mrs. Holstrom began a long monologue, explaining what led to her inevitable doom, recounting to Clarence, old secrets, the skeleton of reality, what she would not have told anyone in a sober state. It was the alcohol speaking. Clarence already knew most of it. Mrs. Holstrom was a lonely white lady, who moved in tiny steps in a one-room refuge in Harlem, sitting in gloom day in and day out, surrounded by her heirlooms... a tiny bottle of Patou perfume, which was a gift from her husband and a picture of a tranquil harbor in Sweden, which hung over her bed. She listened during the day and night to Richard Strauss and Verdi. Her harmonic music often floated into Clarence's window, serenading him. It was Monsieur Albert, the Haitian man and chronicler of faults, who enlightened Clarence about Mrs. Holstrom's history, revealing the myths behind the person, the bones collected in her box. Although Mrs.Holstrom's transgression was not great, it hung heavy over her head for the rest of her life.

Mrs. Holstrom's offense was being tactless in a polite world. She copulated with a black man in an eggshell. She met her American husband in Sweden. He was a high manager for a large corporation. He proposed to her. They married and came, under the magic of beginnings, to the United States to live. Clarence did not know her hopes and dreams, but he imagined she must have been an innocent, naïve young woman, who thought America was like Sweden. She must have come to the United States with an opened heart, believing she could treat everyone she met with the same amount of courtesy and affability. Her husband settled her in a big house in Greenwich, Connecticut and proceeded to neglect her in the luxury of pure emptiness, in his efforts to multiply the loaves...to accumulate wealth. Mrs. Holstrom sought compassion elsewhere. That a black man, a taxi driver laughed his way into her heart did not disturb her. She was from Sweden. She was raised in a tolerant environment. Her polite white upper class friends, for whom pampering was a drug, were on a crusade of the cross roaders, on a warpath, when they found out about the affair. They hit and stabbed her. They abandoned her for falling out of the line. Although it was a bagatelle affair, a small mistake, according to Monsieur Albert, she was forced to sacrifice wealth, privilege and respectability, to go into a second exile. For this shameful and scandalous sin, she was banished to Harlem to spend her days in hopeless thoughts and fantasies of forgotten splendor in the state of Connecticut, of the grand past and privilege ways of her polite white friends. Sex, lies and consumption drove Mrs. Holstrom insane. She found her enemies in her neighbors' garden and they led the way to her devastation. She had a nervous breakdown.

Mrs. Holstrom's black maid was the one, who faithfully cared for her. The black maid rented a small room in Harlem for Mrs. Holstrom and attempted to patch her heart back together. The maid eventually died, leaving Mrs. Holstrom alone in Harlem with her Weltschmerz (*the pain of the world*). Mrs. Holstrom often considered leaving her rare existence in Harlem, but she did not know where to go. She could not return to her husband and children in Connecticut. They had disowned her. She could not return to Sweden. It was a place of her past and dreams, and she was afraid of returning to Europe, a place very different than the United States. She spent the rest of her life in her tiny room, dripping to death, remembering the glance and charm of the past, listening to the floors and walls creak, listening to the movements of her petty neighbors, who pursued their sensual trivialities. The crude polite society became for her a distant dream in the barren world in which she lived. Clarence sympathized with her, because he had a love for butterflies, especially the ones searching for a purpose on gloomy roads.

"When you are young, the sun always shines and you easily begin to believe you will live for eternity. You make mistakes lightly, unaware you will spend the rest of your life regretting them," Mrs. Holstrom remarked, crying with dry eyes, realizing she had weathered in her tracks. She patted Clarence hand compassionately. How could he grasp prudence that came with age? "Suddenly one evening, when I was unaware and most relaxed among my friends, the last refrain of my summer floated past," Mrs. Holstrom said in a sepulchral voice. "It kissed me gently on my lips, farewell. I was too engrossed with living to notice it was my last summer, slipping in evening red across the fields. It was my time to say farewell to youth. I only felt a chill and grabbed my coat to warm me." She spoke of the art of dying. The roses scented the summer air intoxicatingly sweet. The night had matured. Clarence thoughts drifted to Africa. Mrs. Holstrom inquired when he would be departing. She exhorted him to relish every twinkling second of his trip. "Of course, you as a teacher should know traveling is an education itself," she said. The moon hid behind a cloud. Salsa music could be heard on Amsterdam Avenue in the distance. A loving couple strolled pass, oblivious to the rest of the world. "As a young woman, I longed for remote and faraway places," Mrs. Holstrom stated. She raved about the Ramblas in Barcelona and the cafés and canals of Amsterdam, about Paris, Lisbon and Rome. She told Clarence in the past people traveled to learn about the way other people lived and thought. But today people took a trip just to get away from it all, to amuse themselves for fun and relaxation...in an all-inclusive isolation. "I guess I'm a little bit old fashion," she said. "The world I knew, no longer exists...not even in Sweden." They walked quietly out of the rose garden, along Convent Avenue and up 141st street. Before Mrs. Holstrom disappeared into her small room, she asked Clarence to bring her a souvenir from Africa. "Nothing expensive," she stated. "...something small you can place in your pocket." Then she paused for a moment in front of her door with a faraway gaze in her blue eyes. "I have never been to Africa," she said. "But I have dreamed of its fascination." They parted.

Clarence did not realize in this moment that he would not see her again. She died alone in her small room. When he returned from Africa, he found another single, lonely woman of a different race and a different culture, but with the same needs, living in the small room. As Clarence walked back towards the park, he thought about loneliness without boundaries and that the night like life was much too short to waste. He also thought about Antoine, the dreamer, Justine, the seeker, Ms. Holstrom, the defeated one, Monsieur Albert, a pitiful old man, Mr. Sullivan, his petty landlord, the lost children at the school and Babatundi, his almost friend. These were long overdue thoughts. They were certainly not happy in this city of unlimited possibilities, where department stores were not scarce, but scarce were the things that gave life a sense of meaning. On the surface everybody appeared to move gently through the rat race, maintaining a dangerous balance. Each lived his/her life detached and isolated. And they all suffered with a serene stride and an endless smile in the agony of loneliness. Freedom for them remained just a word, as if it would expire with the morning dew in the cornucopia of the cosmos. Clarence did not want to dissect the anatomy of melancholy. It made him sad. He had a garden of thoughts in his head, wandering in his imagination between fields of poppy seeds and sunflowers with Kilimandscharo in view, realizing that life was also a trip, and all human beings were in voyage. He thought about his brother's comment and he felt his brother was right, when he claimed that Clarence was harmony addicted. Clarence believed that to be harmony addicted was not an affliction to take seriously.

On this warm summer night, which was his last night in the city, Clarence wanted just to past his time with a warm man of flesh and blood. He decided to go back into the park during the early morning hours with piousness in his heart, wine in his blood and lust in his stomach. Before midnight, there was nothing in the park but middle aged men, waiting for the approach of decay. The younger virile knights of loneliness came later, in more than a good mood. The park, a pleasure garden, would then be packed with children of the night seeking, touching, and copulating in the early morning hours. Clarence wondered if they had jobs to go to. He concluded that most were unemployed black men, trade for queers of the swamp. The feeling of lust was a torrid feeling for him. It made him itch and made him feel hot in the britches…in flaming need of another human being, seeking incredible encounters in the darkness of the park, because it concealed his shame. Clarence was in reality a victim, suffering his own constraints and deprivations; walking a small edge solely for the purpose of transgression of bourgeois morals…seeking luck that he thought was hidden in the bushes, somewhere in the park. The park was a place for many such animals, a refuge for depraved and repudiated fools. Clarence wandered into it, questioning if he would suffer denial again, before the night took flight. He believed his desire was right and he hoped the warm summer night, the warm breeze would bring him a rich bounty, would bring him a jewel. It was a summer night filled with erotic cravings, casting lustful warmth upon the trees and city lights, upon Harlem, which twinkled and glowed in the valley below the park. The crickets sung and the glow bugs glimmered. Darkness prevailed in the park. The children were all out in heat, carrying on like wild dogs, pissing on the trees, making paths into empty spaces. Hoodlums and juveniles had broken the night lamps in the park in order to lurk better. They were eternal mischievous boys, who would never become men, never reach their goals. Most of them were unemployed or marginally employed and were lost in disequilibria. For queers like Clarence, they were pompous little buffoons, powerless, but exotic toys…exotic boys, who walked an outlaw trail. Clarence forgave them for their shortcomings, because they were all with flaws and imperfections. Would he find a gallant gigolo this night? Would he be hugged or mugged by some handsome prince of love? Was it his life style that caused this risk? Was it only a matter of overcoming aberrant passions? He did not want to think about the thin line between normality and abnormality…no, not tonight. Clarence wanted to saturate his soul with delight and even if it would be a fleeting orgasm and he should die prematurely for having such sinful thoughts…then so be it! He would have at least died for passion's sake. There are no morals in an orgasm. It was the spirit of desire that pulled Clarence, as he saw standing in the moonlight, leaning against a tree, a Lone Ranger. Was this his trick for the night or a fata morgana? The long legs of the man promised only promises and promises of ecstasy. Clarence's fantasies took flight. He wished in this moment that he had the might of a sorcerer, that he could ban the perils of first encounters and rendezvous in the dark. If he could possess such sorcery, he would devastate polite society's morals. Clarence sauntered pass the black cowboy, inspecting his anatomy and hating himself for acting like a horny sissy, doing a Dervish dance around a cock. He touched the man. His touch revealed an immense talent, his toy and his weapon…the measure of all things that made men, men. And yet Clarence knew instinctively that having talent between one's legs was not everything. It could not compensate for lack of intellect or for commonsense. He berated himself for expecting more and searched the sky for answers. The stars were silent. Is this an accidental encounter? The crickets chirped in the bushes. A soft breeze whistled gently through the trees. Clarence allowed his passion to serve as his guide, resolving that words at this moment were much too trivial. He touched the Long Ranger's toy(penis) again and hailed his talent.

"You want me to satisfy you?" This stranger whispered into Clarence ear. Clarence nodded his head, signaling a muted yes. "What's the matter, you're shy?" The cowboy asked. He grabbed Clarence, pulling him into his arms. "Don't be shy, honey," he stated in a husky voice, while rubbing his body against Clarence. "I have everything you want and more besides." Clarence caution floated asunder. He allowed himself to be seduced by this cocksure man, who was black as tar, with glowing coals for eyes and lips so thick that Clarence imagined them swallowing him. In this moment, he would not even have accepted rubies as a substitute for this man. They followed the breeze out of the park, walking towards Clarence's apartment, where they could be alone, where his bed beckoned with liberation. "What's your name?" Clarence whispered softly into the man's ear, as he laid on his bed. Clarence thought it appropriate to know the name of the person with whom he was now intending to share something that was very intimate and sacred, thinking that sex was something special. "I got 11 ½ inches," the man declared. "Do you think you can take it all?" Clarence did not know how to reply to this statement. "I don't know what you mean," he responded, playing coquet. He wanted to flirt with the man, to be courted and embraced, but this man, his trick, did not understand the art of flirting, the moods of the heart. "You're a sophisticated faggot," he said. "Talk is cheap." He quickly disrobed himself, standing like a black Adonis in front of Clarence, posturing naked, splendid and poisonous...smelling like a horse. "I'll bet you one thang," he said, with his penis in his hands. "Mah thang will satisfy you, if nothing else can." Clarence was amused by his comment. It was similar to playing a game. "That is nothing but a useful instrument," Clarence replied, "overwrought and hyperbolic." The broncobuster gazed at Clarence skeptically. "You talk too much!" He retorted in a ruff tone. "I'll choke you with mah thang, if you don't shut up. Now lie on your stomach and let me prove to you what a man is all about."

"It's not my habit to lie on my stomach," Clarence protested, sitting on the side of the bed. "Can't we do it another way?" Clarence wanted to make love and he hoped this man would eventually understand what he wanted; that he would show him the tender side of his soul. But he grabbed his "thang" into his hand, standing before Clarence, slapping him across the cheek with his huge penis. Violence and passion were brothers. Clarence was persuaded. Passion overwhelmed him. He surrendered to the man, falling to his knees as if in prayer, prostrating his ass before this master-man, who soon jostled him onto the bed, mounting him, and riding him high like a cowboy on his horse. They grunted, groaned and moaned with pleasure in a free fall which was a wonderful pain. The sudden end came as a wonder. Their act of passion was quickly over before affection could begin. It dissipated into embarrassment. This sexual itch, which Clarence had had, proved to be evanescent. Human longings floated out of the window. Clarence laid defeated, as his expired lover slept beside him, holding his extinguished bolt (penis) in his hand. Silence prevailed outside of the window, and early morning tranquility ruled, as Harlem and its people slept.

Book II

Africa

11. It Sweetened the Bitterness of the Heart

The enchantment began with the music. African music was for optimists...for the lighthearted. It had a magical craft with a pulsating sound that fed one with imagination. The reveling beat created chimeras in the mind. Its gaiety seduced. A penetrating rhythm and heart-throbbing beat emitted from every corner and abode in Abidjan, as if there could be no existence without the music, as if life was about celebrating, dancing and towing off, as if the music would play until life played out and one ended in a dark hole...called the grave. The music was a style of African life. It was everywhere, omnipresent...in the airport, in the hotel, in the restaurant, on the street, on the market, in the bus, in the post office. The entire city appeared like a musical theater and in every corner, Africans moved cool, real cool, super cool, with a melodic cadence to the rhythms, pursuing their daily chores, loose and relaxed, like paradise birds in the belief in beauty. They did this with their entire hearts, their bodies and their souls. To be, because one was able to think, was nothing. Forget Descartes! He had no significance in Africa. To feel was everything. African music was also subversive... leading one astray, disarming bourgeois decorum and pretensions, braking down rigid fences in the mind. The music sweetened the bitterness of hearts...filling one with cosmic energy and beautiful insanity. Imagine Africa without its music! It would not be Africa! The Africa that Clarence encountered under the blazing sun, with its polyrhythmic grooves, liberated him, making him want to shake his butt and throw his hands into the air; to take a bath in the enthusiastic crowd. The music screamed to the heavens in joy. It spoke of the lightness of being; of light clouds moving over mortal heads...mortals preoccupied with morals and with rationality. Clarence bathed in its joy, cleaning his head of "Western bull shit", dancing his spiritual life. He arose out of ruins, swaying between seduction and delirium, not being able to distinguish between reality and dream, dreaming awake, not being able to hear enough, to see or feel enough, prickling every moment of the day with anticipation from head to toe, like iron on fire. His heartbeat quickened and his pulse raced. His passion was awakened. The hairs on his skin stood at attention. His entire concept of what was appropriate and what was inappropriate was broken into little pieces and his wall fell. It was for Clarence the end of modesty. He felt as if he had landed, but at an extreme altitude.

Africa was a spiritual shock for Clarence, like a fabled garden with a beautiful view. He was bewitched with the African colors. Their outrageous hues gave radiant answers for lyrical minds. The Africans were past being loud. They combined colors harmoniously, rebelliously with a brilliant intensity, like a game without boundaries, in impossible combinations. They floated in the wind, glided through the chaotic streets, appearing not to be of this world, wrapped in the colors of the rainbow, harmonious in movement. Clarence watched in awe this dynamic presentation, as if he was watching a Klee or Kadinsky painting at a museum in Europe or America. His heart laughed, as he walked through the market, entranced, smelling the exotic herbs, watching the Africans haggling about, grasping colors: black with pink and yellow, purple with orange and red, gold with maroon and blue, lime with yellow and silver. This intoxication of the senses forced him to depart from what he had previously considered to be...the measure of things. Clarence became a listener of the night, tossing and turning with tension, gazing out of his hotel window like a star searcher, traveling in dreams, wondering what were the Africans doing on the dark streets below. Were they secretly having fun, while he laid in the luxury of his hotel, trying to force himself to sleep? Were they eating, drinking, merrymaking, craving for pleasure and living a sweet life? Were they making love in their little huts?

The tour guides warned him not to go out on the streets alone at night. They said that it was much too dangerous. But Clarence believed that if he survived New York City, with all of its bloodthirsty bandits, then he could survive anywhere. The comments of the tour guides and members of his travel group placed him in a dilemma, somewhere between the fronts. Clarence found himself inadvertently captive to their nightmares. They conversed about the brutal conditions in Africa, about disease, Aids, filth, poverty, war and crime, the usual afflictions of people of color on this dear earth, many of whom existed in hell, and lived a wretched life. It was better to hold one's tongue in the face of such hard judgment, not to preach about injustices or give a moralizing sermon. Those from the other side of the fence, the comfortable side of abundance, didn't want to be sermonized. They preferred to paint their gloomy pictures, without claiming responsibility for some of the misery. Trying to hover over their judgmental attitudes was useless. Their dismal pictures and cruel opinions prevented Clarence from approaching Africans without prejudice, without fear, leading him to see ghosts where there were none. He was standing on quicksand, which would soon swallow him. The downtrodden didn't have a fan club. Wherever they amassed was considered a dangerous place, whether it was Harlem in New York City or Watts in Los Angeles or the Fravelas in Brazil or the slums of Columbia or South Africa. These were places supposedly full of small time gangsters and abject poverty. White people made an unspoken supposition that any neighborhood with a caboodle of blacks was an unsafe neighborhood. The truth was an invention. In reality, those who should be able to see were blind. They had certain hidden perceptions, which were wrong. The battle was around the optic, the focus, the way one saw the world. Clarence thought about what his dear friend, Antoine had told him in a moment of truth: that a black man going to Africa with a group of Caucasians was like a Jew going to Israel with a group of Germans. They would not and could not understand the sentimental homage of an African-American. He decided not to occupy himself with the guilt and shame syndrome of Caucasians, which was the historical result of telling lies about black people. His thirst to see and to feel Africa...won over his prudence, circumspection and cautiousness. He threw all of the warnings into the wind. The members of the travel group soon isolated him. They had a dangerous arrogance, a characteristic of the rulers of this earth, sitting high on their horse, high on their stool, firmly established above the clouds, judging, appearing holy, and picking out what was historically true from a mass of confused evidence. Who placed them judge of the world? Clarence had a belly full of their opinions, wanting to strike out against them, because he sometimes caught himself seeing Africa through their eyes. They had placed Africa in the shunting yard and expected blacks to wallow in the mire. Africa was a quagmire for them. It was a foreign continent in stagnant waters and they, as tourists, were on an excursion in an exotic nightmare land...on a temporary excursion into a wonderful hell.

After one week on the African continent, Clarence decided to let go of his fear, not to be uptight, to find his way out of the material world. He saw the path clearly. The lightness of existence of Africans, their unbridled gaiety and mirth could not be learned. It had to be discovered. It was like wine that had gone to the head. This was the African spirit and he was convinced that this spirit, despite centuries in the African Diaspora, had never died in him. It slumbered somewhere within his soul. He only had to rediscover it. There were so many unanswered questions... about the African collective madness, about their rituals and belief in magic, in the spirit. How could he get to the bottom of this thing? Clarence often found himself asking, what is real and what a dream is. Could it be that we exist in a soap bubble? Could it be that luck and happiness are subjective and transient? Clarence was obsessed with the African night, in which it rained light, appearing as if the stars were dancing. There was an undeclared mysticism about this place. The Africans appeared to him like ornamental fish that swam in a sea of the soul.

The tour group visited one day a tiny village outside of the city of Abidjan. The village was surrounded by a lightly tamed wildness. Clarence was uplifted upon seeing the dark Djula men, sitting in a circle ring under a Sycamore tree, toning their drums with heat, in total commitment, pulling taut the antelope skins of the drums over a dancing flame of blue and yellow. They were more than exotic decoration. This view awakened his links to a native place, to a magical continent. An orange sun sank on the horizon like a great fireball, illuminating the surrounding nature and the dark Djula men and women. Suddenly, the slit gongs clang in the distance. The Gofé horns, which were of antelope ears, whooped and hooted as if from the heavens. A crowd assembled from the surrounding bush. Little naked Djula children emerged from nowhere, clapping their hands, singing, screeching, and screaming. They revolved in a circle, turning around and around. They kicked red dust into the air, which settled upon their little black faces. Was this a dream, an illusion, a hallucination? Clarence wondered if he had been struck by lightning in an open air theater. Young virgin girls of absolute beauty with wide eyes danced in front of him, spinning about in circles with innocent smiles. A dark jewel with a shaved head and sore eyes, who wore a bright orange print dress and looked like the Blessed Virgin Mary, led the young virgins faithfully in movement. She determined the tempo for the other girls. Each girl wore a different coiffure: braids, corn rolled, string rolled, plaits. They slipped and slithered in rubber slippers, swinging gourds of calabashes that went: Click, click, click; Click, click, click; Click, click, click. Clarence's heartbeat quickened with the swinging melody. He wanted to sit down on the ground, to root, to catch his breath for a moment, when the hunting call of the Gofé horns resounded. The jungle became a large resounding room, where a sensual orgy was taking place. The Gofé horns summoned the old and wise voluptuous women. They wore elegant robes with orange turban cloth tied around their heads. Their faces were worn with wrinkles. Their smiles revealed rotten teeth. They danced like young maidens, swinging their hips smoothly, gliding single file from side to side, as if dancing was life itself. They captivated Clarence's attention. Interspersed between the young and the old women, between seduction and responsibility, were two masqueraded figures in dyed yellow and purple raffia fibers of the Baobab tree. They pranced and danced in a duel between light and darkness. The yellow fibers symbolized the day and the purple fibers represented the night. The singing and dancing continued throughout the night. The drums beat frenzy. The gongs clang constantly, resounding across the tiny village. The atmosphere was delirious, a sensual enjoyment. It was too beautiful to be true.

At the same time, an inexplicable sorrow surged within Clarence upon seeing this spectacle. He suffered bliss of feelings and distress. It was painful to realize that these Djula men and women were singing, dancing and entertaining, only for tourists and these arrogant tourists sat relaxed in cushioned chairs with their cameras in their hands. They smelled of insecticide. They caught the dancers from every angle, watching them performing a perfect art form, observing them twitching their asses, jumping in the air, doing their fancy footwork with body and mind in balance. These comfortable, over saturated tourists were treasure seekers, capturing exotic images with their cameras. Clarence felt sorry for them. They falsified and distorted the meaning. He did not know how it felt to be 'civilized', but he most certainly pitied those who suffered such a plight. The civilized kept a tight rein on irrational emotions. They had lost the joy of movement. They were strangers in their own bodies. They preferred the abstract, mind over matter. Neither rhyme nor reason could entice them to get up and join the dancers, to give free vent to their passions; for they were afraid of making a fool of themselves, afraid of letting their bodies speak. They were afraid of something that existed within their souls. In their hearts, they did not believe in the goodness of human beings. They had lost contact with their spirits. The Djulas later besieged the tourists, expecting a cadou (*a gift*). It was enough to make one sick. Clarence wanted the natives, the indigenous ones, those who were endemic to the African continent, to act naturally, not to try to win or gain by trickery. He wondered why he had hoped that Africans would be different, unfettered and nobler. But despite these things, Clarence became quickly aware that the Africans had a secret life of magic, symbolism and ecstasy, to which he desired entry. It suddenly struck him that as long as he was traveling with a group of Caucasians...moralists, liberals and apologists, the door to Africa's heart would remain closed. Cost it what it may, he was determined to open this door, to swim himself free. The main thing was to be free.

Hotel Ibis on the Plateau in Abidjan smelled like mildew. The rooms were rented to tourists, prostitutes, and their customers. During the late night hours, the prostitutes lingered in the lounge like lost property, unclaimed goods...soliciting. The night seemed to conceal their shame, swallowing their screams in anonymous rooms. Clarence turned the lights out in his dreary hotel room and eavesdropped for trifles that made a difference, for some sign of humanity...the slamming of a door, the footsteps of a bellhop in the hallway or the lustful grunting of a copulating couple in the room next door. The silence, the peaceful quietness was broken now and then by the eerie howling of a container ship with its cargo of pineapples and bananas, sailing through the balmy night for America and Europe. But that was nothing that you could grab onto, like another heartbeat in a bosom that would put an end to his longings. He gazed out of his hotel window over the city, searching the harbor for the lone ship, which sailed from shallow waters into the deep rough sea. In the kingdom of his unconsciousness, he was searching for a myth. The streets below were empty. Abidjan slept. On the dirt road behind the hotel shined a single light. It illuminated a figure in busy activity. Clarence recognized the tiny hut as the eating shack, which served heavy and solid food, the one which he had frequented during the day. It was a dirty place, with filthy plastic thrown over round tables and a floor of sawdust. A big black auntie sat like a matron behind the cash register, looking like a fat meatball with a nurtured roughness and a mysterious and knowing air. She was the owner, holding every movement in the hut in her gaze. "Tell me my brother, where do you come from?" The fat Auntie asked Clarence the first time he entered the hut. She twisted and rolled her eyes, not waiting for him to answer, but began listing nations. "Cameroon? Liberia? Ghana? Nigeria?"

"No, I'm an African American," Clarence answered in a flush of enthusiasm. The fat Auntie gawked at him in silence. "I didn't know that they had Africans in America!" She spoke loudly for anyone in the shanty to hear, laughing into her sleeve. The customers in the shanty laughed with her. The fat Auntie's comment pierced Clarence's heart. He was hurt from the brunt of the fat matron's attack...severely wounded. But he let her remark pass in silence. He just wanted to belong, to belong to anything...a club, a gang, or even a group of idiots who were like him. He wanted to be a member of a collective. In reality, he was a blackbird, a strange bird with broken wings, licking his invisible wounds, and limping to a nest home. Even a temporary home in airy heights under the full glare of the sun would have been satisfactory to him. Clarence wanted to feel at home.

The night was hot and murky. Clarence was hunted by erotic dreams. He tried to read a trashy novel, but the palpitations of his heart distracted him, making him feel like jack in the box. He got out of bed in high tension, put on his clothes. Then he opened the door, peeked into the hallway to make sure no member of the travel group would see him slipping out of the room in the wee hours of the night. They all knew he was glowing lava, "gay", a member of the butt corps and they would naturally assume he was going out to flutter and flirt about, to look for a man, to visit Sodom and Gomorra. He entered the cafeteria of the hotel. It was empty, except for an attractive African woman, a lady-mistress and a hurly-burly white man. The African woman was dressed seductively in a purple and white printed cloth, with wonderful patterns in the forms of spirals and stars. It fell from her left shoulder, revealing her beautiful dark skin. She was black as the night. She wore a matching purple gallee, which crowned her head. Was she a prostitute, Clarence wondered? She was too beautiful, too elegant, and too gracious to be a whore. She appeared to be from another celestial star.

"Bon soir!" (*Good Evening*) Clarence said upon entering the cafeteria. The African woman and the white man, her sponsor, did not respond. They sat, whispering to each other, as if balancing on a wire. She held a cup of blue water in her hand. The white man had a long roman nose, a long chin and bushy eyebrows. He smoked a cigarette, blowing smoke like air attacks in the African woman's face. Their division was cemented. Clarence contemplated if they were lovers, who had forgotten how to laugh or glow worms haggling over the price for a wild passionate night. Was she the girl of his choice? Clarence bought a cup of tea and found a table in the back of the cafeteria, observing the couple and watching the love parade that occurred throughout the night in the lobby of the hotel. The pretty African woman had a breakable blissfulness about her. The accusations and recriminations of her partner broke it. He hounded her with meanness, treating her in an undignified manner, browbeating and domineering over her. She sought protection in silence, while the man continued drinking his alcohol. It was the alcohol that untangled his fantasies and loosened his tongue. His last bastion was in male chauvinism and in macho pride. His voice became increasingly louder, slaying as many as he could within his ear shot.

"I said to get up and get me something to eat." The white man yelled like a thunder god, high and commanding, imposing force from above, as if it was his seigniorial right to demand. The African woman moved slowly in getting out of her chair. But before she could stand, he slapped her brutally across her face. Clarence was her witness for the defense, but he controlled himself, although his spirit told him to intervene, and not to stick his head in the sand. This was not his business, he thought. Everyone has a day of humiliation. He did not desire to dance with this dragon man, like a gladiator in the wee hours of the morning. Small gestures of despotism could be ignored and he knew that a code of morality existed for men, but not for women. The African woman obeyed her muddle-headed king. She was without a lobby. The reflection of her soul was oblique and sorrowful. Clarence wondered in this moment about the secret of the dove, about miscarriages of justice, about the desire to suffer…that it was expected that women bear and forbear. There was no reason to grip, he reasoned, to loose a lot of steam about nothing. He was not born a warrior. He thought about the story that the cute bellhop in the hotel, N'ba, told him about wisdom and the origin of things. Every morning, he would listen to the melodic chirping of a bird that positioned itself outside his window. He asked N'ba, the bellhop, what was the name of the bird. N'ba told him that it was called the Hornbill and he said that when the Hornbill flew into this world, chirping speech, humans were still children in their garden, innocent and free. The Hornbill bestowed upon them knowledge and wisdom. "The only problem is that this knowledge and wisdom flowed from his beak into the ass of a chimpanzee and it was the chimpanzee that gave it then to man," N'ba said. Maybe that was why men acted so stupid, Clarence thought.

The tension in the cafeteria increased. The pale man bullied and maltreated the African woman, faultfinding and nagging. He was a real devil with a sharp tongue, who thought that he had the world in his pocket. Clarence watched the man sling his food down more pig, than human. He had little sympathy for this man. He smiled at the African woman in sympathy, who suffered her pain in a long silence. She returned his smile in a sidelong glance. They flirted with each other, casting furtive glances at each other. Her smile was the smile of a prisoner. Clarence felt sorry for her and it was a deep disappointment for him to witness this scene, this power play. The white man did not deserve her. Clarence tried to act as if nothing was happening, deciding to return to his room to watch the moonlight play with the clouds, which would have been better than to watch the dance of male apes. He walked pass the table where the African woman and the white man sat. "Black bitch…!" The white man said. These heated words caused fire and flames within Clarence, activating him like a battle call, which came from the pit of his southern soul. The words brought back memories within him of injustices of the past. That was the last straw. "Now you wait one minute, mister." Clarence spoke. "You have no right to call anybody that!" Standing face to face with ruin, Clarence wanted to tell this white man that it was the end of the Iron Age, the end of colonialism, sexism, racism and the end of slavery of whatever kind. "Dear Sir!" The white man slurred, flying on waves of alcohol. "I don't want to pick a bone with you." This warning went unheeded. "Where are you from?" The white man asked Clarence, perturbed by his intrusion. "Are you a hot headed American?" He stuck his index finger in Clarence's face. Clarence did not answer the uncouth fellow, figuring that you couldn't tame bears. He spoke instead to the African woman, who was bent from destiny. "You don't have to subordinate yourself!" Clarence told the African woman. She was suddenly shaken awake by a late wonder. A black Don Quixote had come to her rescue in her great need. Clarence grabbed her by the arm and began pulling her out of the cafeteria, away from this deadly pale man.

"You don't need to take this type of abuse, Madame." Clarence told her, guiding her gently towards the door. The white man jumped up from the table, placing himself in the middle of the way. The bad guy role was his destiny. "Are you hard of hearing?" He asked Clarence. "Take your hands off my woman!" The white man yelled at Clarence in a crazy fury, helplessly drunk. "That woman belongs to me! I paid for her lock, stock and barrel," he said wantonly, defending his property in a droll. "I have a right to lead her by the nose, if I choose." He was a comical portrait of a conqueror, a patriarch, a dissolute fellow, a scamp and a good for nothing. Women were part of his luggage and the picture of women in his head was perverted. A good condition was necessary to get pass this raving mad ram. He would not give way. Clarence intensified his course. The white man assaulted him, boxing Clarence on the ear and shoving him to the side. When Clarence regained his balance, he turned and swung at the man, hitting him with a hard left, which should have been enough to send the white man to his brooding place, but the white man quickly rejoined with a hard right that felt to Clarence like iron and steel. Sudden pain shot through Clarence's head. He struggled with the force of gravity, but was able to regain his bearings. The two men clashed, wrestling around with each other in a serious debacle like gladiators in Rome, letting the Gods judge. "Stop it, stop it, Monsieurs!" The agile mother of Africa screamed.

It was a show with an effect, a family hell. Suddenly the white man pulled out a knife. With a sure gripe, he jabbed it in Clarence's direction, threatening him in his safe and sound world. Clarence felt that he had somehow been placed in the wrong scene...that his life now hung on a screw and survival was a question of luck. The situation was critical. The wage for fear was death or kitchen luck. Although there is no peace in weapons, Clarence desperately sought a way out of this conflict, searching in the heat of the moment for a means of protection. Then he suddenly became a fighting machine...a queer, armed with a beer bottle and a chair, battling like a mad dog. Clarence was courageous, but not strong, not a heavy weight boxer. He was just a New York City queer, who was ready to fight for justice and baffled victims...not an expert in the art of killing, but rather, born to be mild. He instinctively knew brutal men had to be taught that there is a stronger one. In a world of men and hens, with poses, nothing but poses of vain, self-confident types, who tested their strength and crushed their enemies, Clarence was a bee that collected nectar by lilies of the valley and primroses in melancholic fields, believing the choice in life was between mildness and annihilation. As the white man attacked, he clobbered him with the chair, and then reinforced this blow with a beer bottle to the back of the white man's head. This was the finishing blow. The ground was cut from under the man's feet. He fell to the floor in a great collapse, contorting his limbs. The drama around a woman ended. The African woman screamed loudly in the voice of the traumatized. She begged Clarence to leave the Hotel with her, grabbing his hand. She pulled Clarence out of the cafeteria, explaining that this was Africa, that the claws of justice were uncompassionate, corrupt and wicked. Fear and desperation were written upon her face. Clarence followed her through the dark streets of Abidjan, across the empty Senegalese Market. There was no traffic, only hawk moths, beggars, prostitutes and callboys, standing on every corner, prowling in the dark. Abidjan was a city like other cities. It had the same dehumanizing quality of big cities.

The African woman led Clarence with galloping seriousness to an ornamental bridge, which spanned over a murky body of water. She found a secluded place under the bridge, pointing for Clarence to sit beside her between mountains of trash. Clarence watched the spirit of her movement, as she strolled down to the water and dipped a dainty handkerchief in it. She approached him, placing the wet handkerchief over his harvested blows. In the darkness, he floated in the wonderful spirals of the African woman's dress, between beauty and trash. "My peaceful American, you have to learn how to practice brotherly love," the African woman uttered. Her voice was raw like that of dubious dames. "What type of love do you practice?" Clarence asked, searching for answers to her desire to be enslaved twice. "When you are ugly, you have to be clever," the African woman responded, accepting her burdens as an African and as a woman. She was not ugly in Clarence's eyes. He saw a creative glowing fire in her face. She had soft red lips, and her brown eyes appeared to light the unknown. She wore a scarab around her neck as talisman. "When you have greedy tongues to feed, you take what is offered," the African woman said, singing sorrow songs. "You are lucky. You are an American; you have a life according to your own wish and taste."

Clarence decided not to dig deep enough to find the truth, not wanting to activate a waterfall of misery. It would surface with the passing of time. "What is the name of that body of water there? He asked, pointing towards the murky water. "It is the Lagoon of Abidjan. On the other side of the Lagoon is Treichville, where I work and live." Clarence and the African woman sat for hours like two cats among themselves, telling stories in a charming rumbling. The African woman said that her name was Hortense. She had a sharp and witty tongue. She told Clarence that the white man at the hotel was Lebanese. She said that they were the gangsters in Africa, the professional thieves, greedy for success, seeking hard cash and ready money. She said that they misunderstood everything in Africa, understanding only the difference between the gross and the net; that they rated everything at its true value, which was less than its true worth; that they knew how to milk the cow and were traders in blood, engaged in a glimmering business with cheap girls and drugs. Hortense said that she wanted to live at all cost. "In Africa, life is not a given," she declared. "This is the other side of Eden. Here you have to struggle to shit." She explained the adversities of African life, and then she observed Clarence in a long silence, asking him his name, but not waiting for him to answer her question. "I shall call you Souleyman!" She pronounced. "You look like a Djula." Hortense told Clarence she sold tomatoes under the wide skies on the market in Treichville during the day. She invited him to visit her at the market place. As dawn was about to break over their heads, Clarence accompanied her across the bridge. He learned that Hortense once had high hopes and that she once could dream and fly, but had given up her belief in Romeo and Juliet...in infatuation and love. She was now imprisoned in her milieu. They departed, promising to see each other again. Clarence watched, as she glided gently through the night and disappeared behind ruins.

It was early in the morning. The hotel was empty, except for a pretty dark seductress of the night, who sat alone in the hotel's lobby. She wore a pink lotus in her jet-black hair. A scratched record of Maurice Ravel's Bolero played over and over again in the background. No one seemed to care about its repetitiveness. Clarence slipped quietly to his room, lying in bed, trying to separate reality from fantasy, thinking about those African ladies of the night, selling love in Abidjan. They were village refugees, who had become hypnotized by the illusions of western ways. They sat in Hotel Ibis on the plateau, sipping Mamba beer, listening to a skipping record of Bolero, pretending to be something that they were not. They searched for anachronistic colonialists, who treasured aristocratic English life style and French cuisine, who gave empty promises that they would one-day take them away from Africa, from Eburnea, land of the forests, to a cold place called Europe or to a battlefield called America. For empty promises, they made love during the early morning hours in tiny rooms with a mildew smell, between African printed sheets. Clarence closed his eyes and felled asleep.

12. We all live under one sky

The next morning, Clarence went to the vegetable market in Treichville. In the center of the huge market were red tomatoes, surrounded by black motherly faces. There were tomatoes everywhere, tons of red tomatoes, round tomatoes in crates, squished tomatoes piled on top of each other, and bruised tomatoes lying beside each other. The tomatoes were interspersed with human forms in colorful cloth and complicated patterns, luxurious forms. African mothers squatted between the tomatoes, breast feeding their babies. They yelled in a singsong cacophony of tribal females, selling their wares. They counted their coins and dollar bills, talking about nothing in particular, gossiping, chatting and screaming every now and then: "E-nee-soh-goh-mah! E-koh-kay-nay-wah! Come here brother and see what I have!" The market women in their glaring mixture of colors mesmerized Clarence. They were flashy and shrill. But all of the market women looked the same to him. They gnarled, but were amiable. They were all members of a magic hood that was recognized by their blemishes. Clarence spotted Hortense, sitting in the middle, as if separating order from chaos. She breast-fed a baby. "Bonjour, Hortense" (*Good Morning*). He greeted Hortense friendly and perched himself on an empty tomato crate. Hortense introduced her sister, Amiraka. She said that they were not sisters in blood, but sisters in spirit. They both sat beside each other like African antelopes, playing a new game of color, dressed in red with silver earrings, and amber necklaces, breast-feeding their babies on the ground. Amiraka was a mirror image of Hortense. Amiraka and Hortense were dressed up like stars, sitting under an invisible baldachin, glowing away. Hortense was the talking machine. Amiraka was shy with a melancholic beauty. She had the sad look of unshed tears. "Souleyman, mon ami (*my friend*)...! This is your destiny day. You have two women, one to beat millet and the other to care for your chickens, goats and hens," Hortense said with a flippant tongue, blowing her horn for all to hear on the market, teasing Clarence about his quiet tactfulness. Clarence watched the commotion of the market as the morning light cleared. Suddenly the sun arose from behind a fog swath, throwing its rays over the market women, sitting between the red tomatoes. A volcano of colors occurred. "Where have you left your brood to hunger?" Hortense asked Clarence. "I have no children." Clarence answered with innocence on his face. "Et la femme (*and a woman?*)...? Do you have a woman?" Hortense inquired. "No." Clarence counted the seconds until the next question came. "Souleyman, mon ami...! Do you like women?" Hortense asked, playing respectless with Clarence's emotions. Dexterity was needed. The market women listened, waiting anxiously for his answer. Clarence responded truthfully and the truth was that which occurred to him at the moment. "I like women, but I love men more," he said. "Well, you will not have to wait long for love, my brother," Hortense declared. "I will introduce you to my brother and with a little bit of labor, your love shall bloom." Hortense smiled, being compassionate and generous. Clarence had not expected this response. The market women chuckled, grinned, shaking their heads in acceptance and agreement. It was the first time in his life that he felt that he did not have to be ashamed for what he was. "We all live under one sky!" Hortense rejoined. This was a wise statement, which Clarence would have expected of an older woman.

Hortense told him that she and her brother came from the north of the Ivory Coast, near the town of Ouangolodougou. Clarence couldn't get Ouangolodougou off his tongue, saying Ouangolodoudou and trying to keep from laughing each time, because it sounded like a place where one would go to do "dou-dou" (*Slang in the American South for to shit*). It was an unconscious slip of the tongue. "Mon frère habite dans Île du Bouley" (*My brother lives on the island of Bouley*), Hortense informed Clarence. She told him that he could take a ferry there from the Lagoon and spend a lazy day on the beach. Clarence recognized that these were strong mothers, who shouldered their burdens gracefully. They did not sit around licking their wounds, but they swallowed their bitter sugar and got on with life, where nothing was as it appeared. They pulled together on a rope, selling tomatoes during the day and sweet passion in the evenings. They knew their worth. "Souleyman, mon ami...! Tonight, we will celebrate a funeral for one of our sisters. She has found peace." Hortense smiled broadly, while mentioning the death of one of her sisters in spirit. "I am sad to hear that," Clarence said. "Don't be sad. Be in a good mood," Hortense replied, inviting Clarence to come to the funeral and suggesting that he might meet her brother there that evening. Clarence thanked her for the invitation and departed. He was beginning to like the Ivorians. They were very natural in their mannerisms, quick to smile.

Clarence walked around the market the rest of the day, collecting impressions, on a trip in a world of sights, sounds and smells that were difficult to adjust to...a mercurial circus, and a royal chaos. Thongs of people pushed and pulled, touched and took unashamed liberties with him. The market traders screamed in an explosive cacophony of voices directed towards him. "My friend...! My brother, come into my stand! My Black American, I have what you are looking for!" They tried to shake Clarence's hand, pulling him into their little shanties, talking for hours, telling fables with hooks and rings. Most of them had the smile of a sphinx. It was a test of strength. One had to have good nerves. The constant assault and the attention, which Clarence received from the traders, left him exhausted. The sun burned his skin. He sought a short refuge under a Mango tree, where a brass caster with his son squatted on the earth, working quietly together. The bare-footed brass caster fired metals, laboring in a makeshift tin-roofed shade, making pots and pans, which were the fruit of his hard toil. Clarence watched him pounding sand, bending over a dirt mold with kaolin on his dark face. He smoothed each grain carefully, drawing water into his mouth, spraying it out like rain droplets. He gathered coal from the earth to fire his hearth. He twisted and turned a bicycle wheel with his foot, blowing air on the hot coals. The metal became molten and powerful spirits were released. Clarence watched him with fascination....using fire, water, earth and air to fashion tools of hand, in a symbiosis of the elements. This was a timeless procedure in an endless world. Nature determined the rules. The African brass caster worked under the tin shade, dripping with perspiration. Clarence wondered about the mysteries of the universe, the mysteries of the elements and he thought how human beings are like the things that they create. If they create weapons of mass destruction, it is because they have mass destruction in their souls.

As night fell, Hortense's brother came unexpectedly to the hotel to pick Clarence up. Clarence did not anticipate this, nor had he expected him to be so handsome. Hortense's brother was a good-looking dark man, whose skin was smooth like silk, which shined and glowed, as if the sun was located directly under it. His face was expressive. When Clarence looked into the fine-looking man's face, he had the feeling of bathing his soul in the sun. He said that his name was Serafin. His nose was wide like that of a horse with lips which were thick and sensuous. There were beads of sweat on his forehead, as if he had been working hard. His deep avocado eyes were a treat to look into...like black rubies, filled with hurt and passion. The pupils were so black that they glittered. He had a bass-baritone voice, uttering his sentences slowly, speaking a little English and French. Since Clarence spoke a little French and English, they understood each other well. The night was warm. Serafin said the funeral of the deceased market woman would start at midnight and that Hortense asked him to accompany Clarence to it. They walked down a long dirt road, which was full of busy African men and women. Every building on the road was rundown, with opened windows and opened doors. High-life music blasted out of the shacks. They entered one of the shacks. Serafin said a Ghanaian man owned the bar with his mother. It was a small hut with only two tables, a long self-made bar and a crackling radio. Serafin ordered Sorba beer. He talked a long time to the bartender, who was a fat black man. The bartender appeared to Clarence to be friendly. When Serafin told him that his "little brother" was American, the bartender became more interested in Clarence, throwing glances in his direction, grinning like an ape.

"I think he wants to go to America with you, little brother." Serafin said, smiling. Clarence did not know why Serafin called him little brother, but it did not annoy him, because Serafin was twice his size. He was a big muscular man and Clarence understood he meant it as an endearment term. "I like to go to America one day!" The bartender yelled from behind the bar. "It is my dream." The bartender's mother sat behind the cash register like a shrewd she-devil with threaded and plaited hair. The tiny plaits stood on her head. She wore orange and yellow African printed cloth. The loud colors accentuated her big bulging eyes and thick lips. Serafin drank first a beer with the proprietor of the bar. He then returned to the table where Clarence sat and drank a beer with him, silently listening to the music from Ghana, Cameroon and Zaire. Every guest that came into the bar would shake Clarence's hand, then go around the bar shaking everybody's hand. Serafin did not have much to say. He gazed at Clarence, smiling once and awhile, amused at Clarence's reaction to the crowd in the bar. He was apparently reading Clarence's mind.

They departed the bar later in the evening, going to a small dirty Marquis to eat. Clarence ordered chicken, but the Auntie said she only had fish. They both ate fish. When the Auntie came out with the fish, it still had its head attached. It was topped with onions and tomatoes. They ate Achakay, a meal-like substance, with the fish, making it into balls, dipping it into the sauce. Loosening up a little, Clarence spoke with the Auntie, a young girl of about 19 or 20, and he spoke to a fellow guest, whom he knew from the hotel. He was also a big black jovial man, who collected the tickets at the swimming pool of the hotel. After they finished their meal, Serafin took Clarence to an old man's house on a nameless dirt road. The old man was a belafon player. He relaxed in his front garden with a small group of men. They worked on their belafons, while teasing each other. Sometimes they would stop joking and played a refrain. The music was soothing, smooth, with an earthy, natural sound. The musicians sat in the dark night, playing heart riveting music like the original Jazz, hypnotizing everyone with the melodic sound.

Clarence and Serafin later left the house of the belafon players, going back to the Ghanaian bar for another beer. Serafin did not speak much. He preferred to observe Clarence. Clarence asked him why he was staring at him. "You look like a Fulani," Serafin said. The Ghanaian bartender agreed. Clarence was now tired of hearing what he looked like. The Africans played a game of guessing the potential tribe of Black Americans. They forgot they were looking at a mixture of cultures, a mixture of Europe, America and Africa. In reality, he had more European blood than African blood. But this did not really matter. He felt African in his soul. They drunk another beer and returned later to the belafon players. Around midnight, the belafon players struck the tone. The moon was full and an old king appeared to sit within the heavens. He had feathers for a head. It was around midnight when the women of Treichville, children of the moon as they called themselves, rushed from their bordellos into the streets. They approached in a group, each one more different than the other, emphasizing their beauty with colors and ornaments, singing synchronized in song. They chanted, while being led down the red clay road near the harbor by a whistle blowing fat matriarch, who twirled a baton in her hand. The women were dressed in colorful African prints, dancing complicated foot patterns in the dust on the dark dirt road, giving themselves totally to the music and the beating of the bongos, forgetting their problems. They danced as if in trance, soaring like butterflies. Illegitimate babies were tied to their backs. The babies slept. They did not cry or whine. Clarence thought, oh what beautiful children they must raise! The belafon players played all night, serenading the mourning women. These were poor village girls, trying to make a living in the big city, in Abidjan. They had fled their tribal villages for the city, laden with bags of unfulfilled dreams. Now they danced frantically to honor one of their own. They deliriously tried to forget their burdens and Clarence realized this time they were not dancing for the tourists, but for themselves. In the early morning hours after the dust had settled, the women of Treichville returned to their bordellos. They drifted silently away with the breeze. The belafon players squatted under a Sycamore tree, playing softly melodies for themselves. They were not tired. Clarence reclined against the trunk of the tree with Serafin dozing to his side. As he gazed into the night sky, there, he saw between the stars, the women of Treichville, the prostitutes, suddenly metamorphosed into colorful butterflies, floating intermingled through the air, soaring over the Gulf of Guinea.

13. Making wild jumps did not mean to arrive

The seat of passion is the heart. When the heart rules, the days burn in flames and the nights are restless, ablaze with longing...jumping from hot to cool, from cool to flaming. Serafin's seductive allures captivated Clarence, leaving him, longing, enamored with love ballads in his head. He became a slave of his heart, dreaming about the geometry of Serafin's body, falling from the ground in the highest of heights. He was no longer master of his own idle life. From the night of the funeral, Clarence knew that life without love would be like life without light. He visited Hortense on the market the next day, inquiring nonchalantly about Serafin, trying to camouflage his curiosity. "Souleyman, my brother is a wandering bird," Hortense jokingly quipped. "He follows the rules of chaos. He has probably disappeared to his atelier in the bush, where a mountain swallowed him." Hortense smiled at Clarence, aware of his emotions. "Shoot your arrow into luck," she advised him, cautioning him that to run after Serafin would be like running after phantoms.

Later that day, Hortense introduced Clarence to another man, who looked like a wild ram. He said that his name was Seydou. Seydou wore tight polyester pants with no underwear, which revealed distinctly his manhood. He constantly smiled at Clarence and appeared to have maggots in his head. Seydou said he came from the steppe in Mali and called himself the hunter, claiming that he liked to hunt leopards, lions and hippopotamus. In reality, he was a shady type, a little bit dishonest...a gigolo. He was an African charmer for female tourists, who worked occasionally as a guide for the tourists. Seydou wore as a uniform a Danga hat with cowry shells on it and small round mirrors that hung from the hat and caught the light. The tiny mirrors flashed with his movements. He was a tall sinewy man with hard muscles, who adorned himself with fetishes and talismans of all kinds. Sweet smelling roots perfumed his body. Seydou invited

Clarence to a damp, dark and musty marquis that night, where they dined in the cool breeze of the African night, eating A-chatay and Fou-Fou. Seydou had not discovered communication. They drank French wine and rum in silence. In moments of euphoria, Clarence caught Seydou's innocence. He appeared to carry the dark night upon his face and the weight of a continent upon his shoulders. His eyes were like stars, gleaming and dreaming of far away places. He grinned on cue. Clarence and Seydou played poker games with each other and other trivial games, as well as, the game of to want and to be. Under the influence of the alcohol, Clarence decided he wanted this man and he did not wait long beating around the bush, talking about the sexuality of elephants, but yearning to be caressed. He invited Seydou back to his hotel room...sure his success was programmed.

Seydou sprawled out across the bed, bestowing his splendid manhood. His eyes were closed. He was both devilish and lyrical, making Clarence nervous and taut with desire. He talked about America and Europe, the promised lands. These were impossible places to reach for him, but imaginable and he was convinced that he would one day go there. "Why do you want to go to America? Clarence asked Seydou, wondering about his motivations. "You would not be happy there. You would probably end up washing dishes and selling cheap wares on 14th Street in New York City." Clarence pondered when Africans would wake up to their folly. "Only when you have crossed the river, can you say the crocodile has a lump on his snout," Seydou responded, surveying Clarence sitting in the chair. "Gold loses its glance for those who have much of it."

The moment had arrived for Clarence to make his move, to take the offensive. He joined Seydou on the bed, lying beside him, caressing his chest without asking for permission. "Do you like girls?" Clarence inquired, seeking the truth. "No, I don't like girls," Seydou answered. This was sobering for Clarence to know. He placed everything on the last card, to unveil and not to conceal. "Are you gay?" Clarence asked Seydou without ornamentation. "What is this thing called "gay"? Seydou questioned. Clarence had never thought about it before, but it was a lifestyle. How do you explain a lifestyle? How do you explain a double existence or male/male sexual encounters? He decided to reduce it down to the lowest common dominator. "It's when men sleep with men," Clarence said. Seydou pricked up his ears. "He who asks questions, cannot avoid the answers," Seydou retorted. "But you said that you didn't like girls!" Clarence declared, wrestling for the right thing to say. "It is the truth, Souleyman, I don't like girls, but I expect to marry and to have children one day. To die without children is as if one has not lived, is to die without leaving ones footprints." Clarence laid beside Seydou caressing him and looking into his eyes. "Why do you allow me to caress you?"

"Souleyman, because you are my friend, my brother and I love my brother." Clarence realized that this what Seydou had just said was genuine. He had often beheld the Ivoirian men on the streets being tender towards each other. He had observed them engaged in an intense public intimacy, which had nothing to do about sex. They held hands. They even kissed and caressed each other. They walked down the streets with their arms around each other's waist. They flirted and gazed deep into other men's eyes. They did all of this in the name of friendship, brotherly love. Friendship between men was held in the highest of esteem. Nature offered all forms. Clarence thought that if this was what friendship was supposed to be like, than he didn't need a lover. All he needed was a friend. He accompanied Seydou to the door, as Seydou got up to leave. His hopes had been dashed and he could not conceal his disappointment that Seydou had decided to leave. Seydou grabbed him around the waist, bewildered by his disappointment.

He kissed Clarence embarrassingly on the cheeks. "The greatest tragedy for an African is loneliness," Seydou uttered. He then placed Clarence's Walkman, which laid on the dresser next to the door, on his head and walked out the door into the hallway. "I like my Walkman," Clarence announced, trying to be diplomatic, hoping that Seydou would give him back the Walkman. "Do you like your Walkman more than you like me?" Seydou asked. Clarence was in a dilemma, not wanting to insult Seydou, but also wanting his Walkman back. "No," he replied, flustered. Seydou grinned and left. Clarence watched him saunter down the hallway, popping his finger, shaking to the rhythm. He remembered in this moment an old African proverb that he once read, which declared, '*you are beautiful, because of your possessions.*'

The days passed each other uneventfully. Although they were filled with activities and excursions, Clarence could not appreciate it. He craved for Serafin, being full of longings for a dark knight, becoming a hunter of confounded passion, and like most birds of prey, he was blind to the suffering of his quarry. N'ba was his next quest of game. N'ba was the bellhop in the hotel. He fluttered from one tree to the next, unaware that he was surrounded by vampires. N'ba was interested only in the world on the other side. As bellhop, he was kept busy satisfying the wishes of the young white sugar dollies in the hotel. He was a hot wire, a continual drip. N'ba had a sexual nature that many white women found appealing. He had large feet and elephant ears. His teeth shined like white gold behind dark skin. His skin was so dark that it looked to be blue. All the other employees in the hotel called him the blue man. N'ba was a pleasant person with a heavenly slowness. He spent his laborious day humming songs. "Have you passed the night in peace?" N'ba would ask Clarence each morning. He had a trace of almandine in his eyes. Clarence replied each morning in the affirmative, not being able to tell N'ba the truth; that since he had met Serafin, his yearning grew; that he was obsessed with the flower of love.

"N'ba, I need to wash my clothes," Clarence announced, with gallons of ideas on how to catch a man. He spanned silk webs in a devious plan to catch N'ba. "Put them in front of your door and I will pick them up," N'ba said, with a nebulous smile, which provoked a firebrand in Clarence. "May I come with you?" Clarence inquired, persisting in wooing N'ba...full of great expectations. "You would not like this place. There are only wretched fellows with empty stomachs, standing half naked in a polluted creek," N'ba responded, coming out with the truth, as if it was a joke. Naked fellows in a creek created pictures of fantasy in Clarence's mind. He thought that it sounded interesting and he, like all queers, would have climbed through a hole in a fence for promises of a rich harvest of men. "That is just what I need to help me wake up!" Clarence said, yawning.

Clarence took a bus with N'ba to the outside of Abidjan. N'ba told him that the clothes were washed in a creek, which was called Banco. N'ba called the naked men in the creek, "Les Fanicos du Banco" (*The fanatical ones of the Banco*). He gave his load of clothes to another African man. He then left, promising to pick Clarence up in the late afternoon. Clarence found a secluded space on a grassy hill, overlooking the black water of the Banco. The creek itself was located between holy hills, birds, trees and palms. In the middle of the dirty creek were the fanatical ones. They were real human beings, of flesh and blood. They appeared to have a love for dirty water. As far as the eye could see were hundreds of naked and half-naked black men, submerged in the dirty water, like a plague of the grasshoppers. They washed their hands wound in the filthy creek, as if their heart blood depended upon it. They were heroes of dirty clothes, sons of the sun. They washed frantically the filthy clothes of the African elite, as if suspended in animation. Neglected, wrinkled old men and raw, virile, young African men slung water in the air. Water pellets flew into their eyes, nose and mouth. The men scrubbed and brushed, pounded and beat the clothes against stones. The soapsuds flung through the air. The plashing of the water echoed between the hills and droplets of water exploded in the air in a silver haze, creating a silver-plated mist over everything. Clarence observed this spectacle... the rainbow above the bowed heads, and the men toiling in sweat for pennies. He watched them as they placed their clothes out to dry in the afternoon, spreading them on the surrounding hills. They then laid their wet, exhausted bodies down to rest under coconut trees, praying silently to themselves.

When the sun began to decline behind the hills, the fanatical boys of the Banco creek gathered their clothes together into heavy loads, treading without a sound to Villas, hotels and mansions, laden with their loads. Clarence watched them disappear behind the hills and resolved, in this moment, that he would never again battle over a crease in his pants or the starch of a shirt. He felt ashamed in his white shirt and white pants, for the frivolity in his head. His attitude in the past was that the best was exactly good enough for him. Clarence recognized in the flash of a second that he was lucky to have been born an American. It was both a blessing and a curse. Upon seeing the poverty in Africa, he grasped the poles in life and understood that he possessed privileges. When N'ba came to pick him up, he returned to the hotel dispirited. "Poverty is slavery," N'ba said, as Clarence recounted to him his shock in the sight of such poverty.

N'ba invited Clarence to his house for diner that evening, after Clarence persisted in inviting himself. He told N'ba that he would like to stay several days at his place. He packed quickly a few clothes, explaining that he wanted to see how normal Africans live, secretly hoping that he and N'ba would sleep in the same bed. N'ba was generous in his poverty, paying for the taxi and for their diner. He lived in a tiny room in a miserable mud house on an unpaved dirt road. His room was not larger than Clarence bathroom in New York City. Pictures of his father, grandfather and great grandfather hung on the wall. N'ba bought fish in a marquioo. They ate it, sitting on the edge of the bed. Clarence asked N'ba how much did he make at the hotel. N'ba said that he earned $100 dollars a month. He had to work the entire day for this sum. Although N'ba had little to offer, he was kind, free hearted. Clarence asked him why he was so generous. "To be without a friend, is to be poor," N'ba replied, shocked at Clarence's question. That night in the shadows of N'ba's room, Clarence laid beside N'ba, becoming weak with longing, letting his hand wander. The shadows in the room were his best protection. N'ba patted Clarence hand gently. He then placed it delicately to the side. Clarence knew when he had been rejected and did not insist. He turned on his side, trying to fall asleep.

During the early morning hours, Clarence needed to relieve himself. He got up out of the bed, searching for the bathroom. N'ba told him that it was outside in front of the house. The bathroom was an open shade with a hole in the ground. Human waste material was scattered around the hole. It was an appalling sight. Clarence pondered how he would do his private business, without getting his feet dirty, without having the feeling that he was shitting on a stage for the entire world to see. This experience convinced him to return to the hotel the next day. He returned to N'ba's room, lying quietly for a long time. He knew that N'ba was not sleeping. "I'm going back to the hotel tomorrow, N'ba," Clarence said. N'ba did not respond. "I am sick, Souleyman," N'ba later said, speaking from his heart. "A curse has been placed over my head."

Sirens sounded in Clarence ears. He saw scenes of a dismal future. He did not ask N'ba any questions, hoping that he would not be told of possible health risks. He did not know why N'ba told him that he was sick. He thought about his grandmother, who would often claim the Lord moves in mysterious ways and that he is continually giving signs. He thanked God in this moment for keeping him from making a deadly blunder. There was a close proximity between sex, poverty and death. For Clarence, it was a lucky end of a catastrophic round. He returned to his hotel the next morning, forgetting N'ba. But he felt only sorry for Ellen, the young American girl in the travel group, since he was aware that Ellen was wooing N'ba in a hard pursuit.

The following days the fever curve fell within Clarence. Death was a stupid idea, he thought. Contemplating it made even tubular stags depressed, aware of their momentary nature. To run, making wild jumps did not mean to arrive. Clarence's obsession with collecting live African art on the continent of living fossils was neurotic. The continual burning inside had little to do with sex. He was yearning to possess the stars in a game of fantasy. The streets of Abidjan during the day were full of commotion, full of chatter. A blue haze covered the murky Lagoon. Clarence walked the streets of the city, searching, collecting images of little worlds and abruptly stumbling upon a weaver in a back ally, squatting under a tin shack, between grass and herbs. The weaver stated that his name was Silvewanna Yao. "I am a man of God," Silvewanna Yao told Clarence, without hesitation. "Are you religious?" Clarence queried. "I am Catholic and God gave me to be loved," Silvewanna responded, saying it with such a mystic faithfulness, as if it was the natural order of things, that Clarence was stunned. His eyes mirrored his soul. "But then, you cannot be an African man." Clarence challenged him in his belief, jokingly accusing him of surrendering his soul to missionaries with crucifixes. He told him that as a Catholic, he, Silvewanna, was not practicing the traditional African religion of myths, ritual and dance. "Bien sûr, monsieur" (*To be sure, mister*), Silvewanna retorted. "I am very African."

Before Clarence was aware of it, Silvewanna's natural countenance had awakened cravings in him. It was this natural glow, the disarming smile and the innocent way Africans encountered one that activated his desire. Silvewanna was beyond being sexy. He spoke with his eyes, with his body and shoulders. Bells were attached to his clothes. He wore a wicker cap on his large fire head. He was in Clarence's eyes a mythical hero, with the jaws of a crocodile and the eyes of a buffalo. Colored beads of glass and porcupine quills hung around his neck. Clarence and Silvewanna Yao talked and talked into the night. Silvewanna Yao spoke proudly about his past life in Toulon, in the French Army, where he served the French cause, and fought for the French Republic. He swore on the past. The present he thrust aside. Absence made his heart forget. Clarence noticed his manly splendor, but he also beheld the reality of Silvewanna's existence. Silvewanna was an unlucky fellow, who squatted under his tin shack, trying to make ends meet, weaving Yasoa and Kondro cloth with whimsical designs. Clarence asked him to explain what the designs symbolized.

"The turtle backs designs are the 'fingers of a young boy' and the mirrors are the 'eyes of a young girl'. The leaves signify 'arguments' and the geometric figures are 'please help me' and 'it rained stones' symbols." Clarence thought about these metaphors of life, which were sewn on a piece of cloth. Silvewanna had obviously discovered the joy of working with his hands. Clarence saw this joy in his eyes. It was a joy that liberated one from the carousel of burdens. Silvewanna Yao was master of his trade and that was enough for him. "Would you consider yourself to be an artist or a worker?" Clarence asked. "I'm just a simple weaver," Silvewanna Yao replied. "I weave during the dry season and work in the fields during the rains." He searched the night sky for a moment, and then he muttered softly. "I'm a slave of life."

"Talent doesn't have to waste away," Clarence remarked, speaking as if he had a bag of wonders, as if he was the savior of destroyed dreams. "When dreams explode, hope goes to the dogs." When Clarence started talking about dreams, Silvewanna revealed to Clarence his secret dream. He wanted to open up a Hamburger restaurant in the city of Man in the West of the Ivory Coast. He said that he had been working hard for it and that he had already saved a little money. He told Clarence that he wanted to go to America one day to buy the equipment that he needed for his restaurant, the typical things that one finds in a restaurant. Clarence listened intently to this farce around the future. With time, Silvewanna asked him if he would send him a price list of the equipment, when he returned to America. "The hand of God will bless you. He will give you a rug full of flowers and the wings of a mythical bird," Silvewanna Yao pronounced. "But I don't know how much these machines cost or even what they look like," Clarence protested. Silvewanna persisted with kind entreaties. His dark eyes shined. Clarence began to believe that Silvewanna was flirting with him. He started a strong wave of attack.

"If I do this for you, what will you do for me? He asked Silvewanna, playing water games with this fish. "What do you want from me, money?" Silvewanna inquired softly. "No, I don't want money." Clarence said, staying on the ball. "I want you." He watched as Silvewanna's eye slits narrowed. He could see him thinking. Silvewanna questioned himself 'if it could be that this man is a colonist?' He thought that colonists wore bow ties and safari hats and had white skin. "What shall you do with me?" Silvewanna asked, hoping Clarence was not a cannibal. "That is my secret," Clarence responded. Clarence's fantasies knew no boundaries. Yet he could not believe that Silvewanna was so naïve as to not know what he wanted to do with him. "Silvewanna, do you know what a faggot is...a gay person...a homosexual...a queer...a pervert? Clarence asked Silvewanna bluntly. "No," Silvewanna answered. "Well, I am a gay person, Silvewanna," Clarence announced, as if it was a battle song. Silvewanna wanted to know what did gay mean. Clarence told him that if he came with him to his hotel, he would show him what it meant. Silvewanna asked for some time to think about it. Clarence told him that when he had thought about it, he could find him at the hotel. He then departed, as if a flood had brought him in and the ebb took him out.

Silvewanna thought about Clarence's proposition on his way home. The next day he came to the hotel seeking Clarence. But Clarence was not there, having gone to Grand Bassam, a little village outside of Abidjan. When Clarence returned to the hotel that evening, the concierge told him that he had had a visitor, who left an urgent note. He handed him an opened and soiled piece of paper. Clarence read it, turning purple in the middle of the coconut. He tore the note up and threw it into the trash can, trying to maintain his countenance. The note read: *"Monsieur, Je voudrais essayer cette chose, appellait gai." (Mister, I would like to try this thing called gay.)*

14. No matter how long the night...

Ellen was doused in orange by the rays of the sun, which gave her a gentle radiance...a dauntless face. Clarence observed her, inhaling and exhaling, unaware that she was sitting in a catapult. There was more in a person's mind than was unveiled on their faces. Ellen sat across from him with an animated smile and a flaming inferno within her heart. She talked about discovering the universe from trees; that they were life giving. And yet her universe was about to fall asunder. They rested under a massive fig tree in the children's cemetery of Abidjan. Although it was very quiet in the cemetery, phantoms appeared to slumber in the air. Hushed echoes of careless laughter and clapping hands resounded in the stillness. If one listened intently, one could detect in the gentle breeze the spirits of the dead, intermingled with the afternoon light. Crooning black hens and bush pigs meandered between acacia shrubs. Snakes, scorpions and goats populated the deserted cemetery. The goats chewed the leaves of the acacia bushes. The small cemetery was littered with discarded batteries, empty tin cans, broken rocks, and pieces of soiled toilette paper. The tiny graves were bedecked with three-forked branches, in the middle of which bowls of holy water rested. Each grave was ornamented with a broken ceramic pot. "The pots were once used to wash cold little bodies," Ellen explained in a soft voice. "They are turned upside down and holes are broken on their side." She picked up a ceramic pot to show Clarence the holes. "The holes symbolize that they shall never find another use. They speak of broken dreams, shortened lives, and saddened mothers," Ellen said with a faraway look on her face.

The notion of mourning mothers appeared to break her heart. She was herself a woman. She understood what it meant to lose a child. Clarence contemplated if he should tell Ellen that she had copulated with a poisonous toad, a flatterer, who had planted an inexorable time bomb under her crust. He hesitated, rationalizing that it was not his place to write someone else's obituary. It was easier to cover one's eyes, to pretend that life would last for an eternity. It was a bizarre situation in this reservation of the living and the living dead. Ellen rested on a stone, her long hair blowing in the soft breeze. She wore ivory earrings, a bracelet of snails, frogs, birds and cow heads. Her silhouette appeared magical against the sun. The sky over her head drowned her in a measureless space. Clarence sought to escape from the silence of the cemetery, suggesting that they should return to the hotel. They strolled through the city, chatting about insignificant things. Ellen was a jovial person, wise from travel. She was a globetrotter. Although she told everyone that she was married, she traveled throughout the world alone. She was a restless wanderer, roaming the world for adventures, for backgrounds and portraits. She was a compassionate woman, not slanderous, nor defamatory. She was the only person in the travel group that Clarence gravitated towards. He believed that they had kindred souls. When they conversed with each other, they both allowed their hearts to speak and their emotions to decide. They huddled together oftentimes in the small opened front marquise near the Lagoon, eating puny chicken wings and drinking Mamba beer. Ellen had many friends in Africa. She had numerous spectacular stories to tell. She was a talebearer. She told Clarence that she had learned Africa's dry heart in the desert of Niger and discovered the significance of life in the creeks of Nigeria. She claimed that she encountered God one day in a hot air balloon over the mountains of Ethiopia. Her stories were novel and genuine. Clarence enjoyed listening to them.

Besides being a curator for the Louvre in Paris, Ellen said that she was a hobby photographer. She gave Clarence tips on how to take good pictures of natives. "The African children are the easiest to photograph, like butterflies," she remarked one day to Clarence. "They are willing, always photogenic. They do not have to learn how to laugh. The elderly Africans, with just a touch of wisdom of age, are the most interesting, but the most difficult to photograph," Ellen claimed. "They want every time a cadou (*a gift*)."Ellen explained it was more useful to use a cheap Polaroid camera in photographing African adults; to give them the inferior picture as a gift and to ask afterwards if one could take another picture. The second picture was then taken with a more valuable camera. Ellen said she sold her pictures to magazines and periodicals in Europe and America, hunters of exotic images. "One can make a living doing this," she asserted. "I don't know, Ellen, I think the view through lenses is something like the view through windows and doors. It preserves an artificial distance." Clarence told Ellen it was very similar to the attitudes of European tourists in Thailand or American tourists in the Caribbean, yearning for summer and sun, playing on the beach, eating coconuts and bananas, while the indigenous population laboriously struggled for their existence in their straw huts. "They are poor and poor people take what they are offered," Ellen said. "Beggars can't be choosy."

Clarence's opinion of Ellen gradually changed, when she told him he should always have gifts for the natives, who do little favors for him. Clarence didn't like the word "natives" nor was he convinced he had to pay each time for services rendered. That was such a materialistic way of looking at life. A simple thank you should have been sufficient. The members of the travel group all had an extra suitcase of gifts for dispensation, which were cheap items they had bought at Woolworth or Wal-Mart. There was joy in the eyes of the Africans when they received these gifts. They were so thankful; unaware their gratitude transcended the value of these shabby items. But this was how the world calculated...buy cheap and sell dear. It was repugnant...a grotesque practice.

The entire tour group was invited one day to the compound of a friend of Ellen. He lived in a small village outside of Abidjan. He was an architect who built castles in the sand, longing for lifestyle and luxury. Ellen was very proud of him. He was a showcase African with a square mouth, a long protruding nose and a domed forehead. Their gestures indicated that he and Ellen had shared beds, had danced the dance of a couple. He embraced and kissed her repeatedly. The architect claimed he had 34 children and eight wives, symbols of his wealth, one for the different levels of his needs. He bragged about being the giver and protector of yams. He discoursed eloquently about the African Spirit. Clarence ascertained that he himself had none. The architect had dotted palms in his hand. He lived with his family in an abandoned concrete house with compartmentalized rooms and closets, a showplace in the jungle for the joy of life. His concrete house had windows without glass and a circular stairway that lead into the sky. The unfinished mansion set behind a thatched roof shack. "How unimaginative it is to build a Western style house in the jungle!" Clarence uttered to himself upon seeing the house. This was a middle class jungle man, who knew his worth. He babbled about being a Waribo, member of the Baoulé tribe. Royalty dwelled within him, he asserted. He declared he was a descendant of Aurare Pokou, the queen who threw her child into the Bandama River to save her people. The architect squatted on the ground, drinking Bangi wine with Babous (*Aliens, foreigners, Whites*). They, Clarence felt, on the other hand, did not have enough sense to drink to his health. Clarence also felt he had become wreathed in mist with a rotten smell penetrating his nose. There was no end to his disillusionment. He was determined to find paradise, if he had to scream for deliverance. A wise healer was desperately sought.

The African night became cool. The architect and his guests sat around a campfire, intoxicated from Bangi wine. Suddenly his numerous offspring ran from the bush, entertaining and beguiling the guests with dance. They pranced with exquisite posture, with patched-up faces, with the eyes of gazelles that twinkled in the night. The spirit of God dwelled within them as they ran, and jumped like antelopes, making music of broken pieces of twigs and grass, with pieces of tin tied around their bony legs. The children were chirping like birds, singing in unison, but clothed in dirty rags, dancing with rhythm and natural grace. They sung, skipped, hopped and shuffled, placing their ears to the earth. Clarence saw them with the eyes of a painter...these children of Africa. Were they hoping for a brighter future? He watched them closely. After they finished their performance, they grabbed the dust of Africa and wiped it across their swarthy faces. In this moment, Clarence craved to learn what it meant to be African. The children then came running to the tourists, gushing and pouring out merriment. Clarence gave them the bonbons, which he had in his pockets. Ellen gazed at him askance, in disapproval. "I don't think it is right to give candy to little African children. It spoils them, turns them into brats. Besides, they don't have dentists here," she later told Clarence, being absolute in her opinion. No one is protected from language. Clarence was shaken awake by these accusations. He thought in the breath of a second, in a world of wrong, who decides what is right? What is universal? He knew there were those, who apply their morals and values throughout this world, without the bat of an eyelash, who act as if they created this world and have the right to destroy it. They imagined they are God's chosen people, high and all mighty on thin ice. They had forgotten they created most of the mist within this world. "Ellen, it is a joke for you to think you have a right to judge," Clarence responded. "The times have changed, honey. There are no longer masters and slaves." This was the smaller of the bold statements which he uttered. "You give sugar to apes. Why not give Bonbons to African children?"

Ellen and Clarence continued their quarrel in the bush bus, driving back to Abidjan. Clarence spoke from his heart. He gave his opinions, but not all at the same time, being a quiet warrior. "Are not children the same throughout this world?" He asked Ellen rhetorically. "Do they not like to play and receive gifts?" Ellen became personal. "You are the persiflage of a man, Clarence," Ellen said, placing her finger in Clarence's wound, seeing the hole in his breast. "I dare you judge me!" Clarence responded. "Allow me the charade of judging you!" Clarence now placed on a battle suit, ready to bleed. Everyone has a different measure of justice. Each person sings a different battle song in the carousel of life. Some believe they are guardians of the earth. Others believe they are guardians of the sun. And others believe they are guardians of civilization or guardians of the moral order. Clarence had had more than his share of protectors and defenders of some valued treasure. "You know, Ellen, I have been meaning to tell you this for a long time. I find your vengeful voyeurism abhorrent. Your capturing of exotic images through Cannon lenses, of naked natives in their natural habitat is for me disgusting," Clarence announced. "You use cold eyes of glass and steel. This only reveals how far you have removed yourself from the human race. I think your needs are psychotic, especially your need to objectify your experiences with a camera, your need to avoid all human contact, except for a selected few, and your need to hide your true feelings. In reality, you only like Africans, as long as they are useful for you. That which you receive is greater than that which you give." This was a hard landing for Ellen. She wrestled for an answer. "Maybe you are too sensitive, Clarence," Ellen said on the run. "Ellen, what particularly disturbs me is the fact that you use a Polaroid camera as enticement, alluring the natives to pose for you," Clarence retorted. "It is similar to the early Portuguese, selling glass beads to Africans for ivory and gold. How can you, Ellen, be so unconscious of history? You are an educated person and a liberal!"

When Ellen and Clarence returned to the hotel with their tour group, Ellen mimicked the offended one. She ran to her room, a parody in a valley of tears. The disagreement with Clarence ended in animosity. The hurting words took on a life of their own. Clarence was accused of being callous. He became a pariah within the group and the white members of the group ostracized him. This was his fate, he thought. He reconciled himself with the thought that no matter how long the night...the day was sure to come!

15. They flew away like two wild fowls

There was a man in the moon with an elephant head and ivory tusks which shimmered. The silhouette played a game of light and darkness, illuminating a proud African mother, washing her infant in a calabash, resting on a flat stone in the middle of a nameless dirt road. Her breasts hung down to her navel. A small group of neighborhood women and men sang and danced in the vicinity, dancing for the pleasure of the moment. Their vocal rhythms gave life to the drab quartier of miserable clay huts. Dirty and noisy children brawled with each other in the red dust. As if propelled by air, Clarence strolled between these gleeful faces, thinking about Ellen. She was now very cool towards him, believing her anger was justified, playing the role of Jeanne d'Arc, who was supposedly unjustly burned at the stake for her good deeds. Clarence's rude words and harsh utterances could not be forgiven. And yet he also realized Ellen could not be held responsible for the crimes of this world. He was tired of being angry, playing the role of keeper of the lyrics, a moral apostle. He became conscious of the fact that he did not have the only window to a native place, and he had to remind himself that he could not be all of his life a bastion against absurd expectations, fighting the battles of the past. His quarrel with Ellen left him drained, sucked dry with a hangover, as if a nondescript, innocuous shadow hung over his head.

"A Salem Aleekum (*Peace be with you*)!"An old man spoke, who smoked a brass crocodile pipe, appearing to be listening to faraway sounds. He was black as the night with geometric designs, which were painted on his owl-like face. A monkey fur hung around his waist. His tubular eyes were possessed, infinitely strange and his hair was stained red by ash and cow's urine. "Aleekum a Salem!" Clarence returned the greetings, astonished to see the humble old man, sitting on a wooden stool like a night watchman, a life-giving spirit. He pondered if this was the archangel of Allah. "I am the secret keeper," the old man said. "I help wandering souls to reach their goals. I sell beads." The old man offered Clarence blue beads, charms and fetishes to buy, to protect against evil spirits. "The blue beads are God, the color of the sky in which he dwells," the old man said, squatting between bones, horns, hairs, wood, roots and seeds. "Cutting words are worse than a bowstring. A cut may heal, but the cut of the tongue does not," the old man told Clarence. Clarence did not want to linger long with this diviner, who with his magic herbs, skulls of dogs, gorilla paws, and red parrot feathers tried to convince him that more existed than that which meets the eye. Clarence did not want to dabble in sorcery and mysticism, since he was not a believer in magic. He also did not believe in random accidents, but in destiny and in the inevitability of events. Clarence decided, therefore, to hear what this old man had to say, and he sat in a lotus position on a mat in front of the old man, allowing the old man to blow consecrated talcum powder over his head.

"Dong, Dong, Dong." The clamorous tinkle of a gong reverberated throughout the little hut. The old man shifted between heaven and earth, falling quickly in a trance, a hypnotic state which revealed the wrinkles of age. The white ashes on his face disclosed deep valleys and furrows. The sorcerer wore a gold Creole in his right ear and a necklace of lapis lazuli. His fallen chest revealed a skeleton basket. He was only of skin and bones, hurling animal bones, buttons and cowry shells across the ground and offering Clarence a bowl of herbs to drink. "You shall marry in the future," the old man declared. "Monsieur, I'm a homosexual!" Clarence exclaimed, impatient with charlatans telling myths. "That is all right," the diviner replied. "There are many forms of marriage and many wonders of the caterpillar." He sprinkled a few drops of gin on the ground. "You shall meet someone who has been sent by the gods to you. You shall travel far away with him. But you must do as I say. You must slaughter a chicken and have the power of faith." Clarence paid to have a chicken slaughtered. The diviner poured the chicken's blood into a dog's skull. He handed it to Clarence to drink. "I do not wish that you depart in fear, Monsieur. I want to warn you." The diviner brushed a long horsetail whisk across his crinkled face as if it was a magical wan. "There are many wolfs in Africa. Beware!" He said. "Travelers are easily fooled."

The warnings of the sorcerer were quickly forgotten, pushed into Clarence's subconscious. He quickly departed the diviner's booth in a cloud of dust, meandering through the streets of Abidjan, which beckoned with commotion and small melodramas like a theater in a tub. Mystery hung in the air and the feeling of a warm summer night lingered. Clarence strolled as if in a hallucination. He was deliriously seeking a holy place, being in love with Africa, which existed somewhere between myth and mysticism. Rowdy French soldiers staggered by, drifting over the ornate bridge towards Treichville. They were in search of a beer and the naked embrace of an African woman. Under the bridge, the water of the Lagoon was murky brown. It stunk of human waste materials. This was the same bridge, under which Clarence and Hortense had huddled together that night when he came to blows with the Lebanese man. In Treichville, Clarence caught the night Ferry to Île du Bouley in a spontaneous moment. The ferry was full of noise. Mothers breast-fed their sucklings. Grandmothers squatted on the deck with heavy loads on their heads. Patriarchal old men rested in forgetfulness with a wisdom, which comes with old age, lucky to be gray and sedate. Market dealers hauled home their bargain merchandise in calculation and anticipation of better business tomorrow. It was a sleepless society on the ship.

Clarence personally sought distance from his problems, to throw his anxiety in the air, hoping the Île du Bouley at night would provide the seclusion, peace and quiet which he sought. He wanted to stroll along the beach with the wind hounds and the sea to his side, to collect his thoughts, the chronology of his Africa trip. He questioned if Ellen was right with her comment that he was too sensitive, and he grasped that he had been sensitive all of his life, as if he lived in the cavity of a rock, which was the universe and a very brutal place. It was a wonder he had gotten through this world so many years, without having a broken spirit, without becoming cynical, calculating, without becoming angry and cold hearted. Maybe it was because he was still convinced in the sanctity of something...that it would one day come his way. Clarence never doubted his worth or the goodness of others. He recalled what the strange diviner in the little hut told him as he left it, heading for the ferry. "There is no such thing as evil people, Monsieur, only evil spirits, which enter like a needle and spread like an oak tree," the diviner said. The brown water of the Lagoon gushed from the back of the ferry, dancing in whirls and swirls.

Clarence leaned against the rail, hunting water bubbles, counting the bubble-like pearls with thoughts of summer wine on the Adriatic, thinking if he would have gone to Italy for his summer vacation, he could have, at least, eaten spaghetti ice cream, enjoying it full of passion, delighting in the *dolce far niente* (*the sweet life*), instead of sacrificing blood in Africa.

Two young cocky boys, who looked like hooligans, or warriors in ritual painting, battled for his attention. They were ruff boys, who threw peanuts at the seagulls. Their goal was to triumph in life, and they burned for contact. They had Clarence in vizier...a rich American, the gate to the west. When they asked Clarence if he was an American, he knew he could either answer in the affirmative or in the negative. If he said yes, they looked at him like he was a piggy bank. And if he said no, they figured he was in the same boat as they were and therefore not worth the headache. Clarence could not conceal the fact that he was an American. Everything about him gave it away.... his Timberland shoes, his Trager bag from Seattle, his Columbia hiking hat, the little smirk at the corners of his mouth which came from the attitude of education or wealth, his dreadlocks, his way of walking and his way of speaking French with the mouth and nasal sound, instead of from the throat. Everything about him shouted that he came from the New World. He said he was called Souleyman to make himself appear less American, less like a bird of luck. He was glad Hortense had given him this befitting name. When he announced that he was called Souleyman, the two young African men reacted bemused. "It's a dog's life, Souleyman," the older of the two young men responded. He offered Clarence a skeptical picture of the people on the ferry. "They live and die like pigs," he said pointing at the passengers on the ferry. The young African man resembled a walrus with a boar's head and sharp cruel eyes. He wore a crest-like hairdo. A gold symbol of the sun and eternal life hung around his neck. He said that his name was Sitti. "They don't seem to be complaining to me," Clarence replied with reservations. "Pas reéllement, Monsieur! (*Not really! Mister*) Do you not have eyes and ears? The tourists and the African elite are the only ones, who like Africa. The rest want to leave." The smaller one of the two young men voiced his opinion with a narcotized gaze.

His name was Alli. He complained about systems and structures. He was a dwarf, with a hinged jaw, bulging eyes, and warts of a warthog. Kinte cloth was tied around his neck. He had metal spikes for teeth. His face was covered with scarification marks. The expression on his face left no room for discussion. "They can't all leave," Clarence argued in jest, trying to make small talk, but not really interested in discussing these problems. Alli and Sitti were the types of Africans he did not like. They were hostage gangsters and camel traders, men on the boundary of sanity. They were the sorts, who were always pushing and shoving, stepping on other's feet. They were the ones, who hated themselves because of their black markings and thus hated everybody. They were the ones, who blamed the white man for their ill fate. But whom else could they blame? Of course they could blame themselves. Clarence recalled a passage from Buddha which said: 'Blame *yourself* for everything that happens to you. Blame *yourself* for all of your problems and you will be on the right long road to enlightenment.' This had nothing to do with self-flagellation. How could he tell these two Africans this, that they were responsible for their problems, without hurting their feelings, without provoking them?

"Luck is round," Clarence said diplomatically, explaining that it goes around and around in a life of appearances and being. "Monsieur, you have the right to come and go at will. We Africans can't go anywhere without a visa," Sitti gripped, speaking with a rattle in his throat. "When you are rich, you are hated, but when you are poor, you are despised."

"Tout à fait (*Exactly*). No one is willing to give us a visa," Alli intoned, doubled up with laughter, but not really laughing.

"We suffer the revenge of the gods," Sitti jested. "Souleyman, is this your first time in Africa?" He asked.

"Yes," Clarence said, defending his right to travel.

"Well, no ill-feelings, Monsieur Americain. To show you just how generous we Africans are, we will give you a cadou (*gift*)." Sitti reached into a mud cloth bag, pulling out two delicate silver chains. He handed them to Clarence "May you wear them well," he said.

Clarence was vulnerable to friendliness, especially when it came from virile males. It had the scent of a promise, the hint of flirtation. When virile men were friendly to Clarence, he automatically disregarded risks and side effects, being always hard on the limit, like on the wings of a bird. The two young African men followed him to a small bar on Île du Bouley, where Clarence invited them to a couple of beers. Later, they accompanied him down to the beach, telling dirty stories about machos and girls. Clarence was embarrassed about his discrete symbols of success, his expensive watch, and his leather bag, as he promenaded between these two impoverished African sharks. The waves of the water of the Lagoon were high and dangerous. A salty wind blew. Islands of stars filled the sky. Clarence felt near to the stars and the moon, and he forgot his initial uneasiness, his fear of rogues and swindlers. Sitti and Alli told him they were from Liberia. They said that they were fleeing from a civil war. They carried the scares of war with them. Sitti asked Clarence if he knew how to kill or how human blood tastes. "I know only how to hurt," Clarence answered. "And since I am not a vampire, I don't know how blood tastes." Clarence wondered if he had fallen into the kingdom of Dracula. "Then you have never been desperate in life," Sitti replied. His eyes reflected the night, the stars, and the moon, possessing a dark shine of emptiness. "Have you ever known fear?" Sitti asked. Alli spoke before Clarence could answer this strange question. "Do you know how shit tastes?" He said, not waiting for Clarence to answer Sitti's question. "I know how it smells," Clarence responded, wondering why these African men were asking him such silly questions. Alli paid little attention to Clarence's response to his question. He dug in the soft sand, as if seeking hidden treasures, preoccupied with some hidden thoughts. The talismans, which hung around his neck moved about with his body movements. It appeared as if he had a trinket for every possible unlucky thing that could happen to him. Sitti suddenly erected himself and walked down the beach to the sea, where he urinated. His head was in the air, but his thoughts were in the sand. He was piously submerged in his own pain. A cool breeze blew from the Gulf of Guinea. Alli whispered to Clarence confidentially that Sitti was forced as a child to kill his parents, and then forced to drink their blood. Alli was an accountant of terror, saying that he also had lost his parents in war. He said that he grew up an orphan. Clarence did not know how to react upon hearing such heartrending information. Should he say: 'Oh, I am sorry to hear that' or should he pat the poor fellow on the back as a sign of sympathy and condolence. It was embarrassing for him to hear the sorrows, the anatomy of horrors from the mouth of this suffering African. Their citadel of dreadful memories became their present jail.

"Souleyman, you have an African name," Sitti declared upon returning from the shore of the Lagoon. "But you have not learned how to act like an African. An African, when he receives a cadou (*gift*) returns the honor by giving a cadou." Sitti's talent was the swift attack. "Now, what will you give us?" He asked, rebuking Clarence for being so inconsiderate. "I'll give you a kiss on the cheek," Clarence said in jest with his usual sharp tongue. "Souleyman, mon ami, we are sure your kisses are sweet. But we Africans believe a cadou given should correspond in value to a cadou received." Sitti was searching for a little luck in Clarence's garden, hoping that Clarence would suddenly become generous. "C'est tout naturél (*It is natural*), monsieur," Alli intoned with his long, opened snout. "How about some bonbons?" Clarence joked. "I have bonbons in my pocket."

"Bonbons are for children, mon ami. We are men," Sitti said. He weighted gold against yams, in a cold fever, making his meaning clear, perfectly clear that he was willing to fight for possessions, to fight for what he wanted. Invisible horns suddenly protruded from his Janus forehead. "Yes, I can see you are men," Clarence assured him. The scanty jokes stopped here. Clarence began to see Sitti and Alli with other eyes, realizing he had flown into the mouth of bears. He told them he was shocked at how time had passed and gradually got up to leave in a desperate salvage operation. Ideas failed him in this moment how to climb out of the jaws of sharks, but he instinctively knew that this was no time to make cheap threats, since he was close to the abyss. Who attempted this was in grave danger. "Souleyman, you must have something of value in your bag," Sitti said with greed in his eyes. He grabbed Clarence's bag. "Hey, it's none of your business what I have in my bag." Clarence grabbed his Trager bag back, out of Sitti's hand. "Besides, these necklaces are cheap imitation silver. I didn't ask you for them. You forced them upon me. Here, you can have them back." Clarence handed the silver necklaces to Sitti. Sitti looked at him in anger. His eyes were threatening, lurking. "Monsieur, a cadou returned is an insult for an African," Sitti said. "I am sorry, but you'll just have to be insulted," Clarence rejoined, ready to sling dirt and lies. This was the end of his illusions about kindhearted Africans. He attempted to leave the beach quickly in full steam, as Alli blocked his path. They struggled over the leather bag, scuffling and tussling with each other. All of a sudden without warning, a gun went off with a bang. Clarence and Alli stopped their duel in their tracks. Sitti held a gun in his hands. To lose one's life over a Trager bag was not the price to pay, Clarence thought. He let the bag drop onto the sand and considered screaming for help in his hour of trail, knowing those who screamed loud enough prevailed. But who would have heard him on this forlorn beach, on this desolate island? Who was observing this battle in a triangle? Were there no heroes near? Had all the heroes returned to their abodes?

Alli grabbed the bag, searching it for valuables, for money and assets. His hands were clumsy, stammering. Clarence thought that this was his day of desecration; that he had landed unintentionally in the butcher's house. He embraced the thought of death in his distressing moment, the death of a fairy queen in the nightshade on the lonely beach. It would be one less person for the earth to bear. Clarence needed now courage, the right nerves. The flood set in. The city of Abidjan appeared far away like a mirage in the distance. From the dark bushes and thicket at the edge of the beach came a male voice, full of strength, arresting, raw, but warm. "Drop the gun, Sitti!"

"Is that you, Serafin?" Sitti yelled. "Don't try to put a spoke in our wheel, man. This is my thing."

"If I grab you, Sitti, I'm going to knock you over," the masculine voice threatened. It was a comical threat, Clarence thought, thinking one had to do more than knock this guy over. Sitti abruptly shot the gun at some perceived point in the darkness, and before he could blink his eyes, he landed swiftly onto the ground with Serafin on top on him, battling for the gun. It was a showdown, a clash between a bat and an antelope. Alli watched them battling, pulling a dagger out of his pocket, waiting on the sidelines, ready to hit and stab. Serafin continued to wrestle with Sitti for the gun. He was brawny, muscular, and stronger than Sitti. He twisted with craft the gun towards Sitti, gazed him for a moment in the eye and pulled unexpectedly the trigger, sending Sitti to the land of the dead. A monstrosity all of a sudden filled the sky with smoke. This was Sitti's evil spirit leaving his body, flying away into the night. This was his anger that took wing. Alli did not wait for Serafin to stand. He started towards him with jumps and leaps, with the dagger in his right hand. Serafin dodged his assault, grabbing Alli from behind by the Kinte cloth around his neck. He pulled it tight, tighter...as tight as he could. Alli collapsed slowly to the sand, dropping the dagger to the ground. They scuffled like dogs over the dagger in a bitter battle to death. Serafin snatched the dagger swiftly. He stabbed Alli one, two, three times, with alacrity and without thinking, as if killing was a prop. Alli's sacrificial blood flowed onto the white sand and he died quickly and hushed.

Clarence stood as if in a trance, finding himself confronted with a horrible crime, staring at Serafin, kneeling in the sand and at the two dead bodies. He mulled about the puzzle of this night, about the game with death and wondered about the creation of human monsters and real monstrosities. Every singer in life was a soloist, singing a song in which each note had a meaning. This horror picture before him was ghastly to behold, worse than horror videos. But hope, the measure of all things, remained in his soul. Hope laid concealed between war, genocide and death. Clarence understood instinctively that he needed to have a strong heart in a desperate situation, but also a quick sole in order to escape. He blamed himself for placing himself in hell's fire. He had climbed up this tree and now he had to find a way how to climb down the same tree. "We have to call the police and the ambulance for them," Clarence pleaded. "That's a lot of wind around the last dirt," Serafin replied, studying the night sky. "I must leave Abidjan immediately. I have no money. Money is sharper than a sword."

"You have done nothing wrong. You defended your right to life. You saved my life!" Clarence tried to convince Serafin he had no reasons for fear. He was badly smitten with him, as if he had fallen into water. "One must talk little and listen much," Serafin said. "Nothing is fair in Africa. They will put me in a prison for life without justice. The only way I will come out will be in a coffin by order of the authorities." Clarence approached Serafin. He looked into Serafin's dark eyes, which spoke a language of space. His secrets were not for sale, and yet his eyes disclosed warmth that Clarence had never seen in the eyes of any man. He was not a warrior. This was a large assault on Clarence's emotions for the prelude. Could it be that he was in love with this man? Would it wither and fade like most things in life. Serafin had done evil and now he expected evil. He believed that to burn in the fire of hell was his destiny. Serafin fought in his mind windmills and dragons. He was the eternal loser, whose belief in wonders was poisoned long ago. What treasures he possessed were hidden in a still place, called the soul. Serafin asked Clarence for money to go to the place of his birth, as if it was a little point in the sky. "There the earth speaks its own language," he uttered, believing he would be safe in his village.

The hour of decision had arrived for Clarence. There were zero solutions. Serafin appeared as if his last hope had sunk into the sand. Clarence was suddenly moved by the force of love. It was no longer important to him what would happen tomorrow, because you could not plan luck. But he somehow instinctively knew that what was happening this night would determine whether he would live near the sun and the stars, or whether he would continue to live in hell.

He told Serafin he had some extra money at the hotel. They agreed to meet later in Abidjan. Clarence intended to go to his hotel, get this extra money, then meet Serafin in the early morning hours. Serafin told him that he would be waiting at the bush taxi station on the plateau in Abidjan. He asked Clarence if he knew where it was located. Clarence nodded his head in the affirmative. Before they departed, Serafin got rid of the two bodies. They were dead, but not yet dead in spirit. Serafin threw their corpses into the sea for the sharks to eat. Clarence worried if the bodies of Sitti and Alli could be washed back ashore. Murder without a body, he thought, was better than murder with a body. "Who cares about a body on a beach? Everyday hundreds disappear in Africa, without a trace," Serafin assured him. "Do not forget me, Souleyman," Serafin pleaded as Clarence departed.

From the ferry to Abidjan Clarence could see Serafin's dark silhouette, standing on the shore of the beach. He appeared to be so near and yet so far. Love comes always unexpectedly. When you wait for it, it never appears. And when you least expect it, it slips into your life. The language of love now dictated Clarence's actions. He saw a way of climbing out of his depressing world. The way was difficult and the path was filled with traps, with risks and hazards. He sat on the ferry back to Abidjan, asking himself many questions. Where was his home? Was home a certain place on a piece of earth or did it exist within the racing heart? He did not know where home was. Was it the small town in the Deep South, populated with human saints and villains, where he was driven by the rhythm of dreams, experiencing joy and frustration, feeling his entire life misplaced, like a coconut that grew alone? Or was home New York City with its urban warriors and meat eating plants which ate too much. They all loved themselves in New York City and each one pursued his and her dreams, with the attitude, 'after us, the deluge'. They all built upon their strengths and paid the cost of an anonymous, isolated and lonely life. This was the New York City blues of fear, money and quality of life.

With the handicaps God gave him, Clarence wanted only to feel comfortable in his skin. Why was it that some people had to fight for the right to exist on this planet? He had to find a home, to find a place to return to, a place where he could feel comfortable and at peace, a place where he could feel he had a stake in the future. This place, where he could live as a black man and as a homosexual, where he would be able to reconcile these two identities within himself, was a fata morgana. Clarence knew this intuitively, but he felt that he had to search for it, this place, if only for the purpose of soothing his soul. The decision was made to follow Serafin into the bush. Clarence told himself that he did not have anything to go back to in New York City, and it was not going to disappear. Serafin was the best thing he had met in his life. He did not know if it was love. Maybe it was infatuation. He had never loved before. How could he know how it felt to love? It was worth pursuing. It would be a learning process. If it did not work out with Serafin, he could always pick up his strings there where he left them. He told himself if he wasn't willing to sacrifice everything for love, then he wasn't worth receiving real love. Since real love was without conditions. Love meant taking a risk. It meant going all the way, not halfway. All of his life, Clarence spent searching, looking for the ecstatic of beauty, obsessed with beauty, which was rare in this world men made. He wanted to have beauty in front of his face, to drown his eyes in beauty and not with hard types. He wanted to smell beauty. If beauty could have been eaten, he would have eaten it, touched it. Beauty meant for him purity of soul, simplicity of form. Serafin was the manifestation of beauty for Clarence. When he gazed into

Serafin's eyes, he saw Serafin's essence, the beauty in Serafin's soul. He felt Serafin was good enough to be ennobled.

Africa was not a paradise. Perhaps it once was one. Anyone with eyes could see the deficiencies on this hot continent under ancient trees. Yet Clarence felt comfortable in Africa, at home. But he would have felt comfortable in the old king's kingdom of Korea, if he would have found a love there. It was more than fascination with the exotic. It was more than sun and fun. Africa uplifted his soul. Africa carried him to another level and showed him another way of looking at the world. It was a spiritual way, not a material way of seeing. There was another path next to the beaten path. Jubilation! A fresh wind blew through Clarence's desert. He drank of a cool stream, remembering he had once drunk of this current before. But that was centuries ago. For the blind to learn to see, it was necessary to drink of this stream again. It was similar to the belief in God. You had to believe in him. You had to feel him within your soul. You had to experience him. Clarence had dreamed one day a man would come his way. He would bring love that was born out of dreams. He would carry him away under a rainbow to his castle on the hill. Instead, a dusky Senufo came, who offered only a hut in the bush and he was willing to sacrifice everything which he had accumulated in NYC to go with this man for the aroma of a promise. But life never turns out the way one expects it to, as if someone greater played a game with the dreams of mortals. Clarence's intuition told him to go with Serafin to the north. His rational mind said, don't be a fool. He would be poor and unlucky, like a fish in a drop of water. Clarence decided to place his fate in God's hands, wanting to believe in love.

He ran into the hotel past the concierge, in the run of his life, in a state of daze. The concierge slept. He did not notice Clarence slipping past him to his room. The concierge dreamed of giraffes, wild bulls, zebras, galloping antelopes and the metamorphosis of insects. In the bar-restaurant, a small group of French tourist sang Karaoke. They were under the influence of Dionysus and good wine. The spirits were busy this night. Clarence hoped they were on his side. He hoped they would ward against evil spirits. Clarence left his belongings as they were, singing a song of rejoice, taking only money, contemplating how his sudden disappearance would be explained. But he didn't tarry long at the thought. Out of sight, meant out of mind and in the eternity of time and the opera of life, the appearance or disappearance of one individual was insignificant, he thought. And the disappearance of a "black gay man" was even more insignificant. Everything would continue as it had, as if he had never existed. Flowers would bloom, wither and die. Thunder would continue to rumble. Seasons would follow each other and stupid men would continue to battle for power. A train of thoughts raced through his mind, thoughts of his mother and father, of his acquaintances in New York. He thought of Ellen, of Alli and Sitti, the demon-like duet that Serafin threw into the sea. He thought of forgetting and forgiving and decided to apologize to Ellen. He had unfinished business to settle. The spirit of his grandmother filled him. "Each breath yu' tak' could be yur last breath," his grandmother often said. "If yu' offend, ask fur pardon and if yu' iz offended, forgive. Life iz too short ta carry uh grudge."

Clarence walked to Ellen's room and knocked lightly on the door. Ellen opened her door sluggish, acting as if she was surprised to see Clarence. She looked at him, as if he had the wrong address. Ellen was afraid of what he would say to her. Clarence felt satisfied to see that she was afraid. He thought momentarily to himself, that even winners had to fear revenge...had to have the courage to relinquish postures of triumph. He could see Ellen was suffering without words.

She was confused in a medley of truths which he had said. His earlier comments had definitely disturbed Ellen in her swallow nest. "Wish yourself something!" Clarence said, trying to break through Ellen's ennui and arrogance, to help her change her mood. "I wish for summer lightening," Ellen replied. "And that we can be friends again."

"Ellen, that's why I like you," Clarence declared. "You know how to wish for the right things." They laughed together. Their laughter bounced off the flower wallpaper, echoing through the empty hallway. They shared a moment in jest together, hanging in a light peace. The comedy of dissension, discord and quarrel dissipated in thin air. "You know Ellen...they say a wonder takes place every day," Clarence said. "I don't know if love is a remedy for muddling through life. But I've been stung by a love bug. I'm now about to jump into the bush with an African man who I hardly know."

"There is nothing wrong with following your heart, Clarence," Ellen answered. "As long as you take some precautions...Don't build on sand, Clarence. It is nice riding a carrousel. But at some point, you will have to get off." Ellen stood in the doorway in a nightgown of taffeta and tulle, digesting what Clarence was telling her. He appeared to her like Cinderella, who had discovered the beautiful life. The heart was trump. How could she tell Clarence that it was only an illusion? "Don't seek the fantastic, Clarence," Ellen advised. "How can you say this, Ellen? You are the one who spends your life seeking adventure in all corners of this world. Don't I have a right to have an adventure?" Clarence asked her. "Yes, but adventures that are affordable, calculable and where you are sitting in the saddle and can control the outcome," Ellen explained. This was a typical thing for a rich white girl to say, Clarence thought. For them it was always about control.

"Have you never dreamed of happiness, Ellen?" Clarence asked in a fit of madness, driven by the rhythm of the drums. "There are no adventures in life and seldom a happy-end," Ellen said. "The comedy of it all lies between the lines. We go through our lives fighting against fading away." Ellen spoke with authenticity this time. She knew personally what it meant to yearn for beauty and a beautiful home. The color of hope was pink. "Follow your heart, Clarence. I will not tell anyone what happened," she said, winking with one eye. It was the only solution for Clarence. The choice fell on him. It was not Ellen's choice to make. The force of love was stronger for Clarence and he felt if he was making a mistake, it was a beautiful mistake. The world was filled with inhibitions and prohibitions, with one prohibition chasing the other. Clarence understood that the only way to break out of normal life was to follow the craft of the sun.

"I want to tell you a secret, Clarence," Ellen whispered, as if she was sitting on top of a volcano. "I have invited N'ba to Paris. We are in love." Clarence was shocked to hear this. N'ba was certainly a handsome black man, but he was poor as a church mouse. Clarence thought Ellen liked only middle-class black men. The consonance of sound settled between the walls of the hallway. Clarence was reluctant to fan unnecessary fears. He did not have an evil tongue nor was he the messenger of evil. How could he reveal to Ellen that the African man, who she circled and wooed in a mating behavior, was terminally sick? "Ellen, N'ba is sick." Clarence blurted out, using shock therapy. "If you slept with him, you need to see a doctor, when you get back to the States or to Paris."

"How do you know this?" Ellen asked. "N'ba told me himself!" Clarence replied. "N'ba has the hope of a second life in America or Europe. This hope is stronger than his fear of the future. Do you understand what I am trying to say, Ellen?"

"I don't understand, Clarence," Ellen responded. "You must tell me more."

"Did N'ba tell you that he loves you?" Clarence asked. "No, he doesn't have to. A woman knows such things." Ellen looked at Clarence from an oblique angle, wondering if he understood the power of a woman's charm to lure. "What about your husband?" Clarence queried. "We have lived separate and apart for years in the same villa. Nothing will change." Ellen explained the end of the romantic, the debacle of a failed marriage, which she saw as a chance. Ellen and her husband were prisoners of the absolute. "No, Ellen, I will say no more. It is not my place to take you out of a beautiful dream. This is the responsibility of N'ba." Clarence kissed her on the cheek and started to depart. "There are no secrets after death, Ellen, except that life is beautiful," he said in hushed tones to her. Their glances faded in departing to join the other faded histories and faded songs of people in hotels.

Clarence slipped out of the hotel without a sound, gliding through the early morning air to the bush taxi station. Serafin sat on a rock like a pharaoh in the Valley of the Kings, patiently waiting. Explosions in the heavens occurred. Serafin and the rock appeared as one. He was rooted in nature. His heart was burden with thoughts of the meaning of life. In this moment, the past, present and future were one. His homesickness was stronger than fear. He tried not to think about what happened on the beach; that he had incurred the God's displeasure and a specter would hunt his house. Clarence approached him like the bringer of blessings, giving Serafin the money for the trip to the north. Serafin showed his gratitude. He gave praise to God for Clarence's appearance, hoping God would redeem him. "Are you surprised that I returned?" Clarence questioned Serafin, his protector and defender. This was the man who had saved his life. "I thought the darkness would have prevented your coming," Serafin said. This was a diplomatic response. "Serafin, I want to come with you!" Clarence stated flatly. He did not dare tell Serafin that he was like a light, which opened his eyes, as he stood helplessly in front of Serafin, joyful of his splendid appearance, his magnificent physique, and his fighting spirit. Honor surrounded Serafin. His valor was pleasing to Clarence. He was worth dying for. "I am now cursed. I will meet misery," Serafin declared. "You should return to your hotel and enjoy what the world offers." The job of convincing Serafin fell upon Clarence shoulders. "Serafin, I have already had many trials in my short life. God has sent me a noble and brave friend. He has given me what I wanted. I know that I will be happy with you," Clarence said. The night sky was illuminated with summer lightening. "I am willing to be your companion in misfortune."

"You will be like a child that comes and goes, little brother," Serafin answered. He placed his arm around Clarence shoulder and hugged him tightly. "Let us go. Pray that the roads will be kind to us." They boarded the bush bus and took an empty row of seats in the back of the bus. As the bush bus departed, Serafin leaned against Clarence. "The God of thunder punishes with lightening," he whispered. He then leaned his head against the window of the bush bus and fell asleep...in the arms of Morpheus. The power of love absorbed Clarence. He observed Serafin sleeping, his beautiful face, feeling like an acrobat in love, feeling like the dispossessed in flight...as they flew away like two wild fowls.

16. One who was born during a journey?

The city of Korhogo bathed itself in alluvial red clay, like a baptism in hell. The devil was the red blowing dust, which blinded the inhabitants, suffocating them. When the dust settled, one could see a small frontier town struggling between Frangi pani trees. Korhogo rested between the anthills of the Savanna. A condemned people, holy folks, the sinful, and malaria carrying mosquitoes populated the town. Over the tin rooftops of the cardboard houses, the insistent chant of the Mullah could be heard, summoning all to prayer. Korhogo was a city, where the rich built private Mosques for worship and the peasants walked barefoot in the red dirt clay. They all did their private business and hygiene on the public streets. Crowded bush taxes and rickety mopeds rushed here and there and a sickly crowing hen awakened all each morning to a living hell.

Serafin awoke this morning in low spirits. He walked to the window of the hotel, gazing out of it. From his hotel window, a picture postcard panorama of Korhogo, veiled in a red haze was framed. It appeared from the hotel window as if it would be a beautiful day. The warm morning sun fought to emerge from behind the red haze. Serafin returned to the bed, seeking to fall asleep. Old histories boiled up in him of the godly and the vulgar. These were not night ghosts, but ghosts of his mind. They hunted his being, hounding his spirit. Serafin was returning to the place of his birth, a place that he once fled...fleeing for a larger life in a bigger world. He wondered if it was possible to return again to a place of peace and tranquility, after all that had happened to him in the last couple of years. Serafin gazed at Clarence, sleeping lightly. He wondered about this American with dual sexual nature, without frame, without composure, without self control, someone, who wore white pants into the jungle and flirted with dangerous situations. Serafin suspected he and Clarence were similar in character...both fleeing a past and an irritating place...both vagabonds between two kindles....both unprepared for life. There was no way to escape the four walls of the hotel room. The clatter of the motorbikes and the crowing hen under the hotel window could not dispel the evil spirits out of his mind. Soundless screams hang in the air. Serafin remembered the drama on the beach, the catastrophe between flood and tide. He recalled his reptile chums, Sitti and Alli, who were absolute underdogs, searching for little bounty. Serafin once treaded with them through Abidjan, engaging in petty crime. Now he was cursed with a fatal deed, hunted by the spirits of the undead. They hounded him from their graves in the deep sea. Only sleep could help him now. In sleep, Serafin was able to climb into another kingdom. He sunk into a deep slumber.

Clarence usually left the hotel in the late mornings, spending the day walking through the dirt-streets of Korhogo. The mornings in Korhogo were cool and the afternoons hot. The unpaved red clay streets were filled with traffic and trade. A variety of vehicles ran across the barren ground, filling the air, the scrubs and the dead trees along the roads with a red dusk. Clarence strolled across the fetish market of elephant tusk, snake skins and dead spiders. A little nappy-headed Senufo boy pursued his trail, begging to polish and shine Clarence's Birkenstock shoes. The Senufo boy waited every day for Clarence at the hotel entrance, refusing to capitulate, tracking Clarence across the city, pleading for the chance to shine his shoes. And everyday Clarence promised him to wear real shoes, so he could spit, and shine them. "I hear America is a rich land. Is it not true, Monsieur?" The Senufo boy asked him in a delicate voice. "Shoo! Shoo! Shoo-away, boy!" Clarence said. "Tomorrow I will give you a big cadou." The little shoeshine boy persisted, attempting to shine the leather strips of the Birkenstock shoes in his desperation. "Monsieur, have you not a small cadou for me today?" He asked, melancholic, half-serious, half in jest. "Tomorrow is a faraway place." Despite Clarence futile attempts to rid himself of the shoeshine boy, he persisted...continuing to follow him and this was the same procedure everyday. The little shoeshine boy thought Americans would be a strange folk with their Birkenstock shoes. They did not even wear real shoes which could be shined.

Clarence's second life began in Korhogo. He had a new look to the world, driven by romanticism, trying to feel his way to Serafin's heart, who was an extreme type of person, but unbelievably tame with a hard shell. Clarence knew instinctively that Serafin was inside soft and tender, like a flower which failed to bloom. Serafin was confused and his heart was a place of loneliness, because he had suffered only defeats in life, instead of rising from the table and winning like everybody else. Serafin only wanted to win. Clarence told himself the gentle approach was the best road to follow with Serafin, not to suddenly assault his masculinity. His destroyed trust had to be rebuilt. Clarence had, like a fisherman, spread a net and accidentally caught a leaping antelope. Now it was a matter of hauling in his net, making this wonderful man fall in love with him. Time would decide. Serafin became sick without warning, spending the days and nights locked in the dark hotel room, declaring that he was just tired from the long travel, telling Clarence not to worry, because it would soon pass like the weather. He said it was something that comes and goes in Africa, claiming he was not surprised when it came and he would not be displeased, when it departed. It was part of his life, he said.

Mohammed, the concierge at the hotel, told Clarence it was Malaria. Serafin later sunk into a feverish delirium on an excursion into hell. Pain became his master. Clarence touched his forehead. He was steaming hot from head to toe and his smile was gone. Clarence proceeded to nurse him back to health, caring for his body and soul. The swirl of time became insignificant. Clarence and Serafin became comrades in dream, dreaming of terra nova, of a home for herons and storks. Clarence was in love and happy, and love brings happiness. He believed Serafin was a satisfying gift to him from the Gods. Serafin brought him joy. Clarence wanted to announce this joy with tubas and trumpets. Instead, he sat by the bed, wiping Serafin's forehead with a damp cloth, helping him to eat, assisting him to the bathroom, placing a net over the bed against the mosquitoes. Then he remembered the tablets against Malaria, which he bought in NYC. They were still in his Trager Bag. He gave the tablets to Serafin, feeling helpless in the face of sickness. Sickness reminded him of human vulnerability, fragility and the brittle presence of humans on this earth. There was no flower which bloomed eternally. Even those that were loved eventually wilted and died. The thought that Serafin could depart this world, leaving Clarence alone to do battle with daily life again, was frightening. It lurked in the back of his mind, making his hands tremble, as he wiped away the beads of sweat from Serafin's merger face. The scent of Serafin's sweat intoxicated Clarence. He wanted to collect it in a bucket for prosperity. Clarence had learned in the past through the death of his mother and grandmother, whom he dearly loved...that even though one felt attached in life to someone, it was best to let them go easily, when the time approached to say farewell. Since this was something he could not prevent. The Gods, cloud traders that they were, gave and took. They teased and played their games with humans like in a game of chest. But Clarence was not willing to let this newfound love depart. He had waited too long in his life to find it and suddenly it came along in Africa and he was transformed. If this love departed, he was resolved to depart with it. Clarence knew he could easily buy the fitting poison on the fetish market in Korhogo. What was life anyway, if not only a moment, which separated one from eternity?

Serafin returned from the kingdom of the sick on a Sunday, after having been sick for two weeks. He was worn down through attrition and he wrestled to understand, to comprehend why Clarence had not forsaken him. When he looked into Clarence rebellious and faithful eyes, he saw his redemption. The ice between them melted. A warm, generous and tender man appeared. Serafin was grateful. "Souleyman, we are strong together," he told Clarence with a smile on his thick lips. "And good friends go over bad roads together." Serafin refrained from making promises to Clarence, knowing promises were not enough. What remained from promises? In his gratitude, he wanted to give Clarence something that was a part of him. "He who is sick will not refuse medicine," he said. Serafin wore a heavy brass bracelet, a fetish, on his left wrist. It was in the form of a Chameleon. He pulled the bracelet off his wrist and offered it to Clarence. "Try on this bracelet. If it fits you, wear it. But if it hurts you, throw it away no matter how shiny," Serafin told Clarence. The brass bracelet slipped around Clarence wrist, as if it was made especially for him. "The Chameleon and the Python were the first beings on this planet. They are the chief messengers of the spirit," Serafin explained. "I believe you are a Gberi."

"What is a Gheri?" Clarence asked. "It is a messenger of God," Serafin replied. "My people say messenger of the spirit. But we mean the spirit is God." Serafin glanced at Clarence. Then he said: "Mutual gifts cement friendships."

Clarence wanted to give himself to Serafin...his heart, his body and his soul. But he wondered if Serafin would understand such a gift. He then removed the two gold Creole earrings, which he wore, which reminded him of his mother, and he gave them tenderly to Serafin. Serafin hung the gold earrings on his leather necklace, which was filled with numerous talismans. "Souleyman, you are like a little shrub that has grown into a tree. You have been named by my sister, Hortense. It is an appropriate name for you. It means a man of peace. But you do not have a family name to indicate your clan, and culture. A person without a clan, without a culture ... has not a home. I will adopt you as my brother. I will give you my family name. You will be called, Souleyman Nyiage, one who was born during a journey. You now have a clan, a culture and a home. You are my brother and a brother is like one's shoulder. Let us hope for good weather tomorrow. Then, we shall leave for my home village." Clarence nodded his head in agreement. He became Souleyman Nyiage. It was no longer just a name for him. He was Souleyman...a man of peace. They slept peacefully this night. Clarence dreamed of meteors, shooting through the sky and he sung in his sleep of his African hero, Serafin, the one without a monument. Serafin dreamed of the thunder Gods.

17. The Mystical and the Earthly

It was no secret that the sun shines perpetually in Africa, parching the soil, wilting the crops, and shriveling wide rivers dry. The sun drenched days laid open the blemishes and numerous skid marks of existence and the progress of life appeared to stall in a void, which languished until sunset. Serafin and Clarence felt incarcerated in their shabby hot hotel room. When the day arrived for them to depart Korhogo, they left the hotel like a great breakout, plunging into the rhythm of the dusty city of Korhogo, glad to be rehabilitated into any society. The bush taxi station was located between the camel market and a mud fortress-like Mosque at the end of a dirt road on a dry stretch of land. The serenity inside the Mosque contrasted with the hectic of the camel market, as if the profound and the mundane coexisted side by side. On the camel market were domesticated flocks of camels, sheep, chickens, goats and weather beaten men, competing in a concert of the clever, trying to make the best deal in a circus of noise and commotion, which was caused by the daily struggle to survive. At the same time, aloof dark men in long boubous prayed in tranquility in the immaculate Mosque.

A corpulent bush taxi driver leaned against a dilapidated Russian four door Lada, which was parked under a glorious Baobab tree. The Lada was a wrack, a patchwork of repairs. A phallic symbol was attached to the front hood of the car, broadcasting manly powers, as if the attribute of virility guaranteed dependability. On the backside of the taxi was written in large letters a catch phrase: "In storm and through snow and ice..." The bush taxi driver, leaning against the Lada, had an innocent boy's visage. He looked as if he had just escaped the age of puberty. His adolescent appearance was, however, deceiving, because he was in reality a sly fish, prepared for all situations, with big ambitions for the future. He was one of those success types that one meets often in Africa, who cared only for themselves, wrestling unceasingly for a profit, drinking millet beer and smiling regularly. His bulging forehead and rectangular shaped face made him appear like an African wood statute with corners and sharp edges. Although his competitors drove leisurely pass him, filled with passengers...overloaded with cargoes of chickens, ducks and sacks of feed, his cocksure demeanor could not be upset, so sure was he of customers. The morning was fresh. He only had to wait for his customers to come. "Toutes directions á nord" (*To all points north*), the bush taxi driver yelled. "Dix minutes jusqu'a la bonheure" (*Ten minutes to luck*), he screamed in a guttural voice.

Serafin and Clarence steered towards the Russian Lada. In the back seat of the taxi perched an elderly man with a metal box in his lap, eating dried bananas. The elderly man wore antelope horns on his head. He was hung with numerous fetishes. Cowry shells on strings hung from his goatskin dress. Serafin and Clarence entered the bush taxi, greeting the old man. But they did not seek a conversation with him, nor did the frail man seek a dialogue with them. They were strangers to each other and strangers remained strange. The three of them waited for the corpulent taxi driver to find a fourth passenger. An hour passed in silence. The bush taxi driver bided his time in the shade of the Baobab tree, eating cola nuts. He was an artist of life...confident he could find another passenger in due time. As the sun suddenly peaked out from behind lamb clouds, a young elegantly dressed woman approached the taxi, appearing in a refraction of light. Behind her, four strong young black men carried a wood coffin on their heads. The elegantly dressed woman negotiated a price with the taxi driver. She paid the four young men, who fastened the coffin onto the hood of the bush taxi. Then she got into the taxi, selecting a place in the middle of the back seat, between the old man and Clarence, as if the seat would have been reserved for her. She greeted Clarence, the old man and Serafin in the front seat.

After the woman was seated, the bush taxi driver got into the taxi, turning on his radio full blast, making rhythmic movements in his seat, shaking his rings of fat, moving his neck to the music...speeding down the red dirt road. His passengers were jammed into the bush taxi like chickens in a cage, on their way to the slaughterhouse. The bush taxi drove towards the north. Clarence imagined the taxi was like a boat, sailing between red dust and heat, sailing through the flat Savanna with the sun to its side. The old man, who sat in the back seat to the left of Clarence, had reddish brown hair which had been bleached with cow's urine. He said he was a sorcerer. His skin reflected the sun, as if a mirror was located just beneath the skin. His deeply set eyes were playful and forgiving. After the bush taxi departed, he shook a small brass container in his hand and sprinkled a few drops of liquid on the floor of the taxi, claiming they were for the Gods. Clarence studied his long fingers, his dirty fingernails, and the brass coiled ringlets on his arm. He appeared to Clarence like a cartoon character, which should have been funny, if he had not been dead serious and real. The old man began rubbing himself with the fat of a python, claiming the fat would guarantee long life. Then he offered some to Clarence, and to the other passengers. "What are you carrying in the box, old man?" The taxi driver inquired of the old man. "It is the ashes of a deceased one. I have been commissioned to bury it under a termite hill," the old man replied. "As you know, my son, in the beginning was the word and the word became flesh. Flesh became the earth, the sky, the wind and the sea."

"I don't believe in you fellows with your bewitchment. You are soul stealers. You make more money then I do!" The taxi driver said. "Monsieur, the devil is not black. I have sweet poison against disillusionment," the old man responded. He stared then at Clarence. "You are a hunter of tones," he declared out of the blue. The taxi driver followed twisted dirt roads, driving like a mad fool. He raced along a muddy river, passing straw huts, and tall women with tin buckets on their heads, who trekked barefoot up a hill. He passed herdsmen, leading their cattle across grasslands and entertained his passengers with music and trivial conversation, teasing and cajoling. "Mother Africa, why is a pretty lady like you traveling with a coffin and a corpse?" The taxi driver asked the elegantly robed woman. "I am taking my deceased husband's body to his homeland, where funeral ceremonies will be performed, where he can take his rightful place among his ancestors." The elegant woman replied, shedding light tears into a dainty handkerchief. "Men die, but their deeds live on," the sorcerer told her. "No one knows the secret of life."

"You should not mourn too long for the dead," the taxi driver teased, sticking his nose into the conversation. "You are attractive, well built and charming." The taxi driver smiled like cherries, revealing his animal teeth. But his thoughts were of ravishing a girl, as he continued on his tour. He told the elegantly dressed woman in mourning that it was useless to mourn over one man, when there were so many good men she could have. "It is a waste for a woman to have frozen passion for a corpse. A corpse is good for nothing," the taxi driver said. "My heart is pure and black in the long lonely nights." The bush taxi driver used boldness as fantasy, trying to lure the woman in mourning with his charm. But he went at it like a bull at a gate, determined to carry off the prize, looking for a bride. "You must find another husband or you will end up in the old women's mill!" The taxi driver said. "One man is enough for a life time!" The elegant woman in mourning responded. The taxi driver shook his head in amazement, at the waste of a useless beauty. "It is the burden of African heritage to honor the spirit of the dead," the sorcerer exclaimed.

Clarence contemplated ancient African traditions. The mystical and the earthly were inseparable in Africa. Serafin sat in silence like a distracted person, meditating and thinking of the secret of graves, of disappointments, of yearnings and sorrows, of the bloody night on the beach, which hunted him. "Father Africa!" The taxi driver yelled to the old man. "Call on your spirits to free us of such tyrants of the highways." He reduced his speed, pointing to three policemen, who guarded a control point on the highway. A fat captain sat in a chair in the middle of the highway, as black as fiction. His two lieutenants, his gun crew, stood erect behind him, as if they had a dangerous addiction to sketch themselves in profile. They held up a stop sign. The bush taxi halted. A lanky lieutenant approached the bush taxi, walking in an exaggerated form, wearing a uniform covered with brass symbols of prestige. "Débarqué, s'il vous plait!" (*Get out of the taxi, please!*) He commanded, rattling his saber in an open show of power. The passengers got out of the taxi. The fat captain, sitting in the chair, beckoned for them to approach him. He was a poisonous midget, a tyrannical autocrat with an official stamp in the service of the government. The bush taxi driver bowed to him. He led his passengers single file towards the captain. Serafin stood at the end of the line. While the fat captain checked their identity cards, his loyal lieutenants searched the bush taxi, looking for contraband, in search of hidden treasures. The police officers were well fed with the arrogant and self-satisfied look of the African elite, who did not request, but demanded, who did not aid, but destroyed. They carried weapons in the service of some arbitrary ruler, some so-called dictator. Clarence understood in this moment what it felt like to be helpless in the face of power. This was a gang of robbers, honorable bandits, for whom Africa was a self-service store. Clarence could not conceal his shock, as he observed the other bush taxi passengers giving the fat captain money like they were buying something in a department store. The fat captain each time nodded his head in appreciation. It was a pact with the devil, a higher insanity. Serafin's facial expression divulged the seriousness of the situation.

Clarence approached the fat captain, who surveyed him from head to toe. Worlds bounced against each other. Clarence held his sharp tongue in check. "Monsieur le Americain" (*Mr. American*), the fat captain said. "Aimez-vous l'Afrique?" (*Do you like Africa?*)

"Oui, j'aime l'Afrique beaucoup." (*Yes, I like Africa very much*), Clarence responded, cool and concrete. He missed a chance to knock the nonsense out of the head of this fat captain, to give him a liberation slap, to punch and to kick, to make a bold stand against injustice. "Vous n'avez pas une contribution pour nous?" (*Do you not have a contribution for us?*), the fat captain asked in full steam. His spider eyes captured Clarence. There was no escaping. Clarence reached into his pocket. He then handed the healthy, fat and immoral captain 50 francs (CFA). "Merci, Monsieur le American" (*Thank you, Mr. American*), the fat captain said, grinning. "Vous êtes très généreux." (*You are very generous.*) The fat captain allowed the other passengers to return to the bush taxi, ignoring Serafin. He was so satisfied with Clarence's cadou that he waved for the taxi to quickly depart. The bush taxi sped down the road, leaving behind the painful incident, departing from fear. Slovenliness, absurdity, nonsense, corruption and deceit were Africa's sickness. This weighed upon Clarence's mind.

The clouds over the Savanna formed formations of dark phantoms, while thunder rumbled in the distance. The faces of the passengers in the taxi were now transformed into the hard stone faces of powerless men and women. They had been mercilessly stripped and denuded, like someone who had just been raped. "Africa and justice...!" Serafin mumbled. "In a court of fowls, the cockroach never wins his case." Serafin did not speak to anyone in particular, but continued to gaze out of the windshield of the taxi. "Mon frère (*my brother*), do you believe that we are all cockroaches?" The taxi driver asked Serafin. Serafin did not answer. "For some, democracy is a dangerous idea," the taxi driver said. A strong wind sprung up from nowhere. The wind blew red dust and debris across the Savanna. Men and women with heavy loads on their heads, rushed along the road to shelter. What the wind blew away, could not be found again. Thunder and lightening filled the sky. Then suddenly a heavy rain came, pounding against the parched earth, against the bush taxi. It appeared as if the rain would never stop, raining rivers. The murky river along the side of the road, which before the rain was shallow, swelled into a stream and the stream soon became a rushing current. The sorcerer held up a crescent with a ram's head on it. He prayed to the spirit of the water goddess and beseeched the queen of the heavens to drive away the rain. The bush taxi stalled on the muddy road in wait for the rain to stop. The passengers inside the taxi waited and listened to the rain in silence. The water around the bush taxi tires swirled, twisted and danced. After a short while, the bush taxi began to float buoyant like a boat without a sail. The taxi became an island between the waters and the rest of the world, which appeared far and distant. The waters swelled. The passengers decided to evacuate the taxi in a panic reaction, trying to reach a safe shore as their last chance. The water flowed timelessly, aimlessly, carrying rubbish in its mist, like the solar system racing towards an invisible goal. The bush taxi submerged into the mud beneath the surface of the water. It sunk to the bottom of the murky waters. Only the wood coffin on its hood could be seen. The black box suddenly broke loose from the taxi and began to float without direction. It collided against the trunk of an impressive Baobab tree, overturned and deposited its content into the rushing water. The elegant woman in mourning, in elegant sadness, screamed a shrill cry. The corpse became entangled in debris, with its head elevated against the rage of the water. A stormy funeral occurred, as the rushing waters carried the corpse downstream. The passengers of the taxi sat on a small mound in safety with their heads bowed in respect for the dead. The rain turned soon into a warm sprinkle and the rushing waters of the river with its great movement abruptly disappeared as it had appeared. The rushing waters had moved much and yet moved little, leaving mud in its tracks behind. Everything appeared as if in a muddy swamp.

Serafin rested on the dry mound, while Clarence sat beside him, watching him...this Shaka Zulu. They were close enough to touch. Did Serafin notice the invisible arrow that Clarence shot into his neck, the flowers strewn in his path? Clarence yearned for his love. The reality of the moment was a dream or was the dream reality? Clarence seldom knew in which domain he breathed. O solé mio! Breathing was an addiction for him and luck was when he held his breath. "Souleyman, you cannot cross the river without getting your feet wet," Serafin said. He looked across to the low hills of the Savanna, which spread its expanse in green and lime. "We are near my home. Let us walk the rest of the way." Serafin and Clarence bid farewell to the other passengers, departing quickly. After the severe thunderstorm, the sun came from behind the clouds. The Savanna glistened, offering a portrait of nature. Serafin and Clarence walked across it. Later they paused to rest and Clarence observed that Serafin had climbed into gloominess again. "You were not afraid of the policemen?" Clarence asked Serafin. "In the beginning was fear," Serafin replied. "But an animal which crosses the river in a herd has not the crocodile to fear."

"I don't believe you are afraid of anything," Clarence joked, trying to coax Serafin out of his sadness. "Oh, my little brother, there are many things I fear," Serafin declared. "I fear the darkness of the night, evil spirits and dying like a chicken." Serafin asked Clarence if he knew the difference between being daring and being reckless. "For me, you are a brave man," Clarence replied. "I am thankful to you for helping me on the beach that night. You didn't have to intervene. Why did you?"

"Tu es très gentil, mon petit frère" (*You are very sympathetic, my little brother)*, Serafin said, grinning, looking Clarence deep into the eyes. Clarence was searching for a spiritual statement. This was less than a declaration of love, but nevertheless, sacred words from Serafin's lips (*Clarence wrongly translated the French word gentil with the English word for gentle*). "Some men are angels and devils at the same time, Souleyman," Serafin declared. "If we do not intend to spend the night in the rain, we should continue our trip." Serafin erected himself, standing next to a termite castle of red dust. "Termites are the masters of the Savanna," he said as a matter of fact, pointing to the termite mold. Serafin and Clarence then continued with bowed heads their journey homeward. After a long while, Serafin pointed to a village nested in the colors of summer, clinging isolated to the side of a mountain, squeezed between nature and wild flowers. Cozy mud huts with straw roofs formed a world in a circle. "That's my village," Serafin proudly declared. He was obviously proud of his birthplace, observing it with harmony in his stomach, fire in his head and yet he was full of misgivings about returning. Everyone here lived in a circle from cradle to grave. For Serafin, it was always like living in a straitjacket. He yearned as a rebellious young man to live wild and dangerous. Now his wish for it was gone. Now he was returning to his home as a hiding place, trying to get out of the way of odious people with cruel tricks, who sawed away at his mast.

"Tell me something about your home, about your family," Clarence asked him. "There is not much to tell," Serafin answered. "Money does not lie on the road. My people do not hunt for lost treasures. They live their entire lives to the rhythm of nature, between the dry season and the rainy season." Thunder clapped in the distance. "Their greatest challenge is to survive." Serafin concentrated on the mountain ahead. He made a farting sound. "What about your father and mother?" Clarence asked. "My father is incorrect.... but still loved," Serafin replied. "He does good and talks about it. He is old, but not wise. He once set a dog at me. I was a problem child, you see. My mother, well, she has a venomous tongue. She is the salt of my life. She was born to be pleasant." Serafin didn't say anything for awhile. "They only tolerate each other." Serafin then stopped talking with this statement and did not say anything else. They continued walking, pausing momentarily in a garden of old granite stones, exhausted and tired. A great silence felled upon them, as they rested, looking at the sky. Later, they continued their trek, arriving in the village in the late afternoon.

Their arrival caused a great uproar in the village. Women danced and old men nodded their heads. The father and son greeted each other. The mother and son embraced. Young men beat their drums and the village was a stage of excitement. Everyone was in a mood for a party. The village was a circle of mud huts with a panorama view, appearing to be a utopia in the Savanna. After everyone had extended their greetings, they disappeared into their little huts anxiously lying in wait of the night, when they would dance Serafin and Clarence welcome. Clarence shared a hut with Serafin in his father's compound. They collapsed exhausted onto two mats around a fire hole, falling asleep. It was during the later half of the night that the belafon players summoned the villagers together. They wore chamois hair as headdress and played hypnotizing tunes. Muscled bound men in loincloths danced in a circle. They were virile from working in the yam fields, covered with cowbells, and hung with cow tails. Brass bracelets ran up their arms. They stomped the ground. The cowbells rang and clang. A well-built man came running from the bush, cracking a whip over his head, dancing in a circle around a fire. He stepped onto the blazing fire, and then suddenly sat in the fire, laid down and twisted in the fire. He jumped up abruptly from the fire, popping his whip in the air, cracking it over the heads of the frenzied dancers. The village chief sat reclining in a chair, fanning himself with Callao feathers. The chief wore a jelaba in black and gray, and smoked a snake pipe. Serafin stood next to the village Chief, leaning against a grand Mango tree.

The male dancers were mesmerizing. Their songs and natural movements entranced Clarence, but he was more than enchanted with the barefooted-black man, called Serafin, who was bursting with the energy of a volcano, leaning against a superb Baobab tree. Serafin had changed his traveling clothes into something more leisurely. He wore tight black shorts, which were torn on the side of his thighs and were too short to be decent. His manhood, his penis, hung down the side, ending at the tip of the shorts. He had on a ripped orange T-shirt with "J'habite ici" (*I live here*) written across his powerful broad chest. Clarence thought, in a delirium... *what are you doing in this jungle, you wonderful black man? Don't you know that if I had you in New York City, I would be more than a Queen! I would be an Empress! Oh, what jewels and what wonders one can find in the bush of Africa!* Serafin was indeed a gift. He was bestowed with a natural brawny strength from hard work, not artificial muscles from a workout in a gym. Clarence surveyed his majestic features, his magnificent horse's nose, and his dazzling white teeth, as he lingered on the sidelines. Serafin smiled in Clarence's direction. Did he know that Clarence was having orgasms of the mind, imagining what was hidden behind those tight black shorts? For another smile, Clarence would have worked in any field, and picked cotton on a plantation. He would have even voluntarily lived in a hut in the jungle...so sure was he of happiness. But Serafin was oblivious to Clarence's sinful thoughts.

A thunderstorm threatened in the distance. Lightening flashed across the night sky, illuminating the sweaty faces of the frantic male dancers and the enraptured crowd. The queen of the heavens reigned on her throne, commanding her servants to bring rain. It commenced to rain. The dancers and the villagers ran to their clay huts for cover. Serafin ran into the bush. Clarence followed him. They found cover together deep within a cliff, secure from the storm, tarrying in the twilight as if they were encountering each other for the first time, standing so close together that their noses touched. Gravitation pulled their longing bodies closer to impending intimacy. They embraced and the rain drops on their bodies became electrified. There was no longer a cover to hide the few last drops of yearning from the depth of their hearts. They both breathed heavy, gaining in desire, lusting after each other. Clarence heard the inspirational sound of gospel music in his head. He was in a state of ecstasy for this son of Africa, who was born in this raw cradle. He knew Serafin would never lead him astray and he had the illusion of freedom inside of a cliff. Serafin squeezed him gently between his arms, for he understood that Clarence wanted him. "Hearts do not meet like roads," Serafin whispered, kissing Clarence delicately on his lips, while Clarence prayed to God with closed eyes that this would be an anchor for eternity. It was highlife for two men making love, meeting at the peak in the nightshade. This was unusual, for men do not love each other, but live according to the rules or war and wish each other short-lived progress. For these types, this was an embarrassment in the bush. Wild dogs howled at the moon. A hyena called into the night. Lions and bats hunted in the nightshade. Night ghosts observed the two men, making love.

After their love act, they laid in each other arms, hearing love songs and feeling love joy, listening to the howling hyenas in the darkness, the sounds of nature. They dreamed of the time when their ancestors hunted mammoths. Clarence dreamed in Serafin's arms, playing with the necklace around his neck, which was filled with leather talismans. The air around their bodies burned. "What do they symbolize?" Clarence asked Serafin. "This one here makes a man irresistible," Serafin said, laughing. "This one protects a man from his enemies. This one makes a man impervious to injury. This one makes a man invisible at night. This one wards off evil words. These two symbolize my heart." Serafin held the two Creole earrings between his fingers, which Clarence had given him in the hotel in Korhogo. They both felt strange in their own bodies, like Daedalus and Ikarus. But together they learned the secret of flying. This was a great discovery for them...to discover love in the night.

18. A Messenger of God

Clarence was delirious the day after his passionate honeymoon night. He awoke in a mud hut, rubbing his drowsy eyes from slumber, wondering about life and its myriad of amazing things and crazy surprises. Had he fantasized the intimate encounter with Serafin? Was the mud hut with the thatch roof in which he now slept and the petite hamlet in the middle of the Savanna real or a dream? Was Serafin an apparition, a figment of his untamed imagination? Suddenly he heard a strange sound, which entered the hut from a cut out window. It was the rhythm of the blacksmith's bellows, blowing air on hot coal, making molten metals outside his hut. This was authentic and the hornbill, which chirped in the distance, was real. This was bona fide Africa, uncorrupted and untamed, disciplined only by the seasons. Clarence was genuinely sleeping on a mat in a mud shanty. An elderly gaunt man entered the hut, carrying a wooden gourd in both hands. As he drew near, he pointed to Clarence to sip water from the gourd, to wash his gums and spite it out. He then ushered Clarence into a large courtyard, where he squatted on the earth, indicating to Clarence to do the same. Clarence and the old man watched together a puny piece of poultry smoldering over burning coals. The old man smoked a pipe, exhaling loops of smoke that encircled him. He wore a tattered stained blue jelaba. In the courtyard, a young woman with hanging breasts pounded grain with mortar and pestle. "Thump! Thump! Thump! Thump! Thump! Thump!" The old man told Clarence the woman was the rhythm pounder. Clarence watched her intently, stomping a rhythm of life. Her body churned with every thrash. An infant dozed in the warm ashes of cow dung at her feet and a juvenile girl reclined in a reverie on a green mat behind her. The rhythm pounder wore yellow beads around her lengthy neck and ivory earrings, which dangled to her shoulders. Two youngsters with expectant eyes waited impatiently on the perimeter. They sat on wooden footstools with chickens scampering between their legs. The rhythm pounder made flour for Fou-Fou and chewed cola nuts while working, thumping the time away. "Thump! Thump! Thump!" A more mature matron stooped on the ground next to the young woman. She winnowed grain with a winnowing tray, getting rid of the chaff. The mature woman and the younger woman did not chatter with each other. They toiled in absolute quietness.

"I am Mafu Nyiage. We are, so to say... relatives?" The elderly man spoke to Clarence. He said relatives, as if he was not sure of its verity, turning his pint-sized chicken slowly over the hot coals, thinking what to say next to this whimsical American, who carried his family name.

Action found sound. "Are you a man or a woman?" The elderly man asked Clarence on an empty stomach, playing the idiot…without delicacy of feeling. "I'm androgynous!" Clarence claimed. "What is that?" The elderly man asked. Androgynous was beyond this jungle man's level of comprehension. "Your hair is too long for a man and you…you walk with a sashay of a woman," he complained in a rattling tone. "This is not the custom here!"

"Oh, that is only outward show." Clarence replied in jest, attempting to maintain his composure. This old man was a little too direct for him. "I am a…I am a messenger of God! As Clarence made this statement, he sought a wonderful provisory for his natural grace, elegant movement and dynamic variability…the purpose of his existence. "What is necessary to see the Gods is a third eye," Mafu said. "You only have two eyes. To have two eyes is a cause for pride, my son, and to have one eye is better than to have none."

"You have two and can't see that I'm a messenger of God?" Clarence asked him. "To believe is to see …to have faith," Mafu replied. Clarence was convinced of his uniqueness. He was… a messenger of God! When Serafin dubbed him this, he grasped that he had suddenly located the piece of the puzzle for his odd existence. He was not…a pervert. He had a rhyme and a reason for living. "I hope our encounter, with God's help, will bring possessions." Mafu uttered, roasting his chicken under a free sky. Mafu decided to wait; to allow time to make known to him, what was this stranger's secret. The experience of life had taught him that every man had a secret. "Children are the reward of life," Mafu rambled on, changing the subject. "God has dealt kindly with me. I have a son and a daughter from my first wife, Kogyma. He pointed to the mature woman on the ground. "…And I have three lads and a lass from my second wife, Kapile." He pointed to the rhythm pounder. "A son is a father's power, more important than money. A child counts more than a king does. Serafin is my first born. He was born with his face down. Hortense was my second born. She was born in the locust season. I had problems with both." Mafu chuckled. "But patience rewarded me. I was afraid they would live a life from the hand to the mouth and die poor. You know, there are three kinds of people who die poor: those who divorce, those who incur debt, and those who move around too much." Mafu puffed on his pipe. He blew smoke in the air. "Serafin and Hortense were both wandering birds. I am happy they are successful in Abidjan. I am happy God has finally sent my oldest son home. This is my highest joy!" Mafu said no more. He concentrated in silence on roasting his chicken, contented in his snug habitat.

A south wind blew over their heads, and a chameleon ran over the roots of the Baobab tree, which grew in the center of the courtyard. Mafu saw his children in the shoes of the winner, which startled Clarence. Was he talking about the great success of a little whore in Abidjan? Did he know that his daughter was a city fox, who lived with other whores in Treichville or that his son, Serafin, made his living with petty crime? Clarence pitied the old man in this moment, deciding to allow him to believe what he wanted to believe about his children…for what one hopes for is always better than what one has. Clarence felt instinctively that Mafu was a dominating man, who preferred to keep everyone under his thumb, possessing the capacity to become instantly brutal and savage; that he was the type of man, who knew how to control and how to bend the will of others. Clarence resolved not to allow him to get under his skin. It was too early in the morning. He had prepared himself for everything, but not for rejection by a bush patriarch. Mafu, on the other hand, decided to let time take its course. He was reluctant to begin with accusations and denunciation of this contrary American, who came into his sheltered world from the barbarous modern world outside.

Serafin introduced Clarence to his grandmother in the following days. Everyone called her Indigo Queen. She was wise, sharp and discerning...like most grandmothers. She had a deep hue, blue gums and blue feet, squatting on a stool behind her hut, pounding indigo leaves in ceramic pots. Her breast hung down to her navel. A simple rag of blue was tied around her head, which matched her blue dress and the plastic beads of blue that she wore as ornament. Her face was covered with potash ashes. In the courtyard were numerous ceramic pots, which contained a murky mixture that smelled of pee. Maggots crawled between the leaves in the ceramic pots. Indigo Queen spent her days working in her courtyard under the azul sky, dyeing cloth with indigo and her nights were spent dreaming especially in blue. When Indigo Queen worked, she dreamed of blue skies, blue huts, blue trees, blue flowers and blue fields of corn and when she slept at night, she dreamed of people with blue gums and blue feet, who lived in a blue world, in a blue universe with a blue God. Indigo Queen dreamed in indigo. She was a master at work, who knew the secret of darkness, the nature of color. She was enlightened...open to the world and she had a dramatic instinct for emotions. Serafin introduced Clarence to her as his companion and friend. Clarence liked Indigo Queen from the bat, since she reminded him of his own grandmother on the other side of the Atlantic Ocean. "I can see you love Serafin," Indigo Queen said to Clarence without embarrassment. "You are two drowning persons, embracing each other". Indigo Queen was happy to see that Serafin had returned home, but she stitched in the sack of the past, instinctively aware that something was wrong. "Serafin was born at the time of a quarrel," she said. "There are always black sheep in a family." Flies hovered around her head as she spoke. She then turned to speak to Serafin. "Your mother, Kogyma, has blue spots from the beating she has had to take from Mafu. She is my daughter. I know she loves to talk, talking and gossiping. I have often told her that home affairs are not talked about on the public square. Your father, Mafu, beats her because he is angry about the passing of time." Indigo Queen spoke plainly to Serafin, while submerged in indigo. "Life has a price," she said. As Serafin and Clarence left her hut, Indigo Queen whispered to Clarence in his ear. "It is an enormous task to love Serafin. Every since he returned from Europe, he hasn't been able to find an oasis of peace."

It was the season for planting rice and peanuts. The men of the village worked in the fields during the day. They called themselves "men of the fields." They toiled like human steam machines, appearing like dark shadows between the cattle and the red dust, swinging their iron hoes to the rhythm of drums and belafons. They protected themselves from the relentless sun by rubbing their bodies with coconut oil, which made their skin shine like hot coals, as if they had an inner light. They glowed. Each had to work for his daily bread, but work appeared to make them happy. The women threshed the millet for porridge, fetched water with calabashes on their heads and searched for the wealth of the forest. In the afternoons, as the sun declined behind the horizon like a large orange ball, the men assembled in the men's house, where they debated with each other and the women gathered under a lucky Barkeli tree, chattering. The children frolicked in the nearby river, bathing each other, washing wet chalk from their bodies, jesting and playing. Their round asses gleamed in the rays of the sun. The wage of work was shared and the motor of life was to celebrate, which was done during the night. The nights were reserved for listening to the sounds of wild animals in the bush, for telling stories, for singing, dancing, and for making love.

One night as an old magic hung in the sultry air, the villagers gathered together to watch the dance of the blacksmith, the "Kouama dance of the Fononbique". The Kouama verged upon the village from the dark bush, dancing behind a heavy mask, stepping to the beat of the bellows; prancing and shuffling around a mound of old discarded metal. His mask was frightening. An awesome snake coiled around its sides. It choked the bird of paradise. The scalp of a chimpanzee hung from the Kouama's neck. He carried an iron staff in his hand, bowing repeatedly to the earth…venerating the spirit of the dead, while his children weep for their mortal mothers and fathers. The villagers danced, sang, mocking the act of mourning. Serafin told Clarence that the dancers were celebrating death, which roamed through the bush this night. He said the dance symbolized his people's hope to die beautifully. Serafin and Clarence, later that evening, escaped into the blackness of the bush for a late rendezvous. They strolled along a small path, reclined on the banks of the Bandama River…star gazing. Serafin talked about his people. "My people live from the hand of the spirit," Serafin said in an intimate voice. "The spirits are in the air."

Clarence could feel the spirits. It was certainly a spirit, which was playing a game of nearness and distance with their bodies. Clarence grabbed Serafin's hand, swimming in dreams. He looked into the night sky over his head, which was a valley of stars. Suddenly a star died in flames. Clarence wished for something special, knowing that he was close to his wish coming true. Serafin kissed him gently, and then he kissed him passionately. The two lonely hearts encountering each other climbed higher into carnal pleasure. The night was a friend of lovers and seekers of high altitude flying. It was a galactic confusion of shape and black holes. At the moment of their explosive bang, Clarence and Serafin dissolved together into light from their hearts. After their act of love, they rested exhausted, observing the heavens. Clarence was warped with the damp of love, wondering if Serafin felt the same way as he did and being the silly love-sick queer he was, he asked Serafin if he loved him, knowing it was a stupid question as he asked it, since he desperately wanted somebody to love him. "Serafin, do you love me?" Clarence asked. "That is outside my power, little brother." Serafin answered with honesty.

Maybe Serafin was just reluctant to use the word love. It was a strong word. A universe existed in this word. This was not the answer Clarence expected, but he could not force someone to love him. He decided, therefore, to accept that which Serafin offered him. In compassion and in deeds, he was more than a lover. "Your father brought me water this morning," Clarence said, changing the subject. "He was just taxing you," Serafin replied. "He was estimating your worth in his eyes. Be careful of my father, he has not yet cocked his pistol."

"You don't like your father very much," Clarence said.

"Oh, I love my father. I just don't like him," Serafin told Clarence. Clarence wondered how was it possible to love a person and not like the person. Then he remembered his childhood. He also loved his father, but did not like him. He thought maybe people love sometimes, because they have no choice, and that they desperately want to love and be loved. "I don't like the games my father plays with people," Serafin said. "My father has a picture in his head of himself as a gentleman farmer, in control at home, as if he has some sort of special rights. He treats everybody as if they would be his property." Serafin had a pained look on his face. Painful memories were recalled. It was difficult to talk about his father. He remembered the hurt, the tears, the disappointment, the weighed malice and the futile battles. He remembered the forgotten war, in which his father had wantonly bruised his heart. And bruised hearts cannot be easily mended or patched together again. The cracks remain for a lifetime. "We all make mistakes in life. I am sure my father regrets his mistakes. Yet water that has flown under the bridge cannot be pulled back. We all have to learn how to forgive and forget," Serafin spoke.

Clarence recalled his father, who was also an unloved heterosexual monster. He thought that all of the pain which he had experienced in the past was now behind him. He was able now to reconcile himself with his past, because he was in love and he hoped for the future. Africa made him hope. Clarence realized now that on the path of life, one would always encounter tyrants… in the family, on the job, at school, in the university, in the church, in the government, and among acquaintances. You couldn't avoid them. You had to fight them every step of the way. "Some folks have a deficient idea of justice and fairness. They believe that justice is meant only for themselves," Clarence said. "You are a wise person, Souleyman," Serafin teased. He grabbed Clarence's hand and squeezed it. "As a child, I often dreamed of expeditions into caves. It was my way of escaping the real world. It gave me inspiration. My home was filled with horror and oppression. The river had to find a new way to flow. When I came of age, when I finished the Poro, I sought my luck in Abidjan. But I was not prepared for war. The river fish's game is not a safe game," Serafin said. "What is the Poro?" Clarence asked. "The Poro is a secret society. A man who walks on the path of the Poro is one who is responsible, wise, and one who uses authority and power with fairness. The purpose of the Poro is to tame, to civilize, and to teach traditions, values and standards of behavior, to ensure that the boundaries between the village and bush do not break down. One who walks the path of Poro walks a sensible path in life. If a man does not graduate from Poro, he is an outcast, excluded from the village affairs. That is why Akadji has been ostracized." Serafin said, playing with his muscles while continuing to talk. "My father forced me to go through the rituals and ceremonies of the Poro. I felt like he was suffocating me. That is why I left my village, left the Sacred Grove for the city." Serafin continued the dissection of his life…an anatomy of horror. The night air was sticky with night ghosts, who exacted a levy. It is always a sad story to hear how a person loses his innocence.

"I was successful in Abidjan. I found a job as an accord worker on the docks in Treichville, a busy harbor. I even had my own apartment. I was doing fine." Serafin's eyes gleamed at the thought of his success. "My job was to load the containers onto the large ships that sailed for America and Europe. My partner was Nimbaha. Nimbaha knew the ropes in the city. He had lived in Abidjan longer. He was a city slicker and he knew how to survive. One day, Nimbaha asked me if he could borrow my identification card for the docks, saying that he had forgotten his identification card at home and that he wanted to leave the dockyards for lunch. He said he would give it back when he returned. When he returned, he calmed he had lost my card. He really put on a big show. I believed him. Nimbaha told me not to worry, that I could apply for a new identification card the next day. I was angry with Nimbaha for losing my card. I couldn't do anything, but get angry. I had no idea that I was just a pawn in an elaborate scheme. Nimbaha sold my identification card to a gang of criminals. They used my card to get into the dockyards that night to steal an entire truck full of unloaded cargo. Since they couldn't use the card a second time, they threw it into the dirt on the side of a road, where the police found it." Serafin tried to bring order out of disorder, trying to understand how he had fallen into a swamp of crime.

"When I came to work the next morning, I was arrested and carted away to a temporary jail on the harbor. I tried to explain to the police what had happened, that this was all a mistake. I looked for Nimbaha. He did not show up for work that morning. He had gone underground. The police threatened me. They beat me. I soon realized they were not interested in handing me over to the city police. They wanted to squeeze as much out of me as they could get. That's politics and responsibility in Africa! They told me they would let me escape if I gave them each 5000CFA. I didn't have that type of money. I stalled for time. I told the policemen I would have to make some phone calls, in order to raise the money. They let me out of the cell. I called several friends and explained my situation. The police listened, while I talked, begged. Eventually they left me in the room alone. They went outside to smoke a cigarette. I later asked them if I could use the toilette. I noticed that I could climb out of the window of the toilette, but I was afraid. It was broad daylight and I had nowhere to run to, nowhere to hide. I returned to the room and started calling again. Later, another policeman appeared. He said he also wanted 5000CFA. They played a game of cat and mouse with me. They put me back into the cell for the night. They told me they would come back the next day with the magistrate. They claimed that if I couldn't get the money together by the end of the next day, then they would turn me over to the city police, where I couldn't expect justice, but a long prison term in a dark cell. They left me in the cell, laughing, like vultures for a great feast." Serafin paused, looking back in anger. "I was desperate, knowing that they were serious. I prayed to God to help me. It was dark outside...dark in the jail. Ships were docked with steel containers sitting on top of each other. Fog covered the harbor. As I lean against the bars of the cell, the bars moved. The bars of the cell were loosened. They could be pushed to the side. In this moment there was no time to think if this was a setup or if I was dreaming. The only thought in my mind was to get out of that cell and to get out of Abidjan as quick as possible. I slipped out of the cell, climbing out of the window of the toilette, running to the nearest ship, looking for a place to hide. The ship was leaving for America the next day. I knew this fact, because I was acquainted with the captain, a Greek man. I slipped onto the ship and stowed away in a room in the belly of the ship. It set sail the next morning for America."

"You were in America?" Clarence asked surprised.

"No, I never arrived." Serafin answered. "But that is another story. I'll tell it to you another time. Maybe now you can understand why I will not be treated with justice in Abidjan for killing those two hoodlums. There is no such thing as justice in Africa." Serafin had lost trust in human beings. This was sad, because to be able to love, one had to be able to trust...unconditionally. "Life is like a learning process," Clarence said. "You trusted someone and were punished for trusting. But you can't stop trusting."

"That I should end up in a dead end street is a punishment of God," Serafin whimpered.

19. A hat that is not yours......

The potter's women of the village prayed fervently to the bush spirit of Chowga, imploring Chowga's forgiveness for intending to unearth clay from the ground...his bosom. They danced in the nude during the night. The potter's women were women without monthly flow. They were heedful not to besmirch the earth for their pillage. These were married bald-headed women with hollow faces, ashy arms and scrawny legs. They proffered alms, beseeching

Chowga's approval. After they hoarded the clay from his bosom and collected it into Kuopin pots, they carried the earthen loads on their heads back to the village, marching along a dusty road single file in song. The potter's women gathered in the potter's quarter of the village the next day, where they pounded glass shards. They squatted in a circle with their legs outspread, sifting clay in woven baskets, mixing grog and clay together, weaving it between their feet, forming with their hands what appeared to Clarence to be phallic symbols. The red clay glided smoothly through their thumb and forefinger. It was coiled round and round, and then fashioned into a thing. The potter's women spun their creations of clay on the gourds of a calabash, burnishing it with the leaf of a Baobab Tree. When they finished their creations, the potter's women rested in delight...for they had conceived with their naked hands their world in pots. There was a pot for every occasion: basi pots for steaming foods, fone pots for burning coals, kobeg washing bowls, puopin water jars for the hut, catol pots for bringing water from the fields, cholo pots for collecting rainwater, nejogo pots for sauces, and ngoun pots for drying and smoking fish. After the potter's women had finished making their clay pots, they hauled them to an ashy pit in a deserted field, where they waited for the vengeful sun to sink on the horizon, the one that beat down mercilessly upon their backs, burning them blacker than coal. Each pot was aligned horizontally in a hollow crater at dusk as the sky turned to a bluish-gray with streaks of orange and the spirits assembled in the bush. The potter's women collected twigs and dried grass, placing the grass over the pots, creating a colossal mound. In the shade of the evening, as stillness pervaded the fields and the tiny village, the potter's women fired their pots. An immense fire burned throughout the night.

Kogyma was a proud potter's woman. She perched nobly on a low stool in front of her hut. The winkles on her face showed that she was worn out from life. She wore a plain bark cloth and a necklace of leopard's teeth that hung around her neck, squatting next to a fire, singing quietly a sad song to herself. To sing was better than to scream. Kogyma prepared porridge for Serafin, Clarence and Kapile's children. Mafu, her husband was making his usual social calls, visiting his pals. Kapile, Mafu's second wife, had journeyed to her relatives in the next village.

Serafin and Clarence planned to trek into the bush to pay a visit to Akadji this morning. Clarence was full of expectations, having heard a great deal about Akadji. Serafin called him "uncle Akadji", but claimed that he was not related to him by blood. He said that Akadji was his adopted uncle, who lived in a faded out garden in the middle of the bush. Kogyma exalted the Gods, upon learning of their intentions. She smiled mysteriously. "Akadji is your father's shadow," she declared, looking thoughtfully at Serafin. "You have already met Mafu," she then said to Clarence. "He can be charming and stupid." Kogyma surveyed Serafin, eating his porridge quietly. "Serafin has sweet water in his veins. He follows a wandering line. A wanderer is always on the axis. Serafin was a difficult birth." Kogyma continued with her chores while talking. "Your father acts as if he shared the birth pangs. He has been working strenuously at increasing his wealth and influence. He and that fool, Nawo, have been patting each other on their backs. Kogyma laughed a quiet laugh. "The sun forces some to stick their heads into the sand."

"What do you mean, mother?" Serafin asked her.

"Nawo and Mafu have decided between them that you shall marry Nookatoha, Nawo's daughter." Kogyma played with time. "You, Serafin...the champion cultivator, married with the chief's daughter! Nawo is the one who allocates the fields; as if it was his sovereign right and your father, Mafu, puffs himself up like a frog at the table, at the thought of his triumph." Kogyma laughed at the absurd thought. Serafin found himself at the beginning, upon hearing this bit of information. He realized that his return to his village would not be a soft return, but he did not know that it would mean war on the ground. He finished his porridge quickly and departed with Clarence. After they left the compound, Kogyma attended to her daily chores. She watered the donkey, dried the grass and hung tobacco under a thatch roof.

Serafin and Clarence tracked across the lush Savanna, walking pass anthills and termite castles, snails and bees, over green hills...across wide fields. They walked away from the tiny village along the pink ridges of a mountain, and then along a river. Wandering clouds covered the sun. They encountered two herdsmen along the way, standing half-naked with white sheets tied around their shoulders. Each carried a stick in his hand. The herdsmen steered bush cows from pond to pond. A symphony of bells occurred as they walked pass them. Later they passed two young girls, who strolled along the river, collecting twigs into bundles for heating and cooking. The two girls were adorned with ochre. Around noon, they built an encampment in the middle of emptiness, drinking tea by a fire in the center.

Clarence was obsessed with the thought that Serafin could eventually marry. Where would this leave him? He had never thought about asking Serafin if he was gay, a homosexual. In his short time in Africa, he had learned that most people did not know what this meant...to be gay. It appeared to be a solely American/European thing. This was not to say that African men and women did not sleep with each other. They certainly did, but they didn't call it by that name. It was not a distinct culture in Africa, just a thing that horny men sometimes did for delight and pleasure and women did for warmth and sympathy. Clarence recalled the time he picked up a so-called "straight man" in New York City, taking him home, where they engaged throughout the night in heated sex. The next morning, Clarence asked the hunk if he was "gay". The man looked at Clarence perplexed, consternated at the question. He responded that he had never thought about it and that he didn't think it was necessary to think about. It was just something he did. Clarence comprehended upon hearing this remark, the difference between him and this man, his trade. For him, it was what one did for amusement. For Clarence, it was a culture. He had a sneaky notion that this was also the difference between him and Serafin, but banned such thoughts out of his head. To think about it made him sad.

Serafin was filled with a profusion of memories. He was in the mist of planning a strategy. He wished not to anger his father, but he also would not allow Mafu to browbeat him for Mafu's dreams. "You know the marriage between my mother and father was a forced marriage," Serafin explained. "It is the tradition of my people to select the first partner for their offspring. The second marriage can then be either for love or for a whim." Serafin spoke slowly. "There is no love lost between my mother and father. My mother loves Akadji. I have the suspicion that I am Akadji's son, though my mother has never admitted this. The problem is that my father also has this suspicion. Because of this suspicion, he fettered and tormented me as a child." Serafin had an anguished look on his face. "Time does not heal all wounds and foolishness has no boundaries," he said.

"It's astonishing for me to hear you say these things, Serafin. You know...my father was also obsessed with the idea that his second son was not his, but from his brother. This belief hunted him his entire life. It drove him insane. He drank alcohol and terrorized his family. I always thought that it was poor low class blacks that acted in this manner," Clarence declared. "No,

Souleyman, it is the animal instinct in humans that make them act this way. Apes kill their offspring, when they are not sure it is of their seed. Lions do the same." Serafin told Clarence. "But aren't we humans civilized?" Clarence asked. "Doesn't civilization mean that we do not allow these animal instincts to determine our behavior?"

"No, we are not as civilized as we claim. There are other creatures on this planet that are more civilized...Dolphins and Whales, for example," Serafin said. "We humans love too little, and kill sometimes that which we love."

Serafin and Clarence did not talk anymore, but continued their excursion. They arrived in the late afternoon at Akadji's hut. Akadji was a spindly elderly man. He beamed upon seeing Serafin, greeting Serafin and Clarence warmly. His bony face was sympathetic, benevolent. Akadji announced that he was the son of Konaku Aka and he said that his father walked upright as men generally do. Akadji was an eccentric person. He lived within a chamber of the mind in which normal men could not fathom. He claimed that he had traveled far and wide, without ever having left the African jungle. Akadji dreamed in colors and in abstract forms. He lived surrounded with plastic, trash and tin cans, upon which he wrote proverbs. He attached them to the numerous trees. Clarence was astounded upon seeing this unusual garden. Akadji had built himself in his old age a proverb garden in the center of the jungle, far away from the nearest village. They called him a fool in the surrounding villages. "A hat that is not yours cannot be placed on your head," Akadji asserted to Clarence. He then strolled around his garden with a slingshot hanging from his gaunt waist, clearing a trail between coffee plants and lemon orchards, braiding the fauns of the palm trees and creating arches in the sky. He escorted Clarence to what he called a fart bush. "The termite mound is the navel of the earth and a shrine to Asei," he declared. Akadji then sat on the termite mound. He was silent for awhile. "When you are waiting for God, you cannot say you are tired. You just wait," he said. On the branches of the lemon trees, Akadji had hung empty Volvic water bottles, plastic Vigor yogurt containers, aluminum foil, paper water cups, which were turned upside down, discarded automobile tires, cosmetic bottles, broken mirrors, spray cans, a dirty T-shirt, pieces of old metal, oil bottles, plastic tops, soda caps, broken snail shells, an empty suitcase and an old radio.

"When will you stop such foolishness, work in the fields like others do, fit in and live a normal life?" Serafin asked Akadji in a teasing manner. Akadji smiled. He had sunken cheeks, rotten teeth, glazed eyes and huge elephant ears. "I have 23 children, 100 grandchildren and 3 wives. My life has not been in vain," he responded. He later guided Serafin and Clarence out of his "Proverb Garden" to his tiny hut, where they discussed the progress of things, shared palm wine and sat together in silence in the dark. When it was the appropriate time to leave, Serafin and Clarence stood, shook hands and left. Akadji gave Clarence the old radio, which hung on his lemon tree and sent his greetings to Kogyma. "Does the wind ever stop blowing?" He asked them upon departing. Serafin and Clarence headed back to the village. Night had fallen. It was a night of peculiar stillness. The moon moved closer to the earth. "Why was Akadji ostracized from the village?" Clarence asked Serafin. Serafin chuckled. "Akadji didn't want to work in the fields. The other men thought he would be seducing their women, while they were in the fields."

The time passed. The heavy rains came and departed. The dry season began and the earth died. It was the time of hunger. The new crops were not yet ripe. The villagers became grass eaters, weeding the rice fields, waiting impatiently for the new yams. The men were freed from their burdens, freed to dream, to pursue their hobbies in the afternoon. They hunted, sounded a mort and claimed that it was freedom for a good thing. They lived and dreamed of killing, dreamed of risky hunts, dreamed of becoming heroes. Mafu claimed to be master of the hunters, praising his skills and deftness. His self- praise stunk.

Clarence learned what living in a village meant, detecting the life-lines of a family in discord, their tears, tragedies and comedies. Despite these things, he lived on an African summit, throwing love darts at Serafin. He was one meter from bliss. The view was heavenly from his spot and he felt as if he was in the shadow of God's kingdom. The village with its difficult traditions was a refuge for him. It provided solitude and provided him with beautiful images upon which to dream. During the long days, he would lean against a granary, observing the young uncircumcised boys of the village, who with the boredom of youth, leaped, jumped and skipped in a circle, playfully prancing backward and forward. They exuded the breath of life. Colorful beads draped their firmed limbs. Their oiled bodies were golden from the sun. They were agile and flowing, gazelles, who dreamed of becoming hunters.

Serafin had not yet taken up his stand, still believing that a father should be exalted like a king and still desperately seeking his father's acceptance. Mafu sensed, however, signs of rebellion within him. Mafu was fixed on a point with a fixed idea in his head. It was a fire pause for the rare battle that was to come. The combatants had not yet declared war. The peace would prove to be short-lived. Mafu summoned Serafin to his hut one morning. He told him to go to the blacksmith, Songileena. "Tell Songileena to make me a hunting spear…a masterpiece," Mafu said. It was a question of honor for Mafu. Although he had ways and means, being niggardly and stingy was part of his plan. He gave Serafin glass beads as barter. "You can take your chum with you," he added insolently, pointing in Clarence's direction.

The blacksmith, Songileena, was covered with charms and protective armlets. An altar and a bloody fetish were in the corner of his hut, which protected him from the spirits of the earth. The blacksmith needed such protection, since he dug deep for iron ore and took treasures from the bosom of Asei. The blacksmith squatted on a fourneau with bellow drums in each hand. He beat music of air, bellowing air onto the hot coals. The bellows created a singsong rhythm, as the metal smelted. The blacksmith sang a happy song while working. He perspired in the swelter of the heat. He shot the fire. The charcoals glowed. The molten metal sunk to the bottom. The blacksmith shaped and beat metal into a blade, sharpening it into a weapon. When he was finished, his daughter, Tyembe, served tea. She was a beautiful figure, not yet woman, but no longer a girl. She wore bangles, bells, and a brightly colored cloth around her waist, which revealed a convex navel. Tyembe had a prickle swing. She was very shy. She kept her eyes to the ground. Clarence observed Serafin watching Tyembe. His eyes gleamed. He was in another space and time. Clarence felt uncomfortable.

As Serafin and Clarence returned that evening to Mafu's compound, Clarence asked Serafin the question that was on his mind. "What did you see in Tyembe?" This was an embarrassing question for Serafin, because he knew that the answer would hurt Clarence. "It is the things she wears that make her beautiful," Serafin told Clarence. The harmattan, a hot wind, surged in the night, blowing across the Savanna and the village. Serafin and Clarence entered their hut, removed the dust from their mats and fell asleep. Serafin's thoughts were on Tyembe.

The hunting season began when the heavens withheld rain and the harmattan wind blew. The villagers claimed that there was a bosom in the bush, somewhere in Africa and that this was the bosom of an ancient mother, which was sacred. It was from this hallowed spot in the bush that the antelope horns summoned for the hunt, announcing the beginning of the hunting season. The hunters of the village congregated around a little hut that was no bigger than a dog's house. They called it the Lozobi hut and referred to themselves as Lozobis. The Lozobi hut was built on the crossroads of three pathways that formed a perfect Tau cross. It was regarded as a sacred shrine in the village, and was covered with fetishes and skeleton remains of slaughtered dogs. It was decorated with pictures of coral snakes, alligators, pythons, chameleons and hornbills...messengers of God.

The night before the hunt, the Lozobis danced indefatigably in a circle, making a lot of surplus noise. A one eyed old man, who appeared to be approaching death, led them around the Lozobi hut. The old man shuffled, hopped and skipped with a cramp in his left leg. His black frail face was painted, scarified. He was outlandishly adorned with a crown of hay on his head and he carried a gun of wood, which he frequently shot, shooting at the wrong things. The crowd screamed loudly in joy at his feeble-mindedness and his poor marksmanship. As the dancing progressed through the evening, the one eyed old man approached Clarence, half-walking and half jumping. He tried to animate Clarence to join his shadow dance. But Clarence sense of smell was offended. The old man's stench followed him everywhere he danced. Clarence pondered how in the world this old man intended to catch his pray. Was it with his odor and funky smell or was it with his wooden gun? The Lozobi hunters were backwoodsmen. They prayed and chanted to the spirit of the wild, begging for forgiveness, for intending to take the life of an animal. A blood sacrifice of a dog was offered. The Lozobis blessed their spears in this fluid of life. Afterwards, they were ready for the kill. The hunt began.

20. Yet the sun was born and must die

Indigo Queen was full of motion this morning, laboring with a measured tempo. She hauled dry grass into her hut, while simultaneously meditating on life and death. The Savanna was dry, arid and barren. It spread before her small hut of straw reed. Indigo Queen wore a light blue cloth with designs of cubes and triangles that appeared to cloak her body. Her dress matched the blue and silver of the morning sky. After completing her daily chores, she perched on a low wooden stool, arranging sisal fray. Indigo Queen could feel the invisible spirits dancing around her body. The spirits did acrobatics and oriental dancing. Indigo Queen knew these were serpents of revenge from beyond the grave and she was not afraid of such spirits. She recognized them for what they were, knowing the power of darkness. A Kpelie mask that was used to chase away such harmful spirits stood in the corner of her hut. Since Clarence had arrived with Serafin in the village, he visited Indigo Queen every morning. She was especially pleased to see him this morning. They exchanged greetings under the early morning star. "Oh, how clever our bodies are," Indigo Queen said. "Something told me you would come at this moment." The early morning light gave Indigo Queen a magical aurora, as if she herself was a spirit and not of this world. She and Clarence eat together millet and rice in the courtyard, discussing the extreme weather, the harmattan and the concerns of the village. After eating her breakfast, Indigo Queen fed her turtles in a small pond in the back of the hut. Then she went into the dark hut, where she graciously got down on her knees in front of an ancestor shrine, which was the holiest place in the hut. She prayed and implored her ancestors for assistance. Clarence observed her intently.

The morning grayed. "I compliment you, Souleyman. You know how to not lose patience in a spider net. Lucky is one who can wait. The spider, you know, is Mafu. He is our devil. How do you explain a monster?" Indigo Queen asked Clarence. She walked around the court yard, talking and arranging things at the same time. "Mafu believes he is crown of creation like most men. He is just a lot of hot air…an old fool, who does not understand the message of the blue, which is the message of life. When the shield wears out, the framework still remains," she said. Indigo Queen paused to let her remarks settle in the morning air. "Old men mourn the lost of their virility. This village is run by old men like Mafu. They sit in a so-called council of elders, juggling rules. They live a royal life, resting in the men's house, making all kinds of rules and prohibitions for everybody else. One prohibition chases the other." Indigo Queen was hard and provocative in her earnest critique." You might think it is an insane notion, Souleyman, but I honestly believe we should give the power to women," she confessed, rejecting the unjust equilibrium of the sexes. "Do you know the origin of things, Souleyman? "I don't think so," Clarence replied.

"Every morning, you hear a bird chirping outside your hut. This bird is called the Hornbill, a messenger of God. It is a bird that flew in ancient times into this world…chirping speech. Before the Hornbill arrived, we were children in our garden. We were innocent and free. The Hornbill brought knowledge and wisdom. This knowledge and wisdom flowed through his long beak into the ass of a chimpanzee. The chimpanzee then gave it to men. That is why men are so stupid. They possess a stupidity without boundaries." Indigo Queen attempted to explain the logic of a thing. Clarence had heard this legend before. He wondered who it was that told him this story. Then he remembered N'ba, the bellhop at the hotel in Abidjan. "Mafu has become an old man and age does not necessarily bring wisdom. He is an arrogant man, an eternal egoist. He loves to tickle his ego. The older he becomes, the more bitter and skeptical he becomes, the more uncompromising and critical of others. He has not withered gracefully and is weather beaten by the misfortunes in his life. Time has not healed his wounds. Mafu is incapable of forgiving. For Mafu, bad deeds are remembered and good deeds forgotten," Indigo Queen told Clarence. She said that she had experienced much distress in her life and because she had suffered, she was able to understand others, able to sympathize with others, who were undergoing mental agony. She said that life had taught her to be liberal and generous. "I was young once," she claimed. "Bad fortune has been my experience. I have encountered all sorts of emotions and I am not innocent of crimes or human faults. But that is now water under the bridge. My misfortunes have not made me into a crippled duck like Mafu. One can also grow wings and learn how to fly. But if I am truthful to myself, I must admit that I have been both victim and perpetrator of suffering. As a young chaste maiden with a faultless spirit, I also married a man I did not love, obeying my parents, because they willed it. This was what tradition proscribed. To rebel against tradition exceeded the bounds of possibility. My husband was not a Senufo. He was a distinguished Djula, a good businessman, who thought that it was his natural right as a man to chastise his wife, when it suited him. He treated me as if I was his property, because he had paid a price for me that was a price above the market rate, and he beat me for the principle of the thing, tying me once to a Baobab tree for the entire village to see, claiming that women were like the Baobab Tree. They angered the Gods, so they ripped it out of the earth and planted it with its' roots above, in the air. My husband believed that women needed guardians and trustees. I accepted his abuse as my destiny and docilely played the role of victim, because it was expected of me."

Indigo Queen told Clarence that she was also a perpetrator of an injustice. She said she was the one who forced her daughter, Kogyma, to marry Mafu, aware that Kogyma was in love with Akadji. "I never liked Mafu. I considered him to be base and mean spirited. But who Kogyma married, was not my decision to make as a woman. My husband stood before this decision. I should have rebelled in this moment, but as a young woman, I did not know that some battles are worth fighting. This is a wisdom which comes with age, a truth, which I did not understand as a young girl." Indigo Queen paused, as if she wanted Clarence to digest what she was saying. "Kogyma, my daughter, was different. She rebelled. It was a clear case of disappointed love. It was a rebellion of the broken. Kogyma obeyed her father. She married Mafu, but she continued to meet secretly in the bush her lover, Akadji. She was so bold as to bring his child, Serafin, into this world, although I advised her against it. This is the origin of their marriage crisis. That Mafu would naturally seek revenge out of hurt pride, and that he mistreated Kogyma and Serafin...I am to blame. I blamed myself for this entangled situation, this mess. When my husband died, it liberated me. I spent the rest of my days trying to make amends for the mistakes that I had made in my life." Indigo Queen poked a stick in the fire. "The rumor has reached me that Mafu plans to marry Serafin with Nookatoha, the daughter of Nawo. Mafu seeks only to increase his powers. I am against such a marriage, even if it means to go against tradition. Serafin is in love with Tyembe and I am going to do everything in my power to prevent Serafin from marrying Nookatoha." Indigo Queen had a resolute expression on her wrinkled face. "My Serafin has survived his father's school. But where he is right now, is in hell. Deep in his soul, he is unhappy, like a caller in the desert, crying for water. He has gone from a folk hero to a tragic figure." Clarence thoughts ran like a racing train. In order to go forward, he had to go backward, to share with someone the bloodstained night which caused them to travel here. He knew Indigo Queen was someone that he could trust. She was a person with absolute discretion, who could listen to the messages of friends and enemies, of those imprisoned in fire, without accusing. "He who conceals his disease cannot expect to be cured," she said.

Clarence told Indigo Queen that Serafin was on the run, running from a crime and he explained how he met Serafin in Abidjan...the fiasco of that meeting. Clarence went so far as to tell Indigo Queen that he loved Serafin. She acknowledged his remark with a discrete smile. Clarence wondered was this a smile of approval or a smile of disapproval. He knew that in some cultures, a smile was used as a mask, to conceal one's true feelings, or to avoid confrontation. "Clothes put on while running, come off while running," Indigo Queen responded. "There are many things that ruin sons and daughters. For every problem, there is a solution. For every ailment, there is a cure. The Lord did not leave us here without help, without a remedy for ills. Our salvation lies in our own hands. Serafin has done evil, now he expects evil. He is wounded and scratched, but a cure is possible. He must beg those who he has sinned against, their dead spirits, for forgiveness. Forgiveness is the world in a word. It is what holds this world together." Indigo Queen mentioned that she knew a man with magical secret powers, who lived just outside the village, a messenger of God, a visitor from another time, who was able to call the spirits, to apply the correct therapy. "He will be able to help Serafin to throw away the crutches and the gloom," she said. "God will show us the way." She then submerged her hands in the stinky indigo fumes, commencing to dye white cloth indigo. "Work is not like a wolf, it will not run away. I have a plan, Souleyman, but do not tell Serafin what we have talked about. Serafin in his stubbornness can sometimes be blind, despite many eyes. I will convince him of the necessity. He will listen to me. God is above all things on earth. He will unchain him." Days passed. Indigo Queen spoke with Serafin, convincing him of the need to cleanse his soul and to placate the evil spirits of his victims. She arranged the meeting with the witch doctor outside of the village. Indigo Queen, Serafin and Clarence secretly left the village in the twilight, after the moon rose and moved closer to the earth.

When there was a problem to be solved, Kapan was the spirit one called upon. The Kapan house with its' conical thatch roof rested in the middle of a forked path. Broken vases were scattered in the front of the house. An old man with a spotted graybeard greeted them upon arrival. He wore a torn Kufi on his head. A bowl of rice and a bowl of water were positioned near his feet. A water gourd, which was turned upside down, rested on a stack of twigs. White, red and black pythons and boro leaves were painted around the facade of the house. Dog collars and skulls hung from the side of the house. A fire flickered under a large tin pot, illuminating the shadows on the wall. The image of a pregnant woman with perturbing breasts and deep sockets for eyes and a long penis man were painted on the inside wall of the house. Skulls of dogs and monkeys were aligned in a row in a corner. The Kapan priest said he was a mediator in the night, a soul washer. He declared he was a healing specialist, who was interested only in the spiritual well being of his clients, and that he could summon protective spirits. "Your soul has been lost in a hell full of violence," he told Serafin. "But you are destined, my son, to rule over other men. Many men will saw at your throne."

He reached into his bag of wonders, pulling out bones, teeth, skulls, skins, stones, roots and clay. "I shall bring you out of your isolation. I shall bring you out of your valley of shadows. There are spirits in the fog. It is terror from the grave. They have knives at your throat. We must drive them away, expel the evil spirits!" The Kapan priest placed his hand on Serafin's head, praying to the spirit of Kapan. He then cut in a delirium the throat of a dog, and cooked its blood over a hearth of three stones. When he was finished, he invited Indigo Queen, Serafin and Clarence to spice upon the blood with yams. Clarence wrestled with vomiting. The Kapan priest said that there was death in the sauce. Serafin fell asleep after the ceremony. Indigo Queen and Clarence let him sleep. When Serafin awoke from his deep sleep, as if from a dream, he told Indigo Queen and Clarence that he had been on an excursion to hell and back. He had a new gleam of silver in his eyes and he was glad to see that it was not the end of the world; that the stone had fallen from his soul. A glow returned to his dark face. "Because the evil spirits were not buried properly, they existed between two worlds, thirsting after revenge," the Kapan priest said. He prescribed for Serafin to construct two wooden dolls and to bury them in the bush. He puffed talcum powder over Serafin's head. Indigo Queen, Serafin and Clarence prepared to leave. They strolled out of the hut. "Every stone is a hero and yet the sun was born...and must die!" The Kapan priest declared, as they departed. He blew talcum powder into the wind. As Indigo Queen, Serafin and Clarence walked down a small overgrown path towards the bush, the Kapan priest shouted to them in an ecstatic cry. "To the glory of God...!"

21. It is better to be subtle than to use a lot of force

It was daybreak. The sky was bright, in different shades of blue, appearing as if it was painted with a light paintbrush. A fresh breeze blew under its expanse. Clarence laid on his mat, dreaming with opened eyes, thinking of the cosmos in a dust corn. He contemplated his eternal search for a home and wondered if this little piece of red earth near a barren cliff could be it, if he had reached his destination. He had at least won the object of his longing…Serafin, and he felt that he was no longer walking down a blind alley; no longer living as a marginal figure at the margins of society. Clarence had encountered love in a tiny hamlet in Africa and it was as if he was riding a golden deer in slow motion. He did not want to know how long this adventure would last or when this dream would end. He savored each moment, counting the days one by one, savoring Serafin's male sensuality, his smile and his compassionate devotion. They exchanged velvety kisses behind the thicket, in the grove and passionate embraces on hot nights…nights full of fire. The experience for both was new. They banded together out of fear that it was a short-lived euphoria.

One day, Clarence and Serafin wandered aimlessly across the Savanna, not far from the village, when a hot wind stirred suddenly from nowhere, announcing an approaching storm. They sought refuge in an abandoned building that was a simple unpainted wood structure. Dust corns blew through the broken windows. Clarence squatted on the floor, observing the flying dust corns and Serafin's body form. "Why do you watch me, little brother?" Serafin asked. "I'm afraid that if I blink, you shall vanish." Clarence joked. "That depends upon the shadow of the room." Serafin said. He stood and approached Clarence, grabbing him up into his arms. "What can you do with an opened oyster? Serafin whispered into Clarence ear, flirting with him. Clarence did not answer his question. Instead, he twittered on the limits of ecstasy, swaying in love-fever in Serafin's arms, looking into his soliciting eyes. They kissed. "You can eat it or throw it away." Serafin murmured after the kiss, answering his own question. Serafin and Clarence then sunk to the floor of the empty room.

"Why is this building unoccupied?" Clarence asked Serafin. "It was the schoolhouse, before the president in a long speech declared all the schools closed. The president was angered by student demonstrations for democracy in Abidjan," Serafin explained. Clarence could not comprehend the light and dark sides of Africa. He wondered why some Africans preferred to climb softly down into a deep hole, rather than to soar high above, and why some Africans preferred to live in shadows instead of light. "Who gives the president the right to close the schools?" Clarence asked, denouncing such high stupidities by the tone of his question. He wanted to yell just once in his life at the gate tower, to confront gallantly and courageously the reality of power, like David against Goliath. "We Africans are not dead and not yet living," Serafin said. "The African politician still cannot separate the political from the personal."

They left the empty school house, after the storm passed. The school house stood deserted in the bush. Clarence thoughts kept returning to it, as they returned to the village. He thought about the broken vases and cow dung that littered its' veranda and about how learning had been abandoned. "That school has become another building without a name and learning is just another privilege taken away," Clarence blurted out to Serafin, as they walked across the Savanna. "Yea, but who really cares on a slow moving train, when the train moves slower than before or when the rain falls denser in the jungle?" Serafin declared. "I care!" Clarence responded without thinking. He held onto the principle called hope. "Sometimes, you have to make a sacrifice to free yourself." Clarence said. "I don't want to throw things into disorder, but I was a teacher in New York City. I could also teach the children here."

"The African has a somewhat different view. The African groans instead of sweating, he laments instead of building," Serafin said. "I have a crazy idea. What if I teach?" Clarence suggested. Clarence believed that this was a good idea; that teaching in this village in Africa could not be as difficult as it was to teach in New York City, where the cheeky young rascals had no reverence for God, for life nor for teachers. Serafin sought to evade Clarence's silly notion. He pondered how he could explain to Clarence the workings of power in his tiny village? Clarence had not yet grasped the role tradition played for the African.

"Our village is divided into separate worlds for men and women. It is ruled by a council of elders, eternal rulers. It's a democratic Mafia. They are all members of Poro, Tyologo (*The senior grade of Poro*). They are the watchmen of traditions. They would decide if you could teach our youth. They don't like to experiment. Nawo and Mafu, my father, have the greatest influence," Serafin explained. Serafin was afraid that Clarence could be marching into uncertainties, but he promised to speak to his father about the matter. Clarence, on the other hand, suspected that Mafu was the real villain. He decided he was ready to clash with villainous boys if needed to be; that he was ready to battle on the ground for an image. Serafin and Clarence walked the rest of the way in silence, stopping to watch in fascination a family of leopards, resting on a decayed log as if they were encompassed in nature. When the moment passed and the evening shadows fell upon the trees, Serafin clutched Clarence's hand into his own.

It was the time of the new yams. The rice fields were weeded. Mafu planned a grand feast with ceremonial horns, trumpets, with singing, dancing and a great meal. He had reasons to celebrate, intending to announce at this feast that he would take a third wife and to announce the engagement of Serafin to Nookatoha, daughter of Nawo. Mafu summoned Serafin to his hut to tell him the good news. They engaged in a long-winded ceremony of greetings, after which Serafin then squatted on a mat across from his father, who sat on a headrest, stretching his limbs. Wart hog tusks hung behind him on the wall. Kapile served them tea in a cowhide robe that made her look like a monk. She wore cowry shells; the symbol of fertility and her skin shined with maize, oil and herbs. "How is your American friend doing?" Mafu asked Serafin out of politeness. Mafu had already formed his opinion about Clarence, the "modern man" as he called him, considering Clarence to be an unutterable absurdity on the boundaries of the uncouth. Mafu was also well aware of the "unmoral relationship" between Clarence and his son. He had witnesses. "You have a refine partnership," Mafu claimed. "Do you know the soul of your chum?"

"He has a good liver," Serafin answered. "He has adjusted well to our ways and customs."

"Yea, but a log that lies long in a river, does not become a fish."

"He only wants to become a productive member, father," Serafin said. "He discovered the abandoned school house and he has suggested that he teach the village youth."

Mafu could not believe his ears. "I had hoped that he would soon leave us," Mafu said. "Now he wants to teach our youth his customs and ways. He is attempting to move in under cover. I will not allow it, as long as God gives me air to breathe." Mafu spited into the fire. "Where there is no shame, there is no honor. He has nothing to teach that would be of value for us. Let us change the subject to more pleasant things."

"He was a teacher in America. He would be a good teacher for our youth," Serafin protested. "He knows nothing of our traditions. He could only teach about progress," Mafu rebutted. "I will no longer waste my time on a little flirt."

"He is not a flirt, father." Serafin objected to Mafu's insulting remarks. "He is my friend."

"This American is a man for all occasions. He claims he is a messenger of God!" Mafu chuckled, as if it was a comical joke. "Is he also a prophet? He will be your ruin, my son!" Mafu was shocked at Serafin's insolent behavior, his soft rebellion and his obvious desire to rush into destruction. In his opinion, Serafin was acting out of character. They gazed at each other for three seconds. There was indignation on both sides. A son was supposed to be a blessing. Mafu thought that he had married into a curse lineage, since Serafin and his mother, Kogyma, caused only problems for him. Mafu regretted that he had not sent Kogyma with her child and her endowment back to her family. He would have done this, if he had not been sure weather Serafin was his child and not the child of Akadji. Mafu had forcefully taken what belonged to him. After they were married, he repeatedly sexually took Kogyma in order to break her strong will. Serafin could very well have been his child. "It is the duty of a father, Serafin, to give advice and to counsel," Mafu declared. "But if a son does not listen, then adversity must teach him."

Serafin was tired of listening to his father. He blamed him for his lost childhood. Pictures shot through his head, revealing traces of his inner world. He recalled that his departure from the village was a painful one. He remembered the time his father beat him with a cowhide whip for being disrespectful. It was the custom for boys to eat their meals in the hut of their father and not in the hut of their mother. As a child, Serafin grew tired of listening to his father complain. He was the great complainer and he always had advice about how Serafin should lead his life. Serafin decided to take his evening meals in his mother's hut. Mafu perceived this as an opened affront to his position as sovereignty of the family. His pride demanded a response. One evening as the twilight dawned and the villagers took their evening meal, Mafu stormed into Kogyma's hut. Kogyma and Serafin rested by the hearth, eating silently their staple food. Upon seeing his father standing in the hut with a whip in his hand, Serafin attempted to escape. Mafu grabbed him and began to beat him as if it was his right to mete out punishment, or to bestow benefits. He hit Serafin, thrashing him with the whip. Kogyma yelled for him to stop. "You will kill him, if you do not stop," Kogyma screamed. She tried to pull Mafu away from Serafin. But Mafu began to beat her as well. Kogyma ran out of the hut, looking for help. Several men came to her aide. They were Poro members. They pulled Mafu off of Serafin, taking the whip away from Mafu. He was in frenzy. Serafin ran out of the hut into the bush, where he remained for one week. When he returned to his father's compound with thoughts of whether to pardon or to retaliate, he avoided Mafu. He moved into his mother's hut. Mafu understood the message loud and clear. "The next time you beat me, you will have to kill me," Serafin told his father. After this incident, Mafu never again dared to raise his hand up against Serafin.

"One falsehood spoils a thousand truths, father." Serafin responded with a sharp tongue of steel to his father's comment about advising and counseling a son. Serafin did not want to shot his powder too early, to irritate a giant. His father had a man in every pocket like chest figures and strong men played music chairs with people. It was better to avoid a showdown with Mafu until the right time. With men like Mafu, you had to be careful when they became angry. Mafu was unyielding, fixed on a point. "I intend to take a third wife," Mafu said. "And your mother, Kogyma, has been defaming me among the village women. I have given her one warning. Go to her and tell her that I will punish her the next time I hear that she is slandering my name." Mafu sipped from his tea, observing Serafin. Serafin sat as if in a trance, as if he was hearing melodies and rhythms that Mafu could not hear. Serafin in Mafu's eyes had become foreign to their world. He preferred to fight rare battles. "I have nothing against men friendships," Mafu said. "Our people have a proverb which says, 'if your wife hurts you, run to your friend.' A man has to invest in his future and he must cultivate his fields. If he does not do this, he will die of hunger. A man without a woman is like a field without a seed. I know that you have been anxiously waiting for me to tell you this. I have made arrangements with Nawo for you to marry Nookatoha. It is a good composition. I have already given Nawo the endowment."

Serafin fell into a deep valley. He realized that his return to his village would not be an easy one. He sought reconciliation, but now he was forced to provoke his father. He had to now tell his secret; that he was in love with Tyembe and intended to marry her. "I don't aim to marry now, father," Serafin declared, fighting against an uncomfortable idea. Nawo suddenly entered the hut with a waddle walk. He congratulated Serafin on landing such a good catch as his daughter. "She is a good woman," Nawo said. "But she eats like a pig. You will have to feed her to keep her happy." Serafin found a poor excuse to flee. He fled from his father's hut, running away like a lightning rod. "Tell that American friend of yours to be careful that he does not find a dead cat in front of his door!" Mafu shouted at him, as Serafin left the hut.

Serafin and Clarence strolled into the bush that night, gazing at the stars. Serafin said that the stars shine more brightly when the moon is not full. He did not tell Clarence what had transpired between him and Mafu. "My father doesn't like you, Souleyman," he finally professed. "Why?" Clarence asked. "Because...of your dual sexual nature." Serafin found a roundabout way to define that which Clarence was. "I thought that I had overcome this stigma," Clarence said, shocked to hear this. "I thought that I was now free to live my life like I wanted to."

"As long as you declare yourself as being different than the majority, Souleyman, so long will you have to defend your existence. For some you are a failed creation. The only thing you can do, little brother, if you are serious about your identity, is to fight, to kick and to struggle. Power is the only thing that a man understands." Serafin was also trying to convince himself of this message. He knew that he would also have to fight for his right to live his life as he willed.

Kogyma lived for the days, in which the visible and the invisible remained present. But her nights were dismal, her bed empty, lost of affection. Gossiping with the other potter's women was her daily life, a way of blowing off steam. Sometimes she told great fibs only to anger Mafu, seeking a bang. Serafin went to his mother with nothing but advice. Dense smoke climbed out of her hut. They rested together on a raffia mat, eating yams and plantains. Kogyma watched her melancholic son with his soft soul, searching for the right words to say. She believed that Serafin was a gift of the heavens to her. "Mother, I come with a message from father," Serafin announced. "He is angered by your remarks about his person in public. He told me to say to you that he will not tolerate it any longer. Should he hear another word about his person from your lips, he has threatened to beat you."

"Who is afraid of Mafu? I will not allow him to muzzle me. He is an old tube who loves to bluff, a paper tiger." Kogyma was quarrelsome this morning. She carried on a constant war of threats with Mafu, a quiet war. Their marriage was a story about brutality, desire and love. Kogyma wanted an avenging angel to right the wrongs of the past. She was angry that she was not allowed to marry her sensual love, Akadji. The thought of it broke her heart. She wished Mafu dead…the quicker, the better. There was great mistrust between them and what remained of life were only thorns. "Mafu is a little man with great ambitions. He and his friend, Nawo, are one of a band," Kogyma declared. "Mafu's pockets have become smaller. That is why he wants you to marry Nookatoha, the daughter of Nawo. I know that it is a question of tradition and rights. But do not follow in the path of your father, Serafin, or you will learn to walk like him. A fool and water will go the way they are diverted."

"Mother, if you step on a dog's tail, he will bite you," Serafin said.

"Mafu walks around with a monkey mask on his face. He is a victim of an obsession…that you are not his child. I have left him to live with this absurd idea." Kogyma unearthed a fresh wound. "His majesty, with a silver filter to protect his nose, is always worried about tradition and style. Does he expect me to lower my head when he passes? I have prayed that his third wife will be cursed with barrenness." These were strong statements. "I do not intend to marry Nookatoha, mother," Serafin stated "And all I can say to you, mother, is that sometimes words of no importance can cause great events. It is better to be subtle than to use a lot of force."

22. The healing power of love…

It became cold and stormy. Kapile, the second wife of Mafu, mortared tobacco in the courtyard. When she saw Mafu run out of his hut, vexed, mean and blowing fire, she fled in panic. She did not want to be caught in the middle of a scrawl between Mafu and Kogyma. The two combatants had reached the breaking point of their marriage. Kapile hurried out of the courtyard, searching for Serafin. Serafin and the youthful Poro initiates labored in the fields of the elders. Kapile urged Serafin to come quickly. She announced Mafu and Kogyma were fighting again and said that this time it was grave, because Mafu had a rope in his hand as he dashed into Kogyma's hut. "I think he will kill her," she said, verbalizing her fears.

Serafin quit his work, rushing with Kapile back to his father's compound. As they approached, Mafu was just leaving Kogyma's hut. He disappeared into his own hut. Clarence stood confused in the center of the courtyard, wondering what to do, not wanting to intervene in a fight which was not his, a conflict that could have a fatal effect. Kapile, Serafin and Clarence scurried into Kogyma's hut. Kogyma hung on a rope from the ceiling in the middle of the hut. Her hands were tied together over her head. She was unconscious. Kapile screamed in horror. Serafin began to weep upon seeing his mother, hanging from the ceiling. He cut her from the ceiling with the machete, which he held in his hand and placed her on the ground, where Kapile and Clarence attended to her. Serafin then ran out of the hut, heading straight for his father's hut. "Go with him, Souleyman!" Kapile yelled. "Serafin might do something he shall regret." Clarence ran behind Serafin, but he did not enter Mafu's hut. He stood outside, listening to their heated argument. "You have arrived at the pinnacle of your failure, my son," Mafu stated. "Did you learn in Europe to disrespect your father?" Mafu appeared to be very calm and confident as he spoke. "And you have arrived at the end of your unkind amusements, father," Serafin said. "You have no right to speak of respect."

"Do you intend to kill me?" Mafu asked, pointing to the machete in Serafin's hand. Serafin looked at the machete in his hand. As he realized it was a weapon, he let it fall suddenly to the floor. "Now we can talk like two civilized men with each other. My son, you are on the wrong track with the wrong friends," Mafu declared. "You must get rid of this unmoral American. He has brought only disorder into our village." Clarence could not restrain himself upon hearing this. He hustled into the hut quickly, intending to defend his reputation. "Come in, my guest," Mafu said graciously. Clarence was weary of Mafu's charms. In his eyes, Mafu was just a dust stumper. "I am sorry to have disturbed your peaceful world, sir! But who appointed you as gate keeper, as the apostle of morals and watchman of traditions?" Clarence asked. "I live my life according to the rules of Poro. I also expect my children to live according to these rules. You are a stranger here," Mafu rebuked. "He is my friend," Serafin said, seeking to defend Clarence. "I, myself, have chosen him as friend."

"If you continue to associate with this American with his labile character, you shall forget the purpose of meaning," Mafu claimed. "He is not worth the dirt he walks upon." Mafu had a threatening bearing. He approached Clarence and spitted into his face. Before Clarence could wipe the spit away and was about to show this man not to mess with a sissy, Serafin stood between him and Mafu. Serafin grabbed the edges of his sweaty T-shirt and wiped his father's saliva from Clarence's face. "What do I have to do to free myself?" Serafin whispered to Clarence in a quiet voice, in a dilemma. "You want to live free?" Clarence responded. "You have to take your freedom. You have to liberate yourself." Serafin turned abruptly around towards his father like a tiger ready to spring. He wanted to slug him, but tradition prevented him from raising his hand. Tradition was stronger than his anger. Mafu understood that although Serafin did not hit him, this was the final breach, which could not be amended. There was a fire pause. Mafu threw Clarence and Serafin out of his compound the next day. They moved in with Indigo Queen, where Kogyma was also housed. When Kogyma regained consciousness, she ran away into the bush, seeking shelter by Akadji. Mafu conspired against Clarence after the incident. He spread rumors like a mischief-maker about him, ridiculing him in public, seeking to instigate the village anger, telling them he was either an evil bush spirit, who brought discord and could cast evil spells or he was indeed a messenger of God, as he himself claimed. He argued that the messengers of God, as everyone knew, were the python, the chameleon, the crocodile, the turtle and the hornbill and that if he should be a messenger of God, then he must have been transformed into human form, Mafu claimed. The officers of the Poro called a meeting in the Men's Meeting House to determine this matter. They summoned Clarence to appear before them, like it was an inquisition.

The Senufo have a mythical explanation for men's control of women. They say that there were two forms in the beginning of time, the circle and the rectangular and that the first power struggle was a mathematical abstraction. The rectangular conquered the circle. Because of this victory, men rested in the shadows of the meeting house, smoking their pipes and women bent over their hearths in the heat of the day. The men's meeting house in the village was built in a rectangular form with layers of straight branches and crooked twigs. A massive tree trunk was positioned in the center of the house. Its branches spread to the ceiling of the house like the outspreaded legs of a woman in wait. The house was cosmic in its symmetry. It was strong and sturdy. But it was not a monument. Each new generation of Poro men rebuilt the house every six years. Within this house, decisions were made democratically. This was the way it had always been. The men gathered in the African afternoon. A tin bell summoned them together. They came in regal form, the old guards in grand boo-boos, after toiling in the fields. The old men and young boys assembled to contemplate, jive, joke, engage in companionship and daydream together in the shadows of the house. And sometimes, they engaged in the ritual of politics in their discrete men's club. They talked about leopards and meant people.

"They tell us you are a messenger of God," Nawo spoke first to Clarence. "Can you also make reptiles fly through the air?" The men chuckled and laughed at Nawo's sense of humor. "If you are a messenger of God, bring us a message. Any message will be accepted," Mafu said. Clarence thought of what kind of magic he could do that would impress them, knowing it would be the game of his life. A powder cloud pushed the sun aside. "I shall make the sun disappear. By the next full moon, the second day of the full moon phase, at noon, the sun will disappear behind the shadow of the moon," Clarence declared. "He is crazy. He believes he is on the same level of the Great Spirit!" Mafu howled. The officers of the Poro consulted. They were the rulers, strong men, African horsemen. They would decide if Clarence would be expelled. They decided to allow him the chance to prove his magic. If he should fail, which is what was expected, he would be expelled from the village.

The month passed. When the hour of Clarence's miracle arrived, everyone in the village anxiously waited. They all gathered in the village square on this day in a buoyant, light-hearted mood, like at a circus, watching the sky for the heavenly spectacle. A black spot appeared on the side of the sun precisely at 12 noon. The villagers screamed in awe. The shadow of the moon streaked slowly across the earth. There where the sun shined, was suddenly a black spot. The spot moved gradually across the sun until it disappeared behind a black void. The day became night and the birds ceased chirping. A cold wind all of a sudden blew. The villagers yelled in panic in a collective shriek. "Bring back the fireball!" Bring back the sun!" The sun suddenly reappeared from behind the black spot and the shadow of the moon moved further. The villagers celebrated. They were relieved upon seeing the sun again. That Clarence was a messenger of God was now an established fact. Mafu bowed to him. He had found an enemy, a good enemy. He scrambled to his hut, where he planned other malicious intrigues, having learned nothing and refusing failure. Mafu did not say much. Since he said nothing, Nawo said nothing. The council of elders followed their example and kept their mouths shut. Bravery pacified them.

"It's official now. You are a messenger of God," Serafin said, approaching Clarence from behind. "How did you know that there would be a solar eclipse?"

"You remember that old radio that Akadji gave me?" Clarence asked.

"Yes, but it would not function without batteries," Serafin replied.

"I had two batteries. They were the only things that I had in my pocket when we left Abidjan and they worked in the old radio. While you were working in the fields, the radio provided me company. I listened often to music and to the News every morning and learned that there would be a solar eclipse. The only thing was that I hoped no one else in the village knew this."

"You were correct," Serafin stated. "You understand the roots of our insanity. You understand that although we Africans no longer live in the Stone Age, many of us still have not arrived in the Age of Reason. We still believe that dramatic changes in the forces of nature are acts of God."

In the following days and weeks, Serafin was often absent. He did not return nights to Indigo Queen's hut. His sleeping mat remained empty. He frequently came in the middle of the day from the bush. Clarence knew the alarm signs. But he could not act like the jealous woman, and demand to know where Serafin was sleeping at night, because he was not a woman, nor was he Serafin's wife. They were just friends. Clarence knew that he had no right to be jealous. He waited for Serafin to tell him what was wrong, and why he was not sleeping on his mat in Indigo Queen's hut. Serafin came one day into the yard, dishevel, sleepy-faced, asking for Clarence. Indigo Queen told him that he was in the hut. "I want to show you the secrets of the Sacred Grove," Serafin said. Clarence followed him into the bush. They walked until the bush suddenly opened up into a forest. Fauns and orchids covered the forest floor. Vines clung to the trunk and branches of tall trees. It was part of the bush, but separated from the bush, secluded, a refuge.

"Before men and women could live together, they roamed the wilderness in groups and feared each other. The old woman, who lives in the heavens, said to them, create a sacred grove and build your villages in the near. Sweep your grounds clean of animals and weeds and live your life in peace," Serafin explained to Clarence. "Souleyman, I want to build my own Sacred Abode. I feel a craving for my own tower. I will marry Tyembe."

Clarence was silent. He had to first control his emotion. If he had had a digger in his pocket, he would surely have plunged it into Serafin's heart. Most homicides are a result of passion. "I thought that you loved me," Clarence said.

"I do love you, Souleyman," Serafin answered. The power was in the word...love. "We are friends."

"But I thought that I was for you more than just a friend," Clarence protested.

"What could be greater than friendship?" You are in my heart, where you shall remain the rest of my life. Just because I will marry, does not change a thing between us," Serafin said.

Clarence twittered on the verge of a nervous breakdown, being an expanse of ruins four stories high. He thought Serafin belonged to him and that he had sacrificed too much to allow someone else to take him away. He suddenly pounded Serafin's chest with his fist, feeling Serafin had betrayed him. This was an unbearable feeling, but only a personal drama in the bush. Clarence searched his bag of wonders and decided if sympathy would not work, then he would offer Serafin luck in New York City. "You don't have to live in this poverty. You could be happy with me in America." Clarence tried to convince Serafin of the assets of the American Way of Life. "What would I do there...live a thrilling life...with a green table decked with abundance?" Serafin asked. "In Africa, we are poor and are slaves to tradition. In America and Europe, you live in abundance, but you are slaves to the market and the market is more vicious than tradition." When Clarence thought about it, he realized that he really did not want to see Serafin in New York City. There he would be just another Bimbo, trying to get over. In Africa, he was something special. He belonged to Africa as Africa belonged to him. You could not separate the two. They were one and the same. If Clarence had had Serafin in New York City, he would have locked him up in a golden cage. He realized if he truly loved Serafin, then he could not wish such a fate to him.

"I once dreamed of going to America. What African hasn't had this dream?" Serafin smiled at the thought of a dream deferred. "Great experiments lead to great failures...or great success," he said. "Being honest with oneself is difficult. I thought that I was lucky to be in Europe, to have escaped the poverty of Africa. But in Europe, I realized Africa was in my soul and spirit. Between Europe and Africa lie worlds, not just material differences, but spiritual differences." Serafin began to tell the story, which he had told Clarence long ago. He started, therefore, at the point where he had finished, as if he had told Clarence this story only yesterday. He decided to tell it to him now in order to make him understand how he felt and why he could not go with him to America. "When I stowed away on that Greek ship, which was sailing for America, my only thought was fame and glory in America." Serafin plucked a brown grass out of the ground and shoved it into his mouth. "I hid in a dark closet in the engine room with nothing to eat and nothing to drink. At night, hunger drove me into the canteen. I stole food. I had never stolen anything in my life, but the will to survive forced me to break a principle of God. This disturbed me more than the fear of dying of hunger in the bottom of a ship. Maybe some people would consider it naïve, but I was an innocent person...not ruined and outworn like so many types that I met in Europe. Since I had some money in my pocket, each time I stole food, I would leave something on the refrigerator in exchange, being so naïve as to believe that it was natural for humans to have sympathy with other humans, who suffer or are in need. When the Chinese cook caught me in the kitchen and turned me over to the captain, I couldn't understand his motivations, since he came from a poor country himself. Why would he wish me ill will? Luckily, I knew the captain, who was my friend. He was from Greece, another poor country. His ship docked often in Abidjan. The captain had sympathy with my situation, after I told him what happened and why I stowed away on his ship. He told me that his ship was sailing for Portugal and then to America, but he could not take me to America with him. He told me that he would have to put me off the ship in Lisbon and he asked me my name. I thought it funny for him to ask me this, since he knew my name. I said 'Nyiage Serafin'. He said from now on you are called Ike Kennedy and you came from Liberia.

"The captain told me that if I had anything on me which would identify me as Ivoirian, to get rid of it immediately...ID cards, money and clothes. Everyday we practiced my new identity and the story of my life. He explained to me what political asylum was. I had never heard of this word before. The captain told me that when the Portuguese police came to take me away in Lisbon, I had to say that I am seeking political asylum and that my name is Ike Kennedy. I was afraid the police would see behind this scheme, because I only speak broken English. The captain said that no white man expects an African to speak English like an Englishman. He said as long as I spoke Pidgin English and did what they expected me to do, I would be all right." Serafin stood, threw the grass straw away and walked towards a tree, where he leaned against the trunk of the tree. He spoke a quiet language in telling his story, how his dreamed popped. "I hoped for a wonder in Portugal," Serafin said, appearing like a sculpture under the Sotoore tree.

"Two policemen, too fat, too satisfied and too corrupt, picked me up in Lisbon. They took me to a place for refugees in waiting. This place was filled with restless persons, lost in room and time, living in a pipe. We did not know on which end we would finally come out on." Clarence suddenly recognized that digging in a wound was not a pretty process, especially if you were unprepared to hear catastrophes and tragedies by mistake. He did not want to hear anymore. The fear of being too similar hunted him. He observed Serafin, the shadows playing a game with his invisible crown. He pictured him blowing a magic flute for the queen of the night.

"In Portugal, I landed between stools, telling my story, telling what the Greek captain told me to say, over and over again. No one believed me. If it had been true, they still would not have believed it." Serafin's breathe faltered. "They played a game with me. What the future would bring nibbled at my nerves. My caretaker, a chubby fellow, took me aside and told me how the system works, saying that Portugal was not a runway for butterflies, but a poor country with many people on hard times. He told me that luck could be bought. He said, 'my friend, political refugees are supported by the United Nations and receive a check every month'. Then he said to me 'do ut des,' which he said was Latin and meant to give and it will be given. Sometimes you have to play a sucker, because luck is not programmed. I promised to give this man my future check and he freed me from bondage. I was officially recognized as a political refugee in Portugal, and even received a passport from the United Nations." Serafin said 'political refugee' as if it was a serious joke.

The Sacred Grove, the Sinzanga, was green and cool with scented trees. It was a place from the dreamtime, a greenhouse in a barren environment. The treetops were entangled. It was a sanctuary, a place of pilgrimage and a place for collective mythologies, appearing to be one step from infinity. Long words and long sentences were out of place here. "I was free to starve. There was no way for me to survive in Portugal, outside of ravaging and plundering, walking the streets of Lisbon, hungry, lost and desperate, far removed from my origins. The dust of Africa was still in my pockets, but I was in Portugal not master of my own decisions... becoming a vagabond, not being able decide when I would eat; not being able to find even dirty work. My existence in Portugal, in Europe was a fiasco without consequences. No one cared if I felled in hunger and died on the streets. After some time, I began to believe death was the gate to life." Serafin's tale of his excursion to hell stirred strong feelings within him. He was a man with a sad song, confronted with the end of a game. It was difficult for him, trying to sift through the chaos of the past, the junk room of memories.

"I was a corpse who roamed trash dumps and dunghills...the last dirt, as if I had died, but was not dead and not even having a hoe to dig a grave. I could not have failed better. A man came to me one day, who was an American, a white man. He obviously didn't have problems with a corpse, preaching repentance, saying that Christ descended from the heaven and we were saved. He said I needed a new belief and it was as easy as that. He told me I needed to be born again to be saved; that God is our salvation, giving me a little book called the Book of Mormon. They claimed to be saviors, to have a vision. They are fishermen in reality, hauling in their net of lost souls, rescuing people after a crash." Serafin paused. Time hung in the air. A hornbill twittered. A turtle inched along a path. Gazelles and wild bulls grassed beyond the Sacred Grove in the distance. A threatened paradise spread as far as the eye could see.

"The Mormons found a job for me. I soon realized that all the men at work, who were all Africans, were connected with the Mormons. It is the Africans, who built glass palaces in Lisbon and lived themselves in dark, filthy pensions. The Mormons promised to take me to America, to see their temple in the desert. Once again there was this promise of a better place. America was dangled in our faces like bait. The Mormons taught us good manners and good morals, and to show our appreciation, we were given the opportunity to contribute 30% of our wages to the church. I did not have anything against this in the beginning, because I was just happy to have a job and a warm place to sleep. I soon learned that the white Mormons contributed only 10% of their wages to the church and they forbade the Mormon women from having intimate contact with us blacks, treating us as if we were their trained and tamed pets. They were not truthful and their benevolence was not honest. I stopped making contributions to the church and soon lost the job. I was the one who offended. This was a clear thing."

Serafin had shared with no one his experiences in Europe. Clarence was the first person, who he told this story. He did not want charity from Clarence. He only wanted to make him understand. “It finally dawned upon me I was just the court’s fool jester and dilettante in Europe. Greediness and fear surrounded me; people surrounded me, who appeared more than they actually were; artificial people with artificial feelings, all of whom treated me as if I was the last dirt. So I stole enough money to return to Africa and began to engage in petty crime in Abidjan. It was better than working as a slave in Lisbon for some white man with thin lips. When I met you, Souleyman, I knew for the first time that I could also be happy in Africa...and in love.”

“I don’t understand you, Serafin,” Clarence said. “How can you say that you love me and then want to marry Tyembe?”

“Souleyman, my brother, I don’t want to fight with you. Life is too short for battles. It is a shadow and a mist. It passes quickly by and is no more. Let us live in harmony together. I love you, Souleyman, my little brother, my friend and I love Tyembe, as well,” Serafin claimed. “Stay with me and go no more.”

Clarence had mixed feelings. He left Serafin, sitting on a rock in the Sacred Grove. The sun light shined through the grove and illuminated his sensuous form. There is no right way of living. Everybody has to find the best way he or she can to get through life. The one with the better counsel wins. This was more than a confrontation with Serafin. It was a confrontation with Clarence’s inner shadow. He had maneuvered himself into a murky corner and was swimming laps in heavy water, in a world that was too wide to answer questions of moral. In his desperation, he used Indigo Queen as his sounding wall, going to her compound, seeking advice. “We are the servants of two masters, the heart and the mind and my Serafin has a heart that is too big for his body,” Indigo Queen declared. “It is not the normal man who can love two persons equally well. You are blessed, Souleyman, to be loved by Serafin. He loves you and he loves Tyembe. It is a selfish desire to demand that he only should love you. Share your love, Souleyman. Be happy that you experienced it in your life time. The healing power of love is like the moving craft of the sun. No one wants to sit in a shadow or to live without love,” Indigo Queen said, at the end of their conversation.

23. On the Wings of Love

Serafin married Tyembe without Mafu’s approval. Tyembe proved herself to be a disciplined little woman, who was excellent in character. Her ways were above board and straightforward. Serafin built his own compound, which included a mud hut for Clarence. They lead a peaceful, pastoral life together, respecting and honoring each other. Clarence was selected by the village to be N’tao (counselor, teacher, and protector) of the young Poro initiates and Serafin was elected into the council of elders. There was no longer talk of Clarence “corrupting the youths” or of him “bringing strange ways into the village.” The fields were tilled in the day. During the night, the villagers sung and danced, as if they were all blessed. Joy was their wealth. Time took its course. Months passed without an event. Before long Tyembe became a little mother. She bore a son on a cloudy day at the end of the rain season. He was a dark complexioned child with curly hair, who was the image of Serafin. Serafin loved him much.

Clarence awoke one gray morning to observe Tyembe in the courtyard. She greeted him with a friendly smile. “If you rise too early, the dew will wet you,” Tyembe said. She rested on a low stool, clutching her child against her breast. Clarence returned her smile, watching her feeding her child, realizing in the instance of the moment that she represented all mothers... mothers in spirit, mothers in deeds, and mothers in need, mothers who wish to be, mothers of the past, present and future. She appeared to have no shoulders, only massive yams for breasts and her lips were extended from her face, as if eternally in wait of a kiss. Her ears were like spherical cups, reposed inside each other, as if she could hear the laments of mankind. She had a coiffure that touched the African sky. Her eyes were like cowry shells...serene, blessing all things seen and unseen. Her neck and arms were lengthy, covered with rings of precious beads, gold and splendid silver. She carried a digger latched to her right arm, for defense...to hedge against ill will. She appeared like an African statute, as she nourished her child and she would have killed anyone who threatened it. The scares upon her face revealed that she was a social being. Clarence observed Tyembe intently and wondered why it was that in real life one could not languish long in one's mother's womb? Why did people eventually learn to moan the day that they were born? Clarence no longer questioned whether Serafin loved him. He could feel his love with every fiber of his body. Clarence was confronted with the question of whether he loved Serafin. This was a more difficult question to answer. He thought that he loved Serafin, the person and the man. He suspected that in reality he loved what Serafin represented...purity of heart, honesty of emotions, the lightness of being, and the beauty of existence. He found all of these things in Serafin. His search had come to an end. He instinctively knew that he could now depart, go back to the "civilized world," enlightened and wiser, in the hope that one day a love would come his way. He knew now what he was looking for.

The planting season started. The yam and rice fields were cultivated. The earth was hot to receive. There were reports of Cholera in Mombassa. Clarence's hallucinations about Africa flickered out. His excursion to a continent was coming to an end. The only souvenirs of Africa that he would take with him would be memories...of facial paintings and scarification, rituals and ceremonies, of traditions, of roots and sorcerers and of Serafin. He realized it would be difficult for him to depart from Serafin. Images flashed in his mind of the moments when they had held each other's hand, slipped kisses in the dark, shared intimacies, and slept in each other's arms. Clarence knew that he had a special place in Serafin's heart and he would for the rest of his life hold a special place in his heart for Serafin. But dreams must end and the reality of survival takes over life. Clarence thought that it was their destiny to have met each other. Now it was time for their destinies to separate. Their paths were only meant to temporally cross. The bottom line was that Serafin was not like him. Serafin was a "normal man", who was destined to found a family, destined to command others. It was also Serafin's nature to lead and to compete. Serafin would take pleasure in his role, naturally subordinating, controlling and demanding. Clarence, on the other hand, was a messenger of God. He would eternally yearn to touch the sky and would remain an outsider on the margins of society for the rest of his life. This is the way he came into this world. It was not his nature to dominate. Although messengers of God were not taken seriously in modern society, because they heard a rhythm that only queers could hear, they were the link to a better world. Clarence felt that humanity would have to travel a long hard road of suffering, before it was understood that it was not about domination and subordination, nor about accumulating wealth, but about love and sharing. For Clarence, there was also a more fundamental problem, which could not be denied or overlooked by him. There was an internal contradiction within his psyche. Although he was fascinated by the collective way of living, which he encountered in the African bush, he himself was not a collective-oriented person. He was an individualist. He was self-centered and corrupted by the principles of the market system and he had internalized the very system that he was critical of. He was incapable of loving, incapable of sharing and he could not learn these things at this late date...as an adult. He should have learned from his parents to love and to share as a young child. But they were too busy trying to survive in the market system. They had had no time to teach Clarence to love and to share by providing an example. And Clarence parent's parents, his grandparents, were also too busy trying to survive. They failed to teach his parents about loving and sharing by providing the example. Clarence wondered about the emotional deficiencies of modern men, and especially the emotional deficiencies of African-Americans. He traced the beginning of such deficiencies, of the paucity of love, back to the period of slavery. This was when this vicious cycle of unloved persons began and it was more vicious than poverty. Clarence surmised it was a post traumatic slave syndrome that he had inherited. And although he was never physically a slave, he had inherited this absence of love, which began with the enslavement of his people and which was transmitted over generations of African-Americans. There was this shadow upon Clarence's soul which made him sad upon recognizing it. He was capable of understanding the problem intellectually and he could explain it in the abstract. But he would never be able to get past the abstraction, since love is experiential. One had to feel it and learn it as a child and not as an adult. Clarence had the disconcerting suspicion that he could only mimic love like his friend, Babatundi in New York City. But then this was another story, which was sadder than the present story.

Suspicion soon felled upon Clarence that he would leave the village and he was already mentally in New York City, although physically still in Africa. He had to make headway with his plans and not allow time to passively control him. It was a good time to return. He would arrive in time to teach the summer sessions at his school. Serafin came to Clarence one day, suggesting that they walk together to the Djula village to watch the weavers. They walked hand in hand to the little village and rested shoulder to shoulder under an ancient Baobab tree. Serafin said the tree was more than a thousand years old. They watched a weaver in utter stillness. The weaver squatted in a loom of twigs, pushing his feet backwards and pulling forward, working with his hands and feet, catching threads. He used his toe and thumb as his guide. He drew thin strings from a revolving spuddle that twisted like a planet in the distance, sending threads of light afar. The heddle pulley gathered and straightened the threads. The man pushed and pulled the comb, which navigated from his left hand to his right hand like a boat floating along the Nile. The weaver weaved cloth. "God said, in your shame you shall wear cloth made of threads," Serafin spoke, breaking the silence between them. "Unlike others, Souleyman, you did not come to Africa seeking an El Dorado, but in search of your roots. You found them. The bird flies high, but always returns to earth. Africa was only a station in the cycle of your life. You understand now that Africa is your native place. But it is not your home. Your home is where you make your living and a cow must graze where she is tied, even if it is an unpleasant place." Serafin placed a straw grass into his mouth that he had plucked from the patch of earth where he rested. He gazed at Clarence, as if he was waiting for a response. Clarence was relieved that Serafin took the burden of being the first to say goodbye. He did not know what to say in this moment and just returned Serafin's stare...looking deep into Serafin's eyes.

"The name, Souleyman, means a man of peace. This is a fitting name for you," Serafin said. "You know I love you. I know what you think and the feelings that you have in your heart. You are a messenger of God, my brother. Don't let anyone ever tell you otherwise. You brought me two messages which I shall never forget. You showed me, even though you were not aware of it, that a paradise can exist in a little mud hut with a straw roof, living the simple life, as simple as breathing. I grasp now that we don't need a gleaming castle and caviar for all the people to be happy. This outlook endangers the future of creation. The second message you taught me has to do with love, Souleyman. I never imagined that I would fall in love with a man. I know here and now that to love is to encounter God, because God is love. You cannot decide beforehand who you will love, where you will find love, and when you will give or receive love. You can only submit, lay down your arms, and exist on the wings of love. Walk the path of God, Souleyman!" Serafin placed his hand on Clarence's shoulder. "Never forget we Africans are a spiritual people. We are a people of God. We live within his shadow and his spirit suffuses us. His power is within us."

Serafin and Clarence returned that afternoon to their village without talking. Clarence thought about what Serafin had told him. What struck him as unusual was that Serafin no longer called him "little brother", but simply "my brother." As night fell, they encountered each other for the last time, rubbing each other's bodies with ochre fat from the bush, making love on the banks of the Bandama. Clarence's announced departure were grounds for celebrating, for jubilation and exultation. The messenger of God was going home. The villagers came together to dance him farewell the night before his departure.

An old fool danced under the full moon, appearing to be not far from sudden death. He had rotten teeth and silver gray hair. He was black as tar. The old man danced butt naked, the way he came into this world, running around in a circle, shaking his ass, with his hands on his hips...defying death to take him, moving in sweat, screaming at the crowd, at the musicians. Despite his age, his movements were somehow perfect. "The music is not loud enough!" He yelled in every direction, playing especially with the children. "Watch me, children! Move! Watch me kick the dust in your faces!" He said. Clarence observed this old fool performing. His dance had a message like all African dances.

"Dance, granddaddy...! Dance...!" Clarence goaded the old man on.

The old man danced the experiences of life, the good and the bad experiences. Each step he took told a story...the little and the big stories of life. The old man was dancing a parody on life...that we all would end up one day like him...wrinkled, fat and ugly, with rotten or false teeth, if we would be lucky enough to live a long life. The main thing in the end was that you knew how to groove, to take the ups and downs of life, to live your short life without fear. Clarence understood the message of the dance and he agreed with the old man dancer...not to take things too seriously, but to believe in the goodness of human beings, to believe in magic, to believe in symbolism, to believe in ecstasy, to believe in the spirit and finally to believe in the spirit of God. It was the spirit that was dancing in front of him and not the old man. It was the spirit that led him to Africa. Clarence understood in this moment it was the spirit which existed in everything in this cosmos, call it energy if you will...and that human beings, first and foremost, are spiritual beings. He understood now what the sorcerer meant, as he, Indigo Queen and Serafin left the sorcerer's hut, rushing into the bush under the full moon night. The sorcerer screamed: "Every stone is a hero".

24. Everything is going to be all right

The time arrived for Clarence to come down from his high plateau. It was deceleration time. He checked into the Air France counter in Abidjan and entered a bar in the airport, ordering a cocktail, trying to pass his time away. A European man hocked on a stole beside him, observing him intently. "How did you like Africa?" The European man asked him abruptly. Clarence noticed the European man had already gulped a couple of drinks and was a little tipsy. He could smell the alcohol on his breath. Clarence hadn't expected this question, however, and did not have an appropriate answer available. "It was ok," he said, in order not to sit embarrassingly silent at the question. "Yea, I know what you mean," the European replied. "It isn't Europe or America, eh? The Africans are so inefficient and totally incapable of learning. I'm an engineer here for Mobile Oil." The European man proceeded to tell Clarence about his horror experiences with a pipeline in the north of the Ivory Coast. Clarence listened to him politely and then excused himself suddenly, leaving the European man in the middle of a sentence...not wanting to hear the usual horror stories about Africa. He went to a nearby table, where a nice looking young white lady sat, who appeared to be more compassionate. Clarence asked her kindly if there was a place free. They conversed for a short time. The young lady told him that she was from Germany. "Die Unverbesserlichen...!" She said all of a sudden in German. "...the undying and unimprovable types! He should have asked you what you learned in Africa," the young lady said. Clarence nodded his head in agreement. "Well, what did you learn?" She asked. "I can't answer this question just yet," Clarence responded. "I can only say for me it was a very emotional experience. Maybe that is because I am, by nature, a very emotional and sensitive person."

"It will occur to you at some unexpected moment, perhaps on the flight to Paris or sitting on the metro." The nice looking young German lady laughed. Clarence laughed with her. "What did you learn in Africa?" He asked the young lady in retort. "Africa made me realize everything is going to be all right, that I have nothing to fear in life, except fear itself. You know, I am German and European. Our greatest fear is being old and poor." She began to grab her handbag, gathering herself together in order to go. "Africans made me yearn for another place in time," she said, as she departed, leaving Clarence sitting along at the table, nursing his drink. Clarence felt that way too! He wondered what it was that made one feel this way. Was it the simple African's reverence for life? Was it their lightness of being? Or was it their spiritualism? He paid for his drink, took a last sip and left, walking towards the sign: Paris-New York.

Back in New York City, the daily routines recaptured Clarence. Babatundi, his buddy and former colleague, called, inviting him to Cape Code for the weekend, claiming he needed someone to drive his Mercedes, since he didn't like driving long distances. Justine Carter, another colleague, called and asked if he wanted to go to see a Spike Lee movie. Clarence took the A Train downtown, sitting in his usual corner, next to the cabin of the conductor. Across from him sat a handsome dark brother, who reminded Clarence of a good-looking camel driver in the Savanna. "What'cha starin' at, faggot...?" The young man shouted in Clarence's direction. He rolled his eyes, stomping his foot for show, trying to make Clarence afraid of his shadow, trying to install fear in his heart. He sprawled out on the bench directly across from Clarence. His hair grew wild. His deeply set brown eyes spoke of longings. He had a look on his face that spoke of his search for a home. Clarence assumed he was another one of those New York thugs, full of aggression and hating himself for existing. Clarence had no intention of struggling with this young man or contesting the order of the world. He ignored the young man's insult and quickly departed the subway on 14th Street. Then it occurred to him...that question again. "What did you learn in Africa?" He suddenly knew the answer. He felt in Africa comfortable with his emotions and comfortable with people. The simple, ordinary Africans made him feel and realize that he was not foreign to this world; that this world belongs to all creation. A sexual orientation was as insignificant as the day one was born and the day one will die. Clarence remembered an African man saying to him, as he was trying to tell him that he was a homo, a queer, a faggot, and a pervert: "It's ok...no problem, brother. Everything is going to be all right!" The African man smiled with no trace of reproachment. This vibrant optimism, this unblemished way of looking at the world, which he often encountered in Africa, amazed Clarence.

He later met Babatundi in a bar in Chelsea, where the hip-hop brothers and sisters were dancing with great feelings, like parrots in paradise. He and Babatundi intended to plan their trip to Cape Cod. Babatundi was all ears, wanting to hear everything about Africa and about African men. "Child, I bet you had more sex than you could deal with," he said. "I'm perfectly jealous!" Clarence did not know how to respond to Babatundi. He had lost the touch and was no longer bitchy and on the edge. "Have you ever had a wonderful dream and upon awakening, you were not able to remember exactly what it was you dreamed?" Clarence asked Babatundi. "Yea, you mean like a good wet dream with a hunk and you don't remember how he looked. You could only remember how he fucked and how it felt," Babatundi stated.

"Sort of like that," Clarence said, perturbed that Babatundi was not able to raise a level above himself. "You can only remember the emotions you had in your dream. So you forget it. But years later, you dream the same thing again and upon awakening, you remember again only the feeling, the wonderful feeling that you had in your dream. But that is all you can remember. Then one day, while doing something very ordinary, it hits you, this dream."

"You mean the hunk materializes?" Babatundi asked.

"It's like déjà vu," Clarence answered. "You say to yourself, but I've been here before. I've experienced this before and you know indeed you have...in your dream."

"Come on, honey. Stop making everything so suspenseful. What was his name and how was he in bed?" Babatundi questioned, somewhat perturbed by Clarence's lyrical way of explaining things.

"When I arrived in Africa, Babatundi, I did not like Abidjan. It was a city like any other large city on this planet and I was intimidated, afraid of the aggressive African traders on the streets and on the marketplace. They were constantly calling, "hey brother", "mon ami" (*my friend*)...pulling me to their stands. They were not afraid to touch me. This surprised me, since in New York we are meticulously careful not to touch each other. I didn't know if I should get angry, refuse or attempt to go along with the flow. I eventually decided to go along with the flow...with the rhythm of life. Then I left Abidjan for the north and got lost in the vastness of Africa. Serafin took me to his little village and I watched them eat, dance, fight and work, feeling oddly that I had been there before."

"Oh child, stop it! You are lucky to be back in New York City, in America! Where you can get what you want and buy what you need!" Babatundi snapped. "Who's Serafin, Miss Thang?"

"Listen, Babatundi. I'm telling you something important. I felt that I knew these people. This was my dream. I had dreamed this all before. Suddenly I awoke in the middle of Africa and remembered my dream."

"What dream, child?" Babatundi asked.

"Africa! Africa was for me like awakening from a long, deep sleep!" Clarence explained.

Babatundi was perturbed with all this silly talk. "Oh child, shut up!" He said. "You still are dreaming as far as I'm concerned. You better come down from your cloud. This is New York!" He popped his fingers three times in the air, making a Z in Clarence's face. Clarence passed over Babatundi's remark in silence. Maybe he was right. Maybe it was just a dream or a fable for adults. Maybe it was just a trip with his fingers on a map, a trip of the mind. Weren't dreams like life...just a bubble? How much was a dream worth? Clarence dismissed the thought from his mind, watching the home-bread black divas and cute black fellows on the dancing floor, jitterbugging...waking up those veins and limbs. Sweet joy was on their faces. They were jovial as their bodies swam in thin air. They had a silk swing...dancing with rhythm and soul...dancing in the spirit like the wild souls of birds. Clarence watched them. He was, somehow, pained and inspired.

www.ingramcontent.com/pod-product-compliance
Ingram Content Group UK Ltd.
Pitfield, Milton Keynes, MK11 3LW, UK
UKHW051130260726
13967UKWH00010B/2958